BLACK SOUL

BLACK SOUL

AHMET M. RAHMANOVIC

This is a work of fiction. Names, characters, places and incidents either are the product of the author's imagination or are used fictitiously, and any resemblance to any actual persons, living or dead, events, or locales is entirely coincidental.

This book was printed in the United States of America.

To order additional copies of this book, contact:
Xlibris Corporation
1-888-795-4274
www.Xlibris.com
Orders@Xlibris.com

74638

To the presidents and governments of the major world powers,
and their puppets in the UN,
who, possessing absolute military and economic power,
allowed and contributed to the genocide
of a small nation of Bosnian Muslims
on the brink of the twenty-first century.

I pray that God gives them what they deserve.

The following story is fiction.
What actually happened was worse.

INTRODUCTION

I wrote *Black Soul* in St. Charles, IL, in 1998.[1] It is a fictional novel based on true events.

For the English language edition, here are a few historical facts about Bosnia and citations from American authors who were involved.

During its thousand year history, Bosnia has been an independent nation, a province of empires – Ottoman and Austro-Hungarian – then a part of the Kingdom of Yugoslavia, and a federal republic in Tito's Yugoslavia. Bosnia has never been a part of Serbia or Croatia. According to the 1991 census, Bosnia had a population of 4.377 million, with 43.5% Bosnian Muslims, 32.2% Orthodox Christians (Bosnian 'Serbs'), and 17.4% Catholics (Bosnian 'Croats')

Following Tito's death in 1980, the majority of federal republics demanded political and economic de-centralization of the nation, which quickly turned into demands for independence. In 1989, at the Congress of the Communist Party, Serbian leader – Slobodan Milosevic – threatened the republics seeking independence that, "In case of the ruin of Yugoslavia, the borders of Serbia must be redefined, because a future Serb state must include all areas where Serbs live." As a response to the threat, Slovenia and Croatia declared

---

[1]   It was first published in America in Bosnian language, followed by the Bosnian publication through the "Svjetlost" publishing house - Sarajevo. For ten years, it has intermittently been on the best-seller list in Bosnia. Thus far, it has been sold in the US equivalent of 3 million copies

independence in 1991. Following a referendum, Bosnia declared independence in March of 1992. Of the entire Bosnian population, some 65% called for independence. In April, 1992, European Union and the United States recognized Bosnia and Herzegovina as an independent state. The same day, JNA (Yugoslavian National Army) and Serbian paramilitary troops attacked Sarajevo. The war in Bosnia had begun.

Richard Holbrooke "Finish the war" page 34

> *"The war had finally come to Bosnia, and with such savagery that, alerted by a few courageous journalist— notably Roy Gutman of Newsday, John Burns of The New York Times, Kurt Schrok of Reuters and Christiane Amanpour of CNN—the world woke up during the summer of 1992 to the fact that an immense tragedy was taking place, as the cliché' went "in Europe's backyard."*
> *An ugly new euphemism entered the English language, courtesy of the Serb: "ethnic cleansing." It meant the killing, rape, and forced removal of people from their homes on basis of their ethnic background. Both Muslims and Croat were targets of Serb brutality."*

http://www.historyplace.com/worldhistory/genocide/bosnia.htm

> *"Bosnian Muslims were hopelessly outgunned."*

Bill Clinton—"My Life", page 509

> *"By then, [after referendum] Serb paramilitary forces had begun killing unarmed Muslims, driving them from their homes in Serb-dominated areas in the hope of carving up Bosnia into ethnic enclaves, or "cantons", by force. This cruel policy came to be known by curiously antiseptic name: ethnic cleansing."*

In September, 1991, The United Nation Security Council imposed an arms embargo on the entire region.

Ibid, page 510

> *"The problem with the embargo was that the Serbs had enough weapons and ammunition on hand to fight for years, therefore, the only consequence of maintaining the embargo was to make it virtually impossible for Bosnians to defend themselves."*

Taylor Branch, "The Clinton Tapes." page 9—recorded October 1993.

> *"Within weeks, the new administration had explored ideas to relax the international embargo on arms shipment to the region, reasoning that the embargo penalized the weakest, most victimized nation of Bosnia-Herzegovina. Unlike its neighbors in Serbia and Croatia, the heavily Muslim population of Bosnia was isolated without access to arms smuggled across the borders. The Bosnian government wanted the embargo lifted so its people could defend themselves, thereby opening a chance for military balance among the antagonists that could lead to a political settlement. Clinton said, U.S. allies in Europe blocked proposals to adjust or remove the embargo. They justified their opposition on plausible humanitarian grounds, arguing that more arms would only fuel the bloodshed, but privately, said the president, key allies objected that an independent Bosnia would be "unnatural" as the only Muslim nation in Europe. He said they favored the embargo precisely because it locked in Bosnia's disadvantage."*

Ibid, page 10:

> *"When I expressed shock at such cynicism, reminiscent of the blind-eye diplomacy regarding the plight of Europe's Jews during World War II, President Clinton only shrugged. He said President Francoise Mitterrand of France had been especially blunt in saying that Bosnia did not belong, and*

*that British officials also spoke of a painful but realistic
restoration of Christian Europe."*

Ibid, page 217—November 1994.

*"[Clinton said] Most of their leaders [French and
British] only pretend to care about the survival of
Muslim nation. He said the preeminent strategic
interest of the United States was to keep the war from
spreading."*

Ibid, page 276

*"Speaker Gingrich breezily declared that he could
think of twenty ways to fix Bosnia without risking a
single American soldier. He and Senator Dole, ignoring
Clinton's pleas, pushed a bill through Congress to break
the arms embargo on Bosnia unilaterally. The president,
explaining again why he was opposed, vetoed it."*

In the fall of 1995, the Dayton peace accord established an entity
called "Republika Srpska" on 49% of Bosnia territory.

Ahmet Rahmanovic   Chicago, January 2010.

CHAPTER 1

"Can you imagine how many women in Europe are making love right now?" Musa whispered to the shadow next to him.

"What?"

"I said, 'Can you imagine how many women in Europe are making love right now?'"

"What the hell?"

"Okay, not all of Europe. Take the ski slopes in Italy and Austria for example. Man! Skiing the whole day, showering in the evening, and then going to the pool or dancing. And, let's see." Musa looked at his watch. It was midnight. "Ah, midnight! By this time, they would be back in their rooms. No worries, no problems. Only love. In the bedroom, in the bathroom . . ."

"Musa, if we get out of here alive, I'm taking your ass in for observation."

"To observe naked women?"

"No, I'll take you to a psychiatrist to have your head examined. You're nuts."

"I'm nuts? Because I'd rather be skiing with a girl than be here with you, toting my head around in a bag for over three years now? That makes me crazy?"

"Keep it down! They should be starting right about now." A disembodied voice floated toward the pair as they waited for a signal.

"This is what *they* call heroism: holing themselves up in the middle of nowhere and hurling mortars at civilians," Musa whispered.

The big guns started firing. The romantic silence of the cold winter night disappeared, replaced by the moaning of multibarreled mortars and the detonations of long-range field guns, firing the music of death and carrying its song to the city of Sarajevo. Mortars left traces of fire in the crystal clear winter sky. Bellowing cannons echoed from the surrounding hilltops, and even while losing the initial shocking thunderclaps, their echoes steadily increased and revisited the valley with a deafening roar. Between the episodes of shelling, a surreal silence descended.

A small open swath divided the forest from the high cliffs, which rose up vertically and stood out clearly against the horizon. Above the rocks, on a plateau, was the Chetnik battle line. The cliff formed an imposing natural barrier for anybody who even considered making the sheer climb. The only usable path to the top, lying to the left of the cliffs, was strewn with mines.

Nine men lay still and silent at the edge of the woods, looking up, gazing at the cold, dark horizon. Chilly moonlight reflected off the white capes, which they wore over their uniforms. White camouflage caps were pulled over each head with eye openings barely large enough to allow each man to peer at the surrounding terrain. It was cold, and their breath blew out like thick clouds of cigarette smoke.

As the men lay still, waiting for the next whistle of death, the whispers among them were forced, tense, and often sharp. They knew that the Chetniks would, soon after firing off a certain amount of artillery rounds on Sarajevo, return to the safety of their trenches. That was when Hamza would give the signal to start the action.

*   *   *

The waiting and ever-hovering death frayed the captain's already overstrung nerves. "It's all right, General. No one said you weren't in charge." Hamza whispered.

The *general*, a professional officer of the former Yugoslav Army, as Hamza ironically called him, was actually a captain who had joined the defenders of Bosnia just a short while before. Hamza didn't have anything against the newcomers, but he had more faith in himself and the people he'd been fighting alongside since day one.

"Listen to me, young man. I am responsible for the lives of these men and for this action," the captain snapped.

"But, General," said Hamza, talking slowly as if trying to convince a child. "No one said you weren't. It's just that this is a bit different from what you learned in officer training. We've been together this whole time, and you can bet we'll pull this one off. If you want to come with us, that's fine. If you don't, stay behind and cover the rear. No one will mind. Isn't that right, guys?"

"That's right, Hamza," the rest of the men agreed.

"C'mon, Hamza, we don't wanna be here till morning. Quit talking and let's go."

Hamza turned to his men, forgetting everything else.

"Dado, take Senad and Dino and head left about thirty yards. You have a dugout with one cannon, maybe ten Chetniks. Kemo, you, Mustafa, and Sakib go to the right. Count on another ten of them. Are you coming, General?" The general nodded. "You, Musa, and I will take the middle. We'll have the main dugout and a couple of cannons. Dado and Kemo, I want you to cut off their trenches."

"How?" Kemo said, worried.

"Fill 'em up with dirt or bodies. I don't care. We'll be neck-deep in shit, and I don't want to worry about our backs too. No one even think about shooting before we do. Twenty minutes is enough for the climb. See that you're in position. We'll only have ten minutes to retreat after we're done before they wise up and turn the rest of the local artillery on us. Any questions?" The men were silent. "Try not to make any noise."

The white shadows split up and silently moved toward the cliffs. Hamza called to Dado, "Listen, if you're looting, check everything carefully—especially any documentation. Stay alert. I don't want any of them left behind us. Is that clear?"

"Crystal," Dado said, grinning wickedly.

Hamza started toward the cliff. He caught up with Musa and the captain. He checked the submachine strapped to his back and the hand grenades at his hip.

*   *   *

"Well, General, this is not a military exercise where you yell out '*Attennnntion!*'" Hamza muttered to himself. Hamza knew the captain was a man of strong moral beliefs, raised in the Spartan way as a professional soldier. Hamza thought with bitterness about what a drawback that was in this situation. No war in history had been like this one. The goal of conquest was usually to gain territory, defeat the enemy, display power, quell uprisings, and control the politics of a country. In this one, the Chetniks' only goal was to exterminate an entire nation. The world refused to understand that. Had they not learned from Hitler? Hamza recalled the false hope that the world would intervene and stop the slaughter being carried out by the army of *ex*-Yugoslavia.

"Is there going to be an intervention?" Musa talked mostly to himself. "Oh yeah, there'll be an intervention. Not the U.S. Sixth Fleet, but the First Fucked-Up Elite Sabotage Unit. There'll be an intervention for these Chetniks in twenty minutes. And then all the rest of them."

"What was that, Musa?" the captain asked.

"Just thinking about whether there will be an intervention."

"Forget about it, son. Just forget it."

"There'll be an intervention, Captain. You'll see." They arrived at the cliffs and began to climb. The cliffs were cold and smooth, covered by a thin layer of ice formed the day before in a short burst of winter sunshine. At first, the cliff offered no resistance, but the climb quickly became more difficult. A few yards below the peak, they found themselves in a crevice of rock with no means of continuing. They had to retrace their steps. Musa cursed quietly. Slowly, they came down small distances at a time, planting their feet carefully on solid outcroppings or small cracks in the rocks. Moving to the right, each man carefully climbed back up the sheer face of the cliffs. This time, luck was with them; the unyielding stone displayed mercy.

*   *   *

Hamza climbed slowly and carefully, trying not to think about the violence that lay ahead. All thought and movement was focused on the cliff that jutted out over and above him. Soon he found himself under the peak. Only a few yards separated him from the plateau. He could go no farther. Smooth ice completely coated the rocks, and he tried in vain to find even the smallest handhold he might cling to in order to climb over. Musa and the captain caught up with him.

"What's wrong, Hamza? Need a boost?" Musa whispered through clenched teeth.

Hamza didn't look at him. Fully focused on the cliffs in front of him, he was deaf to Musa's sarcasm.

Hamza spoke encouraging thoughts to his every muscle. "Easy, take it easy. The others are probably in their places already and waiting for our signal."

He felt as if the whole mountain was on his back and breathed slowly and deeply. Leaning against the smooth cliffs with his chest, he craned his head back to peer at the ledge nearly within reach. Two minutes passed, and he remained still.

"What the hell is he doing?" The captain gave Musa a dark look. Musa put a finger to his lips as a signal to keep quiet.

Hamza observed the cliffs above him. The others were in their positions. He could almost see Dado, Kemo, and Dino lying in front of the Chetnik lines and waiting for his signal. And here he was, standing frozen like an idiot.

Were these two or three yards going to stop him? Would they come this far to end up dead and frozen solid on this unrelenting cliff? He felt the adrenaline rushing through his body. The little adrenaline factory somewhere deep in his brain functioned perfectly. Hamza had heard that, if it could be manufactured artificially, adrenaline would be the strongest drug on earth.

"Let's go, Hamza, let's go!" the men below him whispered urgently.

He turned around slowly, took off his gloves, and handed his sub to Musa.

"We're going." He raised his arms as high as possible.

"I knew it," Musa whispered, mostly to himself.

Hamza stood as straight as he could and ground his fingernails painfully into the ice above him. He transferred all the strength from his 170-pound body to his ten nails and pulled himself up. While holding his balance with the left, he pushed his right hand up and ground it into the ice again and again.

The ice felt like needles under his nails. Sweat soaked his uniform. The muscles he had talked to with such encouragement now trembled like overstretched piano wires. "Just a little more. Just one more step. Just one more." Slowly and quietly, he pulled himself over the edge. He lay flat on his stomach and waited to catch his breath. The Chetnik dugout was straight ahead. Turning back around, he leaned over the edge and gave Musa the signal. Musa took the sub and threw it straight up into the air. Hamza caught it with one hand. Undoing his leather belt, he tied it to the narrowest part of the rifle butt. Then, holding the barrel, he lowered the belt down the cliff. The captain climbed over Musa's shoulders and took the belt. Hamza pulled. Holding on to the belt with one hand and scrabbling for handholds with the other, the captain pulled himself over the top and rested on the plateau. After attaching all three of the subs to one another, Musa pulled himself up the cliff and joined his fellow soldiers at the summit.

The dugout lay directly ahead.

*   *   *

Preparing for the war against Bosnia, the ex-Yugoslav army—now nothing more than a Chetnik-terrorist rabble hiding behind the pretense of conducting military exercises—had dug strategically positioned dugouts for their artillery pieces long before they began their war. Using bulldozers and other heavy construction equipment, they had made roads that functioned as military supply lines throughout the war. These preparations were made not only against Sarajevo, but against all the other major population centers in Bosnia and Herzegovina as well.

The thick logs surrounding the dugout stood out some three feet above the ground. On the right side and behind the dugout were the trenches connecting to the other dugouts in the area. Farther behind the trenches was the artillery. A quiet murmur came from the dugout. Hamza crept closer to the captain.

"Take the door on the left side!" he whispered. "Do you have hand grenades?"

The captain nodded. Crawling, Hamza turned to Musa. "Take the right door, I'm going straight in! Be sure to wait for me!" He tapped his shoulder. "Go!"

Three white shadows split up and began to crawl forward.

Hamza moved carefully. After a few yards, he felt sure that he was going too slowly and might not make it in time. He worried about Dado. He knew that Dado was not going to wait too long. The fireworks could start any moment.

"Fuck it!" he cursed to himself. He rose and ran the rest of the way. The last thirty yards seemed too long, his steps too short, as if standing still. Thirty yards, for life or death. Thirty yards for life . . . for death, for death, death . . .

*   *   *

Suddenly, still running, he realized he'd made it. He jumped the last few yards and rolled to the side of the dugout. While he ran, he retrieved the hand grenades. He looked around the dugout. "What *is* this? Where's the window? It has to be here. IT HAS TO! IT HAS TO! Damn it, I know it's here somewhere!" He feverishly ran the palm of his hand along the walls of the dugout. There was no window. He couldn't toss in the hand grenades without a point of access! From the inside, he could hear muffled laughter.

"Wait . . . what's this?"

He felt a log, about two feet long. It was set between other much longer ones. "Of course! Nobody would keep a window open at twenty below zero," he muttered angrily. Why hadn't he thought of that? Hamza spent hours before a strike anticipating all possible problems, yet he always seemed to miss some minor detail that usually proved important. He stood to his full height and, with all his strength, kicked the bar. He was right. The thick short log was really a window. It buckled and shattered under the force of his kick. In quick succession, Hamza threw his hand grenades through the narrow opening, scattering them across the room. The still of the cold night broke with the sound of savage screams and curses pouring from the dugout, which were lost in the successive explosions. Muffled explosions echoed from the direction of the other dugouts. Hamza felt a nervous smile on his face. Time ticked very loudly in his ears. He ran left, toward the dugout exit. He ran into the c, and they almost shot each other.

"Damn, General! What's wrong?" Hamza asked tersely.

"There is no door on this side," the captain snarled.

"Oh, fuck." They both ran toward Musa.

"Musa, it's us! It's us!"

Musa held his position at the center front of the dugout, where he had located the entrance. The door opened, and panicky shadows tried to make a run for it. Musa met them with a burst of gunfire. Three went down, and the others dove back into the shelter. The captain's hand grenades followed them. As the grenades burst all around, Hamza reached for his submachine gun and ran into the dugout.

"Wait, Hamza!" Musa demanded.

It was too late. Hamza was already in, low to the ground. From the back of the room, machine gunfire echoed. Hamza responded with a long burst of his own. The smoke of gunpowder scorched the eyes. Hamza rose up quietly. Through the thick, acrid smoke, he sensed movement in the corner. Hamza let loose another burst of gunfire. Everything fell silent. The captain and Musa ran inside.

"Hamza, are you okay? Hamza!" they screamed in unison.

"I'm okay, Musa. Everything's okay, General," Hamza offered.

"Huh! We fucked them up pretty bad."

"Yes, Musa, we did. We sure did." Hamza nervously walked through the room, looking around carefully. On the ground next to the stove, one Chetnik sat halfway up, groaning in pain. He struggled to hold in his guts with his hands. The dying Chetnik looked at them without saying a word. From his position, Hamza fired a burst at his head.

"No, Hamza!" the captain screamed.

"What did you want me to do? Leave him here to suffer for hours?"

The captain said nothing. Dust slowly settled. The heavy scent of gunpowder made him cough. At least fifteen bodies lay scattered in different positions. The body of one bearded Chetnik lay across the doorway. Grenade fragments had cut his throat, and the blood poured out of his neck, making a growing reddish black puddle on the floor. At the ends of the puddle, the blood had already congealed and was almost black. On the table was a half-empty bottle of brandy, a few unopened cans of rations, and a pack of cigarettes.

*   *   *

Hamza opened a can and began eating with his fingers. His hands shook. He knew the job was finished; even the sporadic small-arm fire had ceased. He finished eating and pushed the can away. It fell off the table with a hollow echo. Hamza lit a cigarette. Musa pushed a dead Chetnik off the cot, and, lying back, lit one too. Soon, they heard others coming, talking quietly.

The rest of the soldiers entered the dugout and took off their hoods. With faces windburned and hair tangled, they smiled. Their eyes blazed with the glow of life, satisfied that the mission had gone well, the fear each man had wrestled with before going into action temporarily gone. To Hamza, they seemed like a group of friends on a winter holiday. Some moved closer to the fire burning in a barrel. One of them nudged Musa aside so that he could sit on the bunk too.

"We fucked them up this time. Bet they never imagined they could be screwed that hard," the soldier gloated.

"Well, who would have thought it could happen at twenty below zero?" another asked.

"Tonight, even hens and weasels are cuddling up together."

"Pass me those cigarettes on the table."

"Anybody wounded?"

"Nobody," answered Kemo, grinning. "I think we've got about forty of them."

"Look at that one. He looks like he's alive."

"Yeah, from the front. Look at him from the back."

The men carried on a raucous conversation, intent on quieting the rapid tattoo of pulses which, moments before, had threatened to break free of the veins restricting them.

The scent of tobacco filled the room and soon overcame the smell of gunpowder.

"Hey, where did you leave Dado?" Hamza asked.

Nobody answered. Hamza's eyebrows arched. "Did he stay behind again?" A couple of men nodded. Seemingly, out of nowhere, a huge Chetnik lunged into the room. The men inside threw themselves to the ground and drew their guns.

"It's okay, kids, it's okay." Dado grinned from behind the Chetnik. "If you didn't have Dado here to take care of you, you'd all be dead by now." He turned around to find Hamza. "Hey, look who I brought! C'mon Hamza, say something."

"Okay, Dado, take it easy. How did you get him?"

Dado showed off, "He crawled under the dead ones. I almost missed him."

Looking bewildered, a big, fat, barrel-shaped Chetnik, complete with a shaggy beard, fiddled nervously with his pant legs. Hamza figured that he used to be a redneck farmer, probably a village success story. Now, he was a killer, someone who would burn down entire villages. He wore epaulets on his shoulders. Maybe a captain or a colonel? Hamza became interested. If they could manage to bring him back alive, they could exchange him for couple of their soldiers captured by the Chetniks.

This one knew it, and the security of this knowledge and his position slowly dawned on him and gave him an increasing sense of safety and confidence.

"So, Colonel, what's up now?" Hamza asked the prisoner.

"Fuck you, Muslim motherfuckers," the Chetnik blurted out.

"Give him to me!" Musa smiled dangerously.

"Fuck off, Musa." Hamza pushed him aside. "This one's perfect for a multiple exchange. If we make it a trade by weight, we'll probably get back a couple of our guys just to balance out this slab of lard. And as for you, Colonel . . ." Hamza turned to the Chetnik looking at him carefully, "You take it easy. First of all, we fucked you up tonight. Second, you won't be fucking anyone anymore. Your days of fucking are over! Now, tell me your name and rank, nice and slow, or I'll give you to Musa."

"I am a reserve colonel of the Yugoslav Army."

"The Yugoslav Army? Do tell! No doubt, you didn't hurt a fly in Bosnia. You only killed two hundred thousand civilians. Of course, what am I thinking? Just killed Muslims, right? And where'd you come from, Colonel?" Hamza's voice had turned rough and low, threatening, with silent promise of danger.

"From around these parts."

"Hamza! Hamza!" Dino moved close, pulling his sleeve, and whispered in his ear. "I think he's the *Duke* Kraljevac. I saw his picture at HQ once."

Hamza looked at the Chetnik.

"From around here, are you? You mean from here, from the Serbian city of Kraljevo? Better tell me the truth, man." The Chetnik's face paled. Hamza continued, his voice even lower.

"You were the leader of the Chetnik unit called 'The Eagles' in a place called Sweetwater, eh? Saw your *courage* there, against unarmed civilians—women and children," Hamza sneered. "Better talk now, man. We ain't got all day."

"Well, it wasn't exactly like that. You know, our headquarters had orders that the people from those places were to be moved out . . . you know, relocated and so . . ."

"And you wrote on the wall above the dead ones, 'We'll fuck and slaughter every Muslim woman.' And those two girls . . . only twelve years old! You cut off their heads. Maybe it was you who did it with your own hands?"

His worth and Hamza's attitude reinforced his sense that they would not harm him in any serious way. He was important and had value to the prisoner exchange. He began talking, as if telling an old war story.

"Yes, goddamn it, I did it! I beheaded the pretty, little blue-eyed kid myself. First, I raped her in front of her mother and father. All she did was just moan and cry, 'Don't kill me, please don't kill me!' I could hardly come, it was so distracting, and, what I . . ."

Hamza had raised his left hand, palm out, with his fingers spread wide—as if defending himself from the words. His left shoulder rose a bit. Along his spine, hidden from view underneath his uniform, was a Tanto military knife. Its long handle stuck out of his uniform and touched his neck. When he raised his left shoulder, the handle of the knife protruded from the right side of his neck.

Musa caught Hamza's shoulder movement out of the corner of his eye. To him, Hamza's intent was clear.

"No, Hamza!" Musa jumped from the bunk and lunged towards Hamza.

The captain stood frozen and baffled.

*   *   *

Hamza let out a terrifying scream. He grabbed the handle of the knife with his left hand from over his right shoulder. In a single motion, he drew it, swinging to the left, the arc angled slightly downward.

The Tanto was in the air when the captain, figuring out too late what was about to happen, threw himself at Hamza.

"No!" he screamed.

The knife found the Chetnik's neck just slightly under the left ear and kept driving down until it lodged in his right shoulder, all but severing the bragging Chetnik's neck at its base. The shaggy, bearded, leering head fell back, hanging on a strip of skin that refused to detach from a blocky neck. Blood gushed forth in a fountain of gore and tissue.

The next moment, the captain hit Hamza and drove him to the ground. Hamza fell down and the captain toppled over him.

"Idiot!" the captain screamed.

"Oh, damn!" Musa whispered. "Fuck! Damn!"

The Chetnik's body was still stood, blood fountaining into the air. It splashed in the captain's hair and Hamza's face.

Hamza pushed the captain aside and rolled on top of him. He rested the knife's blade against the captain's neck and hissed through his clenched teeth, "Next time . . . next time . . . shoot me or don't get near me."

The captain's mouth was wide open as he tried to catch his breath. He realized just how close he was to his own death. Wisely, he remained quiet. Hamza's face turned white. His eyes blazed wildly. The body of the dead Chetnik finally fell to the ground next to Hamza, and blood continued to gush out of the thick, severed neck. Hamza got up and wiped the blood off his face.

"Dino. Dino! You're crying again? Let's go! You and Senad grab what weapons you can find. Dado, search them and take their documents. We only got a few minutes left." With heavy steps, Hamza turned and walked outside. The cold hit him in the face like a fist. He sighed. Not heading in any particular direction, he walked along the trench. At one point, there was a fork in the furrowed ditch; the narrower path headed towards the woods.

Hamza let his feet take him in that direction. In spite of the extreme cold, he felt himself suffocating. Breathing hard, he tried to focus and calm himself. Nervously, he unbuttoned his uniform. The remaining Chetnik blood slowly froze on his face, stretching the skin uncomfortably. It felt tight and sickening. He looked at his hands and noticed they were shaking. Walking slowly, he came to a tree that canted into the ditch and leaned against it.

While searching through his pockets for a cigarette, he stared off into the distance, aimlessly scanning the frigid, ghostly terrain. The impressive Bosnian mountain chain stretched from the southeast to the northwest. Bare, grayish white peaks, usually covered with snow, exuded a centuries-long peace, as did the immense Balkan forests. Now, from the vantage of the high plateau, the forests seemed like enormous, dark, spreading blotches randomly scattered on the mountainsides, as if they fought to reach and overwhelm the peaks. None of the breathtaking sights reached Hamza's brain. He couldn't register the beauty that lay before his eyes. He tried to concentrate, but failed. His brain refused to focus.

Finally, he started to feel the cold, smell the snowfall coming in the air, and silence made its way into his numbed senses.

Suddenly, along with the sound of the weary, cold wind, he thought he heard someone sobbing. Hamza stopped. He dropped low into the ditch. He hardly breathed. All his senses were sharp again. He'd left his sub in the dugout, but still held the Tanto tightly gripped in his hand. His mouth stretched into something resembling a smile, and he began quietly and carefully heading toward the source of the sobs.

*   *   *

The hidden ditch that echoed the sound stretched toward the edge of the cliff. Hamza pulled the hood back down. With his face pressed against the snow-covered surface, he peered out of the trench. In another ditch—in the direction of the increasingly luminous horizon—he could just make out a shape of a man. He seemed to be looking

AHMET M. RAHMANOVIC

toward the dugout. Hamza made his move. Crouching, he moved through the ditch to position himself behind the man. He climbed out of the ditch onto the snowbank, and slowly crawled forward. From some six yards away, Hamza tossed a snowball in the opposite direction. The man raised his rifle and turned toward the source. Hamza rose. Taking a few silent steps, he threw himself at the man. The stranger turned. Still in midair, Hamza pushed the rifle away and grabbed him by the hair. Falling into the ditch, Hamza found himself on top of the Chetnik. Pulling his enemy's head back, he began to swing his knife towards the neck, and stopped. The pale light shockingly revealed a face of a kid. His arm remained frozen in midair.

"What the fuck are you doing here?" Hamza growled.

The youngster sprawled under Hamza, eyes wide open. He was breathing heavily, unevenly. Taken by surprise and not knowing what to do, Hamza paused for a few moments, just staring at a child's face full of tears.

The kid still had a holstered gun. He struggled to draw it, but his elbow was blocked by Hamza's knee.

Somehow, he grabbed the gun, still in the holster, and fired it. The bullet grazed Hamza's chest and cut a swath along the right side of his face, before flying off into the night. Hamza thought his brain had exploded. Screaming, he plunged the knife into the Chetnik child soldier's head.

Hamza pulled out his knife and jumped away from the body that convulsed in a death spasm. He turned quickly. Not seeing anyone or anything else now, he tore off his hood. Raising his arms toward the sky, he howled into the emptiness of the night. Reverberating, like the long haunting howl of a wolf, a confused medley of anger and sadness.

A howl of anger from the wound of his soul. A howl of sadness for having to snuff out the life of a kid. A howl of anger at himself, at life, at the whole mankind, who silently watched as this cataclysm unfolded.

*   *   *

He removed the scarf from his neck and pressed it against his face. A rough growl rose out of his throat. The initial shock of the incident subsided, and now he felt pain exploding through his brain. Fatigue and the darkness of the night pressed heavily on his eyes. He

24

tried to get rid of it by shaking his head. The pain kept thundering in his brain. He started to lose his balance and was forced to hold on to the wall of the ditch. He pulled the scarf away from his face, and touched his right eye. It felt like it was still there. He staggered back toward the dugout. The others had heard the shot and were running towards Hamza.

"What happened, Hamza?" Breathless panic painted the night.

"Nothing. I'm fine. Let's go, let's go!"

"Hamza, Hamza!"

"I'm fine. Let's go."

The captain came up and hugged him. Blood poured down Hamza's cheek from under the scarf. Squinting his healthy eye shut, Hamza struggled to concentrate.

"It's okay, Captain. Don't worry about it. Get the men together and let's go. The dance is about to begin."

"We didn't take anything . . ."

"Forget it. Run, run!" Hamza pushed them with one hand. "We ran out of time! Don't turn back and don't wait. I'll see you." He added, whispered to himself, "God willing . . ."

The men ran, half-falling, half-sliding. They started down the cliffs. Hamza tried to run, but each step brought on a new wave of pain. He maintained a brisk pace while holding the scarf against his wound. He found it difficult to get oriented with only one eye functioning. He slipped and fell, and hit his head hard on the ground. Lying on the ground, he cursed. His knife had slipped out of his hand. Hamza got to his hands and knees, and groped along the cold ground with both hands, looking for it.

The Chetniks in the surrounding area had finally realized what had happened and began blasting the dugouts.

"Sons of bitches." Hamza thought to himself. "They already had the coordinates down pat."

The first mortar shell fell only a yard or two from the dugout.

Hamza's hand found his Tanto. The feel of the cold metal brought him back, and he dashed for the cliffs.

Explosions tore apart the short-lived silence of the night. As soon as the hissing of the launch was heard, the explosion followed. A reddish yellow flash lit the area for a brief moment, and then rocks, shrubs, and shrapnel would fly in every direction. The idea that somebody would be able to hear the shell coming and then jump out of the way was a movie gimmick. The explosions echoed in rapid succession as if the Chetniks were trying to plow the plateau.

Hamza was only a few of steps away from the cliffs. He had already started thinking about how he was going to get down the slippery side when a mortar shell exploded directly behind him. The impact of the explosion tossed a massive amount of earth, rock, and Hamza himself, into the air. He resembled nothing so much as a rag doll. He knew he had taken a hit—perhaps directly to the body.

"So, this is it."

Darkness overcame him, and he didn't feel himself falling into the trees beneath the cliffs, falling and breaking bushes on his way down, pounding the already tired and injured bones, skin, and limbs. He didn't feel himself hit the ground and bounce like a ball, ending up in bushes near the place where they had rested a half hour before going into action.

*   *   *

Sliding, Musa ran into the captain.

"Captain! Watch out!"

"Watch this, watch this!" Senad rushed past him, sliding on his back, reliving his childhood. He bounced off a tree and began sliding again, trying to navigate with his legs.

The captain tried to stay serious, running and holding on to trees and bushes. He slipped, fell, and started to slide down the hill. The sound of a body hitting the ground made him turn around. Not far away from him, Hamza's body bounced, and crashed in the bushes.

"Musa, over here! Hey, Musa!"

Musa grabbed onto a tree and stopped. He climbed back to the captain, and the two of them started toward the bushes. Hamza lay on his stomach, his back one solid bloodstain. Looking closer, the captain could see that his entire back was a huge, bloody mass. His military jacket had been shredded by shrapnel.

"Oh, man!" the captain cursed.

They turned him onto his back. Hamza's face was covered with blood. Where the blood did not coat him, the flesh was deathly white. His right arm was unnaturally bent.

"Oh, fucking . . . ! Hamza, Hamza." Musa gently slapped him.

"We'll carry him. Turn him back on his stomach." The captain took his coat off and put it under Hamza. He tied the sleeves around Hamza's back.

"Take one side. C'mon, what are you looking at?"

"It won't work this way. He's facedown. He'll freeze, if he doesn't suffocate first."

"Wait, wait. Give me the sweater. Wrap the sweater around his head. First, put the scarf on the wound, so it doesn't stick to the wool. Now, grab a side," the captain instructed.

"Hold on, let me put his arm inside the coat. It looks broken. Okay. Let's go."

The body slid easily down the cliff. They were breaking the slide with their feet as much as possible. They soon came to the ravine where the two cliffs connected. The others were waiting there.

"Hey, what happened?" The chorus of shouts sounded too loud in the frigid air.

"Hamza."

"Oh, damn."

"Is he fucked up bad?"

"I think so," Musa affirmed. "It hit him from the back."

"Now, we're really screwed."

"Your dad's screwed."

Having finished torturing the plateau, the Chetniks were now bombing the forest below the cliffs. The cold had eased, and soon a heavy snow began to fall.

"This is good for us," the captain mused.

"Good for us, my ass! We got at least another five hours to walk."

"That's nothing."

"It would be nothing, if Hamza weren't wounded."

"Fuck you!" They were all speaking over each other, and it was unknown who had cursed whom.

"Have you guys heard the joke about . . ."

"Fuck the jokes. We're in shit up to our ears, and you wanna tell jokes?"

"It's not the first time."

"It's not, but it could easily be our last."

"Don't jinx us."

"Nothing can jinx us anymore. All the bad luck that could have landed on our heads is here already."

"Enough!" The captain barked, deciding to stop the conversation. "Let's see what we can do."

"We can sit here and cry."

"Enough, guys! Go on, captain."

Close by, a shell exploded, and they all instinctively dove to the ground.

"We're headed northwest. Two of us should carry Hamza. Mustafa, you, Dino, and Senad are scouting ahead. And keep your eyes peeled. We'll be right behind you."

*　　*　　*

Musa and Sakib lifted Hamza, and the little group started walking. Climbing was difficult, and once in a while, someone would slip, fall, or slide back down. Musa carried Hamza with his right hand, while trying to anchor himself to the trees with his left.

They had been walking for nearly two hours when the captain called for a break. The men panted, and steam rose from their faces and heated uniforms.

"We're doing fine. If there are no problems, we could reach our troops by tomorrow morning," the captain noted.

"We could've walked this much in half an hour."

"Kemo, that's enough. What do you want, anyway? You've been talking shit the whole time."

"What do I want, you ask? I want a cigarette. Can I smoke, captain?"

"Sure you can, Kemo. With this snow, you could light a fire. Nobody'd be able to see it."

"I wonder where the guys from the patrol are."

"Don't worry, they're somewhere in front of us."

Everybody, except the captain, lit a cigarette. The tension dissipated. Musa sat on the ground and put Hamza's head in his lap. With his fingers, he touched his neck, trying to find a pulse. His frozen fingers couldn't find anything.

"It's time. Let's go." They started walking again. They had trouble climbing up the hills, and going down was worse. Another hill, then another one. The snow kept falling. It was no longer possible to follow the tracks their patrol had left behind.

"Our patrol is not there anymore, captain."

"Don't worry, they have to be somewhere in front of us."

They took turns carrying Hamza. The eastern sky grew lighter, ushering in the dawn. The men staggered along in silence, each occupied with his own thoughts.

Musa had been carrying Hamza for a long time. "Stop, captain. Let's take a break."

"Okay, people, stop."

Everyone had been waiting for that. Musa put Hamza's head in his lap and carefully took the sweater off his face. The scarf covering the wound was soaked through with blood and frozen solid. The healthy eye was closed and the face was a deathly white.

"Hamza, Hamza!" Musa shook him, "Hamza, can you hear me?"

"Musa, see if he's breathing. I can't see breath coming out of his mouth."

"Hamza, Hamza, hey, it's me, Musa. Hamza."

"Musa, I'm afraid . . ." a young soldier announced.

"Afraid of what?" Musa groaned. "Hamza, Hamza." He leaned on Hamza's face, trying to find even the slightest signs of breathing, without success. He shook him again. "Hamza, Hamza." He began to panic. "Hamza, you fuck! Breathe! Breathe! Breathe! You motherfucker, you think you're gonna get out of this so easily? No way! No way, do you hear me. Breathe!"

Musa started blowing into his face, trying to warm him. Soon, the frozen blood began to thaw and melt in pink and red rivulets through his hair. He brushed pieces of ice away from Hamza's shockingly white face.

"Hamza, c'mon. Fuck! Wanna cigarette?" He turned to the others. "Give me a cigarette."

"Musa, you're nuts."

"Musa, leave him alone. What's wrong with you?"

"Give me a cigarette. Give me a damn cigarette!" Musa screamed. He took the cigarette, inhaled a big cloud, pressed his lips against Hamza's and, with all his strength, blew the smoke into him. Then, he did it again, and again. The others looked on in silence.

The captain stared awkwardly at the patch of earth in front of them.

"Musa, take a break."

"Musa, I think he's gone."

"Let's move him aside somewhere. We'll come back for him later."

"What? I would rather stay behind myself than leave him." Panic had overwhelmed him. He cursed, took another drag of the cigarette, and blew it into Hamza's lungs.

"Musa, wait a second, let's take a look," the captain tried reasoning with him.

"Enough! I don't wanna hear a word. Hamza! Hamza!"

It may have been the smoke, perhaps the shaking, but whatever it was, it was definitely a gift from God, for suddenly, from the depths of his lungs, Hamza started to hiss, almost a cough.

"That's right! That's right! Breathe, you motherfucker!" Musa kept roaring.

"Hush," the captain whispered. "I think we have visitors."

*   *   *

"Quiet!" the captain repeated, pointing in the direction of a nearby clearing.

On the other side of the clearing, they could see the Chetniks moving in a line. They looked like shadows in the fuzzy light of dawn, searching the woods. Everybody lay down, trying to blend in with the snow. The captain could feel the snow under him melting and soaking his sweater.

"Don't anyone dare move," he hissed.

The Chetniks walked across the clearing, which stretched all the way to the farthest part of the forest. The captain could hear their voices, but he couldn't make out what they were saying.

"If they find us, it will all be over quickly," he thought with a measure of certainty. The trees around them were sparse and the leafless bushes couldn't possibly hide them.

"Musa!" the captain called out in a whisper. "If they find us, take Hamza and go down the hill. Try to hide somewhere. We'll stay here and try to protect you as long as we can."

Musa stared at him, a question dressing his face. "You know I'm not afraid."

"Fuck you and your fear. Just do what I tell you."

Musa stared at him. That was the first time he had heard the captain swear. He grinned.

"Well, captain, now you're one of us."

"Thank God."

At that moment, they heard excited Chetnik voices.

"Wait." The captain concentrated very hard in order to hear the conversations being transmitted in the thin, cold air. "Looks like they've found the tracks from our patrol."

"Oh, fuck! I hope they won't run into them."

"This is good. I hope they'll go and follow them." The captain calculated rapidly, feverishly trying to predict the next chain of events. "If they go after them, it means that we're safe for now. But, that means that our guys are screwed."

"Don't worry about them, Captain. Mustafa is a forester."

"A what?"

"A forester, captain, a forester. He spent his entire life in forests. They say he used to catch foxes with his bare hands. He just sneaks up to them and . . . wham!"

"I hope so. In any case, there is nothing we can do right now. We'll wait here for sometime. Kemo, you and Sakib go first. Don't go any further than five minutes out. Follow their tracks. My guess is that they suspect that we're on this side too. Just go slowly; it won't do to run into them."

Sakib took his jacket off and gave it to the captain.

"No way." The captain shook his head vigorously.

"Don't fuck around and die from the cold, captain, or you'll be no use to any of us. I'll be on the move anyway."

"Take it, Captain," said Musa. He gently put the sweater on Hamza's head and pulled the sleeve tied to him.

"Let's go, people."

The two of them went quickly in front of the others, while Musa, the captain, and Dado set out behind them, dragging Hamza. Hamza was not heavy anymore; his body slid easily through the snow.

After trudging along for half an hour, they joined Kemo and Sakib, who had been waiting for them.

"The Chetniks are about half an hour away. They're walking fast. I think they're closing in on our guys. I hope Mustafa will sense them before it's too late."

"Don't you worry about Mustafa."

*   *   *

The patrol was a half-hour walk in front of them. After crossing a clearing some hundred yards wide, Mustafa called for a rest. With lighter loads and only their rifles in their hands, they were moving quickly through the forest.

"Not a Chetnik in sight," Dino announced.

"Don't say it twice." Mustafa, superstitious and wise, knew it took very little to bring the nightmare back around.

"What do you think, Mustafa, how far away are we from our guys?"

"Well, about an hour away."

"Should we wait for them, or should we go further?"

"We'll wait until they show up in the clearing."

"Can we have a smoke?"

"Don't. Wait until they get here."

"Mustafa, I'm gonna take a little nap. Wake me when they show up."

"Take a nap, you deserve it. I'll call you when we need you."

Mustafa lay down on the snow himself, looking over the clearing. When their people came, they'd have about two hours to walk, if the battle lines had not moved during the night. He felt exhaustion slip over him. He was in a strange state of semisleep. He knew that he wasn't sleeping, yet he dreamed.

After a while, the wind carried voices to him. He awoke.

Quickly, he realized these weren't his people. The captain wouldn't allow noise. Not in a place like this, a situation like this. He put a hand on Dino's mouth and shook him. Dino jumped.

"Hush! Be quiet. Listen."

All three of them listened carefully, with baited breath.

"Chetniks."

They peered out cautiously and saw a stretched line of Chetniks coming toward the clearing. The snow had covered their tracks fairly well, making it difficult for the Chetniks to decide which way they had gone.

"Listen, when they come to the middle of the clearing, we shoot. Now, spread out. Ten yards to the left and right. One burst. Only one. Then run, and no stopping till the next crest. By the time they figure out what's going on, we'll already be there. Whatever you do, don't let them see you. Another thing, our guys are behind them—the captain and the others. We'll drag the Chetniks off. Maybe everything is going to be all right. Just don't play the hero. As soon as I start shooting, join in."

The Chetniks slowly approached the clearing. There were about thirty of them, their faces already visible. Mustafa carefully put his machine gun in front of him. It was time to play. He aimed and then started firing. A long burst, a few short ones, then a long one again. He felt a certain satisfaction shooting down live targets. The others joined in and started shooting. The Chetnik line scattered. The surprise lasted only a moment, then all dove to the ground. There was loud screaming, yelling, and cursing.

Before the Chetniks could respond, Mustafa had crawled back to the others, and they all ran downhill. Behind them, machine gun bursts and explosions echoed. They crossed the ravine at a run, and continued uphill to the top of the next crest. Upon reaching it, they surveyed the area before them. Not detecting any new threat, from up ahead, they turned to watch for the pursuit. The Chetniks had discovered that they had abandoned their positions and were now moving forward.

Mustafa quickly decided their new position was a mistake. Chetniks could easily guess where they were. They had to move down the crest at least another hundred yards. He was about to say they needed to leave, when the sizzle of a grenade launcher reached him.

"Down!" Mustafa jumped, trying to burrow straight into the ground.

The explosion lifted and threw him into the air. He fell, shook his head, and looked around, dazed. Not far away, he saw Senad. Or rather, what was left of him.

It had been a direct hit.

"Dino. Dino!"

"I'm here."

"Are you okay?"

"Yes. I just got a scratch on my arm."

"Let's move!" They started running.

They ran for their lives. The hillside was not very steep, and the dense forest served as shelter. At a dead run, they came to the end of the forest.

"Oh, fuck!" Mustafa almost ran off the cliff in front of him. The forest ended in cliffs.

"Go right!" They continued running. Behind them, they could no longer hear gunfire.

"It's always easier to be the hunted than the hunter," Mustafa said, still running.

Dino was frightened. He took a little bit of snow and put it into his mouth. He felt better already. They reached another crest.

"Not to the peak. To the side," Musa demanded.

They reversed direction and started towards the side.

"Now we'll fuck them over. Dino, you ever play poker?" Dino stared in the direction the Chetniks were likely to appear.

Without giving him a chance to reply, Mustafa continued. "It's the same thing. If you're good at bluffing, you win."

"And if you aren't, you're fucked."

"Ha! Dino, Dino, who taught you that? Those are some nasty words. You're too young to be using those kinds of words."

"Well, fuck it! I'm too young to smoke, too young to chase girls, too young for beer. Mustafa, do you know the only thing I am *not* too young to do?"

"I know, to die." Musa responded with the weight such a fact demanded.

"Exactly! You have to go for broke, don't you? Only to die."

"Who cares? We'll wait here for them. We fucked them up pretty good, I'd say."

"I don't know where they're coming up with all these Chetniks anymore. In the last few missions, we've killed over a hundred of them."

"Yes. And they've killed two hundred thousand of us."

"Exactly, exactly. But they killed civilians, women and children. And we've killed only their soldiers. Now look, for every real Chetnik they have, they bring along another ten kids."

"They are losing their men, Dino, and they're not recovering well," Mustafa concluded.

"Take last night. We killed I do not know how many of them. And another maybe five now. But we lost Senad and maybe Hamza, as well. Senad was blown apart."

"How can you say it like that?"

"What do you mean, how can I? He died, fuck it."

"I thought the two of you were friends?"

"C'mon, cut the shit." His eyes filled with tears. "If he were alive . . . if he were wounded . . . We grew up together. This way . . . fuck it."

They waited in the snow for twenty minutes. Chetniks weren't coming. Maybe they had lost them. Impossible. Tracks were easy to follow in the snow. Unless, of course, they were planning to surround them. As the thought struck home, Mustafa froze.

*   *   *

Musa never allowed Hamza out of his hands. The captain and Dado took turns helping carry Hamza's lifeless form. Every ten minutes, the patrol would be waiting for them to catch up. The third time, the patrol was running back to them. Out of breath, Kemo reported to the captain:

"Shooting. Twenty minutes away from here."

"We heard it. That's Mustafa."

"That's good. It looks like they didn't catch him sleeping."

"We'll see. Mustafa is definitely gonna drag them farther away. If we continue this way, there's a possibility of running into them."

Musa smiled, a shark displaced. "I'd like that."

"Musa, your only job is to take care of Hamza."

"He's gonna feel better if I kill a few of them."

"Stop it. Kemo, get ahead. I think Mustafa is gonna fall into a trap. Here's the plan: you and Sakib head back in that direction until you see the Chetniks. Leave Sakib there, and get back to us. We'll keep following your tracks for now. When we meet up again, we'll decide what to do next."

Kemo and Sakib hurried along and were soon out of sight.

"We should go too." The captain lifted Hamza from one side, Musa from the other. Dado walked a little distance from them.

After fifteen minutes, it started. Sounds of explosions and automatic weapons echoed through the forest.

"Hand grenades." The captain looked at Musa, worriedly. "It looks like Kemo ran into the Chetniks."

"They can't be smart enough to set an ambush on their own trail."

"I'm going further ahead," captain said, and gestured Musa to be silent with a quick wave of his hand.

"If I'm not back in fifteen minutes, you guys find the way out on your own." Soon, he too disappeared into the embrace of the forest.

"Well, it looks like it's just down to us," Musa bitterly sighed. "Let's get to a better position." He helped pull Hamza behind a group of pines that formed a natural shelter. The foliage was dense, and no snow had collected under the trees. Musa sat down, he took Hamza's head in his lap, and started whispering a song only he could hear.

Dado went to the other side of the cleared area and lay down. He held his gun at the ready, prepared to shoot.

Ten minutes later, the captain returned. Musa waved to him from under the trees. The captain came over. "Mustafa got them pretty good, couple of minutes from here. Kemo ran into the wounded Chetniks and the two guys they had left behind to take care of them."

"Is Kemo okay?"

"He is, but . . . I don't like it. I was taught differently."

"What did you learn differently from the rest of us, Captain?"

"There were no survivors."

"And?"

"No 'and.' There were no survivors. It's impossible that they all died during the fighting."

"Fuck you, Captain. What do you think they would do to us if they could? Where the hell have you been? I'll ask you again when you've gone into a village after the Chetniks have been there. Fuck that 'humane treatment' bullshit!"

"We cannot be the same." The captain held a steady but sad note in his statement.

"And we are not the same. Has anyone of us ever killed a child? Slaughtered women? Not one of us, and not ever. Did you hear me? And these men came at us with guns. You know how sorry I feel for them? Don't even . . ." Musa waved his hand, resigning the subject with an expression of disgust.

"So, what do we do now?"

"Let's head over to Kemo. We'll see then. The Chetniks must have heard the shooting too."

"That's good. They're gonna leave Mustafa alone for a while."

They picked up Hamza again and began walking. Fifteen minutes later, they came to the clearing where Mustafa had waited for the Chetniks. On the other side of the exposed clearing, Kemo waved at them. They hurried across and melted into the woods.

"Any news?"

"Not for now. They're somewhere in front of us. It's gonna be tight if we continue in this direction."

"Does anyone know this area?" the captain asked.

"If I'm not mistaken," Musa said, "this hillside is about a mile and a half long, and ends in cliffs. If Mustafa came to the cliffs, he turned either left or right. He probably went right. If we turn that way now, we'll be able to cut him off."

"I hope the Chetniks don't know as much as you do about all that."

"I'm pretty sure they do. In any case, we'll find out soon enough."

"Okay," the captain thought aloud. "Let's move diagonally. Kemo, you go ahead of us with Sakib. You don't need me to tell you this anymore, but you've gotta be all eyes and ears. If you don't track *them* down before they track *you* down, it's . . ." the captain pulled his finger across his neck with a grimace.

Kemo pulled Sakib by the sleeve, and they disappeared among the trees. The captain reached for Hamza again.

"Let's go, Musa, one day this will all be history."

"If we survive, Captain. My good and honest captain. As you know I am."

"You really don't know how to be serious, do you?"

"There is no way I can be more serious. We have Hamza almost dead and a bunch of Chetniks breathing down our necks. If they catch us, they're gonna slice us and dice us. And you think I am not serious?"

"It's no use talking to you. Dado, what's wrong with you? You are too silent."

Dado, a dismal guy he was, just shrugged his shoulders and took a hold of Hamza.

*   *   *

Chetniks had figured out that Mustafa planned to turn right at the cliff wall, and now they had him trapped in a semicircle. Retreat meant the narrow ravine behind them. If they moved quickly enough, they might make it. Mustafa didn't know exactly what was going on in front of him, but his hunter's instincts, along with those developed during three years of war, told him that they were in serious trouble.

Dino was laying down some ten yards away from him. He was calm. At least he seemed calm. The only thing he feared was falling into the Chetniks' hands alive.

He took his gun out, put a round in the chamber, and put it on the ground within easy reach. Sometimes, captives were exchanged. There would certainly be no exchange for him if he were caught. Not after last night's action. Hamza fucked it up when he killed that duke. But fuck, what would they have done with him the whole night? Dino considered; he had killed him too. What the Chetniks did in Sweetwater could not been seen even in the most gruesome horror movies.

"Fuck it," he whispered to himself. "Mustafa. Mustafa!" he called out in a low voice. "Can you see anything?"

"Nothing. My guess is they are surrounding us."

"Mustafa, are you scared?"

"A bit. But, we've done more than our fair share of killing. They can't kill us fifty times."

"If it gets rough, I'll kill myself. I'm not letting them take me alive."

"Okay, Dino. Fine. There is time enough for that. Just don't rush into it. There is no second chance."

"You're fucking around, but it's my ass we're talking about."

"C'mon, just make sure you see them before they see you, then we'll see."

* * *

The snow had dwindled down and nearly stopped falling. Heavy, iron skies appeared above them and above the deserted area. It was as if someone had turned off the color on the TV—just black, white, and shades of gray. Somewhere in front of them, the Chetniks stalked the night, and behind them the captain, Musa, Hamza, and Dado shadowed them. If the shooting *really* got started, they might hit their own people. Mustafa secretly hoped that the captain would come up behind the Chetniks. They would surely survive in that case. He saw a small movement, deep in the forest in front of them. A bird flew into the air. Mustafa pressed himself against the ground and held his gun ready.

He scanned the forest over the sights on his sub.

"Dino, down there. Next to the fir. Do you see anything?"

"Nothing."

"Maybe it was just my imagination, but I thought someone is hiding there."

"No, not your imaginings, Mustafa. I'm afraid I see one now too."

"Don't shoot yet. I think they have us surrounded. Look to the left. If you're sure, then shoot. Don't wait for me. And Dino, please, see to it that you don't miss."

"Sure thing, no pressure," Dino whispered.

Dino lay flat in the snow, squinting, with one eye half-closed. Then he saw him. The Chetnik was crawling between two trees. Dino aimed and waited. The Chetnik reached a secure place behind a tree. After a moment, he looked out, his gun at the ready. Dino shot and hit. Good. That was only the initial shot. The next moment the whole forest exploded. Hundreds of bullets, like swarms of bees, began to buzz all around them. Dino crawled back a couple of yards down the slope, and ran to the side, shot a burst of fiery death, then did it all over again. Mustafa shot, yelling, and constantly changing his position, that the Chetniks would think there were more of them.

*   *   *

Kemo ran to the captain.

"They're close, in front of us."

"Musa, you stay here with Hamza. The rest of you come with me."

The captain ran, with Kemo and Dado following behind him. They had been running for a few minutes, when Kemo caught up with the captain and pulled him aside.

"Hold it. We're very close. There's Sakib."

The battle was in front of them. They edged closer, moving quietly. They soon saw the first of the Chetnik stragglers. They were lying behind the trees and shooting from time to time. The captain silently motioned to his men to spread out.

*   *   *

Then the first explosion echoed. The detonation blast caught Mustafa and threw him a couple of yards. He landed without a scratch, rolling to absorb the shock to his shoulder and arm.

"Oh, damn . . ."

"Mustafa! Mustafa!" Dino called to him, frightened.

"Get down!"

"Mustafa, those were our guys. That came from behind us."

"Are you sure?"

"Well, the hell else would it be? That was *friendly fire*. Get them on the walkie-talkie."

"You know we're not allowed to use it."

"Fuck the orders! Call them!"

"I don't know the frequency they use."

"Call them on the open channel, quit fucking around! We only have a couple of minutes till they figure out it's only two of us here."

"Mine thrower, respond . . . mine thrower respond!!"

"You still alive, Chetnik motherfucker?" A voice crackled out of the walkie-talkie, along with static.

"It's not Chetniks, it's us. We're on your side."

"Right, right. On our side. Now, you're definitely on our side. Here comes another one."

"Dino, get down."

Mustafa buried his head in the snow as a new explosion echoed.

The real Chetnik soldiers joined the conversation.

"Don't listen to him, my friend. Give him another one."

"No problem, my friend. Here it comes."

"Who is this? Who's on the line? Say it, motherfucker!" Mustafa roared.

"Mustafa, who is it? Who's on the line?" Dino lost it. The thought that his death would come from friendly fire drove him over the edge. Not hearing an answer from Mustafa, he started running in blind panic. The Chetniks saw this panicked dance and started shooting at Dino's running shadow. He dove to the ground and rolled down to Mustafa.

"Give it to me! Give me the goddamn walkie-talkie!"

He grabbed the walkie-talkie from Mustafa and screamed.

"Dino here, Dino here. Who's there?"

"This is Fadil, the legend of Hrasnica."

"Fadil, my friend, don't listen to him. Just flatten him with another one." The Chetniks were back on the line.

"Fadil, this is Dino!" he spoke, trying to catch his breath. His mouth was dry, so he picked up some snow and ate it. "Fadil, listen to me. Remember how I promised you that I'd fuck your sister? Well, if you don't aim just a hundred yards up ahead, I don't think I'll be able to. And then you can be the one to go and explain it to her."

Dino, a grouch and grumbler that he was—as well as the youngest guy in the unit—was a gentle, brave, yet crazy soul. Two months earlier, he got into a fight with Fadil, who was three times his size. After receiving a few *disciplinary* smacks, he made a solemn promise to Fadil that he would fuck Fadil's sister. Every time after that, when Dino had to leave Sarajevo and go through Hrasnica, they got into arguments. Eventually, Fadil got bored of smacking him, so Dino's promise was, unofficially, still valid. In the unit, the guys had already started to make fun of Fadil because of that unresolved situation.

"Oh, it's you, you little douche bag! Here comes another one, and then if you survive, I'll take on the Chetniks myself." A shell exploded right next to them.

"You fuck! You fucking fuck! You're crazier than you look!" Dino's scream had turned into a screech.

"And now, please, apologize to me, nice and loud, so that everyone, even the deaf Chetniks, can hear you. They need to hear it too. They are all talking about how some kid intends to fuck my sister."

"Fadil, please. I'm sorry. Please, dear Fadil. Okay, I won't fuck your sister . . ."

"You're starting again. Do you want another one?"

"No, no! Wait!" Dino talked fast. "Okay listen, I'll bring her flowers next time I'm in Hrasnica."

"She's not in Hrasnica, she's in Germany."

"Even better. I'll ask for time off, and I'll go to Germany with flowers from Hrasnica."

Meanwhile, Fadil had given his mine throwers an order; explosions echoed a hundred yards in front of Mustafa and Dino. The Chetniks retreated, swearing and screaming.

*   *   *

The captain's walkie-talkie buzzed. He heard the entire conversation. Quickly, he waved to the others to come closer.

"To the left!" The captain wanted to get them out of the path of retreating Chetniks. They ran left and got under cover. Soon, they saw the Chetniks running. The captain waited until they had nearly passed them by.

"Fire!"

Guns burst, and a column of Chetniks toppled to the ground. The remaining ones ran back in the direction they had come from.

The captain jumped to his feet and ran toward the place where they had left Musa, Dado, and Hamza. Kemo ran after him while the others went to Mustafa, yelling and calling. A new explosion shook the nearby forest. That was Fadil, randomly searching the forest. The captain cursed. One of the shells exploded in Musa's direction.

"Damn it, that was too close." The captain ran faster.

Through the smoke of the explosion, he saw Musa lying, with a painful grimace, and holding his leg. Not far away, sprawled on the ground, Dado held his gun at the ready, scanning the terrain in the direction of the retreating Chetniks.

"Fadil, cease fire! Cease fire!"

"Who is it now?"

"It's the captain. Cease fire!"

"How many of you are there? I'm aiming a hundred yards away from Dino."

"Cease fire! Fuck Dino."

"Okay," Fadil gave in dejectedly.

"Fadil, send your people over here. We got casualties." It was Dino again.

"They're on their way. Will ten be enough?"

"Yeah, just tell them to hurry."

"They're coming. Don't shoot."

"We won't. Over."

The captain ran to Musa. The muscle above the left knee had been ripped away by shell fragments, and the shredded flesh could be seen through his bloody, ripped pants. The captain took the scarf off his neck and tied it off above the wound. Musa held on to consciousness.

"Everything's gonna be fine, Musa. Those were our guys."

"Fuck them! The Chetniks have been after me for three years, and now *our* morons got me."

"Be quiet, if they hadn't shown up . . ."

"I'm fucked up either way."

"But you're gonna survive. Now, to Sarajevo, and then you'll take sick leave."

"How does it look?"

"Looks like shit, but it's gonna be fine. Your leg will be fine."

"It does hurt pretty bad." Musa tried to stay conscious, but the darkness claimed him, and he lost himself in the blackness.

"Dado, why didn't you look after Musa?"

"He was okay till you came."

"Man, you saw he was wounded."

"Yes, but it was more important for me to look after the Chetniks." Dado stared at the captain coldly.

"Just who am I fighting against?"

Fadil's men arrived with stretchers. They loaded Musa on one, and then picked up Hamza.

"Put him on his stomach. On his stomach."

"Okay, Captain. Damn, he's hit pretty bad."

"He picked up ninety percent of the shrapnel."

"Yeah, sure. Like *you* know what percent he got."

It was already afternoon when Mustafa and Dino came to where Fadil held his position. Fadil hugged Dino like a brother.

"Hey, bro, you were scared, huh? Just you keep fucking with me."

"Cut it out, Fadil. You hit Musa."

"What? Musa? Where is he? Is it serious? Is he alive? Dino, are you fucking with me?"

"No, I'm not. They're coming in behind us."

"Fuck! What were they doing behind you?"

"It's a long story. Just give me some coffee and a cigarette. I've never been so scared in my life."

"Okay, my guys are going to make coffee right now. C'mon, what are you guys waiting for? You heard me, coffee!"

"Get your sister to make him one," said a soldier, and ran outside before Fadil could see who dared offer such a comment.

Fadil's people were carrying Hamza and Musa. Dado was the last one, taking up position behind the caravan of the unconscious and dying soldiers. They were walking close to the position where Dino and Mustafa had been. As the captain turned to have a look around, a bullet struck him in the chest.

"Sniper! Sniper! Get down!"

*   *   *

One of the soldiers carrying Musa was too late. He looked around, confused by the screams. A bullet blew his head away.

"Take cover! Get to the woods."

The men started crawling. A few bullets whizzed above their heads. The sniper was on lower ground, and couldn't hit them while they crawled.

"Quick! Pull the captain!"

"Leave the soldier. He's dead. We'll come back later. Damn it, just leave him."

"Fadil, respond!"

"What's going on now?"

"Sniper. At the place you first found the Chetniks."

"Okay, we're ready. Are you sure none of our guys are there?"

"Positive, just shoot."

After Fadil's men had launched the initial mortars, the Chetniks started retreating fast. One of them, braver, crazier, and likely meaner than the rest, with a sniper's rifle in his hand, jumped into a small natural dugout behind a tree and lay down. He patiently waited to see what developed. After the shooting had stopped, he saw a short line of men. The captain was at the front of the procession, followed by the soldiers carrying the wounded and dying. He thought there might be more of them, and held off shooting while they were in the clearing. Realizing nobody else was coming, he aimed at the captain. He knew that anyone going on a sabotage mission wouldn't be wearing a bulletproof vest—it's just too heavy—and armed with that confidence, he aimed for the heart. He lined up the crosshairs in his scope and squeezed off a shot. He saw the captain stagger and then, before the captain had even fallen, decided to fire on a soldier who hadn't run for cover. This time he aimed for the head. The soldier dropped with a dull thud that echoed off the trees. The others had already run for and found shelter; they were out of reach. He fired a few bullets above their position and backed up, slowly. He felt a great satisfaction. He had come from Russia to Bosnia for money, and was simply earning his pay. When he was far away enough from the screams of the wounded and dying, he began to run. He was out of reach when the next barrage of mortar shells echoed, and a smile sketched itself across his face.

*   *   *

Kemo took off the captain's jacket. The wound bled dangerously. The sniper shot as the captain was turning. The bullet hadn't struck home, but had caused a deep wound to his chest. Somebody handed Kemo a scarf. He tied it to the one he already had and formed a long bandage. Pressing several pieces of gauze against the wound, he tied the scarves across the captain's chest.

"Come on guys, hurry up. The captain's bleeding pretty badly."

"Get down! The sniper is still here."

"He's gone by now, don't worry. That was a professional motherfu . . ."

"You've got guts."

"Fadil, come in."

"What's up?"

"We have another casualty. One of your men was killed too."

"For fuck's sake! All right, I'm sending more people. Is it safe now?"

"I think so. Hurry."

Soon after, the wounded column stopped in front of Fadil's dugout. "Call the doctor! Is there a doctor here?"

"No doctors. Carry them inside."

*   *   *

The small, primitive dugout had been built quickly, and it would not withstand a direct mortar hit. The entrance was in a muddy narrow ditch, making it difficult to carry the wounded inside. Fadil untied the scarves on the captain's chest and examined the wound.

"He's fine. This is nothing."

"What do you mean fine! Don't you see how torn up it is?"

The wound opened again and blood trickled out.

"This is nothing, trust me. A ripped muscle and scraped rib. It looks bad, but isn't really. By the time we get to Sarajevo, he'll be walking, trust me."

"I'll just be happy if he survives."

"Don't worry, my friend. Fadil's seen more wounds in this war than pretty girls before it."

"Oh man, how come you don't have a doctor here?"

"How come we don't?" Fadil repeated the question. "All of those who knew how to so much as give a shot have fled. Those couple of good doctors, who chose to stay in Sarajevo, could do all the work only if they cloned themselves. Please don't bring up the *intellectual patriots*."

"Don't give me that, Fadil. Look at Hamza."

"Huh? Hamza is a thug, not an intellectual."

"Right, as if I don't know what an intellectual is!"

"Well, my friend, if it hadn't been for his dad, he would have ended up in Zenica, in jail."

"That's not true. He finished school by playing by the rules."

"I'm not saying he didn't. I'd bet my life that he did. It is just that you don't know what kind of a trouble child Hamza was. Nevertheless, his dad turned him into a good man. He would take him to different places, to the mosque . . . After a while, he was back on the right path."

"Was his dad tough?"

"No way. He never raised his voice to Hamza. Never hit him or anything like that. God forbid."

"I wish my dad had been like that."

"Now, check this out. This is the best. His dad killed more Russians and Germans than all of us combined have killed Chetniks."

"You're full of shit. What are you talking about, Russians and Germans?"

"Did you hear about the Legion of Ustashas in Stalingrad in the Second World War?"

"No, why?"

"When the Germans came to Sarajevo, they recruited young guys to fight against the communists. Hamza's dad joined them when he was eighteen. Nobody knows what he went through. Anyway, they fought against the Russians. Then he switched around, and fought against the Germans. Once, when I was a kid, I overheard that story when he came over to my folks' place. Can you imagine?"

"We're talking too much. We won't be able to go down Mount Igman before dark. They're butchering us over there with those goddamn anti-aircraft guns from Ilidza."

"Oh, that's right. I totally forgot about that. That's all we need."

"Need it or not, we've got it. Let's go see about the car."

They went outside. Fadil continued talking, more to himself: "Fuck it, Kemo, looks like you're in charge now."

"Thanks, brother. The captain got fucked up, Hamza is screwed, Musa shredded . . . Nobody's left to lead, and now I am in charge. Fuck that honor!"

"You know what, Kemo? I swear a lot, but you're just too much. You have picked up all the profanity there could possibly be in this world. You could write a book. It would sell like crazy too."

"Don't fuck around with me. First thing I learned in the war was to swear, and then to kill. After that, I learned more subtle things, like how to live on nothing for ten days, how to bathe with a bottle of water, how to piss straight into the toilet in pitch black. Would you believe it if I told you I used to write poetry before the war?"

"Yeah. Roses are red, violets are blue, and I think that I am in love with you."

"Go ahead, make fun of me, but I'll write poetry again, about the roses and violets too."

Outside the dugout, a van pulled up. It was a mottled shade of gray with paint scraped off and damaged in a thousand places—a real war vehicle. The only things functioning on it were the tires. They were bald, but had air in them.

"Do you want any of us to stay here with you?" said Kemo, in an attempt to be kind.

"Who would you leave? Look at you guys, you look like zombies."

"Fuck you and your zombies. You really know how to cheer a guy up. Dino was right."

"Don't fuck with me. Get in that van before I change my mind and make *all* of you stay and work."

"Well, then, see you later."

"Say 'God willing!'"

"God willing. That is understood."

*　　*　　*

Kemo jumped in the van and it sped away.

While Kemo spoke to Fadil, the rest of the party ate. They ate a lot. When no one was looking, Dado put a few cans and a piece of meat in the bag. Once in the van, Kemo realized he hadn't eaten anything.

"You guys get something for me too?"

"No, go and sweet-talk Fadil. Maybe he'll feel sorry for you."

Dado took out the can, a piece of homemade bread, and an onion, and handed them to Kemo in silence.

"Thanks, bro," Dado nodded.

"Dado, please say something. You haven't said a word since we left Sarajevo."

"Leave him alone. He didn't have any objections. Everything was just the way he wanted it to be."

Dado looked at him darkly.

"Really, Dado, where are you from?"

"Krajina."

"So why are you here?"

"Because I am a bastard, that's why."

"I don't understand a word you're saying."

"Well, let me explain it to you. The Chetniks killed my whole family in Krajina, and I was caged in the correctional facility in Zenica."

"How long were you in for?"

"Five. Sentenced to seven, but I was paroled after five when they saw that the war wasn't going to end."

"Five years. That's a long time, man."

"What did you do?"

They didn't get an answer. The captain, lying next to Hamza and Musa, unconscious on the floor of the van, opened his eyes.

"Where are we?"

"Near Igman."

"Our losses?"

"Senad bought it."

"Come on, talk like a human being."

"Okay." Dino got serious. "Forty-five percent casualties. Senad dead, Hamza, Musa, and you wounded. Myself, Kemo, Sakib, Mustafa, and Dado are all right."

"Thank God."

"How are you, Captain?"

"I'm all right. Help me sit up."

Dado, sitting with Hamza's head in his lap, moved to one side, and the captain sat up.

"This is a bit more like it."

"Captain, have a cigarette. Fadil's treat."

"Dino, did you steal his cigarettes?"

"To the last pack, my friend."

"He's gonna kill you the next time he sees you."

"As if he's gonna know who it was."

"Yeah, right. He's gonna think Hamza took them."

"Oh, I didn't think of that."

They laughed uncontrollably. For the first time in the last thirty hours, the tension loosened, and they really laughed. The van headed from the ski runs toward Mount Igman. The captain carefully touched his wound and thought, "When it hurts, it will get better, and when it doesn't hurt, then . . ." He shook his head, trying to make the dark thoughts go away. Musa began to stir.

"What are you shouting about? You don't let a guy sleep in peace."

"Ho-ho, are you mad or what?"

"Welcome to the jungle."

"Give me a cigarette."

"A cigarette, a cigarette!"

Dino gave him a pack.

"Fadil's treat!"

"Just keep showing off, kid, he's really gonna kill you one day."

"Dino," Musa looked at him," you really stole his cigarettes?"

"Come on, he's gonna be fine." Dino was a bit worried. "Anyway, fuck him. Who knows if he'll even be alive when we meet the next time? Or maybe, if I'm gonna be alive?"

"Maybe you're right."

*   *   *

Igman, a mountain stretching across the west side of Sarajevo, presents another natural barrier preventing warm winds from blowing into Sarajevo, provided they accidentally break through from the south. Waterless and covered by dense forest, it had mainly been a source of timber for fuel and construction.

The 1984 Winter Olympics in Sarajevo changed its role, and Igman became a favorite winter vacation spot for the people of Sarajevo as well as for tourists from all over the world. The Bosna river has its source near the foot of the mountain. Not far away, at the actual bottom, all but leaning up against Igman, is the community of Hrasnica.

Beside it lies the township of Butmir, stretching all the way to the Sarajevo airport. Sarajevo proper begins on the other side of the airport.

The tunnel beneath the airport was the straw of salvation that Sarajevo breathed hope through, for nearly four years of war.

Igman's road, fairly wide and graveled, was often called the "road to salvation," the last hope," the "suicide lane," or the "path of the dead." It went north for a couple of miles from Hrasnica and then, just as it came dangerously close to the Chetniks' position, it turned back on itself and climbed farther up the mountain. After four or five miles of climbing, the road began winding like a serpent, undulating all the way to the peak of the mountain. Those few miles of the winding road were completely exposed to the Chetnik fire.

The traffic went by at night without headlights, but even so, the chances of getting to Hrasnica, or to the peak of Igman successfully, were slim.

* * *

Not far from the peak, the military police stopped the van.

"Hey, where are you guys headed?"

"Raise the ramp!" Demanded a voice from the van, brooking no argument.

"What do you mean, man? You couldn't go any farther if you were a general."

"Listen, you dumb ass, we have casualties, plus the wounded; Hamza and two others."

"Hamza? The yellow Hamza?"

"Not the yellow Hamza, the golden Hamza."

"Are you serious?"

"We're not sure if he's still alive. Nobody has the guts to check it out."

"All right, all right. Go to the next ramp down there. See how you'll get past that one. They're killing us. They haven't let us open our eyes for two days."

"Take care, my friend."

"Yeah, you too."

They drove further, the headlights off. On the ramp farther down the road, it was the same story. The military police didn't allow them to go any further with the car. In the last two days, too many people had been killed on the Igman road.

"Captain, there is no way we can carry them down there on foot. The slope is sixty degrees and slippery."

"I know, but we can't go with the car either. Who'd drive?"

"Who says we can't?" Dino jumped into the conversation. "I'll drive."

"You'll drive? Do you even have a driver's license?"

"What, you think somebody is gonna pull me over and ask for it?"

"Hold on Dino, this is a serious matter."

"Captain, I swear on my mother's life, I'm dead serious. You just walk down the hill slowly, and I'll take Musa and Hamza down there. We'll go eat first, and then we'll meet you at the tunnel."

"You're serious, aren't you?"

"Yes sir, captain."

"All right, men, get out of the vehicle. Good luck, kid. Keep to the left side."

"Okay."

The captain closed the door and waved Dino on, but the van didn't move.

The captain opened the door. "Come on, go."

Dino mumbled something unintelligible and signaled him to wait.

"Wait a minute, will you? I'm praying."

"You're doing what?"

"I'm praying, I'm saying the surah *Al-Ikhlas*."

"Well, you're not saying it twenty times, are you?"

"No, fourteen. My grandma taught me that. You say it fourteen times, and then you're safe."

"Come on. Get going."

"I'm not going anywhere until I finish praying."

"It's gonna take you half an hour."

"I don't care if it takes five. I'd rather wait and be safe, than risk it for no reason."

"Now, I've seen everything."

"You'll see a lot with us, dear Captain. You go ahead. I'll see you down there."

"I don't understand this," said the captain when he had caught up with the others.

"What is it, Captain? Is Dino saying a prayer?"

"Yep."

"You can joke around all you want, but that stuff works. I mean, you should have seen the mess he went through. One time, a shell went off right next to his ear. He couldn't hear anything for five or six days but that was all. It works for him."

Talking quietly, they began walking down the hill. They were walking down "Rice."

*   *   *

'Rice' was actually an extremely steep hillside on Igman that went directly to the first houses in Hrasnica. Woodcutters used to cut trees and let them slide down Rice. As they slid along, the trees stripped off the rich red earth in their path. Now, Rice was rocks, with only a bit of dirt here or there. The violated hillside, together with the snow and very low temperatures, presented a serious challenge for anyone who would climb or descend. One careless step and the climber would slide down on his chest or back to Hrasnica at a rapid clip.

The small group descended slowly, expecting the shooting to start any moment. Dino was going to need a lot of luck to get down safely. The Chetniks had their anti-aircraft machine guns at Ilidza, and they were zeroed in on the road. All that was left do was pull the trigger and nobody would get to Hrasnica alive.

*   *   *

"Are we ready, Musa?"
"Yes, we are."
"Musa, could you sing for me?"
"What song do you wanna hear?"
"Let's sing *'The water came from one hill to the other'*!"
"No, let's not sing about dead people."
"All right . . . Do you know the one . . . Wait, let's see what Fadil listens to in the van."
"He has a stereo in here? Really?"
"Yes, he does. Let's see if it works." Dino turned the stereo on and put a tape in. Accompanied by drumming, the choir was singing:

> *"To the honorable followers of the faith,*
> *Stand proudly straight as an army,*
> *Guard the light of Islam,*
> *And fear only Allah . . ."*

"Just perfect for this kind of situation." Dino started singing, louder than the radio. Musa coughed a few times, cleared his throat, and then he started singing too:

"Without weakness, without breaking the faith,
Without weakness, without breaking the faith,
Guard the dawn of peace . . ."

The night was quiet. The moonlight broke through the clouds, softly lighting the road in front of them.

"They must have noticed us by now. You know what, Musa? Everybody takes the left side of the road. What do you say we go to the right? I'd think that the Chetniks surely have their weapons targeting the left side of the road by now."

"Dino, do whatever you like. I just hope it's not the last thing you do."

"God forbid."

Dino started singing again. Musa joined him. They came to the place where a pass would protect them from the Chetniks for a minute at least. Dino stopped the car. He turned the headlights on for a moment, and then turned them off and on again. Then he turned them off.

"What the hell are you doing!?"

"Musa, have you read *'Landscape Painted with Tea'*?"

"What fucking tea are you talking about?"

Bursts fired from anti-aircraft machine guns started digging up the road not far from them. Musa jammed his head between his arms.

"Don't be afraid, Musa. They can't get us here."

"Dino, you're crazy. How are we going to get out of here now?"

"Easy. Just like this." Dino screamed, stepped on the gas and the van rushed out from the sheltered area, hell-bent for the bottom of the hill.

*　　*　　*

"Geronimo!"

Heading downhill, the van quickly gained speed. Musa held Hamza's head with one hand, and his shoulder with the other, making sure that his body didn't slide. He didn't dare take a breath. Totally focused, he followed the burning trace of the Chetnik anti-aircraft fire tearing up the sky. The Chetniks would use a tracer after every four regular bullets to adjust their fire, so it seemed as if golden chains were streaking through the air, one after the other.

"Without weakness, without breaking the faith,
Without weakness, without breaking the faith,
Light up the dawn of peace . . ."

The popular Bosnian song played loudly. Dino sang along, as loudly as he could. He held the steering wheel tightly, his wrists white from effort.

"Dino, watch out! Here it comes!"

The Chetnik gunner began shooting from the bottom of Igman and methodically fired all the way up, plowing up the road. Dino veered to the right, as fast as the narrow road would allow him. The van ran into a hail of fire.

A few bullets struck it on the left side, wounding the van but sparing the men inside.

"Geronimo!"

"Let the truth rule now,
Let the truth rule now,
Let it be your white fire,
Let it be your white fire . . ."

"Watch out, Dino! Here comes another one!"

Dino was already at the far right side of the road and the tires were skimming the edge of the road.

BOOM . . . BOOM . . . BOOM . . . BOOM . . . BOOM . . . A heavy round roared into the van.

The windshield blew apart. Dino screamed, let the steering wheel go, and grabbed his shoulder. The van swayed back and forth for a moment, went to the left, and ran into the cliffs above the road. It bounced and continued along at the same speed, scraping against the cliffs with its left side.

"Dino, the steering wheel! Grab the steering wheel! Hit the brakes!"

As if Musa's voice brought him back from the darkness he had rushed toward, Dino grabbed the steering wheel with his right hand, allowing the left one to hang uselessly at his side. He stepped on the brakes with all the strength in his lower body. The van came back to the middle of the road. Two bursts flew above them and missed. The van swerved dangerously on the snow. Dino fought to keep it on the road.

"Get off the brakes! Off the brakes!"

"Another hundred yards, another second, and it's over. It's over!" Dino whispered to himself.

They had made it to the safe part of the road. The road ended in a sharp right curve, where the military police had put their ramp. The van still swerved, accelerating dangerously. It hit the curve out of control, slammed against the ramp, and smashed it. The crash forced the van on its side, and, still speeding, rolled it over on its roof. In that position, it continued to slide, finally stopping as it ran into a warehouse.

"Dino. Dino! Are you okay?" Silence. "Dino!"

"Yes, I'm fine. How's Hamza?"

"He's good."

"Thank God."

"Who showed you the thing with the lights?"

"A guy from the Special Forces. He always t . . . tri-cks th . . . th . . . them that w . . . way."

"Tricks them, my ass. He flashes his lights, and when they start shooting, he drives. You mean that actually helps him somehow?"

"That's right. That's right. It helps, it helps . . ." Dino's voice dropped lower and lower, and became unintelligible mumbling.

Dino fainted.

"Dino!" Musa called to him. No answer. "Hey, is there anybody out there? Hey!"

Musa could hear the angry voices of the approaching military police.

"Let me see the idiot driving this piece of garbage. I'm gonna bust you all, then you can review that driver's ed shit in jail."

Under the beam of his flashlight, the policemen saw Dino bathed in blood, Musa staring off into space, and the shadow of Hamza's body on the floor. He sighed heavily.

"Oh, fuck! Sorry, bro," he said to Musa. He then turned to his fellow policemen shouting, "Over here. Quick! Put them in the jeep and take them to Hrasnica, to a doctor, if you can find one in town. If you can't, make one."

Musa was exhausted from the pain, the wound, and the tension from witnessing Dino getting shot. He fell into a nightmarish trance—neither fully aware nor asleep. He couldn't tell what was real and what was a dream. The rush through Hrasnica, in total darkness, the young, frightened doctor, saying, "Bad, very bad . . . Has to go to Sarajevo . . . Maybe. I doubt it." More rushing.

And his sister? What was she doing here?

"Musa, buy some eggs and cheese, and if you see something else, get it. You know we don't have anything."

"Yes, I will. Do you want anything special?"

Night again. Rushing. He thought Hamza moved, or maybe it was the car?

"God, I'm going crazy. Please, God, let me die." He moved his right leg, and the pain flashed, like a thousand needles stabbing his brain. The curtain of oblivion covered everything, and he joined Dino in blessed unconsciousness.

*   *   *

The captain was swearing profusely. Mustafa looked at Kemo, who looked astounded. The curses were so juicy and diverse that Kemo selected the ones he didn't know that were worth knowing.

"This one's good. Oh, that one's worth remembering too."

The captain cursed at himself for letting Dino drive the van, at Dino for suggesting it, at Fadil for wounding Musa, at the Chetniks for Hamza, at America and England, at Yeltsin and Mitterrand and Sadako Ogata, and at that little Japanese guy Akashi and all the politicians and other functionaries of the UN who were in charge of Bosnia during the war, and finally, at everyone else—living or dead.

They stood in the darkness, by the road that led to the tunnel. Stooped creatures walked past them, obviously overloaded, carrying too much on their backs, shoulders, and in their hands. They were coming silently and disappearing into the darkness, like ghosts.

"Now, all of them are figuring out how much heavier they are," Dado said.

"What do you mean?"

"I mean, how much money they're gonna make on what they're carrying now."

"Are you telling me these people are smugglers?"

"These people are poor people from Sarajevo. The real smugglers are sitting in the government."

"Cut the bullshit, please. You've been listening to the Serb propaganda on the radio again."

Dado waved away his protests and turned away. At that moment, they heard a vehicle approaching. Maybe it's them, thought the captain, and then he saw an ambulance. The captain stepped onto the road and waved it to a stop.

"Have you seen the guys that just came down the mountain?"

"So, these are your people. Or at least what's left of them."

"What are you talking about? Open up!" The captain jumped into the van.

Hamza was on the floor, his head wrapped in a blood-soaked sweater. Next to him, unconscious, was Musa. Dino leaned up against Musa, in a strange half-sitting position, a makeshift bandage over his shoulder. His left arm hung lifelessly. The blood had soaked through the bandage and now oozed through the sleeve. A small pool had started forming on the floor.

The captain wiped his forehead. He sighed heavily.

"Come on guys, get in. You," he said to the driver, "take us to the tunnel entrance."

"Only as far as I can."

"All right," the captain mumbled, without even understanding what the driver really meant.

As they came closer to the tunnel, they had increasing difficulty making their way through the crowd on the road. The area seemed ghostly. A dark night with hardly any moonlight and almost no sounds, despite the crowds, made it seem haunted and spectral.

The captain estimated a thousand people on the road, maybe more. People walked up and down the road in complete silence, all of them carrying far too much. They all had big backpacks on and cardboard racks of eggs in their hands.

"Good God! This is horrible," thought the captain. "My dear Sarajevo, what you have to go through!"

Soon, they could go no farther. The captain called to Kemo, "Go and find the person in charge. Tell him what is going on, and tell him to give you people to help us carry the injured. Instruct him to call the other side of the tunnel to prepare a vehicle. And please hurry."

Kemo looked at him strangely, and the captain wondered what was wrong with all of them. First, the driver, then Kemo, and now even Dado started it too. He concluded that something must be wrong with him.

In a couple of minutes, Kemo returned.

"No way."

"'No way' what?

"You can't get near the person in charge, let alone talk to him."

"Well, then, get the first military policeman."

"What do you think I did?"

"And?"

"There is no 'and.'" He says to wait. Food first, then people with passes, and then . . . ."

"Hold on a second, Kemo. What are you talking about? There's no time for waiting. Did you tell him that we have casualties?"

"Fuck off, man. Where do you think you are?"

"All right, that's it!" the captain screamed so loud that even the smugglers walking nearby jumped. "Why are you all asking the same question?"

He had snapped. "Now, you'll see where *I* live. Mustafa and Sakib, you stay here. You two, come with me."

"Oh yes, I'm liking this. I've been for some payback since last year, but I didn't have the chance to get them, especially that bigheaded one. Kemo, is he there?" Dado whispered.

"He sure is, Dado, it's your lucky day."

"Oh, man, this is the first bit of good news since we started the mission."

"What are you two whispering about? Don't do anything without my orders, is that clear? Don't even blink unless I give the go-ahead. Clear?"

"Hey, don't worry, Captain. You know us."

"That's why I'm telling you."

They came to the house used as an entrance to the tunnel. Kemo and Dado stood next to the captain and forced their way to the entrance. A military policeman stood in front of the house.

"Where do you think you're going, my friend?"

"Take us to the person in charge."

"Oh really? And why would I do that? No way, fuck off."

He pushed Dado's hand away, "I said fuck off!"

The captain looked at Kemo. As if waiting for just that movement, Kemo grabbed the sub hanging off his shoulder, and drove its butt into the polieman's groin. The young man screamed and fell to the ground.

"Leave him. Let's go inside."

Dado jumped over the policeman and opened the door for the captain, theatrically. "His excellency, the captain of the first fucked-up, elite sabotage . . ."

"Easy, Kemo."

The room they entered was very warm. It was filled with tobacco smoke and smelled of onions, smoked meat, and brandy. Behind the large office table in the back of the room sat the commander.

"God help you, Commander!" Kemo greeted him sarcastically.

"Who let you in? Answer me!"

"Commander, we are coming back from a mission. We have casualties . . . ," the captain started.

"Who let you in? What do you want, huh? Hoping to get through the tunnel, huh?, Well there's no way through. No way. Now, get out! When the food goes through, we'll see. Now, get out. Go on, you can see we're busy."

"All right, commander, but when might that be?"

"Maybe at dawn, but definitely not now, clear?" Then, he shouted, "Take them out!" as he motioned to the two men that had just come in, "and next time, knock! This is an office, not a barn."

The captain turned around and started walking towards the door. Kemo and Dado followed him reluctantly.

"Come on, you want me to *make* you move!?" said the policeman with a big head, as he shoved Dado.

From that moment on, everything happened dazzlingly fast, so that those who were present had difficulty recalling the sequence of events and reporting to the headquarters about what had happened, and in what order, in those few moments. The main disagreement was whether the captain had given Dado the sign to start a fight, or if Dado had just taken the initiative himself.

He turned around and hit Mr. Bighead, which then caused the further events. When Mr. Bighead tried to push him away, he ducked and then speared him with his gun straight in the gut, his full weight behind the blow.

The blow doubled him over, and Dado kicked him in the head. Mr. Bighead flew across the room. About that time, Kemo turned around and, in the style of a soccer superstar, kicked the unfortunate policeman behind him directly in the groin. When he keeled over from the pain, Kemo hit him with the rifle butt in the side of the head. The soldier fell to the ground, screaming. With two steps, Dado jumped on another one and sent him to the ground with two blows, first with the rifle to the gut, and then with the rifle butt to the face. The captain held his gun in his healthy arm and he fired a burst dangerously close to the head of the person in charge, who seemed dazed.

Dado and Kemo leaned on each other's back and kept their guns aimed at everybody in the room.

"Come closer, come on closer," Dado ordered the policemen, so that he could keep an eye on them. Kemo grinned and moved his gun from person to person. A single misstep, and Kemo would level the room. Death lay at his feet and waited for its tribute, showing its teeth. Everybody felt its presence and froze, waiting to see what would happen next.

Walking slowly, the captain came up to the commander. Without turning around, he said to Kemo and Dado: "If anyone moves, if anyone so much as blinks, shoot him . . . in the legs. Do you understand? In the legs. And you, you son of a bitch, let's see you now. You will do exactly what I tell you to or I'll blow your brains away personally. Do you understand?"

His low voice held the promise of violence far worse than screaming and swearing could produce. The commander calculated his odds quickly. The incident had already occurred and threatened to become a major catastrophe. He would hardly get out of all this clean, no matter how much support he got from the headquarters.

Even though he threatened to, the commander knew that the captain wouldn't kill him. Wound him, maybe. It was the other two that worried him. Quickly, he decided to save what could be saved. A cold sweat ran down his back.

"Hey, hey, let's just take it easy. What's all the fuss about? What's the problem? Casualties, you say? How many of them did you say? Five? Sabo, get your people up. Where are the casualties?"

The captain looked at him, silently. "The little bitch," he thought to himself, guessing the sequence of the commander's calculations.

"Hey, where are the casualties? It's okay, you two. Put your guns down. Give these men something to drink. Who's gonna show us where the casualties are?"

"Kemo, Dado, keep an eye on him. I'll get the others." The captain tried to reassure his men, "Everything is going to be fine. You're gonna be home in an hour. Now, just take it easy."

Kemo put the rifle down, reluctantly. Dado turned around, looking over everyone suspiciously. Then he stood behind the commander and carelessly leaned the rifle up against his back.

"Watch out, damn it."

"Don't you worry about a thing. Captain, is this good? Captain?"

"Yes, Dado, it's okay." The captain went outside. A dozen people were already there waiting, and he led the way to the van. Kemo sat down next to the wall. He was tired. He put his gun over his knees and started searching through his pockets, looking for cigarettes.

"Dado, you got a cigarette?"

"Why didn't you take one from Dino when he offered?"

"Don't fuck around, give me one if you've got it."

"I have one," said one of the soldiers who remained in the room.

"Catch."

"Thanks, man."

"Could you move that rifle a bit?" the commander asked.

"Not a chance. You heard the captain."

Mr. Bighead, who had been badly hurt by Dado, regained consciousness. He sat on the floor, shaking his head. Blood spilled out of his broken nose and mouth. He carefully brought his hand to his face and touched it. A couple of teeth were broken. Somehow, he managed to get up.

"What the hell did you do to me? I'll make you pay for this. We'll meet again."

He spit blood out of his mouth.

"What's the matter, Bighead, why are you crying?"

"You'll see. When I tear you apart, nobody will be able to put you back together. We'll meet again."

"Why should we wait for next time? We're here now. Kemo, watch out for this one." Dado went around the table and came close to Mr. Bighead.

Kemo carelessly aimed the rifle at the commander.

"Don't even breathe. I'm kind of nervous today."

Dado stood next to Mr. Bighead: "You know what, Bighead? When we meet next time, you'll say, nicely: 'Mr. Dado, I am a dog. Would you please kick me?' So, that's what you're gonna say the next time we meet. And to remember it, you'll practice it now. Come on, now, nice and slow. I'll tell you, you just have to repeat it. Just repeat, you don't have to think. Come on now: 'Mr. Dado . . .'"

Mr. Bighead looked at him. "No way, man . . ."

"Come on, nicely now: 'Mr. Dado . . .'"

"No fucking way, man . . ." Bighead looked at the commander.

"Okay, young man, that's enough now. Hello?" the commander's voice was a wheedling nuisance, but he was clearly unwilling to interfere.

Without any warning, Dado swung his leg, and it seemed that he just grazed Mr. Bigheads shin. Mr. Bighead fell to the ground screaming as if struck by lightning.

"Come on now: 'Mr. Dado . . .'"

"Okay, kid, that's enough," the commander barked.

"Kemo, are you watching him?" Dado asked, without turning around. With his undivided attention, he looked at Mr. Bighead's face, screwed up with pain as he got up.

"Now, shall we try again: 'Mr. Dado . . . '" Again, without warning and in the middle of a word, Dado kicked Mr. Bighead in the other shin, while the first leg buckled. With a scream, Mr. Bighead fell directly onto his face.

"That's good. Now, shall we start again? Huh?"

Mr. Bighead tried to sit down. He couldn't manage it. He tumbled to the ground—moaning—and stayed down.

From the basement stairway, which led to the tunnel, the captain arrived. "Come on, guys, let's go."

Kemo got up. Dado picked up his gun and started walking. He turned to the commander, who had opened his mouth to speak.

"Don't you tell me we'll meet again or that you'll remember me. We are fucking around with the Chetniks up there, and you sit here, make money, and drink brandy all day long. The only thing you're missing here is hookers. That's all. And another thing, tell Bighead that he was lucky. If he starts shit next time, I will put a bullet in his head. Even if it's the last thing I do. Look, Commander." Dado was standing very close to him, "I am not the captain. If it were up to me, I would shoot you first and then the rest of your little group. Then, I would start thinking of how to get out of the situation. This is war, and there is no fucking around."

"Dado, come on, let's go," the captain shouted.

"I'm coming." He turned back to the commander, "and you . . . you've been warned."

While going down to the tunnel, Kemo asked, "Where did you learn that kick in the shins?"

"Jail. Nobody stays standing after a good kick in the shins. But not a straight kick, just graze him on the outer side."

"I've never seen anything like that. Maybe you shouldn't have kicked him that much."

"Kemo, Kemo. You didn't see the people he took care of. This was nothing, trust me."

"Aren't you afraid they could catch you in town?"

"Not him. He'll probably send some of his dogs. But he will never look at me again."

"How do you know?"

"Psychology, Kemo, psychology. You learn these things in jail."

"You've learned a lot in jail. You sure it wasn't a university?"
They hurried to catch up with the others ahead of them.

*   *   *

The Tunnel.

A magic word, which, for years, awoke the hopes of the people of Sarajevo, meant worries for the Chetniks and UNPROFOR, and presented an irresistible curiosity for foreign correspondents in Sarajevo. At first, only people from Sarajevo knew about the tunnel, but the rumors spread further, making the tunnel wider, taller, and longer, putting electricity and even asphalt in it. Some people swore that there was a small shop in the middle, so that people could buy anything they wanted without going out on the other side.

In reality, the tunnel was a hole in the ground, four feet wide, five feet high, running some eight hundred yards under the runway of the Sarajevo airport. After the Chetnik troops, with the shameful help from UN forces, whose commander at the time was the Canadian General Mackenzie, had prepared and executed the total siege of Sarajevo, they patiently waited for the city to fall into their hands. In a city that had had more than half a million inhabitants, the supply of food quickly ran low. The black market blossomed. One egg for $3, a pack of cigarettes from $6 to $9, a quart of oil for $30, a pound of sugar for $40, a gallon of gasoline for $60. For an exquisite gold ring, you could get two eggs. Through mysterious ways, the food from the storehouses of UNPROFOR found its way to the black market.

The soldiers from the Ukrainian battalion were the best at smuggling. Sometimes they even had cigarettes from Serbia. Big profit. In exchange for the food they sold, UNPROFOR's soldiers bought works of art, rare paintings, and rare coins. Books and manuscripts, centuries-old and of tremendous value, disappeared mysteriously from Sarajevo and appeared on sale in Paris and London.

Sarajevo was under a complete blockade. There was one small chance. On the southwest side of Sarajevo lies an airport. On the other side, there was a narrow strip of free suburbs of Butmir and Hrasnica. Above them was Igman—the legendary mountain that transcends every other mountain in the world with the role it played in the war. At the airport, there was UNPROFOR, the UN forces, the Peacemakers. The desperate people of Sarajevo tried to escape across the runway in order to get to Hrasnica where there was food.

Well-rested, well-fed, shaved, and perfumed, the UN soldiers drove around in armored vehicles. They would catch and arrest the desperate runners, as they tried to cross the runway under Chetnik fire. The UN soldiers were there to stop every attempt to leave or enter the city. They tried to make the blockade complete. They used sensors and radars, but some still made it through, under the cover of night.

Faced with a desperate situation, a group of people from Hrasnica began digging a tunnel from the basement of a house near the runway. When the digging was about halfway done, people started doing the same thing from the Sarajevo side, from another basement of a house close to the airport. A tunnel? No, a hole in the ground. The tunnel ran straight, curved, and then ran straight again. From the Sarajevo side, it was supported by metal bars, on the Hrasnica side with wooden ones. Wood was too valuable in Sarajevo. All the parks and trees of the once-green Sarajevo had been cut down—even the tree stumps were gone. Between the vertical beams, there were ribbed steel or wooden bars placed horizontally. On the ground—mud. After a while, they put bars on the ground too and made a small railroad on which small carts could be pushed, for the transport of heavy or bulky things as well as casualties. Sometimes, it even transported the dead, if the family insisted that the person be buried in Sarajevo.

It was rare that anyone insisted.

The tunnel was always wet. Sometimes half-flooded. After rain and bombing had been going on for an extended period, people would get stuck inside for hours. The water would flood to their chests and people would panic, thinking they would drown.

Until the end of the war, journalists could not film it from the inside. CNN offered $5,000 for any camera shot whatsoever. The Chetniks managed to locate the coordinates to the entrance of the tunnel, and they bombed it heavily from time to time. More than two hundred were dead, but people kept on going through. Hunger drove *them. New businessmen opened up food companies. They imported food from Croatia. Magically, they got licenses for transport of food through the tunnel.*

Profits were in the millions of dollars.

In January 1995, world-wide publicity of the tunnel blossomed.

Sarajevo "celebrated," in its own perverse way, the "one thousand days of resistance against the siege of the city". One thousand days under siege. Even Leningrad had not been under siege that long. Fifteen thousand dead. The United Nations passed resolutions. Never in history had they made more worthless resolutions.

For the "one thousand days" occasion, guests came to Sarajevo. Over two hundred mayors of the world's best-known cities and other honorary guests found enough courage and, with their appearance, demonstrated their support for the people of Sarajevo. UNPROFOR tried to stop many from coming. At first, they promised to provide air transportation from the Croatian Capitol—Zagreb—for all the guests, and then accepted only half of them. They canceled flights for others. However, the mayors from all over the world were persistent. They decided to take buses and go through the war zone stretching from Croatia and Bosnia, to enter Sarajevo. The Bosnian Army headquarters decided to let them go through the tunnel. The American network, CNN, phoned Sarajevo's mayor. They had heard about the guests coming in through the tunnel. They were looking for permission to film it. The Bosnian Army headquarters rejected the request.

The whole assembly of mayors took a trip that turned out to be an adventure, something which none of the guests had seen before, not even in the movies. The world watched their epic experience. On the territory of so-called Herceg-Bosna, a fascist creation of Croatian extremists who, together with the Chetniks, tried to destroy and divide Bosnia, extremists stopped the bus. They demanded that the mayors should obtain visas to go through the nonexistent state of Herceg-Bosna. The bus stopped for a few hours. Finally, after all sorts of abuse, they let them go. In Mostar, one of the buses broke down. The police chief in Mostar found another one. Price? It didn't matter. Someday, somebody is going to pay—God willing. In the meantime, the guests recuperated with coffee and tea.

Mostar, once a beautiful town with countless numbers of historical monuments, looked like Hiroshima. The journey continued on the steep hillsides of Igman, where later an American delegation lost their lives when their armored vehicle slid off the frozen road. In the freezing Igman night, the mayors of Budapest, Istanbul, Bursa, Kuala Lumpur, along with a few mayors from different Italian cities, pushed a bus up the hill. In front of the tunnel, the Bosnian soldiers waited for them. They took their luggage. Taping was forbidden. They offered to take them through the tunnel on carts. Istanbul's mayor asked how the people from Sarajevo went through. He was told that they walked. So would he. The other mayors accepted the offer. A representative of one humanitarian organization, who had brought money and medicine for Sarajevo with him, passed out in the tunnel. He was tired, exhausted, and didn't have enough air. They had been traveling for two days without a break.

Then finally—Sarajevo.

They drove from the airport's apartment complex, by the destroyed building of the major Bosnian news agency Oslobodjenje. At the very beginning of the war, in the summer of 1992, the Chetniks destroyed the new, modern-looking building, which was also the location of the printing press of the agency. After that, on a daily basis, they systematically shelled and used tanks in an attempt to utterly destroy this symbol of Sarajevo's journalism. In Sarajevo at that time, more than ten civilians died every day by sniper fire, but Oslobodjenje's journalists, with superhuman efforts, managed to print and personally distribute their newspapers in the buildings and passages of Sarajevo. Oslobodjenje received the Newspaper of the Year Award 1992 by the international press. Likely as much for sheer courage as excellence in journalism.

The mayors reached the only open hotel in Sarajevo, the Holiday Inn. There was a reception of the guests. A small number decided to stay at the hotel, at their own expense—Sarajevo didn't have the money to pay hotel bills for its guests. The others were driven by Sarajevo's cab drivers for free to the houses of inhabitants of Sarajevo, where they would be their guests.

Solidarity. Within the program of the visit, the guests visited the complex called Sokolje, on the frontlines of fighting. There was only one house standing in the whole area. The guests took pictures of it. Unfortunately, the house appeared to be in one piece only if you looked at it from one particular side. In fact, there was only one wall that remained intact.

At the closing ceremonies, the mayor of Madrid said that it was an unforgettable experience. He showed his admiration and thanked the people of Sarajevo. He offered help from his town. Sarajevo became "sister cities" with Madrid and Budapest.

The Chetnik propaganda went crazy. They tried to minimize the importance of the visit. But the whole world wrote about the "one thousand days."

The American Ambassador to Bosnia-Herzegovina, Mr. Jakovich, also used the services of the tunnel on one occasion. Unlike many other world politicians that visited Sarajevo during the war, he never hesitated to tell the truth about the war. That is why when the Chetnik headquarters openly threatened him and did not allow him to use the Sarajevo Airport, he, just as so many Sarajevans, went through the tunnel, across Igman, and on to New York.

After all this, Sarajevo remained under siege for another three hundred ninety-five days.

*   *   *

The air was sticky in the tunnel, heavy and full of vaporized sweat from the people carrying huge loads of cargo. The group with wounded went first. After them, twenty civilians took advantage of the situation and went into the tunnel, pretending to be with the group. Dado and Kemo brought up the rear. The traffic in the tunnel was jammed with silent, steaming bodies. The water came up to their ankles. Dado tried to find something elevated above the water level of the water to sit on. He took out a cigarette and lit it. Someone from the group in front of them shouted: "Put out that cigarette, before I put it out for you!"

"Who is the wise guy?" Dado responded, without looking.

"Me." A huge man rose and stood in the light of a small lamp in the tunnel.

"You know what, big guy? If I get up, first I'm gonna cut you down a bit, just enough to make you my height. Then I'll fuck you up. Just say the word."

"Stop it, Dado, that's enough for one day."

"What's enough, Kemo? Look at those smuggling motherfuckers. Look at how big he is. He could carry a cannon, like I carry a gun. So tell me, what is he doing? Taking money from the poor."

Realizing that he was dealing with a tough guy, the big fellow immediately fell quiet.

The group moved forward. The Sarajevo side was as packed as the other entrance. The fourth motorized battalion went out of the city in groups, following empty carts. The men carrying Musa, Hamza, and Dino put them down in the hallway. The soldiers leaving town looked at them curiously. The captain went to the commander. "I need a vehicle to transport casualties to the hospital."

"I don't have any here. I can call headquarters to have them send me some."

"What are those trucks doing outside?"

"They are loading food for Alan Company."

"Unload it. I need the vehicle."

"How am I gonna unload it? What's wrong with you, man?"

"All right," the captain answered darkly. "I'll show you how. Just . . ."

The commander was about to say something, but the captain stopped him with a move of his hand. "Get out of my way. We had some shit on the other side. Don't even think about starting shit. Just get out of the way. You can write whatever you want in your report."

Dado and Kemo came up to him. "Are we gonna do it again, captain?"

"No need. We understand each other, right, commander?"

The captain went out into the passageway.

"Come on, guys, help me put them on the truck." He pushed several people out of the way in order to get to the truck. The truck was already half-loaded.

"Hey, you two. Would you please take out these few boxes? The others can stay. We can all fit."

The soldiers jumped on the truck and unloaded the boxes very quickly.

"Driver, driver! Who's driving this truck?"

"I'm driving, but . . ."

"Then drive."

"But I can't, I have to . . ."

"Just do as the captain says, okay? Now, drive." Kemo tapped him on the shoulder, just a bit stronger than was necessary.

"I will, I will, but . . ."

"No buts. Just drive."

*　　*　　*

The captain sat next to the driver, as the rest of the men squeezed themselves around Hamza, Musa, and Dino lying unconscious on the floor.

The truck rushed through the night. The entire city was exposed to hidden snipers, and the mortar shells could come from all directions. After three years of constant shelling, they had all the coordinates they needed, and had only to pick a target. They struck every day. Rushing in the darkness, the driver turned into the street going toward the train station, avoiding some overly dangerous intersections, as well as the straight stretch of road from the College of Civil Engineering to Skenderija, which was exposed to sniper fire.

Near the train station, the driver failed to notice the barbed-wire barrier on the street in time, and trying to brake, the truck slid and continued to rush along the icy street. The driver fought for control of the vehicle by stepping on the gas, but that only increased the trajectory of the slide and the truck smashed into a traffic light.

The captain was half-asleep in the warm driver's cabin and didn't see what was coming. When they hit the pole, he flew from the seat and his chest hit the dashboard. He moaned and lost consciousness.

"Hey, maestro, take the tracks!" Sakib said from truck. The driver turned the truck around and continued driving. Shortly after midnight, they arrived at the hospital. Since they were used to casualties coming in on short notice, most of the emergency team was out in the hallway. Seeing the truck breaking outside, the nurses ran to meet it with wheeled stretchers. The transportation process, from truck to surgery hall, had been practiced many times, and worked like a well-oiled death machine—quickly, efficiently, and eerily muted.

*   *   *

The Chetniks, with the blessings of the Christian Orthodox Church, decided to destroy everything that would remind them of civilization, especially Sarajevo hospitals. After abandoning the military hospital in downtown Sarajevo, the roof of which Chetnik snipers used to shoot down unwary civilians, they fired on it with several hundred rockets and almost completely put it out of commission.

More recently, they had attacked the maternity hospital. The building was hit with hundreds of incendiary, armor piercing, and other types of missiles. Doctors and hospital employees were forced to evacuate the newborns into the basement.

After the maternity hospital, the Chetniks targeted the main city hospital. They battered it day and night. 'Miner's lights' were used to illuminate surgeries performed in the basement. Water was carried in plastic containers. The average two hundred new patients per day consisted mostly of those in need of surgery for shrapnel wounds. Every day, the inhabitants of the exhausted city were called to donate blood. Through the shelling, people came and donated blood to save those that could be saved.

Regardless what horrors had visited the city the night before, every morning on Radio Sarajevo, one announcement would play. "Last night in Sarajevo, so many children were born, so many boys, and so many girls." Life went on.

*   *   *

Sarajevo's legend of the surgical division—Dr. Gavrankapetanovich—sat in a chair, eyes closed, trying to relax, to think of nothing. The thousands of operations he had performed during the war did not leave any visible marks on the face of this young doctor, who, during the war, grew to be a surgeon of enormous abilities.

After the first hundred operations, when he had performed miracles on the bodies of Sarajevans and tried to put back together what mortar shell fragments had ripped apart and stabbed through, his facial muscles became frozen and deadly calm.

He passed on that calmness, which reflected a very strong personality and the will to make it to the end, to the other members of his staff. Everyone functioned perfectly. There was no panic, even when they faced the greatest tragedies of Sarajevo—the massacres, hundreds of wounded and dying requiring attention at the same time.

As if from a full night's rest, the doctor got up and looked questioningly at the nurse.

"What do we have now?"

"Four injured."

"Heavily?"

"I don't know. They've been carried for two days."

"See who's in the most critical condition. Prepare him for surgery. Tell the other doctors to try to take care of the others. I'll be right there."

The nurse went out, and the doctor started washing his hands thoroughly, trying not to use too much water from the dispenser.

Mustafa, Dado, and Sakib were standing in the hallway next to the exit. They smoked in silence. Kemo sat on the floor. A male nurse approached them.

"When were they wounded?"

"Depends who you're talking about. The one with the sweater on his head was hit two days ago, the one with the bandaged chest yesterday. Same for the one with the leg. The one with the arm was wounded just last night. What's the situation?"

"Depends which one you're talking about," the nurse replied. "The one with the bandaged chest is going to be fine. He may be coming out now. The one with the arm, not so well. They'll have to amputate it. The one with the leg is all right. He'll be fine in a couple of days. The one with the sweater . . . good God! The doctor didn't know where to start."

"Wait a second, he's alive?"

"We've buried better-looking people. I've been here from the beginning, and I've never seen anything like this."

"It's not really that bad, is it?"

"Well, there have been worse, but those are the ones who were brought in dead, or died an hour or two after they had arrived. Your friend has been alive for two days. By any measure, he should be dead already. The frostbite alone is enough to provide him with a year's sick leave, not to mention the wounds. What happened to his face?"

"Damn! I told him a hundred times, 'If you have to kill, kill right away. Don't hesitate for a second.' Well, I guess he waited two seconds longer than he should have."

"There is another wound. He cut himself under the knee."

"How could he, when he's been unconscious since he got wounded?"

"You left the knife in his hand. We still can't get it out. The doctor says he'll have to give him some kind of a shot to open his hand."

"Oh no, it's the Tanto. Why didn't we see it? Fuck it. Is it a big cut?"

"The wound itself is dangerous, but compared to the other injuries, it's minor."

Clearly, the young nurse was through with the conversation.

The small group continued to smoke and wait for something; no one could have said what.

*   *   *

The captain gained consciousness shortly after surgery. The IV had revived him and left him feeling almost good. He asked the nurse for his uniform. After a short argument, and as he had already risen up from the bed naked, she brought him his bloody uniform. He asked her to take him to Dr. Gavrankapetanovic, who came into the room a few moments later.

"What's happened to my people, doctor?"

"The worst is the one with his back and head blown apart. I don't know about him. It took you too long to get him here. Plus the frostbite. He lost a lot of blood. I really can't tell you anything for sure. He's in God's hands now."

"Oh, Hamza . . . What about the others?"

"The one with the leg is gonna be fine. We might even release him tomorrow."

The hospital was overwhelmed and had no way to provide long-term care for the wounded. The small power generator was used only during surgery. All the wounded not in critical condition were sent home.

"And the last one?"

"The one with the arm . . . We had to amputate it."

"Oh no!" the captain crushed his head between his hands, in desperation.

"He'll be fine, Captain, he'll be fine. He will live."

"How will he be fine, doctor? Do you know how old he is?"

The doctor embraced him calmly. "I know, captain. A lot of our youth has gone through my hands. I've seen a lot worse. It's war."

"What can be worse? How can it be worse?"

"God, help me, it can. Yesterday we had a boy who lost his arm, his eyes, and one leg. It's war." He waited a while. "Can you walk? Your people are waiting downstairs."

"Take care, doctor," said the captain, shaking his hand.

"You too, Captain. Take care of the ones still here."

The captain walked away, nodding.

*   *   *

At the entrance, he met the men. The captain didn't know how to begin. How was he going to tell them? Sadik saw how troubled he was, so he jumped in to help him.

"We know everything, Captain. The male nurse just told us."

"Oh kids."

"Right, as if you are so much older than us," grumbled Sadik.

"What are we going to do now, Captain?"

"Nothing. Go home and wait for me to call you. I'll send you temporary permissions tomorrow. And don't go in, no matter who calls you. If you are needed, I'll call you personally."

"How long are you gonna give us?"

"I'll see. As long as I can get. How are you gonna get home?"

"We'll take a cab."

"You got the money?"

"Dado's paying for everybody."

"You have it covered, Dado?"

"I do, captain. But here's a little something for you, in case you need it."

"No way, I don't need it."

"Okay, in case you don't need it." Dado put the money in the captain's pocket. "Then when you call us, you can give it back if there's something left."

"Where are you going, Captain?"

"I have to go to Hamza's, then Senad's, then Dino's, then Musa's . . . ," he said with exhaustion dripping from each word.

"I wouldn't want to be in your shoes today."

"Me neither, believe me."

"Come on, now, let's get going," the captain ordered, and the little group left the hospital building together.

*   *   *

Mustafa, Kemo, Dado, and Sakib squeezed into the cab.

"Where to, folks?"

"First, to the next available cab. Half of us are going to New Sarajevo, and half of us downtown."

"There is probably a cab at King Tomislav Street. That okay?"

"If you say so, man."

"Dado, how much you got?"

"I don't know, I never counted."

"Approximately?"

"Well, approximately twenty."

"Twenty what?"

"What do you mean 'what?' Rubles! Twenty thousand German marks."

"Bullshit!" Disdain and disbelief sounded in Sadik's voice.

"Really, I'm not fucking around. When it comes to money, I never fuck around. See for yourself."

"Holy shit!"

"Dado, good heavens, what do you need all that money for? You don't know if you're going to survive the next hour, and you're socking away cash."

"Well, you see, this is not for me. This is money for the Germans, Belgians, French, and so on."

"What do you mean?"

"Well, when this war is over, and when we crush them . . ."

"And we definitely will, God willing."

" . . . And when we do crush them, all the real criminals are going to flee to other countries. Then Dado will get his passport and go after them. They'll not sleep peacefully ever again. Never, as long as I live."

"How do you plan to do that? You go to Germany, take the phone book, and there you look under 'war criminal such and such.'"

"Sadik, have you ever been abroad?"

"No," Sadik responded.

"Well, you see, I have. I just did some business." He mimicked the motion of pick pocketing a wallet. "In the West, people will do anything for money. If I had about a million dollars, their police would go to look for war criminals for me. I would just tell them the name, show them a picture if I had it, and . . ."

"Wait a second, Dado? What's this million you're talking about?"

"Listen, kid, our people were rich. Now, the Chetniks are full of our money. When we're done with them, I quickly search them. That's what I call a personal war profit. These thugs downtown, the ones doing all the complaining about it, should come with me, I'll give them half. I swear on my mother's grave."

When he mentioned his mother, Dado frowned, waved his hand, and shut up.

They came to the cabstand in King Tomislav Street. Against his nature, Dado stuffed a couple of German hundred—mark bills into everybody's pocket. The other three took the second cab, and Dado drove off toward New Sarajevo.

*   *   *

As he approached the cab, the captain changed his mind. He would take care of the hardest one first. First, he would go to Senad's, then to Dino's. Only then . . .

"Where to, boss?" the cab driver was in a good mood. The night was calmer than the usual Sarajevo night, which was too often filled with shelling and fires. The business was good too. The pay, which compensated for the fear and risk, was far higher than the usual fare before the war. Driving through explosions and sniper fire was his everyday routine, and he was like a fish in water. He was lucky, for now. As for tomorrow, who knew or cared today?

"We'll take a round trip." He listed the addresses to the cab driver. They were all old parts of Sarajevo, where mostly poorer families lived. The poor saved Bosnia, the president had once said. Unfortunately, nobody did anything to improve the economic situation of those families.

At Senad's, it was terribly painful. Briefly, he explained how Senad died and how the rest of the group was doing. His wound was evidence enough of the complexity of the situation. Senad's father took the news silently. His mother started to cry, but she soon stopped. She made coffee. His father spoke about the situation on the frontlines, about the chances that foreign forces would intervene to stop the war. No one mentioned death. The captain couldn't understand where these people got their strength. He left shortly after delivering the news.

As he left, Senad's father said, "If it would only end! I pray my Senad is the last one to die."

Back in the cab, the captain thought. He had heard those same exact words several times before. 'I pray my son is the last one to die.' At the beginning of the war, journalists interviewed a man whose three-year-old son had been killed by a Chetnik sniper. The father said calmly: "I pray my son is the last one to die. I just want to see that sniper—oh, not to kill him, but to have a cup of coffee with him. I just want to see the man who is capable of shooting a three-year-old child in the head, with a long-range rifle. I can kind of understand bombs, but never a sniper. He had to see my son clearly through the scope. He saw his eyes, his expression, yet he pulled the trigger. I would just like to see what a man who is capable of doing something like that looks like."

There was not a trace of hatred or revenge—just wonder.

*   *   *

At Dino's house, his father cursed, yelled, and swore. Dino's mother was silent. The house was covered in darkness broken only by a small oil lamp. The captain tried to say how the state planned to take care of its heroes.

Dino's father cut him off. He knew how the state took care of things. Their neighbors were handicapped. They didn't have food, while the smugglers didn't know what to do with the money that they made hand over fist. That was the state of things. Everyone knew it.

The captain went outside and took a deep breath of the cold air. He would have preferred heading back to the front, to the task that awaited him next. This was the worst one. He got back in the cab. It was freezing cold. The driver wanted to conserve gas, and sacrificed the heating for gasoline. He trembled, feeling the cold crawling into his soul. He decided not to go to Musa's. He was going to be fine anyway.

"Let's go."

The driver started the engine.

*   *   *

The captain thought of meeting Hamza's father with anxiety. He had heard many stories about the old man. At the headquarters, they had called his attention more to who his father was than to Hamza. They told him to keep an eye on Hamza—that he was fast, often wild, that he was completely fearless, honest, unpredictable, that people love him, that he was . . . the captain couldn't remember everything they had said, but it all came down to the fact that Hamza was a good and reliable soldier, but totally out of control in combat. When the fighting ended, he was a different person—an intellectual.

Indeed, many strange things were said about Hamza. He couldn't remember all of them, but he remembered very well what they had said about his father.

"If something happens to Hamza, and you have to tell his father . . . be careful. Be very careful."

And now, he had to knock on that strange and mysterious old man's door. The cab stopped in front of the house. The captain told the driver to wait for him.

A tall white wall divided the yard from the street. Set into the wall was a heavy, wooden door which seemed at least a hundred years old, with old-fashioned doorknockers never replaced by a bell. The captain knocked on the massive door. The deep thud echoed the sense of dread in his heart. He pushed the door open and entered the yard. The day was breaking. The pale moonlight mixed with the dawn lit the yard.

*　　*　　*

The yard was big, covered with cobblestones. The snow had been cleared away. Near the house was a now-frozen drinking fountain, and in the back, an old oak tree. It was a big, old two-story house covered with clay tiles. Flowers flirted on the windowsills on the first floor. Everything smelled of a hundred-year-old peace. The front door opened, and a large man appeared. He stepped out and pulled the door almost completely closed behind him.

The captain silently observed Hamza's father. Very tall, he stood ramrod-straight. His face was impressive and distinctive. He had a short beard and mustache, almost completely white. His thick eyebrows leaned over his sharp, dark, and piercing eyes. His hair was very short. He was barefoot and wore black corduroy pants. His white shirt opened at the neck with the sleeves rolled to his muscled forearms. The captain could see the muscles rippling under the shirt. He crossed the strong arms over his stomach.

The captain involuntarily shuddered. "I wouldn't want you for an enemy," he thought to himself.

"I am Hamza's captain," he said quietly.

"Avdaga," responded Hamza's father shortly. "Come in, I knew it was you."

"What do you mean 'knew'?" the captain asked, as he entered. He didn't get an answer. Taking off his boots, the heavy smell of dirty socks filled the room. The captain turned around, embarrassed and not knowing what to do. "I apologize. I've had these on for a while."

"That's okay. There is a canister with water down the hall. The bathroom is straight ahead. The oil lamp is in the bathroom, on the shelf to the right side."

Avdaga turned around and went into the room. The captain went into the bathroom, and with the help of a lighter, found the oil lamp.

A thin, short bar made of cork oak, about two centimeters wide, wrapped in aluminum in order not to burn, floated in the oil. A thin cotton cord ran through and burned dimly, timidly lighting the room.

"Who would believe that Sarajevo, a town that had electricity before most other European capitals, would be entering the twenty-first century with this type of lighting?" the captain asked only himself.

*   *   *

Beside oil lamps, the population of Sarajevo had found a thousand ways to survive under impossible conditions. Inventions and new ideas arrived on a daily basis. As the Chetniks progressed in finding new ways to torture the city, the people were finding ways to ease the inevitable consequences of the torture. On the windowsills of the apartments, in pots, cans, and every available type of dish, people grew vegetables. They developed a multitude of ideas inventing carts to transport water.

The one-pound cans from humanitarian aid were used to make stoves on which a meal for an entire family was cooked. Using the same can, coffee could be brewed with only a small piece of wood.

A colored glass bottle, filled with water and set in the sun for a day, would produce water warm enough for a nice bath. Car engines, with no great effort, were converted to run on natural gas and connected to the motors of washing machines. The entire device became a small electrical generator. As this generator had no voltage regulation, the voltage would change dramatically, frequently causing household appliances attached to these generators to burn, especially TVs.

The biggest miracle of the war, however, was the Sarajevan women. Dressed up, as if for a fashion show, clean and wearing perfume, Sarajevo women had a beaty which created the illusion of a normal life, and made everyone's day brighter for the effort.

They solved equations with a thousand unknowns, in the way that only they knew how: how to make dinner for the family over the long four years with only rice and something that looked like pasta—but once put into water turned to a ball of glue—and make it look different every day.

An even more difficult challenge was how to make a cake without flour, oil, butter, sugar, or chocolate . . . Essentially, how to make something out of nothing, something to calm the raging sweet tooth in every family.

A young mother cooked lunch for her three-year-old daughter saying, "Now, mommy is going to make you some eggs." She would bring out a plate with plain rice cooked in water, and put it in front of her daughter. This was the daily routine. In the third year of the war, the father—a fighter defending Sarajevo—came home with a carton of eggs. "Now, mommy is going to make you some eggs." The mother set an omelet in front of the child. The child screamed: "I don't want that, I want eggs!"

After three years of war, a section of Sarajevo, with the help of UNPROFOR, got electricity for a short time. A little boy, born in May 1992, stared at the light, not knowing what it was. When he started screaming, his parents had to turn off the light.

* * *

After he had freshened up, the captain went to Avdaga.

"Assalamu alaikum."

"Alaikumu salam. Please, have a seat." Avdaga indicated a place on the sofa. The captain sat down and sighed. He tried to say something, but Avdaga interrupted.

"Tea or coffee?"

"Tea. It's cold outside."

"Yes, cold." Avdaga knocked on the wall. A woman walked into the room. She carried a smoking silver samovar.

On the tray, there were small teacups, cane sugar, two sugar pastries, and teaspoons. The captain rose.

"Assalamu alaikum."

"Alaikumu salam, my son."

"Azra, this is Hamza's captain."

"Welcome, my son."

The captain was silent, and confused.

"Sit down, sit down." Avdaga's voice was so full of authority that the captain sat as ordered. Avdaga noticed this, and smiled. The captain again tried to say something, but Avdaga stopped him with a move of his hand.

"Take some tea. I'll be right back." He left the room.

Hamza's mother poured some tea into the captain's cup. She poured a bit of extract and filled the cup with boiling water. Her hands were shaking slightly. The captain took the glass, relishing the warmth. He looked into the cup. The tea was dark and shiny. Two golden lines on the cup—hard to notice when the cup was empty—were now shining in full contrast with the dark tea.

Avdaga entered the room again.

"You will spend the night here. I've let the cab driver go."

"I have to pay him." The captain got up.

"It's taken care of." Avdaga sat down. "Cigarette?"

"Thanks, I don't smoke," the captain said, and then suddenly changed his mind. "What the heck, give me one."

Both of them lit their cigarette.

Azra went to the stove, began cleaning it, and put wood in it.

"You weren't sleeping?" The Captain couldn't think of anything more intelligent to say.

"No, we were not. We were expecting Hamza. When you knocked on the door, I knew it was you. Hamza comes in differently."

"I don't know where to start."

"The best thing would be from the beginning. Is he still alive?"

"He was when I left the hospital."

"Is it that bad?"

"Yes."

"Is he conscious?"

"No. Not for two days now."

"You carried him for two days?"

"Yes."

"Where was he wounded?"

"Outside of town, southeast . . ."

"I'm not asking that. I meant, where on his body was he hit?"

"Face, back, chest, legs, arm, frostbite . . ."

"What do you think?"

"It's bad."

"Is he still in the ER?"

"Yeah, Dr. Gavrankapetanovic was the surgeon"

Azra stopped putting wood on the fire. She turned around and silently listened to the captain list Hamza's injuries. He looked at her. Her blue eyes were watering, but she didn't cry. Her face was calm, and only a small wrinkle on her face revealed the storm that was going on in the mother's soul. Avdaga was calm, or at least he appeared that way. He smoked his cigarette and listened to the captain. From time to time, he would take a sip of tea. The captain talked.

He spoke of the mission plan, about his argument with Hamza when he took over command, about the attack itself, about the Chetniks. With a quiet voice, he talked about how Hamza eliminated the Duke, Hamza's first injury, the retreat, how they found Hamza in the woods after the explosion and how the retreat went from there on, about Musa, Senad, Dino, Kemo, Dado . . .

As soon as the captain started talking about the mission, Azra went to the furthest corner of the room, took the Qur'an, and started praying in a low voice. Her voice sounded like a distant gurgle to the captain.

Avdaga listened. He did not interrupt the captain's story, neither with gesture nor word. When the captain had finished, Avdaga got up.

"Azra, it's time to go to bed. We'll be going to the hospital later."

Azra finished praying.

"Sadek Allahul azim." She lightly kissed the Qur'an, said good-night to the captain, and left the room.

Avdaga sat down again. He put some more tea into his cup and the captain's.

"It's war. A lot happens in war. I'm sorry for the boys."

The captain was silent. He felt empty. His tale had exhausted him. He had gone through all the events again and didn't feel any better.

"My Hamza, my Hamza . . ." Avdaga's voice trembled slightly. "I'm going to tell you something. We have time." He started the story. It was the first time he had told his life story to anyone. He spoke clearly, precisely, without too many words. With an intellectual vocabulary, he described pictures and scenes, drawing characters and situations. Images of an entire life flew past the captain's eyes. A life, rich and poor, happy and unhappy, exciting, brutal, and gentle life that with its overflowing contents held enough material for ten normal human lives.

And never after that could the captain understand how a single man was able to go through all that, remain normal, and live. How he didn't explode into rage or insanity, or both.

*   *   *

Avdaga talked on. He talked on through the dawn and stopped around noon.

It was 1941. German troops march into Sarajevo. The Third Reich. The Ustasha Colonel, Slavko Kvaternik, under German protection, announces the independent state of Croatia, and in its declaration, includes Bosnia and Herzegovina in its territory. The Muslim religious leaders, at the conference of the Islamic community, demand the independence of Bosnia and Herzegovina as a state. The Germans agree to this independence, but only under the condition that Bosnians form a military division to go to war under the German command.

It seems the whole world is at Hitler's feet. It's Russia's turn. Communists. The Nazi media plows on full-steam ahead. They hold public meetings, demonizing the Soviet Union. They are looking for volunteers to fight in the holy war against communism. The Ustasha

Legion is founded. The leader of the *independent state of Croatia* tries to serve the great leader of the Third Reich, by offering them the blood of its youth. In the winter of 1941, the Ustasha Legion goes to the Eastern Front. Avdaga, a young man of eighteen, runs away from home to join. He leaves a short letter for his father, a member of the old Sarajevo nobility:

"I'm on the Eastern Front. Listen to the news."

The first and last letter to his father. He never saw him alive again.

The Eastern, Russian Front and glorious, quick victories of the German army in 1941 and 1942. They measure the speed of their advance with the speed of their tanks. Russia is almost at Hitler's feet. In the north, Leningrad is surrounded by German troops, and it is a matter of days before they will march on it. In the center, German troops are right outside Moscow. The soldiers can see the golden domes of the Kremlin in the distance. In the south, they are at Stalingrad. For the first time in history, Russia will be crushed. All the way to Vladivostok.

Avdaga is excited. Victories, victories, victories. He gets his first Iron Cross, then his second. Glory. The German generals are proud of him. Life, this is the purpose of life. Avdaga finds pictures of the massacres he is part of; their meaning simply does not register.

Avdaga is at full strength—six feet three inches tall, and over two hundred and twenty pounds. All the fat boiled off him through the rigors of war. He's a strong, well-trained animal.

Fear? It doesn't exist. Avdaga, with a group of commandos, goes behind the Russian lines and causes tremendous damage to the enemy. He receives another Iron Cross. The Germans are telling stories about the giant Bosnian. Then autumn comes. Winter approaches. The Germans are still advancing, slower than before, but still advancing. Every square meter of conquered territory is paid for with lives.

Winter comes. The fighting doesn't slow. The clash of German Nazism and Russian communism was a clash of worlds. Iron worlds, and in many ways, identical worlds. German and Russian soldiers expected the firing squad for retreating; every fight is fought to the last man.

It does not occur to Avdaga that they are the aggressors and the Russians the defenders.

The Germans are at the gates of Stalingrad. Suburban and industrial areas. Fighting, always fighting. There is no time for sleep. Ten minutes here, half an hour there, between attacks, during a lull in the fighting. It goes on for months. The first cracks in the German perfect military machine are appearing. The Ustasha Legion is on the frontline. The Germans are trying to spare their own soldiers as much as they can.

Half of the legion is disabled, then three quarters. Only a handful of survivors remain. Avdaga is constantly in battle. As the leader of a sabotage unit, he penetrates the Russian rear lines again. Sabotage, murder, blood. Such paradox. His chances of survival in the Russian rear lines are greater than his fellow soldiers' chances of surviving on the frontlines. There is no question in his mind. They're going to win.

And then, for the first time during the war, in December 1942, Avdaga finally sees the true situation of the war on the Eastern Front. Up to this point, Avdaga hasn't stopped in the conquered places. They took the city, town, or village according to their orders. After they had taken the place, they had to move on. On the day of his awakening, they had taken over a small village. A handful of people. Even that small village exacted a steep price in lives. They rest. Avdaga goes into a house that is, strangely, still standing. Inside, Gestapo members are questioning the civilians. They are torturing them. The inhabitants die from the torture without saying a word.

One of them is a girl, seventeen years old, maybe younger. Her curses are gurgles; blood streams out of her mouth, nose, ears. She curses the Germans between shuddering breaths. The torture continues. Avdaga staggers outside. He vomits the image from his soul. After thousands of dead, after killing, slaughtering, after walking in blood up to his knees, Avdaga is throwing up. In his head is a nightmare, in his heart, a horrible seeping wound.

"God, what am I doing here?"

For the first time since leaving Sarajevo, Avdaga recites words of prayer.

The nightmare in his head continues. Night comes. Avdaga goes in the house, where the Gestapo soldiers are sleeping. There are two guards drinking tea at the front. The others are sleeping, three in each room. Avdaga is a professional. He kills them with nothing but a knife.

Quick, deep, fast hits. He goes quickly and silently from room to room. Three rooms, nine Gestapo soldiers, and two guards. He fills his backpacks with the white fur uniforms, waterproof white boots, and food. He leaves the village. To the west, always to the west. As far away as possible.

The German headquarters' report on Avdaga: "Disappeared during the Russian sabotage action. Presumed dead." Nothing more. In the absolute hell at Stalingrad, nobody mentions his name after that.

Avdaga walks for days, sleeping in short intervals, an hour or two at a time, and walks again. Leaning on a tree in his white uniform, he sees German troops passing by. Then the Russian troops. Avdaga is wearing a white uniform in the whiteness of the Russian swampy taiga, then in the Russian forest. He starts to believe he is invisible. He saves food with iron discipline. He eats less than German prisoners do in Russian camps. Weeks go by. Taigas and forests blur past. He comes across a battle scene. The terrible Russian winter has kept the corpses from decaying, preserving their story. Avdaga searches the bodies, looking for food. Slowly, winter fades. The sun occasionally comes out, warming a day or two. By this time, he has experience. He follows the crows. Big flocks, thousands of birds that are so bloated they can hardly stay in the air. The crows eat the dead.

Avdaga is looking for food. If he's lucky, he'll find a piece of stale bread. In one settlement, Avdaga rids himself of the uniform, even underwear—everything German. He puts on the torn clothing of a farmer, and goes back into the woods. He throws his rifles away, keeping only his knife.

Another fifteen days. To the west, to the west, always to the west. Finally, he can go no farther. He loses consciousness, doesn't know for how long. Half-dead, frozen, he is found by children of Russian partisans. They drag him into a dugout shelter and revive him. The partisans give him rabbit's blood to drink. They question him.

Who is he, where does he come from? He makes up a story about being a German prisoner. Yes, he is a Yugoslav partisan. He got away from the Germans. Where? He doesn't know. Nobody would ever guess that he has come all the way from Stalingrad. Not through the foreboding Russian winter. A vote is taken; he is allowed to live.

Weeks later, they take him into action—to mine the railroad tracks. Avdaga shows he's an expert in explosives. He fights with the partisans for a year. He receives the order of the Red Star. The Germans retreat. The partisans attack in groups of three. Avdaga leads one group. The number of successful assaults is growing. His group receives a *Lenin*: the honor ninety percent of Russians would happily die for. Winter comes again.

*   *   *

Near the Romanian border, they capture an entire German unit and a few nurses. Among them, there is an American nurse captured by the Germans in France and sent to the Eastern Front. Two guys each from Avdaga's and Igor's groups take the nurses for questioning to a deserted house. Screams, slaps, and even shots are heard from the house. Avdaga runs into the house.

On the floor are two dead nurses. The American girl is sprawled on the floor, almost naked. Two Russians are holding her legs, another one her hands. The fourth guy is pulling his pants down. Avdaga is holding his knife. He doesn't stop to consider the reasons. It's probably fate.

The Russians are unprepared, taken by surprise. They die with smiles on their faces.

The German artillery finds the village, hitting it with precision. Panic blooms everywhere.

Avdaga drags out the American girl, and they flee from the village. To the west. They pass over the Romanian mountains. Or is it still Russia? On a mountain, days away from civilization, they run into shepherds who don't know about the war. They don't know about the Germans or the Russians. They say they hear thunder sometimes. The two of them stay there for a few months. To rest, to heal.

Avdaga gives the American nurse a Bosnian name: Azra. He patiently teaches her Bosnian vocabulary. Azra is young and intelligent. She learns fast. Together, they invent Azra's life story. In the summer, they move on. They join the Romanians, and go into Yugoslavia.

In the meantime, the war goes from Russia to Romania, Hungary, Yugoslavia, and then rapidly towards Germany. Finally, they get on the train to Sarajevo. The war is over. Military controls are everywhere. Avdaga shows them the Russian orders. Military police greet him with a salute. At last, after four long years, Sarajevo.

His father had died after the German troops had surrendered at Stalingrad.

For the first dead of the Ustasha Legion, the German headquarters had sent telegrams, always about a heroic death in combat, about the immeasurable accomplishments of the German Reich. Soon, they stop that. Silence falls over the deaths of the young men, and nobody dares to go to the Sarajevo headquarters and ask about them.

Avdaga and Azra marry soon after the return to Sarajevo. During the first few years, Azra's accent and inadequate vocabulary are the subject of gossip among their neighbors.

On any question regarding Azra, Avdaga becomes cold and distant. He gets up, theatrically takes the keys to the house, to the store, and gets all the money from his wallet and puts it in front of the curious person.

"There you go. You want the house, the store, the money. Take it. But, don't say anything about Azra. I brought her here for myself."

Nobody ever guessed how much truth there was in his words. The inquisitive person would back off and lower his head. After a few months, nobody brought it up again. Russian medals, and the sparse details he gave about how he got them, secured him a strong image with the new government.

Inevitably, in 1948, the conflict between Tito and Stalin rears an ugly head.

The INFORMBIRO resolution. Yugoslav communists are accused of betraying communism. Stalin calls on the working class of Yugoslavia to stand up against Tito.

Stalin, a role model up to that day, suddenly becomes the enemy. Chaos erupts throughout the country. Thousands, tens of thousands imprisoned, heroes of yesterday. Every pro-Russian ends up in jail. Avdaga is arrested; this strong, silent man who kept himself in the background, who never talked much, who didn't go out much, but had Russian medals. That was enough reason for OZNA to arrest him. The investigation goes on for a month, then two, and three. Interrogation and torture. Who, why, where from; the questions never end. He answers that he cares nothing about politics, that he is a religious man. This makes the OZNA agents even more furious. "Religion is the opiate of the masses!" they spit at Avdaga. "Those are Lenin's words," answered Avdaga. They beat him. Finally, a delegation from Avdaga's neighborhood steps forward on his behalf. People of high regard, the Sarajevo Muslim religious elite. They guarantee that he is not involved with politics. They affirm that he attends the mosque on a regular basis. A religious man can't love Russia. Two months later, he is released.

The investigator asks, as Avdaga is leaving, why the Russians hadn't killed him. He adds, "Don't be offended. It was nothing personal. We in OZNA are defending socialism. We are the iron fist of the proletariat." Avdaga doesn't get angry. After the Eastern Front, nothing ever angers him again.

*   *   *

Avdaga hadn't had much luck with children. First a baby girl, then a boy. Both of them died right after birth. Many years later, a son. Hamza. Hamza, the lion, born under the sign of Aries. A very complex personality type. He had his father's strength, courage, wildness, speed, and his mother's gentleness, affection for the romantic, for poetry. The big, colorful world that he had come into amazed him. Everything was there for him to reach, to try, to taste, to touch. And, that is what Hamza did; he tried, touched, and tasted everything. There was no wall he didn't test headfirst. There was no fence he didn't try to jump over.

Avdaga didn't stop him from doing anything. He let the child do whatever he pleased, and was sure that God's mercy would save him. Azra had always tried to direct him toward different things through disciplined conversations. And while she was with him, everything ran smoothly. As soon as Hamza would go out on the street to play, he would change, bewildering his own and other neighborhoods.

His mother taught him English when he was a baby. It was his second native language. She taught him to play the violin. He was very talented. One day, he came home with a broken nose. One of the neighbor's children had told him that only queers played the violin. He got into a fight. After that, he never touched the violin again.

Avdaga enjoyed him immensely. He justified all his pranks and tricks, never once raising his voice to him. Forever, the boy was "my Hamza." Avdaga paid for the broken windows in the street, ruined trees, broken fences, and stolen sweets in the candy store. By the end of Hamza's childhood, he would pay the owner in advance for everything Hamza would take.

When he played a bigger prank, he would sneak into the house and sit in his father's lap. It usually happened after the sun had gone down, while Avdaga and Azra were drinking coffee. Hamza would sit on his father's lap, and in a low voice, begin the day's confession. Avdaga always thought his explanations to be perfectly logical, and that he would have done the same thing, asking Azra if she could figure out why their neighbors didn't understand the boy. Azra would just smile and send Hamza to take a bath.

On one occasion, Hamza damaged two pear trees in the neighbor's garden. He was with other children, climbing trees and picking fruit. Two girls were with them. To impress them, Hamza climbed to the highest branch to get the pears. The branch broke, and he fell to the ground. The kids were laughing. In order to retain his reputation, Hamza tried to do it again, on another tree. Again, he fell.

Hamza was furious and broke the remaining branches. Avdaga attempted to straighten things out with the owner, and visited him a few times, with no luck. The old man refused to so much as let him in. Finally, Avdaga stopped him at the mosque. Without mentioning Hamza, or the pears, he informed the old man: "My dear friend, I'm going to Kiseljak-town tomorrow. A carriage is coming to pick me up. I would be delighted if you would come along to keep me company."

He had touched the old neighbor's fondest spot. Known for his stories about picnics he used to have, when he would go from Sarajevo to Kiseljak-town, about beautiful wild horses, the homemade bread from Kiseljak-town, about the girls . . . Avdaga knew he couldn't turn down such an invitation. And, the next day, the two of them took a carriage drawn by two white horses and rode in style to Kiseljak-town. They spent the whole day there and came back to Sarajevo late that afternoon, after the sun had already set. No one mentioned the pear trees. And the neighbor never again said anything bad about Hamza.

*　　*　　*

Hamza grew up in complete freedom. The genes from his ancestor-warriors often surfaced powerfully and would have taken him God-knows-where if it hadn't been for Avdaga's and Azra's deep love, which, like a strong centripetal force, always brought him back. As the years passed, he played his tricks less often. Later, Hamza graduated from high school as one of the best students of his generation. Avdaga was bursting with joy. "Soon, you'll be drowning in all that pride," Azra used to tease him. "Oh, my Hamza . . ." Those few words carried tremendous significance for anyone who knew this family and the hearts living within. Hamza attended the university and studied architecture. He wanted to build. During the summers, he worked at a number of jobs as a university student. He helped out in Sarajevo's privately owned businesses, studied the science of life, and fought with Musa.

Born almost on the same day, the two were exact opposites. Hamza was blond, Musa was dark. Hamza was well-proportioned, Musa had very wide shoulders. Hamza liked brunettes, Musa preferred blondes. Hamza was a fan of one Sarajevo soccer team, Musa a supporter of the rival team.

Everything else was in contrast too. Their fights, since childhood, occurred almost daily, and were very serious sometimes. But, they would make up immediately, while washing their bloody faces at a fountain. Once they came to Avdaga's store, with bleeding noses, swollen eyes, and bruises all over. They looked so terrible that even Avdaga wanted to say something. Instead, he just bit his lip and rushed outside to catch some air. He came home late that night and went straight to bed.

Musa's home life was different. His father was harsh and not as understanding when it came to Musa's pranks. As a result, his heavy hand often showed Musa that he had made a mistake. Trying to protect him, Hamza would often send Avdaga over to Musa's dad to talk to him. Right away, at the door, Musa's father would say, "What did they do now?" And Avdaga would have a difficult time trying to convince Musa's father that it was only a childish prank. When he began these visits to Musa's home, it was difficult to persuade his father, but soon enough, Avdaga got the feel of it, so after a third cup of coffee, Musa's dad would start thinking that his Musa was a really exceptional child and he wondered how he hadn't noticed it himself.

"And so you say they're studying now?" Avdaga would answer, "Of course, they're studying. You know when my Azra says something . . ."

Meanwhile, Hamza and Musa, to Azra's great pleasure, were cleaning out Azra's candies, cakes, and every sweet thing there was in the house. Then they would go to sleep in Hamza's room. Hamza and Musa loved to fight each other, as if they were taking measure of their strength. Musa knew Hamza's tricks. Usually, before the fight would come to blows, Hamza would raise his right hand, with his fingers spread out and say, "Hold on a second, why are we arguing again?" And along with the last word, he would hit Musa right on the chin. Musa would suddenly find himself on the ground. Still lying there, he would curse himself for falling for the same trick again and again. When Musa hit first, it was without words, silently. His right hand would flash, and Hamza would be on the floor, shaking his head. "That was a good one," he would usually say, and then jump on Musa.

As a sophomore at the university, Hamza met a fellow who somehow became his best friend and later was his best man. With him, Hamza came to know alcohol, and would come home drunk quite often. Musa didn't like the best man much, but Hamza loved him. He was strong. Almost like Musa. He had long hair and a beard, and always looked unkempt, a bit on the wild side. It was undoubtedly that wildness that made Hamza like him so much.

Shortly after graduating, he sold a piece of land near Sarajevo, very cheaply to Hamza. It was a perfect place for a little cottage. Sarajevo was surrounded by charming little houses.

*   *   *

Then Hamza met Amra, a gentle, petite brunette. She was a music student. They were both very much in love. Avdaga was bursting with pride. He pushed marriage. Not directly, but every so often, he would mention grandchildren and the fact that he was getting old. Two years after graduation, Hamza married Amra. It was a wonderful wedding. A year after the wedding, a daughter was born. It was the daughter that settled down Hamza. All the devils were subdued when he was with his gentle Amra. They opened a small architectural design company. Business was going well. The old house was alive again. Voices, the sound of the violin, Hamza's loud, contagious laughter echoed from the house. Diapers could be seen line-drying in the front yard.

They decided to go to the weekend house and live there until the fall. The fresh air would benefit the little one very much. Avdaga and Azra would visit every weekend. And it was only a half-hour drive from Sarajevo.

It was mid-March 1992 when they decided to move temporarily. Amra wasn't very happy about the decision. She suggested that it would be better to wait until the summer, but Hamza was like a raging flood sweeping up everything in his path. When he decided on something, there was no way to change his mind. And so they moved. Hamza visited his parents almost every day after work. Azra, as all mothers did, wanted to know every detail of his life, his happiness, his little family.

Hamza talked about people from the surrounding villages, their hospitality, the fresh, still-warm milk that villagers would bring to his little one. He told them all about her and everything that she was doing, even the routine and commonplace. And then one night, in early April of 1992, Hamza came to his parents' house with a cut on his head, a machine gun on his shoulder, and a knife—his Tanto—at his waist. He was covered with blood and mud. For the first time in his life, Hamza asked Azra to prepare him a hot tub and a warm bed. She understood. She left the room.

"Then he told me some terrible things. Three days after that, Hamza joined the Green Berets, the newly formed defenders of Sarajevo."

*   *   *

Avdaga had stopped talking. It was noon. The tea had been cold for a long time. Avdaga picked up his cigarettes. The pack was empty. He got up and left the room. He returned shortly, and they lit another one. The captain was silent. Avdaga looked at him questioningly, "Are you okay? You didn't sleep at all."

"I'm fine, Avdaga. I'm fine."

"Look at me. Once I start talking, I just can't stop."

"It's all right, Avdaga. I'm fine."

"Well, now, let me remember why I told you all of this. I know what war is. I know what death is. I have killed. I don't know if God will forgive me. I have looked death in the eye. People died in my hands, friends and enemies alike. It's just, well, now it's somehow different. This is completely different." Avdaga shook his head.

"Do you have to go to the headquarters right away?" The captain nodded, and Avdaga continued, "When you're done there, come back here. If we're not home, here is the key to the house. Take the second room to the left. If Azra doesn't make it home on time, you put some wood on the fire when you get here."

The captain wanted to say something but Avdaga stopped him with a motion of his hand. "Azra and I are going to the hospital right now. We'll see what happens. In any case, we will see you at dinner."

Azra came into the room carrying food. Hot tea and a few crepes filled with canned tuna—the most popular food in Sarajevo during the war.

CHAPTER 2

Hamza's brain stopped the moment the grenade exploded directly behind him. The small gray brain cells switched off, disconnecting the brain from all signals of the outside world. Even the memory centers were disconnected. The seriously injured body chose the only available chance for survival without hesitation. Hamza's complete nervous and autonomic systems were placed on standby. Motor functions dropped to a minimum. The heart beat just enough to keep him going. The lungs worked irregularly, supplying the body with barely enough oxygen, just enough to prevent the critical cells from dying. Life hid and would not reappear, even for a moment. Just like the sharp edge of a razor, the thin line of life separated the blackness of unconsciousness from the nothingness of death.

When Dr. Gavrankapetanovic came to the operating table, Hamza lay on his back, with his head turned to the left. The assistants were trying to clean the wounds and make them ready for surgery. The doctor spoke slowly and in a low voice, as if reading a story. He talked about the wounds and used his hands to help him indicate their severity. The surgical team carefully listened to his statements.

"Life functions are endangered, especially by the high number of wounds on the back and shoulder-blade region. There are fractures to three ribs on the right and two on the left side, near the heart, with a high probability of internal bleeding. There are deep, dangerous wounds in the kidney area, with shrapnel lodged inside. Be careful that none of it stays inside. A few fragments in the neck region. It looks like the spine isn't damaged. A long tear behind the left ear.

"As you can see, the skull has just been scraped. That wound, at least, is not life-threatening. There's a fracture of the right arm, above the elbow, also not dangerous. The right side of his face is shredded from the forehead to the chin. The right eye is not functioning properly, be very careful with it. See to it that the stitches are as neat as possible. If he survives, he'll have to live with that face. Both legs have suffered frostbite, especially at the knees, heels, and toes. There are lots of small tears on both knees. Nothing dangerous, but clean the wounds carefully to prevent blood poisoning. Deep tear behind his left knee.

Hey! What is that knife doing in his hand?"

"We couldn't get it out. His fist is locked."

"Okay. Give him the shot. Nurse, you attend to the frostbite, and you, my friend," he said, nodding toward the male nurse to his left, "handle the wounds at the base of his back. You do the face. Nurse, you can do the legs and that cut. It won't be long before you'll be able to perform these operations on your own. I'll do the back. Any questions? Let's do it. Be prepared to revive him if necessary. And remember, just go nice and slow. With this case, we have nothing to lose. He's survived so far, so I don't see why he shouldn't survive for another few hours."

*   *   *

The surgery lasted for hours. Nurses kept bringing coffee and wiping the sweat off the surgeons' faces. The wounds were cleaned and sewn, one by one. The young doctor worked calmly, with total concentration. Finally, he raised his head.

"This is all we can do for him. If nothing else, everything has been cleaned and dressed. The rest is in God's hands." The doctor was deeply religious and didn't hide it. "Thanks for your cooperation, ladies and gentlemen. Nurse, would you please see to it that he is kept warm?"

*   *   *

Avdaga and Azra came in the early afternoon. The nurse on duty took them to the doctor. Dr. Gavrankapetanovic rarely ever left the hospital. He had just fallen asleep on the small couch when the nurse came in.

"Doctor, the parents of last night's patient are here."

"All right. Bring them in." The weary Doctor was able to put himself in the parent's position and sat up to welcome them.

"*Assalamu alaikum*," Avdaga greeted him.

"*Alaikumu salaam.*"

"So, how are you doing, doctor?" Avdaga's voice was firm and warm at the same time. The whole of Sarajevo knew who Dr. Gavrankapetanovic was, and he commanded both their love and respect. Avdaga knew, without asking, that he had done everything possible for Hamza. The doctor had them sit down, and then explained the nature of Hamza's injuries and how they had treated them. At the end, he said, "we have done our best. In peace maybe we could have done more for him, but under these circumstances . . ."

"Doctor, what do you think, personally?"

"Well, maybe . . . being optimistic, maybe around twenty percent."

Avdaga nodded. Azra listened silently. When the doctor finished, she asked, "Can we go see Hamza now?"

"Sure." The doctor stepped out the door. "Nurse, would you please take them to room fifty-three?" He turned to Avdaga. "If you have any questions, or anything at all, I'm here."

"Thank you, doctor. May God be with you."

"*Alaikumu saalam.*"

They entered Hamza's room. Avdaga looked at the nurse.

"Could we have a few minutes alone with him?"

The nurse nodded and left the room. Avdaga and Azra took the blankets off of Hamza and looked at his body, silently. It had been fifty years since Azra last took care of war wounds on the Russian front. She leaned over and started examining the wounds to her son's head.

Most of the hair behind the left ear had been shaved off, and a long scar went all the way from the top of his head to the neck. Whispering, she made comments on the wounds and stitches.

"He must have been bent down when the shell exploded. The shrapnel entered through the neck and ripped everything to the top of the head. The skull is just scraped."

Azra leaned toward his face. She examined the scars carefully with her fingers, taking her time. "I don't understand this. What do you think, Avdaga? If the shell exploded behind his back, it could not have hit his face and the back of his head at the same time. And this fragment didn't rotate. That's odd."

"This is dangerous," continued Azra, touching the wounds at the shoulder blade. "These wounds aren't sewn, because big pieces of flesh and skin are missing. Rib fractures. I'm not sure, but I don't think the spine is damaged." Azra moved farther down. "He *was* bent over. These wounds were parallel to the flight of the shrapnel from the explosion, that's how the fragments entered his body. Since his back was at an angle, the shrapnel scraped along his body, cut what it could, and went out. It rotated, so that's why pieces of flesh are missing. His legs are fine . . . if there is no poisoning. What do you think about the frostbite, Avdaga?"

Avdaga leaned over, took Hamza's feet, and started rubbing them. He rubbed them a while, and then gently laid them down. "There may be some circulation left." At the moment, there was nothing more they could do, so they covered him, thanked the nurse, and left the hospital.

Avdaga headed toward the cabs, but Azra pulled his sleeve. "Let's walk, Avdaga. There is no shelling."

"Of course." Azra put her arm under his and they started walking along the street. They were silently thinking the same thing.

"Azra, how about I smoke one?"

"Go ahead, my Avdaga, smoke." Avdaga always asked for permission from Azra to smoke when they were walking, and Azra always gave it.

It was winter. The snow crunched under their feet. Thick, snowy clouds covered Sarajevo. Here and there thin lines of smoke rose from chimneys. On the corner, there was a makeshift store—a cardboard box turned upside down. On the box rested a few packs of cigarettes, a bottle of oil, a bag of sugar, and toothpaste—the most sought-after items in the besieged city. A skinny dog, once a valued pet but now just a stray, scavenged for food in the trash can. So was an old woman. Avdaga crossed the street and put some money into her hand.

"God bless you, good man. May Allah protect you and your family."

"You too, grandma."

Heading down the steep steps next to the Sarajevo City Museum, they passed Bakije, a funeral home. The hajji saw him and opened the window.

"Assalamu alaikum, Avdaga."

"*Alaikumu sallam*, hajji."

"I've heard that Hamza has been wounded. Is it bad?"

Avdaga silently shrugged his shoulders and sighed.

"That bad, huh? Come on, Avdaga, everything is going to be all right. God willing."

"God willing."

"It will." The hajji's voice reassured him confidently. "Your Hamza is a good boy."

"Yes, he is. We have to go now. It's cold."

"Indeed, it is!" The hajji shivered for a second as if he had just noticed the chill from standing in the window with only a shirt on. "Stop by when you can, on your way to the hospital."

"I will, hajji. God be with you."

"And with you."

"The house must have gotten cold by now," said Azra when they came to their street.

"I feel sorry for Hamza's captain. I didn't even make him lunch."

"You will have time, my dear. And I think that the captain is more used to the cold than the warmth," Avdaga said, trying to cheer her.

*   *   *

The big room was warm. The captain had arrived before them, gotten the fire going and sat down on the couch next to the window. Looking out into the yard, in the comfortable warmth of the room, he fell asleep. That was how Avdaga and Azra found him.

"Just cover him with a blanket," Azra whispered, "I'll put the beans on the stove. When he wakes up, they'll be ready to eat."

Azra worked efficiently at the stove. Avdaga left her to prepare for his prayers. He headed to the back of the room and began praying. The crackling of the fire and Avdaga's murmur put the captain into a deeper slumber. His loud snores filled the room. When she had finished making dinner, Azra turned to Avdaga. "How about I make us a 'double'?"

A 'double' was a small coffeepot, holding just enough coffee for two tiny cups each.

"You should do that."

Avdaga came closer to the stove and sat on the floor. Azra put the coffee near him and sat down too. Silently, they sipped their coffee. Avdaga liked to say, "A person needs to be like coffee, strong and warm." Avdaga gave Azra a cigarette. It was their little secret. Azra smoked, but only on rare occasions when they were alone, and they had important things to talk about. They smoked for a while in silence. Avdaga was the first to speak.

"What do you think about bringing him home tomorrow?" Azra looked at him intently. "The doctor said he has about a twenty-percent chance. According to what you've said and what we've seen, I would say his chances are fifty-fifty; maybe better, God willing." He was silent for a minute, took another sip of coffee and a puff of his cigarette. "His face looks pretty bad, but medically it's not a major problem. The wound on his head is the same. Frostbite is no big deal. His legs are fine. The only serious wounds are the ones on his back and around the kidneys. The leg and broken arm are not life-threatening either. The back . . . well, his back is, in my opinion, the biggest problem. But, everything will be fine . . . God willing." Azra looked intently into his eyes, trying to see through, to reach his mind, his soul. She knew her Avdaga. Deep inside, he was worried. Maybe he would have cried if she weren't around. But, she couldn't detect the slightest amount of doubt in what he said. He was calm, assured, and composed.

"My dear Avdaga."

"My dear Azra. Do you agree with me? The two of us know as much as the nurses. And Hamza will be more comfortable at home."

"I'll get the small room ready for him. It warms up easily." Firewood was very expensive in Sarajevo.

"And then, yarrow." They both said it at the same time; the comfort of knowing one another's thoughts made the idea of all the work and worry ahead easier to bear.

"Yarrow, I swear. There are so many healing herbs that God has given us, nothing is better than yarrow. Then we press and clean the wounds, then, it'll be all right, God willing." Azra looked at him with love and pride.

"Dear God, please help our Hamza. If not for me, then for the man I love," she quietly murmured.

"What are you saying, Azra?"

"Nothing, my Avdaga, nothing."

Outside, it grew darker, and they finished their coffee in darkness. Through the holes in the stove doors, fire lit up parts of the room, creating strange shadows that danced on the walls. The captain's loud snoring was interrupted by the ticking of the old clock on the wall. The captain shifted his position and continued to snore. Outside, it began to snow heavily; a blanket over things yet to come. The next day, Sarajevo came under heavy shelling, so Hamza had to be transferred home in the evening. The Chetniks, after having showered the Old Town with deadly fire, now turned their attention to New Sarajevo.

*   *   *

The days passed in a blur. For Avdaga and Azra, they were filled with caring for Hamza and prayers. Three times a day with yarrow tea, known for its healing qualities, they cleaned his wounds and spoon-fed it to him in small doses. Few times a day, they changed the compresses on his body, also soaked in yarrow. In the warm room, Hamza was covered with only a thin blanket.

"The air has to pass over the wounds constantly in order to dry them. They have to be completely clean. The best thing is to put the compresses on, leave them on the wounds for a while, and then let the wounds air-dry," Avdaga explained to the captain. As the wounds began to heal, a new layer of skin grew over them. The captain made his new home at Avdaga's. As soon as he finished his work at the headquarters, he came straight back. He would help Avdaga a bit, and after that they would spend some time in philosophical discussion.

Avdaga patiently explained the basic philosophy of Islam. After that, they got into more complicated discussions. The captain had been born and raised in an atheist family. Since his early youth, he had been in military schools where his only religious teachings were of the value of atheism and communism; later, he served in the military that was also officially communistic and atheistic. Therefore, it was understood that he didn't have the slightest idea of what Islam was about. All he was taught was that myriad of different religions were unintelligent and intended for dull and ignorant people. The war in Bosnia caught him completely unprepared. From his post in the south of Serbia, he couldn't understand what was going on. Then he saw pictures of the slaughter and massacres of the Muslim population on CNN. For a long time, he couldn't believe that those people were being killed just because they were Muslims. And even worse, CNN said that his army, the Yugoslavian military, had committed those atrocities.

Then he had been sent on a business trip to Novi Sad. Seizing the chance to get away from the Yugoslav army he felt he no longer belonged to, he crossed the Hungarian border illegally, but was caught in the attempt and detained for questioning. The Hungarian border patrol took him to the Austrian-Slovenian border with Hungary, where the Austrians handed him over to the Slovenians. After a long and dangerous journey, he came to Bosnia and joined the Bosnian Army. He had needed time to realize what terror the entire population of Bosnia and Herzegovina lived in. Deeply saddened for not having been there from the start, he joined the battle for the survival of his people wholeheartedly.

Natural intelligence and logic enabled him to absorb the knowledge Avdaga gave him. He began to understand the real causes and goals of the Serb aggression against Bosnia. He began to recognize the principles of Islam. Partially remembering his early childhood, he recalled spending the summer with his grandparents in their village.

Now, following the bloody experience of this war, the captain was, perhaps unconsciously, but with joy, returning to the faith of his ancestors.

*   *   *

Musa stopped by every day. He used the breaks between rounds of shelling to limp to Avdaga's house. He would usually sit next to Hamza, put his hand on Hamza's head, and smoke. He would smoke so much that Azra would sometimes look at Avdaga with a question in her eyes, which as a rule, she didn't do. Avdaga would get up and open the door that led to the hallway.

"I'll just let out a bit of this stale air," he would say, as if making an excuse.

"He doesn't mind the smoke, Avdaga," Musa would say and continue to smoke.

He sometimes joined the conversations between the captain and Avdaga. Musa was surprised that the captain didn't know the basics of Islam, wisely concluding that "this war was Milosevic's biggest mistake. Man, with people like the captain, the Muslims would have disappeared from this area in twenty years, no shooting or killing required. All of them would have become Serbs. Captain, can you imagine how ironic it would be if the Chetniks caught you and killed you just because you were a Muslim? And you are less of a Muslim than they are. You do not pray or fast. You drink, eat pork, you do not believe in God, yet still they kill you because you're a Muslim."

"That's enough, Musa. It's never too late to come to Islam," Avdaga would say to reassure him.

"Yeah, two hundred thousand people had to die before the captain got back to Islam." The captain did not know what to say, and Avdaga would, secretly, give signs to Musa to stop making the situation awkward. Further conversation would be about the war, the political situation in foreign countries, religion, and history. Avdaga was a source of knowledge that never dried up, and he always amazed the captain and Musa with his thorough conclusions. Everyone enjoyed those conversations. Every day, they became longer and more vivid, probably because Hamza's wounds were healing well, and there was less to worry about. That was true for Hamza's body; but his mind was still in a great deal of danger.

*   *   *

The memories returned first. In Hamza's brain, isolated from the external world for a long time, the first traces of memory started coming back. In the beginning, short fragments appeared and disappeared at random. The images made his eyelids twitch, following the activity and movement.

Avdaga and Azra noticed it at the same time.

"Thank you, dear God Almighty."

As the days passed, the memories in Hamza's brain appeared more and more often and the broken fragments began to connect in a logical pattern. The interruptions in Hamza's brain activity were still very long.

*   *   *

It was afternoon of a sunny April day. After work, Hamza stopped at the post office to pick up a package from his cousin in Chicago.

"Fairly big box, what did he send?" Hamza wondered. He got in the car, placed the box on the passenger seat and stepped on the gas. The car traveled across the miles that separated him from Amra. He always rushed to get home to her. Driving, he started to unpack the box.

It was a Sony camcorder, the latest in technology. Hamza smiled. It was the first time his cousin had gotten in touch with him after years spent in America. According to what Hamza had seen in the movies and newspapers, it was a rough country. A big country where the individual gets lost fast. Drugs, the Mafia, prostitution. No, Hamza didn't like America.

Soon, he turned from the main road onto a narrow gravel path, and after a few hundred yards, stopped in front of the house with a squeal of the brakes. Amra was on the porch. She put the little one nestled in a blanket on the swing. They both enjoyed the sun shining radiantly from the west. The cottage was Hamza's first independent project since he graduated from the university. The big porch that went along two sides of the house was Azra's idea, in true American style.

"Hey, take a look at what our cousin from America has sent us!" he kissed Amra and picked her up. Her long, chestnut-brown hair filled with the sun, and big brown eyes, were in stark contrast to his long, golden-blond hair and blue eyes. He spun around with her in his arms. Amra screamed, and the little one squealed.

"Don't be afraid. Daddy is playing. Daddy loves mommy."

"Amra, look at this." Hamza showed her the camcorder, excited.

"My dear Hamza, this doesn't do us any good here."

"What do you mean?"

"They have a video system different from our European one. I learned that when I was on a student trip with our orchestra. We couldn't watch any of our tapes."

"An apple in a hundred years, and it's a rotten one."

Amra burst out laughing. "It is not that bad. We can convert the tapes to the European system and send the originals to him. I guess he might like to see the old country and relatives."

"You know what? I'll head up to that hill and record the whole area, and then we can tape our house from up close and inside. Tomorrow, I'll record Avdaga and Azra and the old house, so we can send it to him."

"Hamza, what's going on in the city?"

"Nothing. A few lunatics put some barricades on several streets and started shooting. The police will take care of it."

"Hamza, I'm afraid. We are all alone here in the middle of nowhere. Maybe we should get back to town, at least until this gets straightened out?"

"Don't be ridiculous. It's nothing. A few nut jobs, that's all."

"I don't know, Hamza. I'm scared."

"I hope you're not scared when I'm around."

"Get serious, honestly . . ."

"All right, seriously. We are not alone here. The village is right across the hill. My best man is there. If it gets dangerous, he can be here in five minutes."

"I don't know, Hamza," Amra repeated." I've heard some pretty nasty rumors about him. People say a lot of things."

"Let people talk. They talk about me too. Come on, he's my best man. Didn't he give our daughter her name? Huh? The title of the best man, especially for Serbs, is more important than a cousin."

"All right, if you say so. But, please don't be too long. I'm going to make lunch."

"I won't be. It will get dark soon."

Hamza kissed her, got into the car, and drove down the narrow road toward the nearby hill. At the foot of the hill, he parked the car. From there, he walked up the hill in search of a perfect spot from where he could make his first video. From time to time, he would turn around to see if the spot was a good one, and still not satisfied, continued to climb higher. He finally stopped near the top of the hill. He stood for a while, observing the whole area in the beautiful light of the sunset.

"I would get a much better view if I climbed up a tree," he thought to himself. A nearby oak tree seemed perfect. He climbed up quickly. Sitting on a wide branch, Hamza turned on the camera and tried out the zoom. With satisfaction, he realized that he could tape the details of the house even from this distance. He put his eye to the camera and started recording. First, he filmed the house as a whole. He saw Amra going into the house and the little one sitting on the swing on the porch. Hamza went on to tape the natural surroundings. The house was at the edge of a clearing with a narrow gravel road connecting it to the main road. Behind the house was an evergreen forest that ended in cliffs. On the east side, there was a small orchard and garden, where Amra had already planted vegetables. Next to the house was a rose garden, which was Amra's pride and joy. There were many rose bushes, with buds that had been enticed by the early spring sun. Through the lens, he saw a large, white Mercedes. Hamza smiled. His best man was there in time for dinner. That was good. At least Amra and the little one would feel safer. He zoomed in on the Mercedes. It came to a stop and his best man got out.

The other doors opened and another four guys got out of the car. "What the heck are they doing with uniforms and guns? Maybe there's a draft?" Hamza wondered while continuing his taping. His best man yelled something, and the guys headed to the back of the house. Amra came out. She took the little one, who seemed to have started crying, and came down the stairs to his best man. One of his escorts, bald-headed with a beard, explained something to him while pointing at Amra. The best man nodded. The other man came up to

Amra, and it appeared to Hamza, grabbed the little one from her hands and handed her to the best man. The baldy grabbed Amra's hand, twisted it behind her back, and pushed her into the house. Hamza's face went numb; his brain short-circuited. He could not think; he could not move. He just sat in the tree with his eye fixed to the camera viewer.

After a while, Amra came running out of the house. She covered her naked breasts with her arms, and ran to the best man. The best man tossed the little one to one of his escorts. From the sheath that hung on his belt, he took out a replica of a katana—a samurai sword—he had bought in some antique shop in Belgrade not long ago. He brought it up to Amra's arms and drew the blade across her forearms. Hamza saw the blood well up from the wounds. Amra extended her arms. It seemed as though she screamed. Frozen, Hamza continued to record. The best man swung again, hard, holding the sword with both hands. For a moment, the sword gleamed in the sunlight, shone like a diamond, and then cut through Amra's neck, finding little resistance. Her head fell to the ground. Blood fled her dying body in a fountain. Hamza screamed. The best man took the little one with one hand, and throwing her into the air, cut her in half with a single swing of the sword. One of the escorts turned around and started throwing up.

"No!" Hamza screamed and finally moved. He jumped out of the tree, hit a branch, and fell to the ground. He got up and started running. Branches scratched his face, stones cut his legs, but he ran like the wind. Suddenly, he tripped on a rotten branch and flew through the air. Everything happened so fast, he didn't have time to throw up his hands to break the fall. At full speed, he smashed into a large rock and collapsed. He remained lying there for some time. Blood ran down his forehead. The camera was still in his hands. Finally, a heavy, spring downpour brought him about. Completely soaked, he managed to glance at his watch. It was just after midnight. He remembered Amra. He screamed her name and ran toward the house. He ran, fell, slid, got up, and ran again. Finally, he got to the clearing. A thin line of smoke rose from the embers of the burned-down house. Hamza came closer. A dozen yards away from the house, he saw Amra's body. Her head was several feet away. Hamza fell to his knees. He grabbed the headless body and pulled it tight to his chest. The body was cold and stiff. He didn't know how long he stayed like that, but when he looked up, it was still raining. He put Amra down and, on his hands and knees, went over to her head. He slowly picked it up. Amra's eyes were wide open, staring blankly at the sky. On her face, there was a boot print and a frozen expression of terror. Crawling, he came back and put the head against her neck. He tried to stand up, but couldn't. He crawled to the little one. Her eyes were wide open too. He closed them gently. Somehow, he brought the parts of a tiny, cold body to rest next to Amra's. He fell to the ground. Time passed. With his face in the mud, Hamza remained motionless.

Sometime later, he moved. He stumbled over to the burned-down house. He located a shovel with a burned handle, and proceeded to the rose garden. Amra had been working in the garden the day before, and the soil was still loose. He dug quickly. He removed a few rose bushes with the roots and continued digging. When the hole was large enough, he removed his jacket and sweater. First, he placed Amra inside and leaned her head against her body. Then he gently laid the little one beside her in the grave. He positioned Amra's arms around her. He covered their heads with his jacket and managed to partially cover them with his sweater. He began shoveling the earth back on top of them.

He stopped, kneeled down, and pushed the earth away with his hands. He removed the jacket from their heads, and lay down beside them. He hugged Amra and pressed her closer to himself. The move jarred Amra's head off her neck and made it fall to the side. Hamza winced. He sat up and put Amra's head quickly back in place. Looking at the corpses, he stabbed his hands into his hair. For a minute? An hour? He got out of the grave, and, kneeling down, pushed the soil back in the grave. He replaced the roses, roots and all, back into their original positions and carefully spread the rest of the soil all over the rose garden so the grave would remain hidden. The shovel he washed in the muddy water, pulled through the ashes, and threw back into the burned house. The little red signal light on the video camera caught his attention. He took the camera, pulled the tape out, stuffed it in his pocket, and threw the camera away. He headed back to the main road. He had been walking for a while, when he noticed the headlights coming his way.

Despite his numbed senses, he managed to dart off the road and jump into the river. The survival instinct had wakened him just in time. The driver didn't see him. The cold water brought him back to his senses. He waited for the vehicle to pass and continued on. Soon, he saw a barricade on the street. He went down to the river again, and crossed to the other side. He climbed up and circled around the barricade. He decided not to return to the road. He continued slowly across the hill. The rain would not let up. The deathly silence was interrupted only by the steady, rustling sound of raindrops. Suddenly, the wind brought the smell of cigarette smoke. Hamza froze. He lifted his head and smelled the air like a bloodhound. The smell was coming from somewhere around the bend, some twenty yards ahead. He dropped to the ground and crawled forward. He could see a man squatting under a small tree. A guard, he thought. The man was covered with a raincoat, facing Sarajevo, smoking. A machine gun carelessly leaned up against his legs. Hamza kept crawling forward. When he was within a few yards, he picked up a small stone and threw it over the guard's head. The guard turned in the direction of the noise, the cigarette still in his mouth. He wasn't expecting anybody. Hamza rose, made two leaping strides, and was directly behind the guard. With his right hand, he pressed the guard's mouth shut and pushed him against the tree. With the left, he groped at the guard's utility belt. He felt a knife, pulled it out, and stabbed the man through the right temple. It went through like a hot knife through butter. Hamza lowered the body to the ground, taking the machine gun and ammo. He put the knife onto his own belt, and continued walking, not looking back. When he crossed the last tunnel before Dariva, a popular swimming spot just to the east of Sarajevo, somebody shouted, "STOP!"

"I stopped."

"Who goes there?"

"It's me, Hamza."

"Hamza who?"

"All right, man, you can see I've got my hands in the air. Can I come closer now?"

"Okay. Just take it nice and slow. Keep your hands where I can see them."

"Is this good?"

"That's fine. One wrong move though and I'll shoot. I'm not kidding."

Hamza came closer. A young member of the national guard came out of the bushes.

"Are you one of us?"

"Of course, I am."

"He's good, let him go. Hamza, what are you doing here?" It was one of his neighbors from the street, an older and very serious guy.

"Well, you know, I saw that it was getting messy, so I thought it would be better to be here."

"You did well. Things have gotten really bad. People have been killed. Anyway, how did you get the weapon?"

"I bought it from a Serb."

"Buddy, you know you can't have a firearm in your private possession, according to the laws regarding possession of weapons . . ." the young policeman quoted.

"Give it a rest, kid. A tank won't do us much good if this keeps up," the older one interrupted him. "Hamza, just go straight ahead, then turn right at that intersection, and you'll get to Kovaci. There are a lot of patrols, so it's better that they don't stop you."

"All right, neighbor, I'll see you around."

Shortly after, Hamza entered his parents' house without knocking.

*   *   *

Azra was surprised. Though she was terrified to see him dirty and wounded, she didn't show it.

"What are you doing here, Hamza, in this rain?"

"I came for a while, no reason."

"Where are Amra and the little one?"

"They went to Germany. My best man sent them."

"But why, my son?"

"It's getting messy here, Azra. Really messy. Looks like there is going to be a war."

"Hamza, where did you get the weapon?"

"I bought it from some Serb. Azra, could you please run me a hot tub and give me a room? I'm tired."

Azra went out of the room. Avdaga looked at Hamza.

"Tell me."

Hamza started to talk. He spoke slowly and heavily. He stopped, stuttered, tried again, and wiped the sweat from his face. Finally, he finished and looked away. Avdaga was silent, frozen. Hamza added, "Please don't tell Azra anything. It'll break her heart. Let her think they are in Germany. Let everybody think that." Avdaga nodded, and then came back to himself, "You go take a bath and get some rest. I'll come later."

Avdaga came back half an hour later. He looked at Hamza in silence for a long time. With a voice filled with emotion, Hamza did not recognize in this beloved man, Avdaga began to talk. It was a side of Avdaga that Hamza had never seen before.

"You want to go tomorrow?"

Hamza nodded.

"You can't. You'll stay here another three days. Now, take the Qur'an and pray. Don't go to sleep until I come back. Give me that knife."

"I thought I could keep it."

"Of course, you're going to keep it. Now, give it to me," he said in a tone that brooked no argument. "Do you understand? Pray until I come back." Avdaga got up and left the room.

He returned around ten the next morning. Hamza's head nodded over the Qur'an. He prayed in a loud and clear voice, without interruption. Avdaga loved listening to him. He gave him the sign to stop. "*Sadek allahul azim.*" Hamza kissed the Qur'an and touched it to his forehead. Avdaga handed him a complex-looking belt. "Try them on. They work as suspenders."

Hamza got up and put the 'suspenders' on. He placed his hands through the ends of the leather belts. Over the middle of the back, there was a case made of hard leather. At the end of the case was a thin belt.

"You need to secure this belt to your pants. Now, put the knife into the case."

Hamza put the knife into the case and discovered that it lay nicely on his back.

"Listen to me Hamza. You've been in a great deal of fights. You know the tricks. War is different than street-fighting, but you still have an advantage. For the next three days, you have to remember everything I tell you. I'll show you how to use those skills in war. Is that clear? All right, now try to move. Swing your shoulders, get down, try and turn around. That was good. Now, listen carefully. Nobody can really tell if you're left—or right-handed. That's an advantage. Use it. Every advantage you have, no matter how small it may seem, you must use a hundred percent. Just like in chess. If you have so much as a single pawn advantage, you must win the game. Now, pull the knife out."

Hamza reached for the knife with his right hand, over his right shoulder. The handle slipped to the left, out of reach. He tried to reach it with his left over the left shoulder. The handle slipped again. Hamza stopped and took the handle with his left hand behind the right shoulder. The knife, magically, found its way into his hand.

"This is good."

"Great! Try it a few times. You're going to practice that a few times a day. Now, pay attention to this. You don't cut with a knife the same way you do with an axe. The blade has to cut on its way out. No matter how hard you swing, if you cut on the way in, you will soon come to the point where it won't go any further. Try it in the air once. That's no good. Give me the knife. Like this, you see. Swing, then pull it toward yourself and slice. Try it now. That's better. Practice that too. And, by tonight, I want you to be able to do two hundred push-ups. Start practicing right now. Another thing—Azra won't come into this room. When you're hungry, come and eat in the big room. Now, you can go to sleep for a while."

Hamza soaked it all in. He had trouble sleeping and got up in the afternoon feeling more tired than when he had gone to sleep. For the next three days, he went through a military-skills crash course with Avdaga: strength-building, survival techniques, and a number of other things, including crawling, shooting, explosives, mine laying, ambushes, forest food, first aid, concentration, etc.

On the morning of the fourth day, Avdaga announced, "Now, you're ready to go. There are some guys on Bistrik. They call them the Berets. I know some of them, and so do you. Now, go, and may God watch over you. Keep these things in mind: don't drink, don't ever kill women, children, or the elderly, and don't torture your captives. If you have to kill in combat, make it fast and clean. I can't tell you anything more. You know where your home is, so stop by when you can. Don't torture yourself over what's happened. That's going to weaken you, and you can't change anything anyway. It was God's will. Don't think about me and Azra. Your worry and love will only weaken you. There is money is on the table. Take as much as you need."

Azra kissed him without saying a word. Avdaga hugged her after Hamza had left the yard.

"I thought that this was behind us, that I was the last one of our family to go into war. For centuries, everybody from my family has gone through at least one war. And we were good warriors. Now, it's Hamza's turn. He'll be fine, God willing. Don't worry about him."

*   *   *

The guys on Bistrik were one of many groups throughout Sarajevo that got together through the self initiative of the inhabitants. The beginning of the war took the people of Sarajevo by surprise. Nobody would have thought that something like that could possibly happen in their beautiful city—an Olympic city in the heart of Europe. People were confused and expected some kind of intervention—surely from the Americans—that would put a stop to the madness that was going on. People's conversations and comments indicated that the end was expected, if not that week, then definitely the next. The police were the only armed forces Sarajevo had.

The police special forces, called "Vikic's Special Forces"— named after their leader, the famous Dragan Vikic, a Sarajevo legend—led the defense. The police were badly hurt by the departure of, or more to the point the betrayal of, many members of the Serb nationality. They took with them a large part of the special military equipment from the police warehouse, and most of what they did not take they destroyed. The police, together with the civilian units, took over the defense of the city.

Simultaneously, volunteer local defense groups grew quickly throughout the city. They gathered mostly around the black sheep of Sarajevo—the type who had lived on the fringes and were in constant trouble with the law, as well as the famous athletes, karate fighters, judo fighters, and Sarajevo businessmen. Out of the mixed combination of the police, the Green Berets, the Patriotic League, and others grew the Army of Bosnia and Herzegovina. Something that nobody could have expected happened, perhaps for the first time in history. Guys from the edge of the underworld, without exception, stood up to defend their city. The joke circulated around the city that one of them had told the police chief, "Let's beat the Chetniks together. Afterwards, I'll pretend to steal, and you pretend to chase me again."

Some of these guys had strayed from the straight and narrow afterwards, but no matter which way they went, they deserve to be honored for what they did in the first days of the defense of their country. Those self-initiated groups divided the city's defenses between themselves, and had performed admirably.

Juka, Celo 1, Celo 2, Krushko, Topa, Yez, Kan, Caco—each had their own territory while the police covered the rest. The special forces were like firemen, running about and helping out wherever they were needed. They would jump into the fray, get the job done, and rush off to the next job. The response of the youth of Sarajevo, and of Bosnia and Herzegovina as a whole, against the wild, barbarous aggression and unbelievable slaughter of Sarajevo and the entire nation, was spontaneous resistance. Bosnia survived; to the surprise of the entire world, it won battles against the fourth largest military power in Europe. The ex-Yugoslav Army, together with the Chetniks, the White Eagles, Arkan's and Seselj's units, and all the other bandits, murderers, robbers, losers, good-for-nothings, and the Belgrade trash, couldn't wipe out the non-Serb population of Bosnia.

The Muslims paid a high price in blood for their naiveté and trust—around two hundred thousand dead. Most were civilians: women, children, and the elderly. In direct confrontations with the Bosnian armed defense, the Serb criminals usually got the worst of it. A general of the former Yugoslav Federal Army, Milutin Kukanjac, couldn't believe how his troops could lose their positions in and around Sarajevo after he had left the situation in their hands. General Kukanjac is remembered for his statement that the army didn't hurt a fly in Bosnia. While the report on fly casualties is not in yet, the fact is that the same army, with the Chetnik barbarians imported from Serbia, as well as the domestic Serbs who worked together with them, killed and slaughtered about two hundred thousand non-Serbs in Bosnia.

Hamza joined one of those self-initiated groups gathered in the cafe *Butterfly* in downtown Sarajevo. Musa joined the same day. It would be easier when they were together. The other guys were all friends, acquaintances, and people they knew, faces well-known around Sarajevo.

It was normal for them to be there together. In the first series of defensive actions, almost unarmed, they stopped the Chetniks.

May 2nd, 1992: D-Day for Bosnia and Herzegovina. During the previous night, the ex-Yugoslav Army publicly took the aggressor's side. The president of the Republic of Bosnia and Herzegovina, Alija Izetbegovic, together with his escorts, came back to the country after a negotiation session somewhere in the world. After landing at Sarajevo airport, the ex-Yugoslav Army troops captured him and held him prisoner at the military checkpoint near the town. The Patriotic League, Green Berets, and self-initiated groups blocked the military headquarters in the old town—the heart of Sarajevo. General Kukanjac was located at these headquarters too. He cried for help. He called on UN Forces to help him get away. He called to god and the devil. What a shame; a general that was so brave standing above the city shooting unarmed people was crying publicly for help. That same night, Chetnik tanks entered Sarajevo. The defenders watched them. A commanding voice called over walkie-talkies: "If they're just passing, let them through. If they start firing, destroy them."

Easier said than done. 'Destroy them' with what? "Grandpa," a legendary old man of some seventy years, together with Jez, Celo, and the others, stopped the tanks fifty yards from the parliament building of Bosnia. The aggressors' half-burned corpses littered the streets.

Those were the pictures that went around the world. The next day came the exchange. The ex-Yugoslav Army would return President Izetbegovic in exchange for General Kukanjac. The Berets and Patriotic League stopped the convoy that went through Sarajevo, taking General Kukanjac out of town to be exchanged for the president. Kukanjac leaves the city. The defenders seized a large quantity of firearms and documentation on the preparation and goals of the aggression. Everyone finally realized . . . it was WAR!

The fighting grew worse. Parts of the city fell to the aggressors. The defenders took them back. Hamza got out of the city. Musa was with him. They fought on the outer side of the ring that surrounded Sarajevo. The defenders took over Trnovo, a strategically important village. The war went on. Nobody even mentioned intervention anymore. The UN passed more resolutions, great new worthless resolutions with non-binding content. Only the defenders put any real resolutions into effect. Resolutions regarding the Chetnik retreat. The Chetnik terrorists took over the entire eastern and northern regions of Bosnia. Cities, towns, and villages fell like dominoes. The men didn't have weapons; chaos ruled supreme. Unarmed civilians were the targets of Chetnik orgies. The numbers of killed, slaughtered, and liquidated Bosnians grew rapidly. Ten thousand, twenty thousand, fifty! Most of them women, children, and the elderly, slaughtered at knife-point like cattle. The main symbols for the Chetniks were the dagger and the victims—helpless civilians lined up for slaughter.

After more than a thousand days of siege, a group of intellectuals from Belgrade came to visit Sarajevo. The mayor of Sarajevo, Mr. Tarik Kupusovic, accepted their visit. The guests were grim. Coincidentally, the chief of staff of the mayor of Sarajevo was a Serb, a normal human being. One of the group members asked why Sarajevo hasn't been made into an open city, like Paris in the Second World War. They alluded to the hypothesis their media had been selling; the people of Sarajevo had destroyed their city by defending it. To which the mayor coolly responded, "We have amassed the experience of all the towns and villages that the Chetniks have entered. They kill everybody they find who is not a

Serb. That would have been Sarajevo's destiny too, if it hadn't been for the defenders."

* * *

War stretched into yet another summer. The Chetniks have gathered all their forces together for a final assault. Reserves arrived from Serbia and Montenegro. The attack on the mountain ridge Rogoj began, with General Mladic leading it personally. The defenders' lines couldn't take the pressure of the attack and the village of Trnovo fell. The defenders had no choice but to retreat again. It was impossible to establish stable lines of defense.

Hamza's unit had been fighting for ten days. They were surrounded. Ten soldiers, no food, no water, only the mountain. All contact with other units broken. They found a small creek fed by drainage from the mountain. They had just wet their mouths when they heard voices. Hamza ordered his men to fall back. They hid in the bushes. Four Chetniks approached—three young and one older man made up this particular cell. They knew about the spring and came to fill their drinking canisters. Hamza gave the command as if conducting an orchestra: one—two—three—go! They surged forward with their weapons at the ready.

The Chetniks were taken by surprise. Two of them grabbed their weapons. Dado and Kemo were faster; short bursts. The other two raised their arms in surrender. Dado and Kemo stood behind the captives, holding knives to their throats. The others stood in a semicircle around them, facing away from them. They cautiously observed their surroundings.

"Are you from around here?" Hamza asked one of them. The surly Chetnik was silent.

"Are you the guide? Only somebody who's from here can know about the spring."

The captive remained silent.

"All right. You're going to take us out of here."

"Over my dead body I will."

Hamza put a gun to his forehead. "That can certainly be arranged."

"Hold on, I'll take you out of here," the other young captive jumped into the conversation.

"You?"

"Yes, I will. I know the way." He was talking fast. "I'll take you out. Don't kill me."

"All right." Hamza looked at Dado.

Dado had just drawn his knife behind the other prisoner when Dino jumped on him, "Hold it, don't!"

Dado was so surprised that he fell to the ground, tangled together with the Chetnik. Dino fell on top of them. Dado untangled himself and stood. He grabbed Dino's jacket and picked him up.

"You don't want me to kill him? Fine, then *you* think of something! To hell with both of you!" And he threw him on the ground.

"Dino, can't you see the shit we're in? Don't you see there are thousands of Chetniks around us, that we've been trapped? Do you see that, you idiot? Do you see how many of us are still alive?" Kemo was almost screaming.

"Exactly. If we kill him, we won't be able to get out of here alive."

"What are you, some kind of a psychic gypsy?"

"No, but I have that feeling."

"Fuck your feelings. Dado, kill him and let's go."

Dino stood in front of the Chetnik. "Kill me first."

"Hamza, what are we going to do? The kid's gone crazy."

"Fine, Dino. What do you want?" Hamza joined in the conversation.

"Let's tie him up and leave. He can't untie himself in two hours. And by that time, we'll be far away."

"I don't get this, guys." Kemo's voice was bitter.

"I just can't stand to watch people getting killed, and that's it. But if you think that you're braver than I me, then the two of us can go against the Chetniks alone, and then we'll see."

"You would, being the idiot that you are."

"It's all right, people. Dino, here you go. He's your Chetnik. If we get in trouble, because of him, it's on you."

Somebody handed Dino a rope. Dino came close to the Chetnik, still lying on the ground, motionless. He took his arms and tied them behind his back. He tied him for a long time—a hundred-and-one knot. When he was done, he took him to a tree and tied him to it. "That's it. Now, he can't untie himself. Maybe his troops will come to look for him and they'll find him."

On his way to join the others, Dino passed next to the dead bodies of the other two Chetniks. The sight made him throw up. Dado held his shoulders gently. Dino kept throwing up. His face was pallid. He held his stomach. Kemo brought him with a wet scarf. He wiped his face and mouth. Dado took him to the side so he couldn't see the dead bodies.

"Tell me, you don't feel sorry for them, do you?"

"I don't know, I just think it's not fair," Dino sniffled.

"Fuck that!" Dado screamed. Dino started crying loudly.

"I'm sorry, I'm sorry, I'm sorry. I'm really sorry," Dado spoke fast. "I didn't mean it, I'm sorry," he said as he hugged him. "Look, Dino, you don't understand anything. Now, your Dado is going to explain everything to you. You say it's not fair. Well, you see, a couple of years ago, I thought the same way. Let me explain it to you." He came closer to Dino, and started whispering in his ear. "I was in jail because I had killed two people. We were gambling on the train, and I won their money. Then they attacked me and stabbed me three or four times. Seeing this was no joke. I took their knives and stabbed them a few times. The judge ruled that it wasn't self-defense. He said I could have escaped through the window. Hey, the train was moving. How could I have escaped? Well, that's fair."

He continued in a regular voice, "What would you be doing now if it weren't for the war? You would have finished school, found a job, then girls, games, bars. Later on, you would get married and so on. I would have been out of jail by now, and then I'd go back home to Krajina, then abroad to find a job." Dado used his hand to illustrate the motion of pulling somebody's wallet out of his pocket.

"Money, German girls, Dutch girls, Belgian girls . . . Yes, many beautiful girls. Hamza would design houses, and Kemo would cut trees . . ."

"What's that about me?"

"Nothing, Kemo, I swear," Dado said, smiling. "And this way, what are we doing? Fucking around on some mountains, risking our lives, dying . . . and all because someone in Serbia wants to control Bosnia. So, they came to visit us for a while. They're going to slaughter a bit, rob a bit until the Muslims are gone. You think that your mom and your grandma would be alive if the Chetniks had entered Sarajevo? No, Dino, they wouldn't. In my village, nobody survived. I imagine how they led them away for the execution. Grandpas, grandmas, mothers with babies . . . those Chetnik motherfuckers. I imagine how they opened fire. My baby brother's cries. The Chetniks come closer and shoot her in the head. Those images are haunting me. The silence is killing me. I feel a bit better when we're in action. If I could, I'd never come back. You know why I stick around with you? Because of Hamza. There is something that makes him go on, go further, just like me. They killed my father, my mother, two brothers, eleven cousins, uncles . . . Why? Just because their names were different. Just because they were Muslim. Now, let me ask you something . . . have you ever killed a woman or a child?"

"No, Dado. What's wrong with you?"

"I haven't either. And these Chetniks who come here from God-knows-where, with their weapons and their knives to kill us . . . Look at me! I don't know how many Chetniks I've killed. And, every time I kill one, I label him. This one is for my father, this one for one brother, this one for the other brother, that one for my sister . . . Do you know how many of them I have to kill to make it even, just for my family? Not to mention relatives and friends? A whole lot. You think I feel sorry? I don't give a rat's ass!"

"That's enough, Dado. Leave him alone. Let's go. I'm not planning on spending the night here."

"Seriously, Dado, you're acting like a damn professor. You blab on and on, and just can't seem to stop."

"Wait a second, man. First of all, if we're late, maybe we're late for a shell to hit us. Second of all, I have to explain everything to him. Maybe he'll be dead in a minute or an hour. He has to know what's going on. And I don't want him to think that I'm a murderer. I'm a warrior." Dado lifted his arms in the air like a boxer rejoicing in his victory. "A warrior. I am not a Chetnik to sing while I kill the unarmed, and whine and cry when they beat me. I kill silently, and I'll die silently."

"Dado, if he hasn't realized it after two years of war, there's nothing you can say that will help him understand," Mustafa said.

"You see, Dino," Musa said, deciding to say something intelligent, "as far as we're concerned, the war could stop tomorrow. All we need is these guys to turn around and go back to wherever they came from. And about what you said, the 'not being fair,' there is no fair fight with two hundred thousand slaughtered civilians behind us. There is no fair fighting with three hundred thousand hungry people in Sarajevo, who are sure to get the knife if we let the Chetniks get past us. The president can talk as much as he likes, and tell the foreign reporters, "We're going to fight with all allowed means." Well, he can fight like that. As far as I'm concerned, I'll fight with all existing and non-existing means, allowed or not. With a machine gun, a cannon, a knife, my teeth, gas, with the air, the sun . . . can you even imagine him saying "with all allowed means?" That's the same as if you were attacked by ten guys, and you're still trying to fight according to the rules. If I had an atomic bomb . . . if I had ten of them, I would throw them all at Serbia. Let the bastards feel what it's like when your dearest ones die. Look here, Dino. I don't know anything about this Chetnik. But, listen to this now." Dado turned towards the captive. "Where are you from, you hero?"

"From Uzice, in Serbia."

"And who made you come all the way here?"

"The army recruitment."

"Recruitment?"

"The order for military training. They loaded us onto trucks and put the canopy down. When they lifted it, we were in Sokolac."

"And then you came singing, to slaughter the Muslims."

"I swear on my mother I haven't fired one bullet."

"You see, Dino. He hasn't fired a bullet. Nobody has. Whoever you ask, nobody ever shot a single bullet. Then, who is it that's slaughtering us?"

"That's enough education for today. Shall we, Hamza?"

"Let's go."

Musa took out a bunch of wires, made a noose out of them, and put it around the captive's neck. He pulled it.

"Pray to God that nothing happens to me. If I fall, this wire is going to cut your throat."

"Can you loosen it up a bit? I can't breathe."

Musa made a slight adjustment to the tension in the wire. "Better?" he smirked at the young soldier.

The small group started walking. The young Chetnik headed in the direction away from Sarajevo.

"Hey, buddy, Sarajevo is on the other side."

"I know, but we have to go to the east first, because in front of us and to the west are my troops. When we go back, maybe a couple of hours, then we'll go to the south. We'll have to walk for a while—about five hours—and then turn due west and northwest. I've looked at the attack map kept at the headquarters. Don't worry. I'll get you through. You know, before the war I was a mountain hiker. In the military, I was a scout."

"That's great. Just remember, it's your ass on the line too."

With a start, Dino looked around.

"Where is Dado? Where is Dado?"

The rest of the group looked at each other. A short machine gun burst echoed from the direction of the spring. Dino threw his rucksack and ran back. After twenty yards, he ran headlong into Dado.

"Hold on, Dino, where are you going?"

"Dado, you killed him!"

"I didn't, I swear by my mother. I just fired a burst near his head, because we told him not to try to untie himself but he was trying to."

"Don't lie to me! You killed him!"

"When I tell you I didn't, then I didn't." Dado's voice had taken on a deadly quality but forceful tone.

Dino pushed him aside and tried to pass him, to check. Dado waited until he had gotten just past him, and then hit him with the butt of his rifle. Dino dropped without a word. Dado kneeled, picked him up, and put him over his shoulders. He carried him back to the others. "Congratulations, Dado. When you screw up something, a hundred people can't fix it."

"Quit fucking around and help me carry him."

"Why did you kill him?"

"Who said I did? I just shot near his head."

"Tell that to somebody else."

Kemo came closer and grabbed Dino's legs. Dado got his shoulders. They moved carefully, clinging to the woods, the valleys, and the passages. After a couple of hours, Dino regained consciousness. Never saying a word, he continued to walk with the others. They continued south and had been walking for several hours when Hamza ordered a rest. Everybody dropped. The young captive turned to Musa, "Are you going to kill me?"

Musa was silent. The prisoner asked again, "Are you going to kill me?"

Musa looked at him carefully.

"Who were those three guys?"

"The young one was my neighbor. He was going out with my sister. The old one is from around here. He was the guide. I don't know who the third one was. Are you going to kill me?" Musa noted the barely controlled fear in the young man's voice.

"If everything turns out right, I don't think so. We won't need to."

They started walking again. The moonlight was strong enough to read by. Hamza moved closer.

"How much farther?"

"We're almost there. You see the lights in the distance? Those are your guys. You have about an hour and a half, maybe two."

"Where are your guys?"

"Somewhere back there. About two hours. Are you going to kill me now?"

"Are you sure that your guys aren't closer?"

"A hundred percent. Are you going to kill me?" This was clearly the only important thought in his mind.

"You know what? You probably won't understand this now." Hamza pulled out his gun and cocked it. The prisoner sat down and closed the eyes.

"Later you'll understand that I just did you a favor." Hamza fired a single shot.

The prisoner screamed and fell over on his side. Blood bubbled up through the bullet hole in his knee. Hamza crouched next to him and tied off his scarf above the knee. Musa handed him his scarf too. Hamza bandaged the wound, tightly. The young man clenched his teeth and mumbled. Tears streamed down his face. Dado brought a long stick and gave it to him without a word. He pulled out a gun. Hamza jumped.

"Hold it, Dado!"

"What's wrong with you? I won't do anything to him. He's brought us through all right. Here, kid, take the gun. It's loaded." Dado swung and threw it about twenty yards away. "Take it when we leave. When you come closer to your guys, shoot. They'll pick you up. This shit is over for you. You're going to be crippled for a while, but fuck it, you won't have to be a soldier anymore. And, tell your people in Uzice that the Chetniks have killed half of Bosnia. Maybe they'll feel better. It hurts when somebody you care about dies." Dado turned around and left. The others left too, and soon, the darkness of the forest swallowed them. The young man sat for a long time, watching them leave.

It was a quiet summer night. The moonlight hugged the mountain, the immense forests, the occasional fields, and the bare peaks. Somewhere in the distance, an owl hooted. Stars twinkled in the coverlet of the sky. Crystal-clean mountain air. The young Chetnik with a newly injured knee sighed, "Oh, what the hell! I got off easy. As long as I don't bleed to death by the time I reach my side, that is." He got up and started walking, leaning on the stick. His leg hurt. Every few minutes, a tear would roll down his cheek. He passed the gun without picking it up. The Bosnian drama was over for him.

*   *   *

From the dark hallways of oblivion, the terrible pictures of the war played out before Hamza's eyes, flickering briefly, then disappearing again. All the horrors flashed before him: the missions, attacks, retreats, deaths, the military cemetery in Kovaci.

Whenever he returned to Sarajevo, it was filled with more dead, as though there was some perverse connection between his arrival home and the number of tombstones. His crowd of friends grew smaller. Someone wrote a song once:

> . . . *Heaven is overcrowded*
> *with my generation,*
> *one by one*
> *we'll all get together . . ."*

A whiteness rolled over him. A whiteness over the whiteness of all things, and a white fog over white regions. The mountains were white and the forests were too. Even the sun was white. From the white clouds, a white horseman on a white horse came towards Hamza. His face was white and so were his eyes and hair. A white shield, a white sword. Behind him, two white images approached—a woman and a child. They floated, glided through the white surroundings. Hamza knew that it was Amra and the little one, but he couldn't take his eyes off the horseman.

* * *

"Avdaga, something is happening," the captain whispered.

Avdaga leaned over Hamza's face. Drops of sweat had begun to appear at the roots of Hamza's hair. His nostrils grew wider, and he began to shake slowly, his eyes flickering under closed eyelids.

"Now, he's on the edge. He will either leave, or he will stay."

"Wipe his sweat. Call to him," the captain urged.

"No. It's his decision. Even if an unconscious one."

"But . . ."

"No buts, my friend. To choose death is not always the worst solution."

The captain still didn't understand a thing.

Musa kept smoking silently.

* * *

The white horse was already above him and Hamza felt its hot breath on his face. He heard a voice, though the horseman was not moving his lips. The voice came like thunder, "Hamza! Hamza! Come, let's go. Stand under my flag. I'll take you to the green fields, where crystal clear rivers flow. I'll take you to a place where there is no pain, where there is no death. You'll be happy forever, with those you love. Hamza! Come with me. It's time."

With a superhuman effort, Hamza turned his eyes away. Amra and the little one were looking at him, smiling.

"I can't go yet, Amra, I can't. There is something I still need to do. Wait, please don't leave," Hamza said, without hearing his own voice.

He screamed, but no sound came out of his mouth. He was desperate. The horse reared, and began prancing backwards. Amra and the little one began gliding back. Hamza watched them leave with helpless desperation. Just a bit more until they were swallowed by the whiteness. He had to stop them. They had to hear him. "Hold on! Stop! Wait!" Nothing. And then, with all his strength, a scream broke out of him: "Amra!"

*   *   *

His scream woke Avdaga. Musa jumped off the bed, leaned onto his wounded leg and fell to the floor, moaning. Azra ran into the room, went back to the kitchen, and returned with a wet towel. She started wiping big drops of sweat off Hamza's face, all the while whispering the prayer:

> *"La illahe illallah, Muhammedu Resullullah,*
> *La illahe illallah, Muhammedu Resullullah."*

It was the forty-second night since Hamza was wounded.

*   *   *

After they had amputated his left arm, Dino started to regain consciousness. When he woke up, he didn't know where he was, or why he couldn't stand up. Dr. Gavrankapetanovic slowly explained the condition in which he had been in when brought to the hospital, and what they had had to do. "What are you talking about, doctor? An amputation? I was just grazed. Do you know that I drove the van to Hrasnica? I was just grazed, nothing more. Musa knows. Ask him. That's right. Ask Musa. Ask him!"

They quickly gave him a shot.

When he woke up again, night had fallen. His left shoulder hurt badly. Sitting up in the bed, he looked at it curiously. At the place where his arm should have been, there was nothing. The truth sank in: amputation! Dino screamed. When the nurse ran in, she found him pounding his head against the iron bed frame. Blood streamed down his face. She tackled him.

"Doctor!" Her cries for help echoed through the hallways. Dino was released from the hospital a month later, in a difficult mental condition. He locked himself up in the house. He refused to see anybody. People from his unit came by—Dado, Kemo, Musa all visited—or tried to. They talked to his father for a while. Dino was nowhere to be seen in the house.

*　　*　　*

"It'll be all right, with God's help. It'll be all right." Avdaga was gently touching Hamza's hair.

"You see, Captain, now he's dreaming. You see how his eyelids are moving? He'll be fine, with God's help."

*　　*　　*

It was autumn. Hamza was outside Sarajevo, on the Nisic plateau with the group, caught up in a heavy battle. The Chetniks had been there since the beginning of the war. If they could manage—just once—to move them from their positions, they wouldn't have time to establish new ones. Not since the Chetnik lines were so well-entrenched.

Finally, the Bosnian army tricked the Chetniks and broke their positions. The Chetniks withdrew in panic. The army of Bosnia took over a huge territory, including a few Chetnik villages. In the houses, they found a pile of washing machines and TVs—war trophies from the plundering of Bosnian towns and villages.

Outside the village, in the ditches, Hamza sat with his men and smoked. From time to time, somebody would look towards the Chetnik positions.

"Hey, somebody is headed for us." Everyone moved into ready positions. Sadik had a long-range rifle. He aimed at one of them, then lowered the rifle.

"Hold on, boys. These are our guys."

"What do you mean *our* guys?"

"What I said, ours. A patrol. I think it's the Zenica brigade. They have a prisoner."

Soon, four soldiers approached them, leading a prisoner between them. Hamza went to meet them.

"Hey, wait a minute. Where are you guys from?" Hamza questioned.

"From Zenica."

"And you came all this way on foot?"

"Don't fuck with us, old man. Can't you see we're dead tired?"

"Let's get you some coffee. It'll be ready in a minute."

"Really?"

"See for yourself."

The patrol went into the dugout. Kemo put the coffee pot on the *sarajka*, a very popular stove made from humanitarian aid cans. Sadik went outside to keep watch. As promised, after a few minutes, the pleasant aroma of coffee filled the dugout.

"So, how is it in Zenica?"

"How should I know? I haven't been there in ages."

"And where did you catch this one?"

"Over there." The soldier pointed into the distance.

"Is he the talkative type?"

"Yeah." The leader of the patrol started laughing, "It's just that now, he's got no tongue, just weight."

"What do you mean he's no tongue?"

"Well, like I said, he is dead weight to us now. Good for exchange. We don't need him any longer. We know everything we need to know."

"Huh, so, that's the deal. Well, uh, you know, uh, if you don't need him, uh . . ." Hamza acted as if he didn't know how to begin. "I mean . . . what I want to say is, if you don't need him, why don't you sell him to me."

Musa, Dado, Kemo, and Mustafa looked at each other, not understanding a word. What was he up to now? Dado gave them a sign to be quiet.

"Are you nuts? How am I going to sell you a human being?"

"Well, you know . . . It's our first time outside," Hamza lied. "I would really love to have a Chetnik. My friends back in the city would be speechless. Come on, sell him to me."

"And how much would you give me for him?" the leader asked in disbelief. He knew that some of the new guys in the army could be a bit off and he still wasn't sure if it all wasn't some kind of a joke.

"What do you say about a carton for each one of you?"

"And just how did you get cigarettes up here?"

"They're not here, but in Visoko"

"You want us to wait here for you to go and get them?" They laughed.

"No. I'll give you the money right away, so you can buy them yourself."

"How much?" one of the soldiers asked.

"The carton was twenty dollars."

"Yeah, before the war. Now, there is nothing below fifty."

"Yeah, minimum fifty," added the other Zenica soldier.

"Fine, four times fifty is two hundred. Ah, what the hell, I'll give you two hundred fifty, so you can get some coffee in town. Dado, give them the money."

"But, you can't tell anybody we sold him to you," the first soldier added cautiously.

"Of course not."

"Say, 'I hope I step on a mine if I tell anyone,'" the leader of this band of questionable soldiers demanded.

"Are you serious?" Now, Hamza began feeling concerned that they might be messing with him.

"Dead serious. You have to say it, or no deal."

"I hope I step on a mine if I tell anyone."

"That's good. So, we're going to go now." They stood to go. One of the soldiers kicked the captive as he passed by. They went out and disappeared into the downpour which had started up violently, as if the sky had opened and sobbed with grief of the last months for the lands below.

"You really are out of your mind." Dado looked at Hamza, not approving what he had done. "Look what we gave two hundred and fifty for. He doesn't even have a hundred and twenty pounds in him."

"Let it go, bro. See if they've left."

Musa went out of the dugout and came back inside quickly.

"No sign of them."

"Now, don't look at me, and don't ask me anything. And forget what you've seen. I've got some debts from before the war."

They fell silent. They had been together for too long to ask any questions. What Hamza did with the captive no longer interested them. Hamza moved to his newly bought prisoner and picked him up by the collar, "Let's you and I go for a walk." The prisoner turned pallid and led the way out of the shelter. They walked through the rain towards Chetnik positions. After a few minutes, they came to a sparse bit of forest.

"Hamza, please, don't do it."

"What's wrong with you, Neno? We have been friends forever. Are you nuts?" Hamza untied him. He shook his head. "Listen to yourself, 'Hamza don't!' You really are out of your mind. But anyway, how are you? What's new on your side? How's my best man?"

Neno turned a sickly shade of green. Hamza pretended not to notice.

"Hamza, you don't know . . ." Neno was almost whispering.

"I don't know, I really don't know. I've never been captured. But, then, I would never be captured, because those on your side don't take prisoners. They kill them all."

"It's not that, Hamza, I'm sorry . . ."

"I am sorry too, Neno. Now, get out of here, before any of my guys show up. Give my regards to my best man from me. Thank him in my name."

"For what?"

"For sending Amra and the little one to Germany. Hey, being a best man ain't peanuts. And tell him that you're a part of my debt. God help us, if we survive, we'll meet again. Now, get lost. I'm sorry about the weapons, I can't give you any."

"Fuck the weapons, I didn't need them anyway. Oh, Hamza, Hamza . . ."

"Try to get them to send you somewhere else. It's senseless for us to shoot at each other. And I can't be anywhere else but around Sarajevo."

Hamza turned around and started walking towards the dugout. Dino waited for him at the door. He smiled.

"I'm really glad you let him go."

"Kiddo, you really don't know anything. You have to pay back your debts. Isn't that right, Dado?"

"That's right. Everything has to get paid back."

"Well, how deep exactly are you in debt?" Sadik was clearly worried. "I mean, how many Chetniks do we have to 'catch and release' before you pay it all back?"

Hamza didn't answer.

*   *   *

One morning, after tending to still-comatose Hamza, Avdaga and the captain sat down for coffee. Relaxed on the sofa, they enjoyed the dark, warm liquid and a cigarette. The captain had begun to smoke heavily. The gentle rays of the March sun hugged Sarajevo. Though it was cold, the icicles hanging from the roof were losing their smoky color in the sun, turning a shiny translucent color. At their ends, the water dripped, catching the sun's rays for a moment and reflecting the colors of the rainbow—like a diamond—and threw themselves to the ground. Another spring was on the doorstep in Sarajevo's war.

"You don't have to go to the headquarters today, do you?"

"I don't, but I have some things to take care of."

"Take care of them tomorrow. Right now, let's go to Bakije, the two of us. I promised the hajji we would come two weeks ago. Azra, we're going to Bakije."

"Isn't it too early, Avdaga?"

"No, the hajji comes in early. Let's go, Captain."

At Kovaci they offered a prayer for the fallen soldiers, then walked on down to the city. It was early, and Bascarsija was almost empty—a few people walking, a couple of cars moving along the quiet streets. They stopped next to the mosque and went into the Bakije.

"*Assalamu alaikum*, hajji."

"*Alaikum mu Sallam wa Rahmetullahi wa Berakatahu!* What's going to happen? Is it going to snow or what?" Not waiting for an answer, he turned to a young boy who sat on a small couch. "Get up, you scamp, let the people sit down."

The boy blushed. Avdaga looked down and the captain felt sorry for the boy.

"What are you doing there? Sit down! Don't worry about the boy. He's one of us. We drink coffee here every morning." He turned to the boy.

"What are you waiting for? Go put on some coffee. They're going to leave without having coffee. Sit down."

"This is Hamza's captain."

"Well, well, welcome! A captain, you say? A professional, or one of these new, self-declared ones from the war?"

"Professional, hajji. A real captain. He was serving in Serbia when everything started. Hamza always says good things about him."

Coffee and conversation were served.

*   *   *

Bakije, the name of the Muslim funeral home in Sarajevo. Located in the northern corner of Bascarsija, "Bakije" is an institution founded almost a century ago through donations from the prominent people of Sarajevo. Ever since, they have carried out funerals in accordance with Muslim customs, with a minimum number of employees. During the communist era, it could be a dangerous job. The government looked on their work with suspicion, but ultimately decided against interfering. With the arrival of 'democracy,' the employees hoped they would finally be able to work in peace. Almost the same day, the war started. For foreign reporters and TV crew who always sought to find and present a new aspect of life in besieged Sarajevo, the work of Bakije had remained outside their interests. Or perhaps that aspect would have been too painful and bloody to the average person in the West, who was lulled by a life of almost surreal abundance.

The number of Muslim funerals in Sarajevo before the war was between eight hundred and one thousand two hundred a year. The local joke was that the hajji had supposedly commented at one of the annual committee meetings that, "The death rate is tapering off, but remains at a satisfactory level." At the beginning of the war, the vast numbers of dead civilians and defenders quickly exhausted the burial supplies of Bakije. From that point, until the end of the war, the employees scrounged for the necessary materials in all possible and sometimes impossible ways.

They bought construction wood from the people of Sarajevo. They got a circular saw and made the traditional "tabuti" stretchers and "nasloni" supports in the front yard of Bakije. From the Bey's mosque, which had been in the process of being remodeled when the war broke out, they took the scaffolding and used the boards for their simple traditional wooden open coffins. After that, schools donated wooden tables from the classrooms. People took the surviving seats from the Olympic Cultural Sports Center "Zetra," which had been fire-bombed by incendiary shells. They would tear the plastic lining off the seats and use the wooden boards for coffins. The plastic and rubber were given out to the people for heating.

Over the three and a half years of the war, Bakije handled the burial of nearly fifteen thousand Sarajevans. The other serious problem for Bakije was the fuel for the vehicles. The City Parliament gave as much fuel as it could, but even they were limited. The military headquarters was occasionally somehow able to get fuel for the funerals of their fellow soldiers. Bakije bought fuel on the black market. Wealthier families would bring fuel for the funerals of their beloved. Finding fabric for wrapping the bodies was also a problem. Everything was a problem.

After a large massacre, the back yard of Bakije was filled with bodies of the unfortunate Sarajevans. Foreign TV crew came to film. A young Austrian reporter carefully picked her way between the corpses. She spoke into the camera, choked up, started crying, and finally fainted. They brought her into the office and gave her water to revive her. Throughout the war, Bakije buried their fellow citizens. They drove across town through shelling and sniper fire, sometimes picking up the bodies of unfortunate people on the streets along the way. The chairman of the society died from a mortar shell attack while on his way to his home.

Before the war, Sarajevo had two active cemeteries—"Bare" and "Vlakovo." Bare was located in the part of the city constantly under fire, and Vlakovo was in Chetnik hands. On the southeast side of the sports stadium Kosevo and the Zetra complex—where the opening and closing ceremonies of the Olympic Games had taken place—were a few soccer fields, tennis courts, and a running track. During the war, the entire complex was converted into a cemetery. Long lines of fresh burial mounds crossed the fields diagonally. Additionally, the old Sarajevo cemeteries were reactivated. Within the hundreds-of-years-old cemeteries with cultural and historical value and beauty, new burial mounds appeared.—the burial mounds of the defenders of Sarajevo as well as those of its inhabitants.

Putting much effort into killing as many civilians as possible, the Chetniks regularly fired at funerals as well. Many died while saying their last farewells to their loved ones. It was decided that the funerals should be performed at night. Bakije operated under such circumstances throughout the war. The personal courage and dedication of the employees, together with their faith in God, made it possible for those people to maintain a healthy spirit and sound mind. Thus, Bakije became a regular place to go to for a cup of coffee any time of the day. People would come to talk for a while, to laugh a bit, to find out the news, and to absorb some of their peace and faith. Superficially, it seemed that those people had become numb to death, which was partially true. The hajji used to say, "Yes, we've become numb to death, but you can never become numb towards the death of children. No matter who you consider as the guilty party for the war, the children most definitely don't enter into it. For example, last spring we brought in two kids from Kobilja Glava. They had been picking cherries when the Chetniks killed them with anti-aircraft guns. That was really hard."

*   *   *

"So, he is a good man, you say?"

"A good man." Avdaga fell into his trap without thinking.

"Well, do you know, what should be done with good people, my Avdaga?" All of Sarajevo knew that joke. "Good people need to be . . . so they multiply, and there are more good people." The hajji burst out laughing.

The captain got up to leave, but Avdaga stopped him.

"Hajji, hajji, at your age . . . ."

The hajji was still laughing.

"Hajji, you've changed since I last saw you."

"You mean I've fucked myself up. Yes, I sure have. Pretty soon these pants are going to walk all by themselves." He finally got serious. "And you, my dear Captain? Is this your first time in Bakije? What did you expect it to be like? Did you expect to find all the saints here, floating around and praying? Huh? We're far from the saints. Anyway, relax. Don't be angry with me. I didn't mean anything bad."

"He's new." Avdaga said.

"You mean a new Muslim. There are no new Muslims, Avdaga. All Muslims are born as such. He was just lost for a while. But, God will help him. He'll be fine. He's with you, so he can't be anything else. Just don't be one of those newfound zealots who started going to the mosque yesterday, and suddenly become saints, giving lectures to everybody else."

"Are more people coming to the mosque, hajji?"

"Those that used to be here are still here. Now, tell me Avdaga, you're a smart man. You know everything. When do you think this is going to stop?"

"You mean the war?"

"Yeah."

"Well, it's a bit of a stretch to say that I know everything. I do understand some things."

"Well, then, please tell me. Every day, all manner of wise men come here and talk. Some say this, others say that. Now, I'm really interested in hearing what a really smart man thinks about all this."

"That's pretty high praise to be saying in front of all these people."

"People? Where?"

"Hold it, hajji. It's enough that you're joking about me and the captain here. Don't go any farther, please."

"All right, fine. Are you going to tell us when this is going to stop, or what?"

"Why not, my good hajji. Well, this is how I see it. First of all, I know that this is hard for everybody. But you know Einstein's Theory of Relativity. When you're in nice company, five minutes fly by in a second, and when you're holding your hand over fire, then five seconds seem longer than a year. These four years of war are very long for an individual. For the history of a people it's nothing.

They are a mere moment. Well, now, we, as people, are holding our hands over the fire, but that'll also be over. And when is this going to stop? When we talk about the war in Bosnia and the relationship between the world and us, first of all, we must distinguish between governments and people.

"Everything I say is related to the governments of states, because all the people in the world, excluding maybe Serbs and their *big brothers*, the Russians and Greeks, are on our side. Did you see how many mayors from the entire world were in Sarajevo for the one thousand days of resistance celebration? While Chetniks are killing themselves bending over backwards just to bring some Greek mayor to visit? Even the citizens of the small countries are on our side. But nobody asks them anything. Just like the people in big countries, nobody asks them anything either. And, who does get asked? The big powers get asked, like America, Russia, England, France, or Germany. Others like Italy, China, Japan, a bit too. Those are the main players.

"The main division of power works like this—Germany pushes Croatia, and Russia, England, and France push the Chetniks."

"Wait a minute, Avdaga. The French and English have been here from day one." Someone threw in.

Avdaga looked at the man interrupting him for a moment and then continued, "Milosevic is a big player, and it's the world's luck that he's not the president of a bigger country. He is insane, but at the same time, he is very smart. Don't worry, he'll take his Serbia to rock bottom eventually. It's not time yet for that. Milosevic and his advisers calculated everything perfectly before they attacked Bosnia. And his mentors helped him in his analysis. Russia is not nearly as big a power as it once was. Second, the European Union is in its early stages, but already wants to be independent of the USA. NATO has lost the direction and significance it had when the USSR was powerful. The USA is a bit tired of being the world's policeman, yet wants to show Europe and the whole world that nothing can be done without its help. What else has happened? There have never been so many mediocre people in such high positions, never in the history of world—remember that, never. Let me mention a couple of them. Let me start with Boutros Boutros Ghali, an Egyptian, the Secretary General of the UN, a man who deeply and truly hates

Islam and everything associated with it. He'll do anything to be able to do nothing.

"Then there's Yasushi Akashi, who comes running after every massacre to establish the number of casualties, and then goes and kisses Mladic and Karadzic. Then there is Sadako Ogata of the UNHCR. Sarajevo's children aren't allowed to leave Sarajevo in empty planes, for security reasons. They have to take buses to go through Serb-held territory, so that the Chetniks can kill even more of them? My God, can somebody explain why the children of Sarajevo couldn't go on the planes? The children are here, the planes are here, and the planes leave Sarajevo empty. And the children are starving. The plane wouldn't even feel their weight and wouldn't spend any more fuel than usual." Avdaga turned to the hajji.

"Is the coffee coming, hajji?"

"It's coming, Avdaga. Hey kid, where's the coffee?"

A young man enters the Bakije. The conversation stops.

"Good afternoon."

"Good luck to you," the hajji answered. "What good news do you bring?"

"Well, it's not good. My father died."

"My condolences . . . come, sit here. What was your father's name, where did he die?" The usual questions went on and on. The young man answered sadly, and the hajji wrote down the information about the deceased man. At one point, the guy started sniffling.

"You know, I would like . . . I would like something . . ."

"You mean you want a big funeral—several imams, men and women versed in the Qur'an . . ."

"Yeah, I would like that, my father was a good man, you know . . ."

"I see. As soon as I saw and heard you, I knew right away how nice your father was. Listen to me, kid, if you're asking for my advice, I'm going to explain to you how and what you need to do. First, when you enter the Bakije, you don't say 'good afternoon,' because it is an inappropriate way of greeting a religious man, and the Bakije is a religious institution, so, we say '*Assalamu alaikum*' Second, your father didn't die; he passed on. The only thing you can do for him is to pray for him. Not to pay other people to do it. Pray once, or ten times, but pray yourself. Do you know how to pray?"

"Yes, I know *La Illahe Illallah* . . ."

"That'll do it. Don't worry about the funeral, well take care of everything. We'll bury him tomorrow night."

Avdaga continued his dissertation, " . . . and the world is lucky that he is the president of a small country. I won't bother you with the historical and the geographical causes of this war and all the other wars in this area. Let me just tell you a few facts. You all have learned about when every one of the Serbian nobility of the past few hundred years was married and to whom; and when the duke's daughter received Belgrade with the region of Macva as her dowry, and when she was divorced and returned the dowry, namely Belgrade and Macva. But we don't know anything about our own history. At best, we know something about the battles during the Second World War. We don't know about how, during Illyrian times, wars were fought on this territory, and that the line between the eastern and western churches was drawn, and that Attila, the Hun fought wars here. No, nobody knows about that.

"In the thirteenth century, Bosnia fought against Hungary. And did anybody know that the Bosnian Army fought in their famous Kosovo battle, together with the Serbs, against the Turks? Yes, they did. Other than the Bosnians, there were the Poles, Albanians, Hungarians, and others. I'm not sure, but I think there were seven different armies fighting against the Turks. And the Turks won. Then, there were the rebellions against the Turks, against the Austrians, then the world wars, and so on.

"Currently, there is a conflict of interests among everyone living under this sky. I will only mention a few parties representing different interests. If we go into detail, it would take us three days to get to the point. So, Catholicism, East Orthodox Church, Islam, East, West, North, South, NATO-Warsaw Pact, Russia-the West, America–Europe, the European Community, England, and France vs. Germany, and on and on. Some of these conflicts are just historically there, without much action at the moment, while some of the others have just erupted. Europe, with the old and tired nobility, void of ideals, noble goals, or anything else worthy of mention, have only the armor of their bare economic strength and high standard of living. When was the last time you heard of a famous writer, painter, musician or any other artist from Europe? There aren't any left alive."

"For God's sake, Avdaga, what do writers and musicians have to do with our war and when it's going to stop?" A voice came from somebody on the couch across from them.

"Ahem," the hajji cleared his throat, and the speaker fell silent.

"So, it would be better if this 'United Europe' weren't united. The only thing they agree upon is that Germany will back Croatia, and that France and England will back the Chetniks and Karadzic. The European countries are trying to hold on to the division of power that was made after World War II.

"The English are in a desperate panic about the possibility of the German sphere of influence reaching the Balkans, or even farther east. So, now they are trying to do anything to help Karadzic and the Serbs, to eliminate or at least stop the German rise. France hasn't played an important role in the world for a long time. Italy has problems of its own. The Scandinavian countries are so far away that they are not even interested. They are helping our refugees more than anyone else, but that's about it. Regarding the other big powers in the world, Japan is completely uninterested. They're going to do as America says. China doesn't have interests of its own, but they're going to try to get something from America for their vote in the UN."

"And what about America, Avdaga?"

"Well, that's the key. America is the main player. America is on our side too. Don't look at me like that. That is the truth. The others can show off as much as they want. But in the end, it's going to be as the Americans say."

"So, why don't they say anything? What are they waiting for, us to disappear?"

"They have their own problems too. But, you know that the Americans have always been on the right side."

"What about Iran?"

"Yes, Iran! That's the exception that confirms the rule, even right here and now. For the first time, America and Iran are on the same side. That's hard for America. They'll need time to swallow that. They'll become friends, but it takes time."

"Good heavens, Avdaga."

"Now, the most important thing is when is this going to stop? Since England, France, and Russia are on the Chetniks' side, we can kiss intervention goodbye. At least not the kind we expect. This is going to stop, my dear old friend, when we nail the Chetniks, when we start taking over real territory, and I don't mean a couple of villages, but cities and towns. Actually, when we get close to doing that."

"You think they're going to intervene against us?"

"Exactly. Everybody is going go crazy trying to stop the war. Really, they are going to jump in to protect the Chetniks."

"But, Avdaga. They've established the War Crimes Tribunal. Everybody is going there."

"Never. Remember that. Never. None of the big ones are going to that court.

Sure, they're going to catch a few camp guards, a psychopath killer, but the real criminals, never."

"Avdaga, I think you see this one too black. France and England have been here the whole war. They help, they get food. Thank God they're here," somebody offered.

"You think so? Do you remember when the Chetniks caught those UN soldiers and tied them to the bridges and factories like dogs? And what did their generals do? Nothing. But when one of our guys took their vehicle and two bulletproof jackets. The bastard commander of UNPROFOR shut off the water, electricity and gas and stopped the delivery of humanitarian aid for the entire capital of a sovereign and recognized state, for three hundred fifty thousand people, and kept it up until those items were returned. As they said, the pride of the UN was at stake: the pride of Generals Smith, Nambijar, Morillon, and the bastard MacKenzie. They don't know about pride. An old lady digging through the trash for something to eat has more pride than all of their governments combined. Isn't it so? Do you know that the word 'pride' is not even used in cartoons in England and France anymore? Then they say that their youth no longer have ideals, that they get into drugs, don't show respect for the elderly, and so on. Come on, do you really think they should take General Morillon or Janvier as their ideals or role models in life? They are such perfect role models."

"Well, you didn't really make us any happier, Avdaga." the hajji was serious.

"Well, it's not that bad either. And when is it going to happen?" somebody interjected.

"God willing, in the fall."

"You mean, this fall?"

"God willing."

"What about Serbia?"

"What Serbia? It's become the Land of the Rotting Stench. It'll happen slowly. They did kill, slaughter, burn, rob, destroy, maim, on and on, but that is nothing compared to what awaits them. Can you imagine when these robbers, arsonists, and murderers go back to Serbia? Everyone of them would kill their own families for a dollar, because in Serbia, murdering and robbing are considered virtues, and raping is a duty. Whoever robbed and killed in Bosnia is going to continue doing it when he gets home, especially when we take the economic state of Serbia into consideration. It's going to get so bad that ordinary people won't be able to live there anymore. Then somebody with an iron fist is going to appear, somebody like Seselj. And they are going to vote for him. And then he'll really show them the meaning of 'rock bottom,' just like Hitler did with Germany.

"The only thing is, the Serbs are no Germans, and won't be able to recover morally in twenty years. They are going to stay in much of their own shit forever, and they will never be able to get out of it. Any state that declares their war criminals heroes doesn't have a snowball's chance in hell," Avdaga ended.

"We're off, hajji. Please give our regards to your family."

"You too, my dear Avdaga. And don't get angry, Captain. Listen, you drop in even without Avdaga whenever you're passing by. There's always somebody here."

When they had left, Avdaga asked the captain, "So, Captain, what do you think?"

"I couldn't have imagined that there was such a place in Sarajevo. Is it always like that there?"

"Almost always. Before the war, it was better. Now, everybody is a little nervous."

"If they're nervous, then I'm ready to be hospitalized."

"You see, that is the Muslim way of dealing with death. Think about it. Is there anything more natural in this world than death? With our own birth, we're sentenced to death. In most societies, when somebody dies, there is crying and screaming. Don't you think that it's a little illogical?"

"Well, when you look at it like that."

"Remind me to tell you more about death and dying."

They entered the front yard. Azra was hanging Hamza's sheets out to dry.

*   *   *

After he opened his eyes for the first time, Hamza's condition became better day by day. Whether because of the prayers, Azra's soup, the herbs, or a combination of everything, it did not really matter. Ten days later, Hamza was able to sit up straight and enjoy the long conversations between the captain and Avdaga. He slowly joined in, until the day when Musa told him how their mission had ended up, how Senad had died, and that Dino, the captain, and Fadil's men had been wounded. He told him about the situation on the front lines, in the city, about how the state took care of the wounded.

From that day, Hamza closed himself off and was silent. He would answer briefly when asked something, and fall silent again. Musa kept bringing news about the fighting and the goings on in the city. Hamza turned to books, falling deep into depression. He would spend days reading books from any genre, anything he could get his hands on. He read Aristotle, Plato, Hegel, Ibn Khaldun, Marx, Mewlaana, Sheikh Saadi Shirazi, Shakespeare, Miller, as if trying to find answers in those books—answers to the questions that bothered him. Avdaga and Azra watched his transformation, worried, but refraining from commenting.

One morning, Hamza informed them that he was going into the city. He got dressed, took his grandfather's cane, and, refusing to let Avdaga or the captain help him along, left. The war cemetery held many more fresh graves. He prayed for them for a while. Walking down the street, slowly, he enjoyed the fresh air and the warm May sun. Shops were open, mostly bars and cafes. He saw strangers pass by, uninterested. The girls were dressed up. A few soldiers wore parade-worthy military outfits.

"Look at that Rambo," Hamza thought. "Those guys are not going into battle. Skinny ones, tall ones, bitter ones—they're the fighters. These, the smiling ones, are just for show. The fools."

Gradually, he came as far as the town market and turned into a passage on the right side. He went into Momo's bar. Momo was a Serb, one of the rare ones Hamza would stick his neck out for. Momo's bar had three little tables with three chairs each and a bar, where two more people could sit.

When they were all together, Hamza's crowd would take up the whole bar. The coffee was good, and the prices decent. Hamza's friends used to gather at Momo's and leave messages for those who missed the gathering. When Hamza entered, Momo was busy at the bar. When he saw Hamza, he ran to him and hugged him.

"I can't believe it's really you!" He kissed him and turned to a table where two young men were sitting. "Come on guys, we're closing. Let's go, you don't need to pay, it's on the house." He nearly ran them out of the bar. Then he sat Hamza on a chair and looked at him closely. Along the right side of his face, over the eye and forehead, was an ugly, wide scar that ended at his hairline.

"It got you pretty bad. But thank God you're alive. That's all that matters. I'll get you a coffee now. Not even Azra makes a better one."

Momo started making coffee at the bar. Hamza relaxed and looked around at the faces in the bar, all new faces. Behind one table, there were three big guys eating and drinking brandy. On the table was cheese, salad, and grilled meat, among other things one would not expect to find in a besieged town. Hamza looked at Momo.

"Things are changing, Hamza." Momo spoke a bit nervously. "There are many new faces in the city—businessmen." He spoke more, but Hamza's thoughts had wandered off somewhere else. He stared through the window. Suddenly, he stood up.

"Businessmen? We used to call them smugglers before the war."

Suddenly, and very loudly, Musa came into the bar.

"Well, well, well . . ." He came to Hamza and clapped him on the back very hard. Hamza's eyes filled with tears of pain.

"Take it easy, Musa, or you'll have to carry me home."

"It wouldn't be the first time. Momo, get me some coffee and a coke. We're celebrating!"

"Hamza doesn't come every day," Momo added.

"Fuck Hamza. It doesn't have anything to do with him. I just decked an idiot at the market. It really made my day."

"Who did you hit? You can barely stand on your feet. The last thing you need is a beating."

"They're nothing, man, nothing. I could take five of them at one time. You know what happened? An old lady was going through the marketplace, looking to buy some sugar. And the prick tells her twenty-five dollars. 'How come it's so expensive, my son?' she asks. And he goes, 'The siege isn't ending anytime soon, granny. Hoped it would, huh? It's twenty-five, take it or leave it.' Then, I came closer, transferred the crutch to my left hand, and cracked him so hard he dropped on the spot. I was just getting ready to fight him with my precious crutch here, and he, he shut up. Didn't say another word."

The three big guys eating in the corner rose. One of them took out a big wad of cash, "I'm paying. These soldiers' bill is on me too."

"No, thanks, there is no need for that," Hamza said in a low and dangerous voice.

"You just tell me how much. We know how it is to be a soldier."

"The man just told you nicely that there is no need to"."

Musa got up from the chair when Momo got in between them.

"Thanks, guys, but it's on me today. Thanks a lot, and please, come again."

He saw them to the door. When he had closed the door, he turned to Musa, who looked at him with fury in his eyes,

"Man, Momo, why didn't you let me? I was really looking forward to it."

"Why didn't I let you what? Look at you, man, you can't even go to the bathroom without a crutch. Besides, I have to live and work here."

"Yeah, Hamza, do you see this?"

Hamza stared through the window, silently. Somewhere in the distance, heavy explosions echoed.

"That's it for today," Momo said, giving his expert opinion. "The Chetniks have changed their tactics. Instead of shelling all day long, they just shell a few times in the middle of the day at places where they see or assume there are many people. More people die that way."

"Let's go, Musa. Take care, Momo."

"See you. I'll tell your partners you stopped by, Hamza."

"Have you seen Dino at all?"

"Nobody has. Why?"

"Just asking." They went outside. After the explosions, the streets were empty except for the odd person darting from one shelter to another. Musa pushed Hamza along. "Should we hurry too?"

"No need to. You never know if you're running from a bomb or towards one. This way is best, and then if it's meant to be, it's meant to be."

With the help of a crutch and a cane, the two of them walked on. They enjoyed the air, the sun, and the empty streets.

"You'll see, Musa, one day we'll remember these days with nostalgia."

"Nostalgia? Are you nuts? I just hope it stops, so we can stroll down the Saraci normally again. I don't need anything else."

"Just remember what I told you, Musa—with nostalgia. The war itself is a piece of cake, compared to what awaits us."

*   *   *

The summer of 1995 passed slowly in the streets of Sarajevo. The Chetniks launched a major offensive in Krajina. They wanted to destroy this little pocket of free Bosnia, together with the Bosnian Army's Fifth Corps, defending it. During the heaviest assault, Dudakovic, the commander of the Fifth Corps, launched a surprise counteroffensive, taking over a significant piece of territory. He captured weapons and food, then retreated. The shelling of Sarajevo continued. The Chetniks used modified aerial bombs loaded on rockets. One of those, at Alipasino Polje, ripped a building in half.

A direct hit destroyed an entire part of the TV Sarajevo building. Another one destroyed the health center near the "Sarajka" shopping mall.

The Bosnian Army counterattacked. Successes in the beginning, but then they retreated. Exhausting fighting took place on Mount Treskavica. The Bosnian Army took over the peak called "Djoko's tower," only to retreat three times. The lack of adequate heavy artillery turned out to be the deciding factor. Their attempt to break the siege failed.

Just as the fighting around Sarajevo eased, the Chetniks, under the command of the war criminal General Mladic, entered the town of Srebrenica. The little town northeast of Sarajevo, although under siege for almost three years, had resisted Chetnik attacks heroically. The UN persuaded them to hand over their weapons under the condition that the UN will guarantee their safety, by making the city into a "safe heaven." On July 11, 1995, the Dutch battalion surrendered Srebrenica to the Chetniks without a fight. Further, the commander of the UN troops in Bosnia, General Janvier, ruled out any kind of action by NATO forces, according to the orders of French president Chirac. So, while the hunt for civilians was going on in the forests around Srebrenica, the Dutch officers, together with General Janvier, were seen making a toast with the war criminal General Mladic.

The Chetniks killed ten thousand civilians in Srebrenica in days.

The war in Bosnia continued.

Fall came. Like the Phoenix rising from the ashes, General Dudakovic and his already legendary Fifth Corps went on. The Chetnik strongholds were crumbling. The Fifth Corps approached the towns of Banja Luka and Prijedor. In the Western countries, which were on the Chetniks' side, there was panic. What if the Muslims freed Banja Luka? What if the plan for the destruction of Bosnia fell apart?

For the first time in almost three years, they admitted there was an actual war in Bosnia. Until now, there had only been the killing of Bosnian people, so the West kept silent about it. When the Army of Bosnia finally captured enough weapons to be able to fight against the Chetniks with equal force, they fled on all fronts. Even then, the Western countries remained faithful to their dishonorable role in Bosnia, and presented an ultimatum to the Bosnian Army. "If you don't stop all military operations, NATO troops will attack the Bosnian positions. The Bosnian Army stops. Why? The unique opportunity to force England, France, and Russia to finally stand openly on the side of fascism was gone.

Afterwards, in many academic discussions, those countries tried to justify their actions by stating that it was done to protect the Bosnian people. The West used the International Tribunal for War Crimes in Bosnia as a "threat" against the Serbs. War criminals like Karadzic and Mladic were never going appear in that court, simply because the truth would come out about who sponsored and supported them, encouraged them, and promised them that they would do everything to stop any measures that the UN might instigate against them. The world would find out what Bosnians and the people of Sarajevo have known for a long time, the role that Butros Butros Ghali, Yasushi Akashi, Mitterrand, Major, Yeltsin, and others played in permitting the genocide to take place.

The war in Bosnia was, at long last, coming to its dishonest end.

*   *   *

Hamza withered away. Dark circles grew under his eyes. Without appetite, cutting himself off from the rest of the world, he would sit on the sofa, smoke, and drink coffee. It was early July. On a small radio, Hamza listened to the news from Srebrenica—direct reports of genocide. The tens of thousands of inhabitants of the town became the target for the Chetnik murderers. Using a primitive radio transmitter, a journalist from Srebrenica asked the leaders of Bosnia and Herzegovina, "Does this mean that we're left to our own devices? Have you written us off?" The commander of the UN troops in Bosnia, the French General Janvier, did not permit NATO air attacks to prevent the genocide.

The units of the Bosnian Army grew quiet on all fronts.

The Chetniks entered into Srebrenica.

The captain entered the front yard.

"Captain, what's going on?"

The captain was silent. He just shrugged his shoulders.

"Captain, the Chetniks are going to kill everybody. They're going to slaughter them. Why are the Sarajevo and Tuzla units quiet? Why isn't anybody headed towards Srebrenica? Why doesn't anybody try to open a passage for those people? Captain?"

"Enough! How am I supposed to know? How am I supposed to know?"

"Go ask them!"

"Who, Hamza? Who am I supposed to ask?"

The veil of silence and oblivion slowly fell over the bodies of ten thousand unburied people of Srebrenica.

Hamza closed himself off again, this time for good. He answered all questions tersely. He was silent. Avdaga told him once that he looked better when they brought him home from the hospital.

*　　*　　*

The summer months slid by quietly. A mild autumn had arrived in Sarajevo. At some point, in mid-October, Azra called Hamza into the house. Avdaga sat in the big living room. Azra poured some coffee into cups and all three of them lit cigarettes. Hamza was surprised to see a cigarette in Azra's hand, but he didn't say a word. Avdaga took a few puffs and finally started talking:

"Hamza, my son, it's not going to work out this way."

Hamza opened his mouth to say something, but let it drop when he saw Avdaga's face. Avdaga continued:

"Azra and I were thinking. We think that it would do you good to go abroad for a while. What do you think of that?"

"I don't really care. I know that I haven't been the most enjoyable company for the two of you. I'm sorry that I've disappointed you."

"God forbid, it isn't anything like that, my Hamza. Azra and I are very proud of you. We have been, your entire life. A lot has happened, but I have never been ashamed of you. It's just not going to work out this way, Hamza. You're ruining yourself. I've already told you once that you looked better when we brought you home from the hospital. You were covered with wounds, but at least your soul was healthy. Now, it's the other way around. I've got almost everything ready, if you're willing?"

"I'll do anything you want me to," Hamza answered in a resigned voice.

"Azra, could you hand me the papers please? All the papers are here, along with the permission to leave the country. Officially, you're going to Italy for rehabilitation. In Italy, you're going to stay with a friend of mine. There, the affidavit regarding the family ties with our cousin in the U.S. will be waiting for you. You need it to get into the United States. You'll have to go to the U.S. embassy for interviews, and then if they let you in, you'll go to your cousin's in Chicago. Travel around the U.S. awhile, get to know the country, the people, the customs. The prophet Muhammad, peace be upon him, once said, 'Travel in order to be healthy'" We, Azra and I, hope you'll find new meaning in your life in America, new motivation to go on, God willing. We had problems too, but we had each other. Try it. You can come back whenever you want. You don't have to worry about us. We're fine and healthy for now. If you apply for a passport tomorrow, you'll be able to go in a few days."

Avdaga sighed, tired from all the talking. Hamza looked at Azra. She drank her coffee in silence, but after a while she spoke:

"Try to find yourself, my dear. The U.S. is a big country. It has everything. If you know what you're looking for, you'll find it for sure. It's going to be lonely here without you, but, with God's help, you'll be back again."

"America?"

"America."

"All right. I'll apply for a passport tomorrow."

It was Sunday. Hamza had packed his small military rucksack. Underwear, pants, a sweater; a small package. Avdaga handed him a book wrapped in cloth, "Here's the Qur'an. Pray sometimes. If you pray carefully, you'll find all the answers in there. Now, go. Give my regards to Dervo, and don't pay too much attention to what he tells you." Azra kissed him in silence. Hamza hugged her. Finally, he set off down the street. He said a prayer for the soldiers at the cemetery and continued walking.

Musa came out of the bar at the bottom of Kovaci and joined him.

"Where you off to?"

"America."

"Well, good luck. I'm not going anywhere. No way. I would die without Sarajevo, like a fish out of water."

"Don't screw around, Musa."

"I'm not. They're going to bury me here."

"Well, America is not the end of the world."

"Avdaga says you're going to Chicago?"

"I have a cousin there."

"Take good care there. They say there is crime, drugs, the mob. Every once in a while somebody gets killed over there."

"Their mob is kid stuff compared to Chetniks."

They came to the taxi stand. Musa thrust his right hand into Hamza's hair. He pulled Hamza's head close to his.

"Okay, my friend. Now, go to Berlin, and then all of you can go to Chicago together. I'm kind of sorry you're going. I thought Amra was going to come here. But, it doesn't matter as long as they're fine."

Hamza put his bag on the ground. He said nothing, averting his eyes from Musa's. Musa started feeling uncomfortable.

"What's wrong, man? Is everything all right?"

"Nothing. Nothing is all right, brother. There is no Germany. There is nobody, Musa. Nobody."

"What do you mean there is nobody, what are you talking about? Hamza, what's wrong with you?"

A terrible doubt hit him like thunder. He grabbed Hamza's hair with both hands.

"What's wrong with you? Didn't we talk about how we were going to visit them once this whole thing was over? How we were going to take the little one to the zoo, and visit Vienna, Munich, Budapest . . ."

Musa talked fast, trying to stop Hamza's answer with a torrent of words. He could already feel the answer.

"Shhh, Musa. There is no Amra, brother, no little one. There is nothing anymore, Musa. Nothing! Best man killed them at the very beginning of the war."

"What are you talking about? Did somebody tell you that? That can't be. And you believed them right away . . ."

"Musa. Musa! I buried them. In the rose garden behind the house."

They were standing next to a cab, heads almost touching. Musa's eyes became glassy. Darkness fell over them. Silently, tears ran down his face. They momentarily paused at the tip of his chin and fell to the ground. His jaw shook, and he tried to stop it by grinding his teeth.

"Well, I'd better be going."

"You go on, Hamza. I'll just sit down for a minute."

Hamza entered the cab. On his way in, he tossed his cane to Musa, and closed the door. The cab drove off. Musa sat on the sidewalk. He sat with his head down. Silent sobs wracked him. The tears kept flowing, soaking the pavement. It started to rain.

After a while, an old lady came out of the house across the street, carrying an umbrella,

"Oh, son, you're going to catch a cold if you keep sitting there. Get up, come on, get up. I'll make you some coffee so you can warm up a little bit."

"That's okay, ma'am, thank you."

"Thank God, my son. Just get up and take it easy, if you don't want to come in for a coffee."

Musa got up, thanked the old lady, and started walking down Bascarsija aimlessly. The rain, now accompanied by strong winds, started falling even harder. It seemed like waves were crashing over the Old City. The people caught in the rain stood under the awnings, looking curiously at the young man who walked by slowly, taking no heed of the rain.

CHAPTER 3

Hamza's journey to Rome was made up of several stages, each one an unforgettable experience in its own right. Hamza arrived at the tunnel in a cab, walked through, then took a military jeep to Hrasnica. The walk up Igman was difficult for him. Especially "Rice.". It was already late afternoon when he got to the pass on Igman. The military policemen on the ramp were people he knew. Coffee, stories, memories. The policemen were bored. Only a few people were leaving Sarajevo. Sometime before midnight, his bus for Tarcin arrived. The bus was a wreck, windowless and sporting holes from shrapnel and every caliber weapon. The passengers prayed before going inside. That night, they were in luck and, except for having to duck a couple of times when they came close to Chetnik positions, the trip went well. Although, driving without any lights, the driver did actually have to bring the bus to a halt a few times just before it went off the cliff, but that was just another part of the driving routine.

Tarcin. A small town outside Sarajevo. Before the war, it was known for its sanatorium for respiratory diseases. During the war, it was the most important crossing to the free territory. The driver announced that they were stopping until dawn because the ramps on the way to Kiseljak, Visoko, and Zenica were closed at night.

Everybody went into a cafe. In a house next to the road, a housewife—whose husband had died in the war—had opened up a cafe in her living room. People traveled, and all of them had to wait in Tarcin. They either waited for night to come so they could go up Igman and then to Sarajevo, or they waited for day to travel towards Zenica or Mostar. The room was warm, the coffee strong, and everybody felt at ease. The place was open 24/7. Instead of stools, chairs, couches and sofas littered the room. The walls were covered in handmade bags. People traveled, and those going into Sarajevo had food on them. The best way to get that food through was in a bag. "The business is going great, thank God," said the lady owner. Hamza drank a few cups of coffee. In the corner of the room, a new business was booming. An older gypsy woman read the future from a coffee cup for a fascinated pair of girls.

When dawn arrived, the trip continued. Every five to ten miles, there was a new checkpoint. The Bosnian Army and HVO—the Croat Military Council—controlled them, alternately. Kiseljak was a Croatian stronghold during the war. From there, the soldiers had gone to Ahmici and other villages, completely wiping them out. The food in Kiseljak was relatively cheap, so the passengers used the opportunity to stock up with all they could carry.

Hamza didn't bother going out. In Visoko, they changed buses. The next one was almost new and was comfortable for a change. Even the stereo worked. It was beautiful. That afternoon, they reached Zenica. Before the war, the thirty-hour ordeal used to take an hour. Hamza bought a ticket for Split for the next morning. A number of new travel agencies were open. The travel agency owners were mostly Croats, because buses went over the HVO-controlled territory and through Croatia. He spent the night at a friend's house At 5:30 a.m., he left for Split.

The once quiet villages between Zenica and Travnik now painted a very sad picture. Croatian fascism had broken out in those pleasant regions for incomprehensible reasons. Remains of charred houses were evidence enough of these barbaric acts. The International War Crimes Tribunal at The Hague would later indict some of the leaders of the so-called Herceg-Bosna state for the crimes they had committed in central Bosnia. Several days before going to The Hague, a number of the indicted were awarded the Croatian Order of Merit by the president of Croatia himself, Dr. Franjo Tudjman.

Split, the pride of Dalmatia, as well as the cultural, industrial, athletic, touristic, and every other center of this part of Croatia. As Split is situated at the crossroads of very important routes, it had always been the goal and dream of many world travelers. Good roads, the port and the airport accommodated their arrival. During the war, Split was one of the biggest losers. An international and cosmopolitan city before the war, Split became a Balkan village, poisoned and buried in fascism, nationalism, and chauvinism. Even the pleasant and friendly Dalmatians were confused by the sudden arrival of the west-Herzegovinian barbarians in Adidas sweatpants, white socks, and dress shoes—the official uniform. Most of the domestic population tried to live a quiet, unobtrusive life, spending most of their time indoors and avoiding attracting attention when they had to go out.

Step by step, Hamza walked to the Split harbor. He was lucky. The ferry "Rijeka," run by the Jadroplovidba Company, was headed for Ancona that same night. Hamza bought a ticket and a few magazines. He sat in a cafe. Flipping through the headlines, he decided not to read. Smoking and drinking coffee, he waited for the night. The ferry "Rijeka" had three decks plus sleeping rooms. Hamza decided on the upper deck, which held the restaurant and a duty-free shop. He sat comfortably and spent the night trying to take a nap. A cold, gray dawn welcomed him to Ancona. Italian customs officers boarded the ferry. The passengers waited in line to take care of the customs formalities. It was Hamza's turn. After they had asked him a few questions, they pulled him aside. He waited patiently for hours. Finally, when the last passenger had left the ferry, they questioned him again—why was he traveling to Italy, who was he going to stay with, did he have his address, how long had he known the man, did he have money, how much, etc. Finally, the custom officers agreed to let him enter Italy.

It was nine-thirty when Hamza stepped onto Italian soil.

*   *   *

Hamza had all the time in the world, and walked through the town slowly. He stopped at a café, then a pizzeria, then a café again. At some point, he made his way to the train station. In the early evening hours, a train left for Rome with Hamza on board. It was a tourist train, without cabins. Loud Italian guys were discussing politics, the soccer championship, school, past and future vacations. The noise lulled Hamza into a deep, recuperating sleep.

The train station in Rome was crowded. It was impossible to tell it was well past midnight. A number of souvenir shops, restaurants, and fast food joints overwhelmed the senses of the unwary traveler. On the plateau outside the train station stood several "ladies of the night." A bit farther down stood the pimps, observing the work. At a newspaper stand, Hamza saw newspapers from Bosnia. He walked around the station, drank a few coffees, and waited until ten in the morning. Then he took a cab, giving the cab driver Dervo's address. Soon, the cab left the busy downtown area behind, and headed for the suburbs, where beautiful, rich-looking villas were commonplace. That part of Rome was on one of the "seven golden" hills, and held a magnificent view of the city.

The cab stopped at a large gate that separated the private property from the street. The gate, made of heavy steel, was painted black. Hamza looked for a bell, and not finding one, opened the gate, and entered the yard. A gravel path led from the front gate to the house. The path itself headed straight for ten yards, and then split off in two directions, finally coming back together again right in front of the house, making a perfect circle. In the middle of the circle stood a stone fountain, probably as old as the house itself, and framed by a rose garden. Tall trees flanked the house on both sides. Narrow, pebble paths led from the house and disappeared behind the house, deep into the park. The house itself was a very impressive building, with the left side covered in ivy. The main door, the color of old amber, had artistic engravings and helped divide the house into two symmetrical parts. On both sides of the first and second floors were six windows, most of them shut with heavy, green, wooden shutters. In front of the central part of the house, stone pillars supported the porch. All in all, the house seemed to hold a whisper of reserved dignity which gave the house a personality before Hamza ever set foot inside. He thought of it as a house that could be loved, a house where happy people could live. A doorbell stood next to the main door, embedded in black marble. Hamza rang the bell.

Soon, the door opened and two glowing, black eyes and a magical smile appeared.

"Si, signore?"

"I, uh, would like to speak to Mr. Dervo," Hamza stammered.

"I don't understand." The girl seemed amused by Hamza's confusion.

"Mister, signor Dervo?"

"Oh, *signor* Dervo, *si signore*." She motioned to him to come in.

In the back of the house, a door slammed and a deep, male voice started swearing at the girl in perfect Bosnian. The girl just shrugged her shoulders, as if saying "He's like that, and there is nothing we can do about it."

After a few moments, an old man appeared, standing in front of Hamza.

Dervo.

All Hamza knew about this man was that he was Avdaga's long-time friend. Avdaga had neither discussed nor explained anything about him, at least not in front of Hamza. Dervo was an elderly man, in his mid-seventies, gray, a bit hunched over from age, but still looking very strong. He was freshly shaved, wearing a white dress shirt, a tie, heavy robe, and leather slippers.

"*Assalamu alaikum,*" Hamza first said.

"*Alaikum mu Sallam.* So you are Avdaga's gold, huh? Hold on, let me get a good look at you, turn around." When he saw Hamza's confused facial expression, Dervo burst out laughing.

"Come on, now, don't get all upset. You're definitely Avdaga, all right. Different hair, smaller face, all in all, a bit gentler, but still, I'd say, definitely Avdaga. Avdaga's gold. Ha-ha-ha. Come on, get in, get in.

Sabrina! Sabrina! Oh my God, look at this Tunisian of mine. Sabrina!" While he yelled, Dervo didn't notice that the girl had already entered the room, and looked at him, smiling, from the door. "Oh, there you are . . ." Dervo babbled something to her in Italian, and she went upstairs. "I told her to make you some coffee and breakfast and to prepare a room and bath for you. Let's go into the salon, I feel most comfortable there."

The salon was in fact a huge room that was used as a dining room and reception area for major feasts. Along the right side lay a long dining-room table intended for twelve, although it could have easily held twice that many. A little farther down were a sofa, loveseat, and an armchair, set around a small table. An antique dresser with bottles of liquor from all over the world and a dish for ice stood by the wall. Several glittering crystal glasses were arranged on top. Set into the opposite wall was a fireplace of marble and quarried stone. A few logs crackled in the fire. The floor of the whole salon was covered with three enormous Persian rugs. Two soft leather armchairs stood in front of the fireplace. Dervo sat Hamza in one, pulled the other one close, looking carefully at Hamza.

"Avdaga's gold, huh? Avdaga's gold? Ha-ha-ha-ha . . . well, I really am happy I didn't die last summer. Hey, hey. I haven't gotten a better gift in twenty years. So, that ass Avdaga keeps you a secret who knows where, for what, twenty-five, twenty-six years. How old are you?"

"Twenty—seven."

"Well, there you go." Sabrina came in, carrying a tray of hot coffee, milk, cookies, and cake. She smiled at Dervo, looked at Hamza, and left.

"If not for that smile, I probably would have fired her a long time ago. She doesn't do anything, but her smile is worth double what I pay her."

Hamza looked around the salon. Everything was perfectly clean, from the doorknobs to the windows, curtains, every piece of furniture, so he thought that what Dervo had just said couldn't be very true. Dervo poured coffee into the cups, waited for Hamza to light a cigarette, and started talking.

"So, tell me? How is Avdaga? How is his American girl?"

"What American girl?"

"Your mother, Azra. Hey, hey, hold on a second. Don't tell me you don't know your mother is American?" Dervo burst into laughter. "The old fox. I thought he sent you over to tell me what was going on, and in fact he sent you so that I could tell you what was going on. So . . . ," he squinted. "Did he by any chance tell you not to talk to me?"

"No. He just told me not to listen to you too closely," Hamza answered warily.

"Avdaga's gold. Avdaga is so happy to have you. Well, tell me what happened to your face?"

"From the war.

"I can see that it's from the war. It's not from kissing. But, how?"

"I was wounded."

"Oh all right. I see you don't want to talk about it. Only if you want to, Avdaga's gold, only if you want to. If nothing else, in all these years I have learned not to ask too much. Let's go back a bit. So, what do you really know about Avdaga and Azra?"

Hamza looked at him, at a loss for words. What did this strange old man mean by that? What did he know about his own mother and father? What didn't he know in spite of growing up between them for so many years? He knew what all children do about their parents. Dervo was excited as he guessed the flow of Hamza's thoughts.

"You know what, Avdaga's gold? You can tell me everything. Seriously. These walls don't have ears, and everything you tell me I'll take with me to my grave; and that's not all that far off."

"Well, I don't think you're headed for the grave anytime soon." Hamza was polite, but still uncertain how much this man could be trusted.

"I am not, you know. Watch this!" The old man took out a coin, put it between his thumb and index finger, and pressed it. The coin bent easily.

"Huh? What do you say to that?!" Hamza just stared at him. "Now, you try. Touch it, it's real." Dervo laughed as Hamza continued to stare between the old man and the coin.

"Anyway, I have an idea. You go and freshen up, and I'll wait here for you. Sabrina! Show him his bathroom and bedroom. Avdaga's gold, I'll be here when you're done."

Hamza was used to the wealth of an old Bey house, but this place was something else. Money had never been an issue in the house. In spite of the opulence he had already witnessed, he was surprised when Sabrina brought him to his room. The city stretched outside his window. Rome basked in the autumn sun. The bathroom was a combination of black and gold. The big black tub was made of marble, and the faucet gold-plated. The bathroom alone was worth as much as a decent house in Sarajevo. He filled the tub and sank into the hot, perfumed water. After a long while, he came down to the salon. Dervo sat, staring at the fire, absorbed in thought.

"Let me ask you a favor. Would you please take your things out of the bag?" Hamza looked at him. "You know, for a long time, maybe twenty years, I regretted not having anything with me from the old house in Bosnia. I used to always think about what I would have brought with me if I'd had the chance. I am really interested in what I've been missing."

Hamza took his belongings out of the bag, silently. The underwear, two pairs of socks, a shirt, a sweater, pants, a small bundle, and the Qur'an.

Dervo came closer. He took the Qur'an, opened it, and started flipping through the pages.

"Very nice. An Arabic-Bosnian version. Do you know how to pray? What am I saying, of course you do. What is this?" Dervo opened the tobacco box. A small video tape was inside. "Memories?"

Hamza nodded.

"And this?" Dervo opened a small package. It had a few belts, a case, with a knife handle sticking out of the case. Without saying anything, he looked at the belts and the knife case, and finally took the knife out of the sheath. He touched the blade of the knife, examining how it sat in his hand in the upright position—sideways and downwards. He turned to Hamza, and stared at him, as if seeing him for the first time.

"You must be a good warrior. Also, equally good with both hands," he stated.

"How would you know that?"

"So, Avdaga made this for you?" Dervo answered with a question. "Well, you see these two squared engravings on the case and these two iron rings? Those are on the left side for right-handed people and on the right side for left-handed ones. You have it on both sides. You see, Avdaga and I came up with this design. It's an invention from the Russian front." Dervo slowly nodded, deep in thought.

"It's sad. For twenty years I have been packing and unpacking that bag, changing what I would take with me, if I could do it over again . . ." Dervo sighed. "Tell me, can you drive?"

"Yes, I can."

"Have you ever driven a Ferrari?"

"No. What kind of a Ferrari?"

"A red one. A Ferrari has to be red in order to be a Ferrari. Same as a Mercedes has to be black and a Jaguar, silver. What do you say we go for a ride now? We'll go to Piazza Navona, and then after that, we can go to Caffe della Pace. Let's go, we'll talk in the car. Sabrina!"

Sabrina seemed to be the exclamation point at the end of Dervo's sentences. Every conversation seemed to end with "'Sabrina!'"

Sabrina entered the room which seemed to become brighter. She had changed into denim pants and a jacket with a fur lining. The white fur on the collar was a nice contrast to her black hair. The turtleneck, the same color as the jeans, accentuated her large breasts. Hamza thought the sight of her should be prescribed for cases of serious depression.

"Si, signor Dervo?"

"We'll take the Ferrari. You can take some other car. Don't worry about lunch and dinner. We are going to eat out. Be good."

"*Si, signor* Dervo." Sabrina kissed him on the cheek and left the room.

"Ah, if only I were forty years younger," Avdaga sighed. "Let's go, Avdaga's gold."

"Why do you call me Avdaga's gold all the time?"

"Because you're golden. You know, when somebody looks at you, they think of gold. Secondly, that old fox is the dearest friend of mine. This way at the same time, I call you and say his name. If it bothers you, I can call you Hamza instead."

"I don't mind, I'm just asking."

"You can ask me anything, Avdaga's gold."

The Ferrari was parked in the driveway in front of the garage. A little black horse on the car was a status symbol for the man who driving it.

Hamza sat behind the wheel and started driving carefully. After a couple hundred yards, he pressed down the gas pedal a bit more to see how the car would react. The tires squealed, and the car shot forwards as if out of a cannon.

"Wow, easy, easy." Hamza stepped on the brakes. Dervo laughed.

"If you're anything like Avdaga from the old days, we're going to collect a few speeding tickets on our way to Navona. Did you know, I haven't spoken our language in years? Now I just enjoy the sound, it's like music."

Hamza relaxed, driving slowly and enjoying it.

"So, you really don't know that Azra's American?" Dervo asked him in English. Hamza automatically answered in English.

"You see? You don't even notice that you're speaking English. That's because it's your native language. Did you ever ask yourself how a woman, in those days could speak English so well, or play the violin?" Dervo sat comfortably in his seat, and fixed his sunglasses.

"Avdaga and I got along like a house on fire. If you saw one, the other one wasn't far behind. I was older when I met him, so I taught him how to act like an adult. Those were the best years. Then it started in Europe, the war that is. I was older than Avdaga, and was interested in politics. I'd had enough of our rotten government, and the politicians, corruption, bribes, connections, and intrigue. The whole country was like a very sick patient. The situation of the Muslims in the Kingdom of Serbs, Croats, and Slovenians was particularly bad. Then I started listening to the man who showed up in Germany. He spoke about work, order, and discipline. He called for better living conditions for his own people. At that time, Sarajevo and Bosnia seemed like a cage to me. I went around in circles, with no way out. The blood of a twenty-five-year-old flowed through the veins of a man who wanted something more, stronger, longer-lasting. I wanted to take the whole strength of the world, to concentrate it, to make the people work and live according to law and order. You see, I'm not ashamed to admit it. When you've passed eighty, you don't need to lie anymore, not to yourself nor to others, or to find extenuating circumstances for what you have done.

My opportunity came when the Germans entered Sarajevo. The speed with which the Kingdom of Yugoslavia crumbled confirmed my convictions. I was the first one to sign up for the League. Avdaga was the last one. He ran away from home, attracted by the adventure. He was young, eager to prove himself. He took off at the gates of Stalingrad. He killed a number of GESTAPO officers and got away. The German command reported him as "missing in action, after the sabotage of Russian units." I knew he'd fled. There was no soldier that could capture him. Kill him, maybe. But capture him? Not a chance. And somehow, strangely enough, I knew that he would cross Russia and survive, and that we would meet again, sometime. So you see, he fled and I stayed, all the way to the last day. I was captured by American soldiers in Hamburg in May 1945. After the war ended, majority of Germans regretted what they had done. They hadn't intended it, they didn't know, etc. I didn't regret it. All right, I was deluded by the idea, but so was half the world. Then the following years were spent in camps.

They moved us from camp to camp, interrogated us, tortured us. I couldn't stand the interrogations anymore. I demanded that they kill me or let me go. I could influence neither the beginning nor the end of the war. If it had been up to me, it would have been different. But, I was a soldier, a warrior. I had my ideals and fought for them to the end. I never said a bad word about the officers or the army during my time in the camps. You wouldn't believe how many countries offered me asylum—America, Canada, Brazil . . . I think everyone except Russia. I didn't even think about going back to Bosnia. I chose Italy. You know, it was close. Now I'm asking myself, close to what? At that time, life in Italy was hard. I did all jobs imaginable. I loaded ships, worked on the railroad, made roads. I realized very quickly that this would ultimately take me nowhere, and take a lifetime in arriving. So I enrolled in school. I studied and worked. I graduated, got my Master's, then Ph.D. I kept getting better jobs. I became the co-owner of a company, then founded my own and so on. Everything just sort of happened. Now I have everything money can buy, and it's as if I didn't have a thing. I don't have a family, I'm not married, and have no kids."

"Where did you find Sabrina?"

"The people from the employment agency sent her to me to work in the house. She was a little girl. She's from Tunisia. So, day after day, her smile would pull me out of my depression. There's nothing between us. What could ever happen between us?" he smiled. "So to make a long story short, I made her go to school. She graduated from high school in record time. Then she enrolled in university. Another year or two, and she'll be a medical doctor. I'll be sad when she graduates."

"I thought she was a cleaning person."

"That's our game. I pretend to yell, she laughs, and so the days go by. Usually she drives this Ferrari. I left her some money in my will, so she can start something on her own when I die."

"Now, why don't you tell me something about Avdaga and Azra? It seems as though I don't know much about them at all," Hamza asked.

"Well, when Avdaga left the village that we had been occupying . . ."

Hamza drove all around Rome. He was in the Vatican, then a minute later would find himself at the Via del Fiori Imperiali, passing the magnificent Coliseum. Speeding on, he found himself at the Piazza del Popolo, on Del Corso street. He passed the sign for the fountain di Trevi . . . Dervo talked on. He spoke slowly, quietly, just like an old man. Hamza drove in silence, absorbing Dervo's monologue carefully.

" . . . and they visited me once. A long time ago. At that time, you could still buy plastic raincoats and gondolas. I begged them to stay. I cried, offered, threatened, and blackmailed them. I offered Avdaga the company, I offered to buy them a house, anything that could possibly be given, just to make them stay, just so we could be together. He said that he couldn't live without Sarajevo air. I could . . ."

"So, I am half-cowboy."

"Well, something like that. Although Azra never mentioned where she's from, her name, or anything along those lines."

"Maybe she has, to Avdaga?" Hamza knew the two of them were nothing if not lifelong best friends and confidants.

"I doubt it. Anyway, where are we? Wait a minute. Turn right here. A few more miles and we'll be at della Pace."

Caffe della Pace is located in the street next to Piazza Navona, one of the most elite places in Rome. This cafe has been open consistently for over one hundred years. Nobody really officially announced it, but quietly, della Pace had become the place where the crème de la crème of the elite met when staying in Rome. Actors from all over the world came here, athletes, sons and daughters of the rich, idle wives of the richest men in the world, with their all the more idle lovers—old rich homosexuals, followed by their young and poor Apollos. Essentially, everybody who had money to throw around, free time, and felt the need to be seen there. They all pretended to be bothered by the paparazzi who surrounded the cafe, trying to catch something new and sensational. Names like Stallone, Tomba, Naomi, or Schiffer were no surprise here.

"Come here a few times with a Ferrari, and the whole of Rome will know you. Within these circles, of course. They think that my Sabrina is a descendant of some Tunisian king," Dervo whispered while the waiter escorted them to their table. Hamza sat comfortably in the chair, lit a cigarette, and looked around the cafe. He sat in the midst of status symbols and brand names. Watches, rings, glasses, shoes, suits, ties, tie clips, everything was there. Everything and everyone was on display, clamoring to be seen.

"Maybe it's just my imagination, but tomorrow, there will be at least three guys who will be walking around here in military jackets with big patches on the back."

Hamza was silent. He thought about Dervo's story. It sounded incredible, but somehow everything fit. He had never met anybody from Azra's family. And many songs that he remembered from his childhood were in English. There was also the fact that Azra played the violin. She rarely talked about her childhood, and even when she did, it was foggy experiences and ambiguous stories. The experience that the two of them had gone through explained the great love they had for Hamza. Only people who had gone through truly difficult times can separate real problems from imaginary ones. In that sense, Hamza's childhood pranks, which used to drive the entire neighborhood crazy, must have been only amusing for Avdaga, in no way a real problem. They stayed at the café for several hours. Dervo told him, in a low voice, about the guests, who did what, where everybody lived, and so on. All in all, there weren't that many ordinary people in the café. After that, Dervo took him to a typical Italian restaurant, whose name Hamza couldn't recall. They ate pasta and fish, and drank wine. They came home late and Hamza went to bed with thoughts of home, parents, and secrets in his head.

*　　*　　*

While waiting for the interview at the American embassy, Hamza spent his days with Dervo and Sabrina. The two of them had probably made an agreement not to let him out of their sight, even for a minute. The days passed by in quiet peace. After almost four years of war, Hamza felt like he was at a crossroads between the real and surreal, between dreams and reality. It was a world of the whitish haze. He would wake up without explosions in quiet Rome. Hamza woke early in the mornings nestled between autumn and winter. He didn't have to do anything, didn't have to go anywhere. He was in a time vacuum, together with this strange, yet amazing old man and the Tunisian beauty Sabrina. They floated, displaced in time and space—Dervo because of his age, Hamza because of the hell he had come from, and Sabrina because of the fact that her existence had been secured and her great love for the old man. There were no time limits. They would leave the mansion without any rules or order. In the early dawn, they searched for an open restaurant in the villages around Rome. Late at, night they would eat fish and crabs in Fiumicino. At midnight they would drink coffee while standing under an awning at Fontana di Trevi, watching the rain shed tears on the monument.

Sabrina would show Hamza Rome's tourist attractions. He was fascinated by Michelangelo, the Coliseum, the streets and the piazzas. One night after coming home late, and after Sabrina had gone to bed, he stayed up with Dervo, talking. At some point that night, he told him the story about the war and the tragedies in Bosnia, about the games that the West played, about his own tragedy, so similar to thousands of others. Afterwards, Hamza wasn't quite sure why he had done it. Perhaps because of the complete atmosphere of the darkened room, on whose walls the shadows cast by the fire danced while the cold wind moaned outside, or because of Dervo's childish curiosity and questions that poked his soul, like finger in the eye. Perhaps it was because he had been in the relaxed atmosphere of a normal life for over a month. The burden that lay on his soul didn't pressure him as much in Bosnia, during the war, but now, it tore at it, and he had to share it with somebody. Hamza couldn't find a better listener in the whole world.

Dervo sat next to him, partially turned toward him, staring at a fixed point above the fireplace, with a clenched fist on his chin. When Hamza finished, he looked over at Dervo. He wasn't sure whether he had listened to him or had relived the pictures of the hell he himself had gone through.

*   *   *

The interview at the American embassy in Rome was brief. After checking his documentation and the reason for his immigration request to the USA, the officer shook his hand, "Congratulations."

"Have I been accepted?"

"No, we say: 'you have been approved.'"

*   *   *

The day of Hamza's departure was fast approaching. One ominously dark and cloudy morning, Dervo announced that he was having guests over that evening, and that he would like Hamza to be there.

"Would you do me a favor?"

"Name it." Hamza knew he would do anything for this old man.

"It would mean a lot to me if you could be dressed appropriately. So, if you wouldn't mind, you and Sabrina can go and buy what you need."

They bought a classic black suit, white shirt, necktie, and black dress shoes. Sabrina remarked on how good he looked. "Especially, from the left side," Hamza thought wryly.

The guests started arriving at a few minutes before eight. The driveway was filled with limousines, shining beneath the garden lights. As soon as they came to a halt, the drivers would open the doors. Dervo and Hamza stood beside the door and greeted the guests. Sabrina took their coats and hats. Only five guests came. After the last one had entered the house, Dervo looked at Hamza, and the two of them proceeded into the salon.

"Is no one else coming?"

"No. Everybody is here. Every one of these people is worth a thousand others."

Hamza didn't understand what Dervo had meant, but he figured that those five men, along with Dervo, were at least five hundred years old. The old gentlemen—three Italians, one Hungarian, and one German—sat by the fireplace. All were impeccably dressed, perfumed and clean-shaven. Sabrina entered the room, wearing a long black dress and carrying drinks. She left them and returned to the kitchen. Three professional cooks had finished the dinner preparations shortly before eight. After they had taken their drinks, the old gentlemen came back to the fireplace. Dervo stood up. He spoke in English.

"It is my honor and my great pleasure to see you all here tonight. Gentlemen, let us drink to that. Cheers! At the same time, I would like to remind you of my great friend Avdaga. You know him from my stories, and you, Vittorio, know him personally."

"He hasn't died, has he?"

"No, fortunately he hasn't." Turning to Hamza, he explained, "At our age, when you mention somebody, the first thing that comes to mind is that he has left us. No, gentlemen, Avdaga is, thank goodness, alive and well. I have the honor and pleasure to introduce you to Hamza. Avdaga junior."

Vittorio, an elegant elderly gentleman, once standing at six feet four inches, was hunched over from the burden of his years. He had to lean back to see Hamza's face. When he did, his long white hair touched the back of his black suit. He blinked a few times.

"There are only a few people that I remember with such pleasure as I remember Avdaga."

One by one, they rose and came to Hamza. They shook hands again. Hamza smiled while shaking their hands. He could see they were all nice old gentlemen.

"Well, I've been waiting for this since you came to Rome," Dervo said happily.

"That's enough, leave the boy alone," the German guy said, speaking in English with a strong accent. "Sit down, our young friend. Please sit down, and make us old men happy. You know, we rarely get a chance to speak to anyone under seventy that is not family or a business partner."

Hamza sat down in the armchair. Somebody handed him a glass, and he drank it in one long draught, without thinking, and coughed. The gentlemen laughed.

"You see, young gentleman, we would like to talk to you for a while. I think that's the reason why Dervo invited us. We usually meet every three months. You must be something special. That's to be expected, considering the fact that Avdaga's blood runs in your veins. If you would agree, we would like to talk a bit about the war and history of Bosnia. I think that you can tell us a lot about Bosnia, and we are going to try to present you with views of historical events, which are slightly different from those that you learned in school."

Hamza took out his cigarettes. He looked questioningly at Otto.

"Oh, go ahead, young man. At our age, there are no harmful things. Most of us smoke as well."

"While I'm not running away from a free exchange of opinion, I would like to ask you to forgive me if I'm a bit harsh. It's just that I'm sick of the West." Hamza noted.

"We would expect that to be the case. Allow me to begin." Otto walked in front of the fireplace, with his arms clasped behind his back. "First of all, we spent our youth in World War II, equivalent to yours in Bosnia. You see, the six of us fought in four different armies, on two different sides. Can you recognize any former warriors in us? Hardly yes? At that time, Germany in the thirties, that was enthusiasm all right. Now we may call it collective madness, but it can never be repeated again. I'm not talking about small groups, but millions of people. Hitler took power during some of the hardest times for the German people, and united them around his ideals. Millions lived with the same heart and soul. I'm glad I lived to experience it. Now, you see what remains. Dervo and I are the remainder of what used to be a powerful army marching out to the east in the summer of 1941. Look at us now, we're just old men living out our last days.

"Vittorio was a partisan from Naples. De Villa and Sebastian fought for Mussolini and changed their uniforms in 1943. After that, they fought against the Germans. Janos, the hero of the Red Army, was accidentally in Russia when the war began, and fought for Stalin the whole time. And look at us now—we've been together for a long time. You're coming from a war too. You fought. You were a warrior. You killed. The battle scars on your face say as much.

What is in your soul? What remains in the soul of the warrior after all that? Do you still feel hatred? I am deeply convinced that the war itself was not a mistake. Humanity needs war to purge itself, to find spiritual values again. With time, humanity becomes mired in wealth and opulence. People grow corrupted, whole nations and countries even."

The old De Villa got up. "I would really like to show you a different point of view of the same history. I don't intend to try to impose my opinion on you. Let's look at, for example, the Soviet Union or Russia. You think that the Russians were better off winning the war, the war for the homeland? We talked about it for a long time, and finally decided that they're not. We think that Hitler wouldn't have killed twenty or so million Russians that Stalin did after the war. Besides, Hitler gave the Russians something no one had ever thought of. In war, you die like a man. Hitler gave Russians the opportunity to die for an idea, for freedom, for Mother Russia. You know what Stalin gave them? For him, it wasn't enough only to kill people. From his perspective, you needed to break people—destroy them while they are still alive, and then eliminate their very existence from the role of humanity. Are you familiar with the fact that all the twenty million people killed during Stalin's purges admitted to being CIA agents or spies for other imperialist and capitalist powers? Just imagine all those poor souls who were convinced, through torture, that they were 'enemies of the state.' Those people could hardly wait to be killed, since they were proven to have been spies. No. I don't think that the Russians would have been worse off with Hitler.

"Or take France, for instance. Otto's troops conquered France, in . . . Otto, was it five weeks?" Otto waved his hand in agreement. "Five weeks, give or take a day or two." De Villa continued, "You Bosnians fought against Serbia and Croatia for almost four years. How is this possible? I think that it could be explained by the fact that the French people didn't have an ideal to fight for. Or, in other words, the French actually begged the Germans to march in and set up some order."

"What are you talking about? What 'order'? Millions of dead begged Germany to come and kill them? Europe, Asia, Africa.

Exactly what order are you talking about?" Hamza asked with a puzzled look.

"Bravo, bravo. But look here, now. I told you about Russia. And France, well, let's just say they hadn't exactly exhausted themselves fighting against the Germans. You agree with me, of course. So, look what happened in Africa. What human or divine law said that Africa had to be French or English, and not German or Italian or African? Do you know that some states in Africa saw the Germans as their liberators? And speaking of the dead, the majority of German soldiers, or soldiers of any other army in the war, are just soldiers, warriors. That is how we used to kill too. In battle, on the attack or on defense, we were killing other soldiers and warriors."

"Carrying out orders?" Hamza said sarcastically.

"Just like you, young man. Did you decide where you were going to attack and why? No! You received orders and carried them out to the best of your ability. Or, did you really have to kill all your enemies? Maybe you could have captured them, or wounded them? I know, I know, there was no time to think about that. It was war. However, that is no justification to the dead ones. He would not mind waiting for you to think it over."

"Wait, this is crazy. I think I know history. The things you're talking about here, the way you are thinking, you are turning everything upside down."

"Everything *is* upside down, young man. One more thing, while the war drums beat loudly and the war flags are hoisted all over the country, all the leaders love and care for their warriors. But once everything calms down, the others surface. Smarter, or meaner, it doesn't matter. They get their positions by kissing up to someone or by being humble. Then the leaders see that it is easier with the new ones than the warriors that had surrounded them before. Soon the leader realizes that, in fact, he is infallible, because for God's sake, everyone around him is amazed, and hangs on his every word. Books are published with his wise thoughts according to genres—from hunting and fishing, to economics and philosophy. Unlike the warriors who always used to criticize him and make him feel like an ordinary mortal."

"I'm sorry, but Bosnia . . ." Hamza interjected.

"Hold it! Hold it, young man. Don't disappoint me now, please. Just don't tell me that it's different in Bosnia. You know, we're old, we've seen it all. And what you wanted to say, that would have been a miracle equivalent to the one that took place 1995 years ago, when the great star appeared in the east."

At this point, Hamza stopped his protesting.

"What we are actually trying to explain to you is that you should try to observe things from different perspectives. If nothing else, it's more interesting. Sometimes the devil isn't as black as he seems. And all the warriors in the world are brothers. Be careful, however, and hear me correctly: warriors, not murderers."

When the guests had left, Dervo motioned Hamza to stay. They sat next to each other. Dervo put his hand on Hamza's knee, "Avdaga's gold, I know how you feel. I'm just sorry that you didn't come to visit me before the war. As you have seen, my friends are very strange indeed. So am I, for that matter. One of the reasons I have never married is that my hands are bloody. We get together once every three months and have a discussion on whether we are soldiers or murderers. And, everybody always finds a justification for his own fight and his own side.

"So, this tonight was also an attempt, by pitting our opinion against yours, hoping to prove that we were right, although we know we were not. All warriors are damned. Those who attack as well as those who defend. I am not talking about the murderers. They are always the same, in every war. Ever the vultures and hyenas. Let me give you a piece of advice, a benefit of old age. Look for love. It's the only thing that can save you. Not in others, but from yourself. I figured it out too late, unfortunately.

"Anyway, there's another thing I would like to tell you. Here, take this credit card. I have never used it. I'm giving it to you for one day. On that day, whenever that is, you can buy whatever you want with it."

"How much?" Hamza laughed.

"A thousand, a million, it doesn't matter. I have only one condition. When I get the bill to pay it, I want to know that you were happy that day. Money doesn't mean anything to me. I don't even know how much I have in my accounts. Even if I tried hard, I wouldn't be able to spend but a small part of it. All right, that's it.

I have nothing more to tell you. Let's go to sleep now. Sabrina is going to drive you to the airport tomorrow. I won't see you again. These past days have been a very happy time for me."

Dervo patted Hamza on the knee and, with a contented smile, left the room.

* * *

The engine of the jaguar roared silently as they drove towards the airport. Sabrina would glance over at Hamza every once in a while.

"I don't like the fact that you're leaving."

"We almost never do the things we want to."

"What do you really want out of life, Hamza?"

"If I knew that, I wouldn't have left Bosnia."

"Is it normal to want more than a family, wife or husband we love, children, a home? To grow old and watch them grow up?"

"I don't know."

"So, why are you leaving?"

"I don't know."

Silence lingered on. The check-in line stretched on. With two hours before the departure, they made their way to a small café inside the airport.

"Are you going back to Tunisia once you graduate medical school?"

"No, not while Dervo is still alive."

"What are you going to do?"

"Nothing. I am going to live like I do now. Be with him."

"You really love him, don't you?"

"Yes. The same way you would love a grandparent. He pulled me out. I would have probably ended up on the street. I know how that goes."

"You know a lot," Hamza observed.

"I'm no saint. I have a lot of bad in me, but all that regressed when Dervo came into my life. He showed me a different kind of life."

"The life of the rich?"

"No. Money is a good thing. With a lot of money, Dervo actually showed me that money isn't important."

"Are you happy?" Hamza turned a piercing gaze on Sabrina's beautiful and calm face.

"Why are you leaving? We could have been together."

"Maybe, if things had been different, if I had met you before. Now, it's too late."

"No, it isn't for me."

"I know. I wasn't talking about you."

"Dervo says that you're a warrior."

"He told me that too."

"You really know how to interrupt a conversation."

"I'm sorry." Hamza saw the twinkle in her eye as she teased him out of his shell. Hamza pulled out Dervo's credit card.

"Please, return this to Dervo."

"Ha-ha-ha," Sabrina laughed gaily. The whole café turned and looked in their direction. "I knew it. That's exactly the way you are."

"And just how am I?"

"Dervo taught me to always say what I think. He always says what he thinks and thinks what he says, which is good. You don't have to think about what the point was."

"That's an advantage of old age," Hamza said dryly.

"He really meant what he said when he gave you the card."

"I know he did, but I don't need it."

"You don't need anything. Dervo would be very disappointed if I brought it back to him, and I wouldn't want to do that. Keep it as a souvenir. And if you love him, and would like to make him happy, use it when you're happy."

"If I ever become happy, I won't need anything."

"So, do it to make an old friend happy. Give me a cigarette."

"I thought you didn't smoke."

"I don't. Give me a cigarette."

Sabrina took a few drags off the cigarette. Snuffing out the tip, she rose. "I'm leaving. I hate saying goodbye."

"Nobody likes to say goodbye."

"We didn't even shake hands when we met."

"I didn't want to touch you."

"So you wouldn't get dirty?"

"So I wouldn't get *you* dirty."

Sabrina hugged him, pressing her whole body against his, as if she wanted to crawl beneath his skin. She trembled. She pressed her lips against his in a long kiss, and stepped away from him.

"Think about me sometimes."

"You can be sure of it."

Sabrina turned and left the cafe. In the airport hallway, she started running. Her high heels echoed throughout the huge hall—a lonely tapping of a lonely heart.

The airplane was full. The passenger conversations became an indistinguishable murmur. Hamza thought about how, in novels and movies, in a situation like this, people think about their lives or their unpredictable future. Hamza found out that it wasn't true for him. His thoughts were empty. Nothing. He just waited for the plane to reach the cruising altitude and the flight attendant to announce that they could unbuckle their seatbelts and smoke.

CHAPTER 4

The airport in New York and the press of humanity, streaming in from around the world. Refugees were visibly marked with big badges. The procedure was fast and efficient. Bosnian refugees received all the necessary papers upon entry to the U.S. They received permits for unlimited stays, for work, for building their lives anew. The only thing they couldn't do was vote for the president. "Maybe I'll even like it here." Hamza held on to the notion that everything could not be as bleak as it appeared.

The other refugees were mostly entire Asian families with many members. Three or four generations all came together. They reminded Hamza of the old Charlie Chaplin movies about immigrants. He had two hours until his flight to Chicago, so he drifted to the first floor of the airport where the food court was located, and despite its size, was mostly full. McDonald's, Burger King . . . America! Hamza stood to a side and lit a cigarette. At the same moment, as if sent by the devil himself, a large female police officer appeared next to him.

"Sir!" she yelled out. "Put that damn cigarette out!"

Hamza was surprised and confused. "Sure, sure," he hurriedly replied. "Would you please tell me where I'm allowed to smoke?"

"Nowhere!" the police officer answered roughly and marched down the hallway. An older gentleman sitting near him, pointed to the exit.

"Only outside, young man."

Hamza thanked him and went outside.

"Fuck America," he thought. "The airport is bigger than all of Sarajevo, and there is nowhere to smoke."

Outside, it was dark and raining. A few stretch limousines stood parked in front of the airport entrances. Hamza lit a cigarette. As he smoked, he mused, "Big country, big limousines, big female police officers. Truly American." Everything that was big, good, and strong used to be labeled as "American" in Bosnia. Standing next to him were a dozen other unfortunate guys, also forced to smoke in the rain. After his third cigarette, Hamza felt the cold creeping under his skin, and returned to the building. He walked from one restaurant to another, one souvenir shop to another, and finally entered one that appealed to him. He ate and leafed through a magazine, wondering why half the pages were covered with advertisements. He took a cup of coffee and walked outside for another cigarette. When he returned, he found that his plane for Chicago had left ten minutes earlier.

The problems with his ticket began. Explanations, and yet more explanations. In the end, he managed to get another ticket for Chicago, the plane leaving in an hour. "Very good," Hamza thought. "This is like the bus station in Sarajevo. You miss one bus, the other one comes right away." On the plane to Chicago, Hamza found out that smoking was banned on all flights within the U.S. and so he decided to get some sleep instead. An attentive and kind flight attendant woke him up when they were over O'Hare International Airport.

O'Hare, the biggest, the longest, the widest, the most attractive, and surely the most frequented airport in the world. Planes arrive and depart every few seconds in all possible directions, and from Hamza's viewpoint, in no order whatsoever. Just as one plane would land, another would take off, and so on endlessly. Waves of passengers traveled up and down the concourses. Hamza retrieved his bag and left the building, lighting a welcome cigarette as he did.

"Big country," Hamza muttered. "They have an airport the size of Sarajevo, their female police officers are bigger than wrestlers, limousines like buses . . . Their rabbits must be the size of bulls, or at least rams," he laughed to himself.

Entering an available cab, he gave his destination address to the driver—Schaumburg. It sounded more like a German than an

American town. Soon, the cab pulled up in front of his cousin's house. Hamza paid the driver and got out. The house was big, and it was clear his cousin had done well for himself. The front door, located in the middle of the house, was flanked by a pair of windows. The same general layout was on the second floor. On the right side was a two-car garage. The lights were on in the house. Hamza crossed the lawn and rang the bell. A middle-aged, chubby woman opened the door.

"Are you Hamza? The cousin from Bosnia?" she inquired.

"Yes. Good evening."

"Good evening. Please come in. We've been expecting you. No need to take off your shoes."

Hamza put his bag by the door and followed her. They entered the living room, where a fire burned in the fireplace and gave the place a welcoming ambiance. Hamza remembered his cousin as a stubborn young man, never satisfied with his achievements, who one day decided to leave for the U.S. When Hamza entered the bright, warm, and welcoming room, his cousin stood. He smiled and came to him with open arms and hugged him.

"Welcome, cousin."

"Thanks, cuz."

"Let me look at you. You look the same as the last time I saw you. A few wrinkles around the eyes perhaps. Are you still shoeing monkeys?"

"People go through phases."

"We have another guest here. He came from Bosnia recently too. Let me introduce you." He hugged him and walked him across the room. "Hamza this is Srdjan. Srdjan, this is my cousin Hamza, the one I told you about."

"Nice to meet you." Srdjan extended his hand to him.

The typically Serbian name put Hamza on his guard. "Where exactly did you come from?" Hamza asked without extending his hand.

"From Ilijas."

With a stone-cold and unreadable gaze, Hamza looked at his cousin. He turned and left the room. Cousin followed him.

"Hamza, where are you going? Come on, man, what's wrong?"

Hamza responded without turning, "Ask your friend." He took his bag and left the house the same way he had entered.

"Stop! What's wrong with you? Where are you going at this time of night? Hey, come on, stop."

*   *   *

Not looking back, Hamza walked through the front yard headed down the street. Rain was falling again, and he pulled up the collar of his jacket. The street ran into a bigger one, and that one ran into a bigger one still. It was well-lit, lined in shops. Hamza walked slowly, looking at the store windows, never stopping. In some nameless fast-food restaurant, he ate a couple of sandwiches, took a cup of coffee, and went outside. He walked, smoking and drinking coffee. The hours passed. In downtown Chicago, he tilted his head back, trying to see the roofs of the buildings disappearing into the fog. It was dawn when he finally stopped and looked around.

He was in a neighborhood that seemed dirty, with decayed rows of houses and two-story buildings. On one of them, he saw a big sign that read "Apartments for Rent". Without a second thought, Hamza went into the building. He was looking at the mailboxes, looking for some sign of where he might find the owner or the manager of the building. An old black couple was walking down the hall.

"Excuse me, could you tell me who I can see for an apartment?"

The couple looked at each other, surprised. Silently, they pointed him to the door at the end of the hall, and left, still looking stunned. Hamza scratched his scar, thinking that was the reason for their strange looks. He knocked on the door. Soon enough, he heard voices on the inside, and a fat black guy opened the door.

"You have an apartment?" Hamza asked, offering no preamble or introduction.

"For you? Are you alone? And, you really want an apartment?"

"Yes."

"And you really want a place *here*, in this building?"

"Yes."

"Ha-ha-ha . . . you really want a place in this building?"

"Right here." Hamza began to wonder if this was the right door; maybe he had gotten a tenant instead of the manager.

"Okay." The black guy got a little serious. "One-bedroom or studio?"

"What is a studio?"

"Ha-ha-ha . . . What is a studio? That is a place for one person to stay."

"Then, I'll take the studio."

"Okay, wait a minute." The door closed, and a few minutes later, the manager reappeared. He was carrying a large group of keys.

"So, what kind of studio do you want?"

"Any kind will do."

"Fine. So, you really want a studio here? All right, I don't care and I'm not asking anything, it's none of my business. Here we are. This is a great studio."

Walking into the studio apartment, Hamza found it to be pleasantly warm. There was a large room, a kitchen, and a small bathroom. It didn't seem too bad.

"Okay. How much?"

"For you, three hundred a month."

"Two fifty."

"You must give me the first month's rent and deposit upfront."

"What is a deposit?"

"In case you destroy something, I can pay to repair it."

"And if I don't destroy anything?"

"Then I'll give you the money back."

"When was the last time you gave somebody their money back?"

"I don't remember," he smiled cheerfully.

Hamza pulled a roll of cash out of his pocket. He counted five hundred and handed the packet to him.

"Okay. Here's five hundred."

"Thanks, I'll get the contract tomorrow, so when you go out, stop by and sign it."

"Fine. No hurry."

"Another thing. Hide your money. Carry about ten dollars in your pocket, no more."

"Why?" Hamza was clearly puzzled by this interesting offer of insight.

"Because people lose their lives for less money then you got there. I didn't see anything, and I don't know anything. You can bring a girl over, if you want to. I just don't want any trouble, all right?"

"Sure."

Hamza closed the door and set his bag down. He went straight to the bathroom and took a long, hot shower. After getting out, he dried himself with his shirt and put on clean underwear. He lit a cigarette and lay down on the floor next to the radiator. He woke up later that same afternoon. He brushed his teeth and, returning to the radiator, he lit a fresh cigarette. The warmth felt good. It felt good not to think about anything. That had taken a lot of practice. He let his thoughts flow easily without any particular order or content. After the first cigarette, he tried to make himself think. He found that it took a lot of effort. He forced himself to concentrate.

"Okay, so now you're here. You wanted America, you got America. Let's see what needs to be done, and in which order. First, I need to have some kind of identification card. That's needed in every country. Then I need to look for a job. The only thing is, I don't know where to look for one. Maybe there is an institution or something that can help with that. Maybe those guys from Catholic Charities know something. That's it. First, I'm going to go to Catholic Charities."

Without standing up, he rolled onto his stomach and did twenty push-ups, then a few more sit-ups. He then did a few more simple exercises. He felt himself getting tired very quickly. He'd have to increase the intensity and the number of exercises. America is a country for the strong, physically and intellectually. He had to be strong. He realized that he was not angry at his cousin at all. His cousin probably couldn't even guess why he had left. He was still living in the good old times of Yugoslavia. Brotherhood and unity. Sleep crept up on Hamza. He quietly and gently shut his eyes.

*   *   *

He woke very early.

Once the sun had fully risen, Hamza went outside. In the hallway, he ran into a few black guys. "The white people must sleep longer," he thought. He stopped a few people on the street and asked them about the Catholic Charities. Nobody knew anything. Finally, he saw an officer. The officer asked him for his ID first. After he had carefully looked through his passport, white card, plane ticket, and everything else that Hamza had on him, he kindly explained to him where he needed to go. Hamza thanked him and started to walk away.

"It's quite a way, if you're walking."

"I'm not in a hurry. I have time."

After hours of walking, Hamza finally got to his destination.

Everyone at the Catholic Charities was nice. The young man that received him welcomed him to the United States. Slowly and patiently, he explained the first steps that Hamza needed to take. Physical examination, alien registration number, ID card, public aid . . . In the end, he gave Hamza the addresses and phone numbers of all the institutions that he needed to go to. He complimented Hamza on his knowledge of English and assured him that he would succeed in the U.S.

On his way home, Hamza bought a coffeemaker, coffee, sugar, and milk. "I'm moving in," he thought. Once in his apartment, he made coffee, smoked a few cigarettes, and went to bed. He used his jacket as a blanket. Rising early the next morning, Hamza went for his physical examination. After two hours of walking, he finally stopped a cab. That day, he almost finished the physical, leaving the last few details for the next day. On his way home, he bought a pillow and a blanket. During the next few days, he filled out paperwork for Public Welfare, a social aid for financially disadvantaged Americans. All refugees who arrived in the U.S. received this aid for the first few months. It consisted of money and food stamps. While receiving this aid, refugees are obligated to participate in English as a Second Language classes. Hamza welcomed the opportunity.

Unlike Catholic Charities, people at the Public Welfare were rude and arrogant. Hamza felt like "a pig in Tehran," as if he came to steal something. He could barely wait to finish. He left with a bitter, metallic taste in his mouth. He returned home by cab. A group of younger black guys stood in front of the building entrance. Hamza greeted them and passed by. Nobody answered his greetings. He saw a big guy opening the door across from his apartment. He greeted him too. This time the guy said "hey" in response.

*   *   *

Once in his apartment, he put coffee in the coffeemaker and went into the hallway. He knocked on his neighbor's door. After a minute, the door opened a crack, and his neighbor peered out.

"Hi, I just made some coffee. Do you have time to have a cup with me?"

The guy seemed not to notice him at all. He looked out into the hallway cautiously. When he realized that the hallway was clear, he looked at Hamza angrily.

"Fuck you and your coffee!" and slammed the door.

Hamza stared at the door, not understanding what just happened. He shrugged his shoulders and went into his apartment. He caught himself shrugging more and more these days.

"Damn, Hamza, where have you come?"

He sat next to the window, leaned on the radiator, and lit a cigarette. He sipped the coffee slowly. It had begun to snow, the first snow that year. He turned with a start as his door opened slowly, admitting his neighbor into the apartment. Closing the door, the man approached Hamza. Hamza smiled.

"He changed his mind," he thought. Silently, he poured coffee into another cup and handed it to him. The neighbor's surprise was evident on his face, Suddenly, he swung his right hand and slapped the cup out of Hamza's hand. The cup flew across the room and smashed against the wall. The coffee splashed all over the wall. He glared at Hamza furiously.

"Who are you, baby? Huh? What the hell are you doing here?"

Hamza looked at him. He was over six foot five and some two hundred seventy-five pounds of muscle. His curly hair was braided into countless little braids. His shiny white teeth and two black eyes gleamed wildly. Unconsciously, Hamza felt respect for that raw, concentrated strength that towered over him.

"I am your new neighbor."

"Neighbor?" the black guy screamed. "Neighbor? What are you doing here?"

"What do you mean?" Hamza patiently continued to counter questions with questions of his own.

"What do you mean what do I mean, baby? You have been here since Monday, and you ain't been killed yet. Get out of here. Tomorrow morning. Do you understand?"

"How about coffee now?" Hamza smiled.

The black man clenched his teeth and rolled his eyes toward the ceiling, helplessly. Hamza handed him another cup of coffee. The black man got up, locked the door, took the cup, and sat across from Hamza.

"I'm new here. I've been in the U.S. for only five days," Hamza offered.

"And you've spent all those five days here? Baby, do you know where you are?"

"I'm in Chicago."

"Chicago is big. Where exactly . . . ?"

"I don't understand the question."

"Man! Baby, you're in Kedzie, South Chicago."

"So?"

"So? White people don't even walk around here during the day. And if they accidentally end up here, they lock their car doors and try to get the hell out as fast as possible."

"I don't really understand what you're talking about," Hamza explained.

"Let me put it to you this way, baby. Black people live here. This is the worst neighborhood in the U.S. You can't live here, not for long, anyway. It's a miracle that you're still alive. You see this door, this lock? It don't mean shit! If a couple of guys show up, take everything you own, kill you, or just beat the shit out of you, nobody is going to show up. Nobody is even going to call the police. You're on your own. Do you understand now? Move tomorrow morning."

"Move where?

"North. Anywhere."

"North Chicago. How far north exactly?"

"Around five thousand north. Those are better neighborhoods. Another thing, you don't call people over for coffee, not nobody. A neighbor and coffee? Never even heard that shit before."

Hamza shrugged his shoulders, insecurely. The black guy rose to leave.

"Get some sleep now, baby. I'll keep an eye out for you tonight."

When he was at the door, Hamza asked him, "What's your name?"

"Whatever you like." The black guy smiled and left.

Hamza locked the door, put his pillow next to the radiator, covered himself with the blanket, and fell asleep. At some point in the night, he heard a noise coming from the hallway. He turned over and went back to sleep.

*   *   *

The morning was cold. It was still snowing with ice-cold winds. The Windy City is the name given to Chicago in a moment of inspiration. Hamza woke at dawn. His morning routine was made up of the physical—coffee, exercise, and showering—and emotional—pleasure in the aroma and taste of the dark brown brew. Thinking about what his neighbor had said, Hamza realized that he was right; he shouldn't tempt fate. He would look for an apartment in a better neighborhood. The streets of Chicago, usually busy, were deserted. Hamza walked through the fresh snow on the sidewalk. Nobody had passed since the snow had begun to fall. Ten minutes into the trip, a car pulled up next to him, with a few young men inside. The guy in the passenger seat rolled down the window, "Hey, man, you got a couple of dollars?"

Hamza didn't understand what the young man wanted, so he turned toward the car. Seeing the long ugly scar on Hamza's face, the young man mumbled something that sounded curiously formal like "have a nice day," and the car bolted down the street.

"I must look like one mean guy."

Hamza hailed a cab and drove to about 3500 North Chicago. It was different in this part of town. People walked down the streets and there was traffic. Used and new car dealerships, fast-food restaurants; life had a different synchronization here. Believing this street to be too noisy to live on, Hamza walked along the side streets. As he turned from Kedzie and headed west, he soon found himself in the quieter neighborhoods. The houses were beautiful and most had big porches with plaster or brick pillars. He walked from street to street and came to one street that did not run straight as the others. The generally romantic feeling of the neighborhood was partially ruined by the sight of the odd pile of garbage that could be seen on the street every now and again. Besides, there was an ugly three-story house on the corner of the street looking badly neglected. About a hundred yards from the street corner, Hamza saw a beautiful stone house. Heavy beams held a wide porch, and stone stairs led to the yard. In front of the house, there were two big oak trees. The whole house had an air of antique beauty and subtle elegance.

In one of the windows on the second floor hung a sign: "For Rent".

"It must be very expensive," Hamza thought. He was about to continue the search, but changed his mind and went to the door. He rang the doorbell.

"Come on in . . ." responded a voice from inside.

Hamza turned the doorknob and went inside, stepping into a wide hallway. On the left side was a wide stairway leading upstairs. On the right, a smaller hall, which led to the apartment on the first floor.

"Hello, anybody home?" Hamza called to the disembodied but social voice.

The first door opened and an older black man came out into the hall.

"Good morning."

"Good morning. I saw the sign you're renting out an apartment, so I thought . . ."

"Come on in."

They entered the kitchen, which led to the dining room and the living room.

A large black lady worked at something next to the stove. The room was filled with pleasant smells.

"Mary, honey. This young man is looking for an apartment."

The woman turned around and her eyes went wide at the sight of Hamza.

"Hey, Don't Worry Andy, you know what . . ." Mary stopped in the middle of her sentence, not wanting to talk in front of the newcomer. "Excuse me, young man, would you mind waiting in the living room for a couple of minutes? Would you like a cup of coffee? Of course, you would. Don't Worry Andy, take the young gentleman to the living room. The coffee will be ready in a minute."

"This way please." Andy let Hamza pass in front of him. Hamza sat in a leather chair, took out his cigarettes, and looked at Andy as if seeking permission. Andy nodded. Mary brought Hamza a cup of coffee and excused herself. Taking Andy's hand, she led him back to the kitchen. Although he didn't want to listen in, Hamza overheard parts of their conversation, " . . . that's trouble . . . you're not thinking . . . you weren't afraid of trouble before . . . I was thirty years old then, now I'm fifty-five and I want to sleep soundly . . . he looks so sad . . ."

Hamza got up and went to the window. The roads had been cleared of snow, but the front yards were still covered in a blanket of white.

"Very nice neighborhood," he thought. "Just what trouble are they talking about?"

"Ahem," Andy cleared his throat behind him. "Where are you from?"

"Bosnia."

"Oh, Bosnia, I know."

"Everybody knows."

"There's a war going on over there."

"Yes."

"How long have you been in the U.S.?"

"It's my sixth day today."

"That short. Your English is excellent."

"Thank you. So, what's with the apartment?"

"Mary is a bit afraid of foreigners. Did you fight in the war?"

"Yes, a bit."

"How long is a bit?"

"Three and a half years."

"That's not a bit. So, what are you?"

"What do you mean?"

"Are you Christian or . . ."

"Muslim. Why?"

"Were the Muslims the good guys or the bad guys in the war?"

"The good guys. Definitely the good guys."

"I see, I see. Wait a minute."

"Can I see the apartment?"

"You'll see it. There's plenty of time." Andy went returned to the kitchen and Hamza could do nothing but wait. He went to the window in order not to hear anymore fragments of fear and pity. He heard Andy's loud voice anyway.

"Yes, I think that's the way it should be."

Soon, Andy came back into the room.

"Okay, now we look at the apartment."

They went into the hallway and then continued upstairs. The apartment had a living room, bedroom, a kitchen with a dining room, and a bathroom. The living room was big, bright, and faced the street. The entire floor was covered in nice, light purple carpet, and Hamza's feet felt pleasantly padded on it.

"I like it."

"Of course, you do. I like it, too."

"I think I'll take it. How much is it?"

"With the heat, gas, and electricity?"

"Altogether."

"Three hundred fifty."

"Three hundred fifty? That's not too much."

"Depends on the person. When can you move in?"

Hamza put his bag on the floor, "I just did."

"I mean, when are you going to bring your furniture in?"

Nodding toward the bag on the floor, he said, "That's all."

"Hmm . . ." Don't Worry Andy was silent for a heartbeat. "If you want, I have a mattress, a few dishes, and a coffeemaker that I can lend until you settle in."

"That would be great. Let me give you the money now." Hamza took off his jacket. He took a bunch of bills out of the hidden compartment in the collar. He counted the money and gave it to Andy.

"Um, this is seven hundred dollars," exclaimed Andy, a bit confused.

"I know. The deposit."

"There is no need for that. But, if you have extra money, you can pay me now for two months. It's like saving your money for tomorrow."

"All right," Hamza agreed.

"And don't be mad at Mary. She's precious as gold, but afraid of problems."

"You won't have any problems with me. So, I'll go get some food and other things I need."

"Have lunch with us."

"No, thank you. Maybe some other time." Hamza buttoned up his jacket and went outside. He wandered around the city for a while and bought a pillow and a blanket again. He purchased a tablecloth to eat on. Hamza loved to eat on the floor. People who eat on the floor can't get fat. If they eat too much, the stomach presses up against the lungs and it simply hurts too much; these people have no choice but to stay slim. He bought a couple of towels, shampoo, soap, and purchased a few magazines and some food. It was late afternoon when he came back. Andy let him in and gave him the keys. A mattress and some blankets had been moved into the bedroom. In the kitchen, there were some dishes, a coffeemaker, and a microwave. After putting away the food, Hamza took a shower. The warm water felt good after the long, cold walk. He worked out for a while, and returned for another shower. He prepared a few sandwiches and went to bed just as darkness pulled the shades on his sixth day in America.

*   *   *

In the next few days, Hamza wandered around the city; he bought a map, and quickly discovered that everything was simple once you knew east from west. The streets ran on a grid from east to west and from north to south. There is a point zero in the center of Chicago, and all the streets are either, north, south, west, or east of that point. This system made it quite easy to find out where each street was located. Hamza decided that Americans had figured it out pretty well. He wandered through Chicago, traveling by bus or train, to the shores of Lake Michigan and then back inside the city. He found out that the Sears Tower was the tallest building in the world and Michigan Street was the heart of Chicago. He would go into dark bars in dangerous parts of the city as well as into glamorous clubs downtown.

To the casual observer, he appeared uninterested in this deluge of experience and sensory input; yet his brain collected the information, and sorted it according to area and quality. He knew where to get good food cheap, where the cheap stores were, which bus or subway line could get him closest to home, which streets have prostitutes, drug dealers, and so on. He never talked to or spent time with anyone. He was unnoticeable and faceless. He blended into the masses that rolled down the streets of Chicago. Only his scar made him different. Everything was fine as long as people approached him from the left side. But his right side would have people backing away. He thought it was funny, yet his scar protected him from trouble. On the streets, the bums didn't ask him for money, and in the better restaurants he was served faster. Cab drivers never tried to overcharge him. The scar really did look terrible. A quarter inch wide, it turned white in the cold, and it looked like his face had a white stripe going through it.

The following Monday, he set out to look for a job. He decided to walk and look for "Help Wanted" signs in the windows. Eventually, the wandering had brought him in front of the Catholic Charities building. He decided to go visit the nice guy that had shown him what to do when he first got to the U.S. Paul Kerr was working that day and was his typical warm and friendly self. Hamza felt glad to see him from the moment he recognized him. "This is what I call a surprise," he said, shaking Hamza's hand." Have you earned your first million already?"

"I'm on my way. I'm looking for a job."

"And? Are you looking for anything specific, or just a job?"

"Any job for any kind of money."

"Are you sure?"

"Definitely." Hamza was nothing if not certain of how to survive.

"Wait a minute. A friend of mine works in a hospital, and they have openings every once in a while. It's a janitor position, but it's not bad. And it's inside, nice and warm."

"If they have anything, I'll take it."

"Wait here a moment, please." Paul stepped out of the office. He came back shortly with an address. "What can you actually do?"

"I can do anything." Confident and certain was Hamza's natural state.

"And what is your profession?"

"I'm an architect."

"Wow! Then I don't know about this cleaning job. You may not be at all satisfied pushing mops and buckets around."

"Don't worry. Cleaning is fine."

"Okay, well, you got the job. You start at 7 a.m. You will be earning $5.50 an hour. It's not a lot." Paul sounded apologetic to Hamza.

"That's fine." Reassuring, calm, and certain, Hamza conveyed the idea that it truly was fine with him.

"Here's the address. Ask for Miss Melin."

They talked about the weather and car prices, and Hamza left. He decided to walk to the hospital so he wouldn't have trouble finding it the next day. The next morning, he was at the hospital shortly before 7 a.m. Miss Melin was a nice older lady, with white hair and gentle eyes. She took him to the supervisor. The supervisor was an energetic, self-confident man, and showed Hamza what needed to be done. "What we're looking for from you is to be on time, to be clean, and to finish the listed jobs during the day." He gave him the list of his assigned duties. "Now, let me show you around, and then you can start tomorrow." Hamza's area of cleaning was half of the third floor—sixteen rooms and bathrooms, hallways, and the dining room. The supervisor explained the phases and order of the jobs. "So, first, clean the rooms, then the hallways, and the dining room. Then you need to come back for the bathrooms. Make sure there's always plenty of toilet paper and rubber gloves. Then the windows, doors . . ." Hamza listened carefully, trying to take in all the details.

As Paul said, the job wasn't bad, but in cleaning, eight hours a day seemed like eighty. Time went by unbelievably slow. Hamza realized that time went by faster when he worked at a faster pace, so he worked as fast as he could. At the end of the day, he had enough time left over that he could clean the windows in one of the rooms. After two weeks, his section gleamed. Returning from work one day, Hamza passed by a three-story house still under construction. Through partially fogged-up windows, he could see the carpenters working. Hamza knocked and went in. The room was pleasantly warm.

Three guys were cutting wooden two-by-fours and putting them in place.

"Hi. Is the electrician in-charge anywhere around?"

One of the workers came up to him. "No, why?"

"I'm an electrician, and I'm looking for a job."

"He'll be here the day after tomorrow. I can tell him that you came by, and you can also stop by later if you want to." Hamza came by two days later. He quickly made a deal with the boss. He'd try out for a couple of days. If the boss was satisfied with what he saw, Hamza would get the job. The pay would be $6.50 an hour in cash, more than what he was making cleaning rooms, windows, and floors.

The knowledge that he had gained during summers working with Sarajevo's contractors came in handy. Electrical installation in the U.S. was the same as in Europe, although the process was different. Hamza saw, for the first time, how they bent and put pipes in place. His boss was quite satisfied with his work and aptitude for learning. He told Hamza that he had never seen anyone learn so fast. When he was able to work independently, they would talk about a raise.

The staff of the hospital was sad to see him go. His supervisor told him that if he had only three workers like Hamza, he could fire the rest, and if he ever needed a job, he could always come back.

The new job was a challenge for Hamza. It felt like a constant I.Q. test. He enjoyed each part of the work and finding the best and fastest way of doing things. The days passed quickly. The other workers were very nice to him. After a few days, he would stay at the construction site after hours to finish up the job. They went on to a different building shortly after.

A month later, he asked the boss for a raise, and found his first disappointment in the U.S. The boss, who had been very nice and outgoing up until that point, changed completely. He kept telling him about the crisis in the U.S., about feeling lucky to have this kind of job, not having to pay as much tax as he did, etc. In the end, however, he agreed to raise his wages to seven dollars an hour. From that day forth, it seemed that nothing Hamza did was ever good enough. Complaints and criticisms kept piling up. Why this, why that? You're falling behind, you should have gotten twice as much done. Every day brought a new problem. Hamza took the abuse for one week. The next Monday, when the boss started complaining again, Hamza put his tools away and walked up to him.

"Okay boss, you win. I'm not working here anymore."

"What? You can't do that. You can't leave just like that! You have to give me two week's notice. In fact, you have to work until we get this building done."

"I don't have to do anything. Finish it yourself."

*   *   *

He walked down Michigan Avenue for a while, stopping in an Italian restaurant to drink an espresso, then bought a carton of Marlboro reds, and headed home. By the time he arrived, it was late afternoon. At the corner of the street, on the stairs of a large building, sat six or seven black guys. They had a paper bag that they passed around and regularly drank from. Probably whisky. Hamza passed by, one of them called to him. "Hey, you, come here!"

Hamza glanced back and kept walking. He was agitated. He tried to understand the reasons for the boss's sudden attitude change. He couldn't understand that a simple half-a-dollar raise was the reason for everything. On top of that, he knew that he worked more than the boss himself did. The stress and agitation had numbed his reflexes. He didn't hear the steps behind him. Two hands grabbed him across his chest and held him firmly. He was completely taken by surprise. As he tried to turn his head to see what was going on, someone crashed a knotted fist into Hamza's stomach. He moaned from the pain, and his bag fell on the ground. The first punch was followed by a series of blows to the stomach. The pummeling was concluded with a hard hit to Hamza's chin. Hamza's body relaxed and the one holding him dropped him to the ground. Hamza sprawled on the pavement.

Through the fog he saw the man that hit him leaned above him. From a distance, he could hear:

"Hey, you son of a bitch! When Big Mike calls you, you run over and say, 'Yes, sir.' Do you understand?" A hard kick in the ribs followed. Hamza rolled away from the kick.

"What are you doing here, huh? Come on, speak up!"

Hamza choked. His mouth was full of blood, and he couldn't breathe. With an effort, he spat it out and took a breath. He tried to say something, but the blood just kept on coming. He lay on his stomach and tried to spit the blood out. The black guy leaned over him, paying no attention to his condition, and rifled through his jacket. He smiled when he found a wad of money. He took his watch, then put a hand inside his shirt, looking for a necklace. Not finding one, he kicked him again. Hamza regained consciousness. He was breathing with his mouth wide open.

"So, what did you say you're doing here?" he kicked him again, pulling back a bit this time.

"I live here," Hamza mumbled.

"What, now you're gonna lie to me?. As far as I'm concerned you're not living here, you're dying here. Ha-ha-ha." He came closer to Hamza and looked at his jacket.

"Take it off!"

Hamza shook his head

"What, you don't want to? I just told you not to think. When Big Mike tells you to do something, just do it. Understand?" Mike kneeled down and punched him in the chin. Hamza's head bounced off the pavement with a crack.

"Do you understand now?" Another punch to the temple. The skin split above his eye, and blood started gushing fast. Mike looked at his own fist, full of blood, with disgust. He wiped it on Hamza's jacket and kicked him again.

"You dumb son of a bitch!" He went back to his friends on the porch.

Hamza was on the edge of consciousness. He opened and closed his eyes, trying to regain some focus. His left eye was swollen shut and blood streamed down his face. One of the assailants came over to him. He took out a tissue and wiped his face. He pressed it against the wounded eye and placed Hamza's hand over it to hold it.

"It's all right, man, you're alive. That's the important thing. Most don't survive pissing off Big Mike. Let's get you off the sidewalk."

He propped up Hamza by the shoulder and carried him to the fence. He leaned him up against it and Hamza slid to the ground, his back resting against the fence. He held the tissue never realizing it was in his hand.

"Why didn't you just give him the fucking jacket? Those kicks before weren't dangerous, but the last couple of shots got you bad. You could have been dead, man."

Hamza spit the blood out of his mouth. He tried to smile.

"You'll have to kill me for this jacket," he whispered.

"Stupid, he almost did."

"Almost, but that didn't get it done."

"For real, what are you doing here? This is a black neighborhood. White people don't come around here."

"I'm black."

"No, you're not."

"Yes, I am. Inside."

The young man, who had kept the conversation at a whisper so that Big Mike couldn't hear him, burst into laughter.

"Hey, Big Mike. You were wrong, man. This is our black brother. It's just that he's black on the inside."

"Black Soul? Ha,-ha-ha," Big Mike laughed out loud. The rest of the gang joined in. Suddenly, he became deadly serious and looked at Hamza. Big Mike was the king of the neighborhood where Hamza lived. His place of birth—the poorest neighborhood in Chicago—combined with the color of his skin, had already put him at the bottom of the social ladder. As a child, he had quickly learned the only law of survival: "Eat or be eaten. If you don't take from others, others will take from you."

Thanks to his enormous physical strength, he assumed leadership very early. His territory at first extended only to his street, but it slowly expanded. He was born to be a leader, to be the master of this semi-underground world. Very tall and extremely strong, he was a leader without mercy. Mercy meant weakness, and weakness was for nicer neighborhoods. Now, he looked at this strange white man, and found that he didn't like something about him. He'd had a chance to see a lot of people beaten up and defeated. The one bleeding in front of him was beaten up, but he didn't have that defeated look in his eyes. Big Mike dismissed the notion with a wave of his hand. During the night, the son of bitch would probably move to some quieter area, anyway. Most likely, he'd never see him again.

Hamza used all the strength he could muster and got up, holding on to the fence. He walked over to the bag, which lay in the street, and took out a pack of cigarettes. Painfully, he walked down the street. It took him a while to get to the house. Don't Worry Andy met him in the hallway.

"Hey, what happened? Are you all right?"

"Everything is fine," Hamza said, trying to pass him.

"What happened?" Andy was insistently dogging him.

"I fell. Hard."

When he had entered the apartment, he locked the door, leaned on it, then sat on the floor. He felt his body burning and his head bursting into a thousand pieces. With his eyes closed, his thoughts returned to his childhood.

It was a very warm summer day. They were picnicking by the river—green fields, golden sunshine, crickets. Hamza ran with a kite. He kept that image in his mind like a photo. He consciously caught and held his breath, and soon his pulse and breathing returned to normal. The pain started to ease. He wasn't sure how long he had been there. He got up, turned on the coffeemaker, and went into the bathroom. The water made the pain return with a vengeance. Slowly, his body got used to the water, and he was able to relax. It washed the clotted blood from his face and body. As he came out of the bathroom, he avoided looking into the mirror. He poured the coffee, sat next to the window, lit a cigarette, and looked outside. It was dark and pleasantly warm in the room. Outside, he could see the snow falling hard. By the morning, there would be another ten inches of snow.

*   *   *

Three days later, Hamza emerged from his home. He had lost some weight, his cheeks were hollow, and dark circles hung under his eyes. Paul Kerr helped him find another job, repairing roofs in Skokie. After that, he changed jobs quickly. He worked as a maintenance man in one building, then renovating houses in the suburbs, then with electricians in the questionable areas of South Chicago, then at a bread factory, and then again as an electrician.

* * *

When it was initially founded, the city of Chicago was strictly situated on the shores of Lake Michigan. The rapid development of the city, characteristic of a U.S. metropolis, soon wiped out the borders between the city and the surrounding towns. Since those areas around the city were suburban, Americans demonstrated their practicality once again, and simply called them "suburbs'." These towns and villages maintained their autonomy, retaining their own city halls, police force, etc. In recent years, more and more inhabitants of Chicago, especially the more well-to-do crowd, decided to move away from the city, willing to pay the price of the long drive to and from work.

* * *

The spring of 1996 arrived without warning. One morning, instead of a cold, icy wind, a warm one blew in. The trees seemed to blossom overnight, and the entire city became green in a few days. Chicago changed its face. More people were walking downtown; the girls looked happier. Along the shores of Lake Michigan, more and more people were out jogging every day. Hamza worked on a renovation site on the West Side. For him, the days were all the same—waiting for something he could not define. At winter's end, Rachel Barton, the famous violinist, was to perform a concert in Northern Chicago at The Ravinia. By chance, Hamza had read about it in the newspaper. He ordered a ticket by phone. After work, he took a train and cab to Ravinia.

Ravinia itself was right on the shore of Lake Michigan. Hamza was surprised by the number of people who had come. The tickets were expensive, even by American standards. The basic necessities of life were cheap in the U.S.—food, clothing, survival necessities.

AHMET M. RAHMANOVIC

But everything else was very expensive. Similar concerts were well-attended in Sarajevo, but the number of attendees was limited by the size of the theater. Hamza found an empty seat at the beginning of the third row. The young violinist came out onto the stage to thunderous applause, and soon the crystal sound of the violin filled the place. Hamza sat comfortably, enjoying the the music, as well as the skill of a world-class musician. His spirit left Ravinia on the wings of music and flew to Sarajevo. He was at one of the concerts where Amra used to play. Concentrating on the memory, he ceased to notice anything around him. The concert ended, but Hamza, with his spirit in distant Sarajevo, hadn't noticed. He was still looking at the empty stage.

"Excuse me." A girl stood next to him, waiting for him to get up, so she could pass. Her words didn't reach him. "He's really rude," she thought, while squeezing past his seat. When she had passed, she turned around. The long, ugly scar on the face of the stranger caught her attention. She took a closer look, and saw a teardrop roll down the scar, running down his face. The girl stepped back, then took a tissue from her bag, and silently put it in his lap. She left the theater quietly.

*   *   *

June G. Thomas was born on the first day of a new year in Montana. She was the fifth child of the Thomas family, and a big surprise. Her mother and father were well over forty and her three brothers and a sister were almost grown when the newest addition to the family arrived. Her family treated her like a toy. Although the family business and the farm took up a lot of their time, someone was always in the mood to play with her. This way, passed from hand to hand, June grew up surrounded by happiness and love. She was the little princess of the Thomas family and the happiest creature on the face of the Earth.

Every member of the family had their own area of interest, and tried to explain it to their little princess. Her father taught her the economics of business and the household. Her mother would explain the secrets of cooking to her. Jeremiah, her oldest brother, would take her swimming. She would go horseback riding and hunting with Jonathan. Her youngest brother, Pitt, would take her to the library and find her books filled with beautiful stories about little princesses like herself. Her sister Catherine taught her how to act like a lady.

June grew up in absolute freedom, and from an early age knew exactly what she wanted, and never gave up until she had achieved it. So, when, after graduating from high school, she announced that she was going to Chicago to study medicine, her family could only nod, since her statement wasn't a question or a request for permission. She was simply informing them of her direction. Her father just nodded silently. He knew that any attempt to stop her or try to change her mind would crush everything they had taught her from birth—"Life doesn't give you anything. You have to take things. You have to fight for what you want." It was the family way.

She spent the last summer on the family farm preparing for the trip and a life away from the family. Since she had grown up surrounded by the care of her entire family, June had to learn how to live independently.

"Money is not the most important thing in the world, but you have to respect and spend it rationally. You see, we can afford to pay for your college and living expenses, so you don't have to think about money. However, I would like you to work and earn a part of it yourself. You'll see afterwards that this is the best way. You'll have your college and basic expenses paid for, and you'll just have to take care of the rest. If you can't, if you really need more money, just call us."

June was a Thomas, and she would never call to ask for money.

Her brothers taught her everything she would need to know in Chicago. First and foremost was physical strength in combination with self-defense. They all had graduated from colleges all over the US, and they explained to her the basics of functioning in a big city and at the university.

And so, in the fall, armed with knowledge and will power, June left the big stone house and a farm the size of a small European country, and traveled to Chicago. The Thomas empire changed without its princess. "She'll be back one day. Happy and smiling like always. Nobody who was born and raised on the slopes of the

Rocky Mountains can stay away forever. She'll be back, and she'll probably bring somebody with her," her father concluded at the family dinner after having said their good-byes.

"I would like to see that," Jeremiah grinned wildly. "That son of a bitch is going to have to prove himself worthy."

"Not everything is decided with fists," said Pete, the family intellectual.

"True, but if you can't back your words with fists, you can't stay in Montana."

"Take it easy, kids. She just left. It's going to be slow and lonely without her."

*　　*　　*

Chicago is a strange city. It has a lot going against it, and almost nothing for it. First, there is the climate—a terrible climate with cold, windy winters and hot, steamy summers full of humidity and mosquitoes. One of the biggest cities in the world, Chicago is full of the vices that are a part of every megalopolis—crime, drugs, and prostitution. However, everyone who comes to Chicago is captivated by something magical within its embrace. Nowhere in the world can a person make more friends, and at the same time be so lonely. Although June had received many attractive offers from different medical centers, she decided to stay there upon finishing her studies. She never regretted it.

She finished in record time. She couldn't say that she had studied very hard. She simply had a great time. Just like some people enjoy collecting stamps, fishing, or rock climbing, June enjoyed learning about the human body. She was fascinated by psychiatry and surgery—psychiatry for the secrets of the human soul, and surgery for the secrets of the human body. By the end of her education, she had her own view of medicine. Some of them weren't necessarily backed up with science, but she was convinced that a psychiatrist had to know the most, and that a surgeon could help the most. She was convinced that everything was in the mind—in sickness and health, happiness or sadness, satisfaction or depression. She was surprised to discover that ninety percent of all people were not satisfied with their looks, and the other ten percent lied. Some wished their noses were a bit shorter, narrower, wider, their ears smaller, their breasts higher or larger. Some wanted to be a bit thinner, some a bit bigger. At the end of her studies, she knew she wanted to specialize in cosmetic surgery. When she picked up the scalpel for the first time, she thought that it would be the easiest thing to do and that anyone could do it, similar to watching a top figure skater on the ice. Everything looks so simple and natural, as if anyone could duplicate the movements. But it is only when one actually stands on the ice that they realize just how difficult those simple-looking moves truly are.

For her specialization, she was accepted to a famed Chicago clinic. She had her own method of preparing her patients. In the first stage, she tried to get into the mind of her patients. She carefully studied their files—occupations, hobbies, favorite colors, and a lot of other, apparently unimportant, information. She made sketches, studied photos from their youth, and compared them with the way they currently looked. The actual surgery was the last stage of an extensive process.

There is such a thing as a face without character. Technically speaking, there is nothing wrong with such a face: the nose, eyebrows, mouth, eyes, everything is exactly as it should be. However, there is something is missing, almost as if their personality was somehow erased, and only the waxen face of a mannequin remained. June was successful in her attempts not to destroy or change the physiognomy or the character of the face. She quickly became well-known and highly regarded.

Physically, June was perhaps the average American girl, perhaps a bit more attractive. It didn't matter if she wore jeans or an evening gown; her feminine figure was not to be hidden. Her face was not as beautiful as it was interesting. It was the most interesting thing about her. Thin eyebrows with small wrinkles in the middle of her forehead set off her beautiful, sea-green eyes. Her nose was long and straight. Full lips, a chin that projected slightly forwards, and high cheekbones, made up her visage. Her face was framed by long, hazel-brown hair, which fell over her shoulders. It was the kind of face that artists could observe for hours on end, and always find something new.

She spent most of her time at the hospital. In her free time, she read medical magazines. Like thousands of other people, she regularly went jogging along the shores of Lake Michigan. Every once in a while, she would treat herself to a Chicago Bulls game. They say there are fewer and fewer people in America that are believers. Such is not the case for Chicago. Absolutely, everybody firmly and resolutely believed in the Bulls.

June also loved music, any music. Perhaps she loved classical music more than rock or blues, but only a bit more. She was proud of her CD collection, especially her foreign music. "I'm going to the gas station," she would say when it was time for her to go visit her family in Montana. That was truly what her visits were like: filling up the tank of her car. She couldn't function without them. Those visits became holidays for everybody. She was like a tender shoot that got all its strength from her large and powerful family tree. Her entire family would wait for her arrival, and afterwards would see her off, all the while expecting to hear something about her coming back home for good.

"One way ticket?" her father would ask.

"Not yet," June would answer.

And all the talk about her eventual return home would be over with that short question and even shorter answer.

Men would come into her life from time to time. They were short-term relationships, after which she would appreciate her freedom even more. From childhood, she could not tolerate anyone setting limits for her. Invariably, all of her relationships would eventually reach the point of "you should" and "you could" conversations. No, her freedom was much more precious. She was preoccupied with her job so much that she didn't feel ready for any kind of a serious relationship. That spring of 1996, at the concert in Ravinia, she saw a strange young man. She would think of him once in a while, probably because his scar had seemed so cruel and contradictory to the tear that had rolled down his face, belying the apparent image of toughness. She would love to be able to see the left side of his face. The picture would probably be completely different. During that summer, she had the feeling that she had seen him a few times along the beaches of Lake Michigan. However, every time she would finally manage to make her way through the crowd, he would be gone. Or perhaps it was never him to begin with.

*   *   *

The days were getting very warm. Hamza loved to go to the beaches of Lake Michigan. He felt good surrounded by so many relaxed people. He would usually go to one end of the beach, just near the jogging trail, sit on the hot cement, and put his feet in the water. He would smoke, drink a Coke, and stare at the water, thinking about nothing in particular. Since the start of the war, he had been practicing how to escape reality. In the beginning, it seemed impossible. Try as he might, his thoughts would always return to the very things he tried not to think about. With time, he was able to push the negative thoughts aside. They would shut off, letting the thoughts simply float away like hot air balloons. They would bounce off each other, barely touching the issues he didn't want to think about, and then float away. He felt that all the negative information was being stored somewhere in his head, and he would inevitably explode one day.

Perhaps one day, but not today.

On a particularly hot day, Hamza took off his shirt. He soon noticed that people were staring at him and whispering. His face, the long scar along his chest and back were drawing attention. Hamza got dressed and left the beach. He didn't return for days, and never again took his shirt off in a public area.

In July, Hamza figured out that he really needed a car and that it was about time to stop the masochistic walks, as well as the forays by train and bus. He had been thinking about a car since winter. Money wasn't a problem. Besides his regular income, he also had the money he had brought from Sarajevo, and he lived extremely modestly. Besides the rent, he had almost no other expenses. Food was cheap, and he mostly ate at home. He smoked a lot, but that wasn't a big expense either. After a while, he had over ten thousand dollars in his account.

While money wasn't an issue, Big Mike and his gang were. Since the night they beat him up, he hadn't had any major problems with them. Once or twice a month they would stop him, and he would have to give them all the money he had on him. But, except for a few smacks, they no longer troubled him. Don't Worry Andy suggested he move to a better neighborhood, but Hamza liked the apartment, and more than the apartment, Hamza liked Don't Worry Andy, his Mary, their friendship, and unobtrusive kindness. He especially loved the way they treated each other. On the surface, it looked as if the woman nagged and forever started small, senseless arguments. But looking past the surface, he saw an enormous love between them. From time to time, the three of them would have dinner together. Hamza had consciously avoided any bonding with people and, as much as possible, tried to avoid those dinners as well. When he had no choice, he would sit with them, forgetting Bosnia, and everything else, and enjoy an ordinary American dinner.

He knew that no matter which car he bought, Big Mike and the others were going to steal it or break into it the very same night. He looked around the used-car dealerships and, in mid-July, found what he was looking for. In a western suburb, a few miles out of Chicago, Hamza found a large dealership for new and used cars. As he slowly walked between the cars, a salesman approached.

"Good morning. It's a beautiful day."

"It sure is."

"If you tell me what you're interested in, maybe I can help you."

"I'm just looking around. I'd like to buy a car."

"Good for you. Good for you. Are you interested in a new or used one?"

"I really don't know."

"If you would like a new car, we have very good rates on Fords. 1.9 to 4.9 percent financing, and we have a big selection of used cars too. You can see here, there's a Taurus, an Explorer . . ."

Hamza had already seen the old pickup truck at the end of the lot. He slowly approached the truck while talking to the salesman. The truck looked like it had spent the whole war on Mt. Igman. It was of a strange, ambiguous brown color that couldn't have looked good even new. The doors were extremely rusted with a couple of holes. It was a miracle the door would stay closed at all. The fenders had rusted-out holes in them the size of a fist. All in all, it was a piece of junk that should have gone to the wreckers a long time ago. The thing that attracted Hamza's attention were the new tires and exhaust on it. It appeared that somebody had taken care of it.

"Does it run?" Hamza cut the chattering salesman off mid-sentence.

"If you mean can it start? Yes, it can. All vehicles here are in running condition. But, I can't guarantee you that it can run more than a few miles."

"How much do you want for it?"

The salesman glared at Hamza with an insulted look on his face. Even if he sold him the truck, his commission couldn't be more than fifty dollars.

"I don't know, I have to take a look in the book."

"Then let's take a look."

They went into his office. The salesman looked through his books for a long time and finally at Hamza.

"Two thousand dollars."

Hamza laughed. "You have to be joking."

"Well, I don't know, but that's what it says here."

"Could you look a little more carefully?"

"I'll check with my boss." The salesman left. He came back after a few minutes.

"You were right. I checked with my boss. He said he could give it to you for one thousand six hundred."

"Let me give you my offer. Four hundred and fifty dollars. Cash, right here, right now."

"That's very little. I don't know . . ."

"Can I talk to your boss for a minute?"

"Probably. Come with me."

The boss was a textbook example of an American businessman. Young, healthy, with a wide smile, white teeth, and a tan. He looked as if he had just come back from the Carribean. When the salesman told him what Hamza's offer was, he turned very serious.

"That's not enough."

"Please, can you tell me how long it's been standing over there?"

"Well, not too long."

"Let me show you something. There's grass growing around the wheels, which means it was here last summer too."

"All right. What's your best offer? I just can't give it to you for $450."

"$520, right now, cash."

"Sold! Get him a receipt. But, you need to know that we can't give you any guarantee on it."

"Of course. Thank you. You made a good deal."

The boss shook his hand reluctantly.

When he had signed the contract, Hamza came out with the keys. The interior of the truck wasn't as bad as he thought. The seats were torn, but not rotten. He put the key into the ignition, but it wouldn't start. He went into the office again and asked the salesman to give him jumper cables. The salesman smirked with mean, personal satisfaction, but came out to help him anyway. The truck started, and Hamza pulled out and headed toward home. On his way, he stopped at a local service station to change the oil, spark plugs, cables, and belts. The old mechanic asked him how much he had paid for the truck. When Hamza told him, he looked at the truck and then told Hamza he had gotten a good deal—as long as he was not interested in appearances, of course. Then he added that the car could go for another fifty thousand miles without any major repairs.

Three days later, coming home from work, he ran into Big Mike. As before, they took his money and a carton of cigarettes. One of Mike's buddies gave him back one pack, to have for the night.

"So, you have new wheels?" Hamza looked at them silently. "You know what, Black Soul, you're not as crazy as some think. You bought some good wheels. The thing runs, and nobody is going to steal it. There is nothing to steal from the inside or the outside. You're not crazy."

The truck ran great. It could go over eighty miles per hour without a problem. However, it was, hands down, the ugliest vehicle on the streets of Chicago.

*   *   *

All the inhabitants of Chicago, long-time residents as well as the newcomers, agreed that the fall was the most beautiful time of the year in their city. The temperature would drop significantly, yet remain pleasantly warm. The humidity would disappear and even the mosquitoes would go away. The countless parks in Chicago would change color day by day, from a tired green to a soft yellow, red, and maroon. The leaves fell and the wind danced them around the streets. The social and cultural life, slowed by the blistering Chicago sun, would begin to wake. While nature began preparations for its winter hibernation, people were getting ready for new events. The concert season began. Concert sponsors made every effort to supply both their regular and occasional visitors with the concert schedule for the fall and winter season. June spent several days enjoying the process of picking out the ones she wanted to attend.

*   *   *

Hamza was surprised to find an envelope addressed to him. Nobody knew his address. It was the program for the fall-winter concert season. Hamza remembered having given them his address when he had made the ticket reservation. They had sent him a program because he was a potential concertgoer. "Look at that! There's somebody out there to write to the colonel." He was surprised to find that the letter had actually made him happy. He looked through the program carefully. Most of the best-known names from the world of music were on the list. Finally, he made up his mind and circled two concerts. The first one was in September. It was the Chicago Philharmonic Orchestra.

The Chicago Symphony Auditorium was already full when Hamza arrived. He had spent a long time looking for a place to park at. "The best business in Chicago is owning a few acres of land and building a parking lot," Hamza concluded as he finally found a parking spot a few blocks away from the concert hall. The concert started, and he had to repeatedly excuse himself as he squeezed his way to his seat. While the people were standing up to let him by, he noticed a young woman who looked at him with particular interest. Hamza went out of his way to excuse himself to her.

"I do apologize."

"Never mind, we're all late sometimes," the girl answered without taking her eyes off of him.

"Maybe there's something wrong with me?" Hamza thought. He smiled to himself. "But of course there's something wrong with you, Hamza. Never let yourself forget."

As the conductor came out onto the stage, the musicians stood up. The audience applauded. Hamza joined the applause. The concert was performed to absolute perfection. The conductor was outstanding, the musicians excellent. Almost all throughout the concert, Hamza could feel the young woman looking at him. When he would turn around, their eyes would meet for a second, and then the young woman would return her eyes to the stage. After the concert had ended, June looked around and searched for the young man with the scar on his face. Where had he gone? She thought about talking to him for a bit. Hamza had left via the aisle on the other side and had disappeared into the crowd.

June swore that he wouldn't get away the next time. If she ever saw him again, that was. That night, she dreamed of performing surgery on several patients, all of them had the same long, disfiguring scar on their faces.

*   *   *

Hamza finally settled down with a company that processed plastic components. He worked as a maintenance mechanic. A little bit of experience in fixing things, together with his natural intelligence, helped him adjust to the job quickly. He soon became one of the most reliable workers in the company. The employees were a bit reserved towards him, but he didn't care much for their company anyway. That isolation suited him just fine. During the working hours, he dedicated himself to fixing and studying the machines. The days passed by quickly, in a monotonous way, and it seemed as if every other day was Friday. Voluntary isolation from the world and long hours of being alone hadn't left a mark on his soul. At least not yet.

The rare article about Bosnia in Chicago newspapers didn't leave any room for optimism. Anytime he read one of those articles, he would become depressed for several days. Although he deliberately avoided people, he had managed somehow to make a few true friends. One of them was Ekrem, a soldier from Kozarac, a little village in northwestern Bosnia, which became well-known during the war when the Chetniks slaughtered nearly all of its inhabitants. Hamza had found out about him in *Zambak,'* a magazine published locally by a group of Bosnian enthusiasts in Chicago. Ekrem was a survivor of the Chetnik concentration camp "Manjaca"." Every once in a while, Hamza would stop by Ekrem's apartment, where he lived with his mother, wife, and son. His son was two years old when the Chetniks had captured them and hauled them off to the concentration camp. He now attended second grade and was one of the best students in school.

Ekrem had been captured in battle. The fighting had been going on at such a rapid pace that he had forgotten to save the last bullet for himself. In the camp, the Chetniks had exterminated all men in Ekrem's family, in ways known only to them. One day, while in an extremely "good mood," the Chetniks had lined the people up in front of the barracks. They took ten men and liquidated them immediately, with shots to the head. The others were made to watch. Then they took Ekrem.

"Now you're going to see a Balija scum Muslim die slowly."

First, they broke his ribs with the blunt side of an axe. When he had fallen, they sliced him up. He instinctively held on to the worst cuts. Together with the executed prisoners, he lay the whole day in front of the barracks. At dusk, a group of prisoners was sent to remove the corpses to the back of the camp. Two days later, another group of prisoners was to bury them. Carrying his body, one of the prisoners noticed that Ekrem had twitched his eyelids. They asked one of the "good" guards to let them take him inside. They would pay him, of course.

"With what, when we've taken everything from you?"

"New guys arrived. We have about two hundred marks and a watch."

"Take him." The "good" guard let them take Ekrem back to the barracks.

Ekrem told Hamza that his friends urinated on his wounds to sterilize them, since they didn't have anything else. God himself wanted him to survive. To this day, he doesn't like doctors. He says that all doctors are Chetniks. In the Manjaca camp, a Serb doctor used to pick out prisoners in bad condition, and send them to be "cured." He would kill them himself. Ekrem had refused to go for a physical examination in the U.S. until they found a Bosnian doctor in the Bosnian Refugee Center, who had also survived a concentration camp. The doctor had survived a camp run by the Croats.

Ekrem was a living corpse when the Chetniks exchanged him for their soldiers. For the next two weeks—in the hospital in Zenica, a town near Sarajevo—the doctors struggled to keep him alive. Now he was in the U.S. and received a long-term disability pension. One part of his brain was slowly dying from the blows that he had received. When the weather began to change, every part of his body would ache. The pain would get so bad that he couldn't so much as stand up. When the weather was stable, he could work and earn a few dollars here and there. He worked for what he called "a good Croatian guy." Ekrem was an artisan—a ceramics expert—before the war. If he was lucky, he could now manage to work five or six days a month. The Croat boss paid him well—ten dollars an hour. At least this way he could earn some extra money for cigarettes. He would send part of the money to the Bosnian army but didn't want his wife and mother to know. They pretended they didn't know. Ekrem said that the West was not satisfied with having allowed and assisted the Chetniks to kill Muslims. He said that the West was giving them the title to their property.

The right to take everything that belonged to the expelled and murdered Muslims.

He claimed the West had given the Chetniks the title for his house and his grandfather's fields.

He said the West had given the Chetniks the title for his uncle's barns and cows.

He said the West had given the Chetniks the title of his sister's dowry.

He said, "Fuck the West!"

God willing, there would be war. Ekrem would go back to Bosnia.

In the spring of 1997, Ekrem returned to Bosnia with his family. Until then, he had been a refugee in the U.S. He was now a refugee in his own country. His village, Kozarac, was under Serbian regime, according to the decision of the great powers, which rewarded genocide.

*   *   *

October was beautiful. It seemed as if the Indian summer had decided to stay in Chicago forever. Long, warm days wandered around the alleys, boulevards, and avenues. Nature had settled down, awaiting colder days, and everything seemed to be in a state of foggy expectation. The people of Chicago tried to use every sunny hour, knowing the cold and the long winter was inevitably coming. The streets were always crowded, and along the shore, there were thousands of people of all ages jogging every day. It was especially crowded on weekends. Hamza would come to the lake around noon. He liked to go to the end of the beach, where the trail ended and the beach began. He would sit on the warm cement, put his feet in the water, and smoke while drinking his Coke. Behind him, people jogged, rollerbladed, and rode bikes.

Looking at the water in front of him, Hamza felt alone in the world. That Sunday in early October, Hamza felt a bit melancholic, so he let his thoughts fly freely, and, with the speed of light, they returned to Bosnia. This time of the year, the big oak tree in front of the Bey's mosque was losing its leaves, as were the chestnuts in the main city park. Tito and Vasa Miskin Streets were full of people walking. Old married couples holding hands would be walking slowly and elegantly. They would stop from time to time to greet other also older married couples. Young mothers pushed their babies in strollers, constantly fussing about them. The fathers looked after the older child, always running away and disappearing into the crowd. Lovebirds were walking, hugging, and holding each other. They would stop by the store windows to look around, and kiss each other once more. At the cemetery on Kovaci, spouses, grandmothers, mothers, and sisters of dead soldiers would be tending the graves of their loved ones and whispering prayers.

*   *   *

"Excuse me!" somebody tapped his shoulder.

Those two words, said quietly, burst like an explosion in his head. Hamza, startled by the sudden intrusion and the return to reality, almost fell into the water

The girl apprehensively moved away. Hamza stood to his full height.

"I'm sorry, I didn't mean to frighten you."

"No, no, I'm sorry I startled you!" the girl stammered.

"I do apologize, you took me by surprise."

"It was my fault."

Hamza looked at her more closely this time. Her face seemed familiar, especially her eyes. Surely he'd seen those eyes elsewhere . . . He couldn't remember where, but he was sure he had seen her before. The girl wore sweatpants, while the guy she ran with wore shorts and a T-shirt.

"Do we know each other?" he asked.

"Well, not really. I've seen you at the concerts a couple of times, but I don't think you've noticed me."

"Actually, I think I have." Hamza remembered the girl who had kept looking at him during the concert.

"Should we move to the side a bit?" The other joggers were forced to go around them, and kept bumping into the people running from the opposite direction. Hamza picked up his shoes, and they walked onto the beach.

"It's a beautiful day," June said.

"Yes, a fine Indian Summer."

"Are we going to go on?" asked the guy impatiently. He had been jogging in place the whole time. Hamza looked at him more carefully. He was a bit taller than Hamza, and at least a dozen pounds heavier. His hair cut perfectly, with a clean business look, dripped with sweat. He was strong, with well-defined muscles, broad shoulders, and a broad chest. He had a high forehead and dark, determined eyes. While speaking, he showed his strong, white teeth. Hamza perceived him as the stereotypical American dream. From his war experience, he knew this was the type who snapped first. Guys like this one—strong, young, healthy, extremely honest, with strong moral principles—shattered like icicles when faced with the cruel reality of war.

"So, you're jogging?" Hamza asked, just for the sake of continuing the conversation with this enigmatic woman who stood measuring him with her unforgettable eyes.

"Yes, the weather is beautiful."

"Maybe you should try running a bit instead of smoking. Cigarettes are bad for your health," advised the young Apollo.

"Snipers are bad for your health," Hamza returned, not recalling anybody who had died of cigarettes, but many who had died at the hands of snipers.

"Excuse me?" The face of the young was often a billboard advertisement for their lack of information.

"Never mind. I was talking to myself."

"All smokers are the same. Smoking is a sign of insecurity and weak character."

"Hey, JK!" the girl tried to protect Hamza.

"No, no. Do you know how many people die each year from cigarettes?"

The girl looked at her running partner disapprovingly. Hamza looked at him, narrowing his eyes. He had the desire to smash that perfect creature that radiated health, intelligence, and sweat.

"Less than ten percent, in any case." During the war in Bosnia almost ten percent of the Muslim population was killed.

"Excuse me? I don't catch your drift."

"I didn't expect you to. I don't run if I don't have to. But in any case, I think I am still faster than you."

"Huh! That'll be the day!" The young man looked at him, suspiciously.

"Would you care to race?"

"Please! This is pointless," the girl interjected.

"We don't have to do anything protracted, just to the lake. You see those two sitting next to the water? First to the towel wins, okay?"

"Are you serious?"

"Would you give us the start signal?" Hamza turned to the girl. "And please look after my shoes. The winner buys lunch. Deal?"

"You mean the loser?"

"No, it wouldn't be fair to you." Hamza took a drag of his cigarette, and put it out in the sand. "Ready?"

The girl stepped to the side.

"Ready? Go!"

They ran. JK, as if on a racetrack—slightly bent, widely spreading his arms in the run—ran forward using long strides. Hamza ran bent over. His chest almost parallel to the ground, he pushed off with his legs as if trying to jump, and would certainly fall flat on his face if he didn't place his other leg down just in the nick of time.

After only the first ten yards, he knew that he would win.

215

"Well, Apollo," he thought to himself with a vicious grin, "you've obviously never run the one-hundred-meter sniper dash."

At the finish line, some forty-five yards away, Hamza beat his opponent by nearly two yards. He touched the towel and turned to JK.

"Congratulations!" JK shook Hamza's hand firmly. "But nevertheless . . . ," he breathed loudly, "nevertheless, what I said about cigarettes still stands."

Hamza patted him on the back.

"I repeat, snipers are dangerous, cigarettes are not."

They walked back to the girl.

"Hey, JK, maybe you should start smoking."

"I have to go back to the hospital. I'm sorry about lunch," JK shook Hamza's hand.

"It was my pleasure. Maybe, we'll have a rematch?"

"I'm always here when the weather is nice."

June was about to say that this wasn't true, since she'd been looking for him all summer, but she stopped herself in time. JK ran off down the trail. The two of them were quiet for a second.

* * *

"Well?"

"Lunch?"

"Sure, if you too don't have to go back to the hospital."

"How do you know I work in a hospital?"

"I assumed he was your colleague."

"Correct, but no, I don't have to go to the hospital."

"My truck is a bit north of here."

"We can take my car. It's right here on Huron."

"Okay." Hamza put his shoes back on, and they walked down the trail. Hamza walked while she ran, sometimes a bit ahead of him, sometimes a bit behind. They walked underneath Lake Shore Drive, the street running along the lake, from north to south, and separating the shore from the rest of the city. They soon arrived at her car. It was a small sports car, a gentle green object shining in the sun.

"Beautiful car."

"It's not beautiful, but thanks, anyway."

"It is a beautiful car."

"You can't buy a beautiful car for $14,000," June chuckled wryly.

"Maybe you should try buying one for $500?"

"Are you kidding me? The tires cost more than that."

"I'm not kidding. I'll show it to you one day."

"Five hundred dollars? Really?"

"Well, actually, it was $520."

"I never even heard of such a thing. You want to take this one for a ride?"

"I'd like to try."

"Okay. Let me just get changed."

June jumped into the backseat. She took off the top part of her tracksuit and wrapped a towel around herself. She put a shirt on over her head and took her bra off with her hands beneath the shirt. Checking to make sure that Hamza wasn't looking through the rearview mirror, she changed, slipping into a pair of jeans.

"All ready!" she said, jumping into the front seat.

"Ready." Hamza started the car, backed up in order to get out of the parking spot, shifted into first gear, and stepped on the gas. The tires squealed, and the car launched forward. Hamza shifted the car through the second and third gears, keeping up the pressure on the gas. They were already going seventy mph. Hamza eased off the gas pedal and slowed down to twenty-five mph.

"Phew," June breathed a sigh of relief.

"I told you this was a good car." Hamza was satisfied with the way the car performed on the road.

"Maybe you have never driven a real sports car."

"The last one I drove was a Ferrari."

"What kind of a Ferrari?"

"A red one. A Ferrari has to be red in order to be a Ferrari."

"Really? How about a Jaguar?"

"That has to be silver, and a Mercedes must be black."

"Black?"

"Black."

"Are you some kind of a lord?"

"My family used to be Beys."

"Beys? What is that?"

"Something like a lord."

"Are you serious?"

"Yeah, always."

"Where are we going?" June wiped her wet curls with the towel.

"Not far, Giordano's. The restaurant is good, and you can smoke too."

June laughed. "I know. I like the place, too, though I don't smoke. Where did you learn how to drive stick?"

"Where I come from, all cars are stick."

"So, where do you come from?"

"Bosnia."

"Bosnia? Wasn't there a war going on over there?"

"Yeah."

"Were you in the war?"

"Yes."

"That scar? Is it from the war?"

"Yes."

"I'm sorry. I ask too many questions."

"That's okay."

"How long have you been here?"

Hamza smiled.

"Well, I have to talk about something!"

"It's all right. Almost a year."

"Your English is perfect."

"It's my native language."

"So, where are your parents from?"

"My mother is from the United States."

"Okay, but where in the U.S.?"

"I don't know, she never told me."

Hamza found a parking spot, right in front of the restaurant.

"You're lucky. I never manage to find a spot."

"Yeah, lucky."

They entered, and the waiter led them to a table in the smoking section.

"The largest pizza there is, with all the toppings, just no pork."

"No pork?" June raised her eyebrows.

"My religion . . ."

"What are you?"

"Muslim."

"Muslims don't eat pork?"

"No."

"Why not?"

"Does anybody ask Robert De Niro or Michael Jackson why they don't eat one kind of meat or another? Muslims avoid eating just one kind of meat and everybody asks why. We just don't and that's that."

"All right, jeez. Why so defensive?"

"I'm sorry. Muslims don't eat pork because it's prohibited in the Qur'an. It's not for us to figure out why. There is definitely a reason for these prohibitions. The same thing goes for gold."

"What do you mean?"

"Men are prohibited from wearing gold."

"What does that have to do with anything?"

"I guess there is a connection. A couple of years ago, the Swiss discovered that gold causes prostate infections and possibly cancer."

"Really? I didn't know that. But nobody puts as much gold on themselves as the Arabs do, all those rings and chains. They look like Christmas trees. Aren't they Muslim too?"

"They're Muslim too."

"Then I don't get it."

"There is nothing not to get. Most people take what they like from religion, including the Arabs. In fact, the biggest crimes in history were committed in God's name. So what?"

"Well, nothing. It's just kind of funny."

"What, the crimes committed in God's name?"

"No, that we're chatting like old friends."

Hamza shrugged his shoulders.

"And you don't even know my name."

"I am Hamza."

"I know. I heard you when you introduced yourself to JK."

"So, what's your name?"

"You'll laugh."

219

"No, I won't."

"Promise?"

"I promise."

"June."

"June?"

"Yes, June."

"Were you born in June?"

"No, in January."

"Um, you're going to have to explain that one."

"Why June? I've asked my father the same thing."

"And?"

"And, he said that January wasn't an appropriate name for a girl."

"It's not a what?" Hamza's lips quirked into a hardly noticeable smile. He struggled to contain the laughter bubbling up inside of him, for fear of offending this American woman with an odd name, but his shoulders began shaking, at first only a little bit, and then more and more visibly, until he burst out laughing. He laughed long and hard. When he saw an insulted look on her face, he started laughing even more. He hadn't laughed out loud in a long time. For years, his happy, humorous side had remained closed off from the terrors of the war. Once the shell cracked, it was hard to contain it.

"I'm sorry. I'm sorry, please . . ." tears were flowing from his, eyes and he grabbed a glass of water that stood on the table. He tried to drink it fast, in order to stop the laughter, but ended up spilling it all over his face and shirt instead. This only prolonged his laughter, as he laughed at himself, the name June, the absurdity of hate and war.

"Serves you right," June said, still feeling insulted.

"I'm sorry. It's rare that I break a promise."

The waiter brought the pizza, and they started eating.

"So, where are you from?"

"From the U.S."

"All right, come on. That's enough."

"Montana."

"The Rockies and the prairie?"

"Bingo!"

"That's good."

"Not good enough."

"So, did you run to Chicago or did you catch a plane?"

"Very funny . . ." It was plainly obvious that Hamza would have to earn June's forgiveness.

"Really, what are you doing here?"

"I work in a hospital."

"Ah. Have you been in Chicago for very long?"

"Almost ten years."

"Do you like it?"

"Do *you* like it?"

"All I know about America is Chicago. I'm tired of this flat land."

"Are there mountains in Bosnia?"

"Absolutely! It's all hills and mountains. We had the Winter Olympics in our country."

"I can faintly remember something about that. I was a kid then. You would like Montana, then. Mountains, rivers, and lakes . . ."

" . . . and pretty girls."

"Thank you."

"For what?"

"Nothing."

At some point Hamza looked at his watch. "Wow! Time really flies. I think it's time for us to go."

"Do you want me to drive you to your car?"

"That's all right, I'll walk."

On the street, June got into her car and rolled down the window.

"See you."

"See you."

She stepped on the gas and pulled away. Hamza began walking in the opposite direction.

About fifty yards down the road, June stepped on the brakes. "Shit! Shit, shit!" She hit the wheel with her fists. "'See you?' How am I going to see him when I didn't even get his phone number? He didn't ask for mine either." She hit the wheel hard one more time.

"Never mind. I'll find him. When it is time, I will find him."

Her odds were a mere one in eight million.

*   *   *

Next Sunday, the weather remained sunny. Hamza came to the lake, and as usual, sat, took off his shoes, put his feet into the water, drank his Coke, and lit a cigarette. Occasionally, he would turn around, but June was nowhere to be seen. She was at the hospital that Sunday. Tired of looking around, Hamza returned to staring at the water. He hadn't talked with anybody the way he had with her in a long time. She was interesting, and they had hit it off as if they had known each other for years. She was outgoing, open, and somehow his. He smiled inside. Maybe he'd see her at the concert. The only problem was that there were nearly ten concerts in Chicago every day. Should he look for her in the hospital? Nah. If she had wanted to, she would have given him her phone number. Still, he would like to talk to her again. He didn't want to think about how he had laughed out loud for the first time in an eternity. June? A strange name, but maybe his name seemed strange to her too. "Excuse me." Somebody tapped him on the shoulder. This time Hamza remained calm. He learned that lesson the last time. He smiled and turned around.

*   *   *

He found himself face to face with an old, well-dressed gentleman who stood looking down at him. He wore a khaki suit, a sandy brown shirt, and a tie with a green design. His hat was the same color as the suit, and struggled to contain his long white hair, which jutted out from beneath it. He looked like an aged Lawrence of Arabia.

"Don't worry, young man, she will be here. Maybe not today, but she will definitely be here again."

Hamza got up. He looked at the old gentleman, confused about how he had read his mind.

"Excuse me?"

"Allow me to introduce myself. Mark H. Simon. My friends call me 'the Colonel.'"

"I am Hamza. Nice to meet you."

"Come again?"

"My name's Hamza."

"I'm sorry I am approaching you so directly."

"No problem."

"You know, I live in that building over there." The old gentleman pointed to the building across the street. The old, exclusive building shone with elegance and dignity. Hamza quickly estimated that an apartment in that building must cost over a million dollars. "The tenth floor, balcony without flowers."

"Yes, I see it."

"It's not that I don't like flowers, just that there is too much work to do with them. And I forget sometimes . . . Shall we walk?"

Hamza nodded and put on his shoes.

"I have a rather ugly hobby, you know. As you can see, I am old and can't go out as much as I used to. Yeah, I go for a walk every day, especially now that the heat has gone. During the summers, however, I go out only when it gets really dark, once the heat lets up. It's a lot more comfortable to sit in a room with the air conditioning on."

"You were talking about a hobby?"

"Yes, yes. I forget things sometimes. I almost started talking about something entirely different. Yes, that hobby of mine. Somebody might think it's a bit odd . . ."

"From your appearance and the look in your eyes, I don't think anybody could say there was anything odd about you."

"Thank you, young man. It is nice to hear that. Anyway, my hobby is to look out my window onto the beach, with binoculars. Well, actually, it is a telescope. I have binoculars too, but I can't see the details through them."

"You look at the girls?"

"No, no" He chuckled, "At my age? Although, there are many beautiful girls, it seems to me that the older I get, the prettier the girls get. No, I don't look at the girls . . . Well, maybe sometimes. I look at people, situations. For example, a family comes to the beach. The mother changes into her bathing suit. Then the husband puts suntan lotion on her, and she settles herself into her position and instructs him on what to do. Of course, I don't hear what they're actually talking about, but I can tell by their gestures and facial expressions. Change the kid, put suntan lotion on him, don't look at those tramps, watch the kids, bring me a Coke, light me a cigarette . . . blah, blah, blah. There aren't that many real men."

"Oh, I don't know."

"I have been watching you almost all summer."

"Am I that interesting?"

"Yes, for a number of reasons. First, you're the only one wearing a jacket, and a military one at that. Don't you ever expose yourself to the sun?"

"Sometimes."

"Second, if you'll pardon my mentioning it, that scar of yours. It attracts attention."

"I can't do anything about it."

"Yes, of course. You see, Chicago is an enormous city, and there are many odd people in it. Soon enough, you get used to all the weirdoes, and they seem normal to you. There is this one guy who every day . . ."

"And the third reason?"

"Oh yes, the third reason. You have been either in jail or in war."

"How did you come to that conclusion?"

"Only people coming out of a prison or war can sit and stare at the water as much as you do."

"Huh?"

"I would say that you've come from war, one very far away. Your English confuses me, but I'm sure there is an explanation for that. Yes, I'd say that you've come from some war. That's where you got that scar. When you look at the water, smoke, and think about nothing, does it make you feel good?"

"You seem to know a lot. Like a guru."

"Ha! Know a lot? I didn't read it, young man, I lived it."

"What did you live?"

"That staring at the water. When I came back from the camp."

"What camp?"

"Korea. I was in that war, and then a prisoner in a prison camp. I acted just the way you do now. Did I miss anything?"

"Not really. I do come from war."

"The last war I know about was in Yugoslavia. Not including the East and Algeria. And by the way you look, I wouldn't say that you're from the Middle East."

"I come from Bosnia."

"You know young man, I would like to apologize on behalf of my country, if it means anything."

"Why? What for?"

"What we did, actually, what we didn't do in Bosnia, is a disgrace. I, as a citizen and a former officer of this country, am sincerely ashamed."

"There is no need for that. The others did worse, or didn't do anything. At least, America . . ."

"No, no, young man. America is America: the first, the greatest, the one and only. The biggest, the richest, the most beautiful, the strongest. My country, which I have, thank God, served my whole life. America: the last hope for people starving for freedom. My beloved America. All other countries are second-class players. Believe me, I am perfectly aware of our strength. I know what we are capable of doing. I know what we should have done, and didn't. I just pray that God, and your dead, will forgive us. Instead of stopping that Butcher of the Balkans, as one CNN reporter called him, within five days, we spent years debating whether our fear of a new Vietnam was justified. You see, that little dwarf, Vietnam, had stung us so bad we still haven't recovered. Additionally, the United States hasn't had a president like Washington, Roosevelt, or Lincoln for a long time. Anyway, if you have time, we could go to my place and have a cup of coffee."

As they were walking, they had already reached the colonel's building.

"That would be a pleasure."

The entrance to the building was also the entrance to a private parking lot. The security guard immediately came out of his booth when he saw Hamza.

"It's all right, he's with me."

"Of course. Good afternoon, Colonel."

Hamza was amazed at the colonel's apartment. It had a magnificent view of the endless blue waters of Lake Michigan.

"Would you like coffee or something else?"

"Coffee please."

While the colonel prepared coffee in the kitchen, Hamza looked around the room. The ceiling was very high for an apartment. Built into the wall next to the window was a huge fireplace, flanked by book-filled shelves on both sides. The other walls held a number of paintings. In the corner rested a large silken American flag. Hamza looked at the books. He had already seen many of them in Avdaga's library.

"We have the same library, Colonel," Hamza shouted to the old man still in the kitchen.

"Really? That's great. Nowadays, people usually read junk." The colonel entered the room, carrying coffee.

"Does the fireplace work?"

"Of course, it does." The colonel went to the fireplace and pressed a button. Cheerful flames began dancing immediately.

"Gas?"

"Yes. It would be a bit difficult to carry the wood up to the tenth floor every day and then take the ashes back down afterwards."

"I hadn't considered that."

"About those books, I tried reading romance novels a few times, just to see what it is that people like about them. I have never been able to read more than twenty pages."

"People like light stuff."

"Yes. Instant this and instant that. At some point, we lost contact with other people, with nature, and with humanity. I fear we are becoming an instant society more and more every day."

Hamza went to the bookshelf and took a book out at random: *The Roman Empire*.

"What do you think caused the fall of the Roman empire?" the colonel asked, recognizing the book from a distance.

"Well, let's see," Hamza coughed. For a long time, his conversations had been about food, work, and the weather. "I see it like this. The Roman empire, just like all empires before and after it—the Mongols, the Ottoman empire, the USSR—crumbled from within. Those were all strong empires, impervious to external threats. But just as in construction, a building can fall to the right or to the left, or it can come straight down. The latter usually happens when the base can't support the building. That is exactly what happened with the Roman empire and all the other empires that I've just mentioned."

"Very good, young man. The base couldn't support the building! Does that mean that the same problem threatens the U.S.? We are a big empire too, you know, though we are a democratic one."

"You caught me off guard. I wasn't thinking about that. Let's consider for a moment. The American governmental system makes it virtually impossible for the president or congress to gain too much power, since they are mutually dependent on each other. The term limit on the presidential office also doesn't allow for the creation of leaders like Mao Tse Tung, Tito, Stalin, Gadafi, or Castro. He can be the next Lincoln or Washington, but after eight years, he is history. On the other hand, the president has enough power to prevent the U.S. from becoming a bureaucratic state, where congress has all the power and the president is just a figurehead. After all, the biggest crime here is not paying taxes to the state. The state comes first, then everything else. Finally, in such a political framework, everything is subject to being proven in practice, from ideas to means of production to distribution. Looking at the United States from this rather simplified standpoint, I don't think that there is a danger of it collapsing from within."

The colonel looked at him with interest.

"I haven't heard something as brief and good as that about America in a long time. Even though it's superficial, it shines with optimism. I can't really reject anything you've said. I could add a bit here and there, especially regarding politics at the lower levels, but that wouldn't change your portrayal significantly. Yes, I, too, think that America has a good future in the next century. Our ancestors did a good job in laying the foundation of this country. I hope that future generations will know how to cherish and improve it. So, what do you think about Cuba?"

They talked late into the night. At some point during the evening, Hamza made "poor man's noodles'" using Dervo's recipe. Noodles, a bit of oil, and tomatoes. The colonel was fascinated. It was almost midnight when Hamza got up to leave.

"I almost forgot. About the girl . . ."

"What girl?"

"That girl of yours, the one I told you was going to come again. That was the reason I came downstairs in the first place."

"What about her?"

"I watched her the whole summer too. She would usually leave a bit before you'd arrive. It always seemed as if she was looking for something or somebody. And you know what? Trust my age and my military experience here, son; she has found precisely who she's looking for."

"You think?"

"I don't think. I know. Love is a strange thing. Well, now you know where I live. Just come and visit me anytime. I'm not inviting you to be polite. Really, do come."

"Will do. It was a real pleasure."

"The pleasure is all mine."

*   *   *

The bright early days of the Chicago winter were replaced by dark, gloomy days full of rain. The smell of snow was in the air. From time to time, Hamza would get homesick. There was nothing specific in his thoughts of Bosnia. It was more like a foggy feeling that he wasn't where he was supposed to be. One rainy November day, while he was in one such mood, he found himself near the restaurant "Jaran," whose owner was a man from Sarajevo. Hamza knew him from before. He entered, sat at the table, and ordered a Turkish coffee. Even though the "No Smoking" signs were clearly visible, everybody in the room was holding a cigarette. A young man talked about the need to vote in the elections that were going on in Bosnia. The way he stood and moved, his theatrical way of talking, the phrases that he used, and the constant gestures reminded Hamza of the activists in the County Councils in socialist times. Hamza found the guy's tone irritating.

"Calm down, Hamza, you came here to have a cup of coffee," he kept telling himself.

The young man talked about the "to be or not to be" for Bosnian Muslims, about the big opportunity to win the elections, about the democracy that was finally coming to Bosnia, about a fantastic political program that would change Bosnia and bring it shoulder-to-shoulder with Switzerland. When he started praising the SDA

("Party of Democratic Action") and listing all their merits, Hamza couldn't take it anymore.

"Take it easy, will you? I didn't come here for a political meeting, just to have a cup of coffee in peace, if I can."

As if he had been waiting for a comment like that, the young man got up and looked at Hamza. "You see what I'm talking about? He is one of those whose fault it is for this happening to us. You like it over here, huh? You don't care about our people suffering over there, do you? Our party bothers you? It doesn't bother you? Of course, it's easy for you to look at it from the outside and talk. Why didn't you pick up a gun and fight?"

"Are you done?" Hamza cut in. "Let me tell you something. Never mind who carried a gun. Whoever did, did! Tell me, have you heard of Haroon Al Rashid? You haven't? You little turd! Is there really a man who hasn't heard of the righteous leader of the faithful?"

"What did you say?"

Hamza didn't pay attention to his threatening tone of voice.

"Now, I'm going to teach you a little something. I won't charge you for this. 'Free of charge,' as Americans say. They say that a long time ago, there was a ruler in Baghdad named Haroon Al Rashid. He ruled for twenty-three years. From the age of twenty-six to forty-nine. History says that before and after him, there never was a more righteous ruler in the world. He used to dress like a beggar and go around the town. He would walk around poor neighborhoods, knock on rich men's doors, and listen to what people were saying. At every moment, he knew what was going on in his country, so he didn't have to rely on his ministers' reports. Good trick, huh? Even today, his name is a symbol of righteousness. Do you know what our leaders are going to be known for? For *not knowing*. For making out of the SDA, out of its historical role in the preservation and progress of Muslims in Bosnia, a party for the enrichment of a dozen people and their families. For profaning the idea of the first Muslim party since the Second World War to such an extent that they are going to lose the next election. For having, for the first time in the written history of the world, the slogan: 'Either honest incompetents or competent thieves.' And for choosing the 'competent' thieves.

"What are they thinking? That the people are that stupid? That we don't have honest and capable people among us? No, my brother, it just isn't so. We do have capable and honest people, but they don't want to play the way these bastards tell them to. Do you think that anybody cares that our intelligent young people are leaving the country every day? Nobody does. They don't need the smart ones. They only need the 'sheep,' the ones who will be obedient. Do you hear me? Obedient. If they continue that way, and it certainly seems that way, they are going to eat themselves up from the inside. Just like Tito said: 'The thugs from our own party are going to crush us.' And they did. The SDA is also going to be crushed like that, and without a party like the SDA, Bosnian Muslims are going to go through more suffering and massacres. Only next time it will be for good. And, as for the president . . ."

"Don't you dare attack the president!" the agitator screamed.

In the corner of the restaurant, a man sat alone, with his right arm unnaturally twisted. Hamza read the warrior history in his eyes as soon as he entered the restaurant. Likewise, the man had read the same thing in Hamza's. Now, the man rose.

"Don't interrupt, kid! Go on, man."

"What is our president going to be known for? Again, for not knowing! That's what he will be known for. He didn't know that there was going to be war? The Chetniks had settled in their tanks and sharpened their knives, and he told us there wasn't going to be a war. It takes two to have a war. That's true for a proper war. However, it only takes one to kill. He also didn't know that most of the people whom he had put in crucial positions were getting rich from the war. He didn't know what the humanitarian organizations were doing. He didn't know that the people in charge of humanitarian aid turned those organizations into aid and employment for their friends and families. He didn't know that the Chetniks were going to kill everybody in Srebrenica. He didn't know that those people needed help. He didn't know that the families of fallen soldiers didn't have anything to eat or that the disabled veterans of the war were starving. He didn't even know that the government spent so much money for its ministers to sleep in five-star hotels. They could have supported the families of the fallen soldiers and disabled veterans of the war. At least in Sarajevo. When, in the end, those poor, unfortunate souls came out onto the streets protesting, he said, 'I didn't know.' Can you believe it? He didn't know that his soldiers, disabled war veterans, people who had fought and defended the country of which he was president, didn't have any bread to eat?! What did he know? What the hell did he know?

"Recently, they've sent people from around the world to figure out where the money is disappearing to, the money that the world has been sending to Bosnia. And you know what he says? 'If the allegations of corruption are proven to be true, the government will blah, blah, blah . . ." If *what* is proven? What everybody knows already. That some ministers and people in charge, the ones whom he had put into those positions or had approved for those positions, came out of the war richer than the Rockefellers.

"But him? He didn't know! Bah! He didn't want to know. Aside from the defense of the country, nothing is more important than the families of the fallen and disabled veterans of war. Absolutely nothing! If, rather than going to one of his pointless meetings where he saw the same people over and over again, he had just gone to the home of one war veteran who had lost his legs on the mountains around Sarajevo, he could have found out everything. He would know the facts: what people thought and what needed to be changed. But he too thought that those people were stupid, and only he and his pals were smart. And he said it too. At one conference, he said, 'The smart ones will understand what we did, in three years. The others will never know' Well, it has been two years, and I still haven't understood anything. It must mean that I'm stupid. Well, that may be, but, I don't like anybody telling me that, especially not my president. And please let him explain just what that genius thing they did was, so that we, the stupid ones, can understand it too. What I do understand is this: two hundred thousand dead, maybe half a million wounded, and 1.2 million refugees. A burned and destroyed country, corruption and crime. Yeah. He will be remembered for not knowing."

"Do you think that our president steals?"

"I don't think so. I know that he doesn't steal. But, I also know that the newspapers have been writing for months about the criminal activities of individuals in the government. They even print their full names in the newspaper. What does the president do about it? Nothing. Not a goddamn thing! Well, someone should be going to prison. Either the journalists are lying in those articles or the ministers are stealing. Look at the system here. We're in America. Anything can happen until it reaches the media. Then you're screwed, whether you're the president or a refugee. That is a functioning legal system. And you? What are you getting upset about? Did you come to the U.S. at the beginning of the war, through the SDA, to study? Huh? To study English a bit, huh? Well, of course. That's why you're getting so upset. You've been here since 1992, and you still don't do anything? Am I right or what? The money that you brought from Bosnia lasted you a long time. Where did you get it? Did the SDA give it to you, or did you sell guns to the Chetniks? Now, you want to go back to Bosnia, but you need a reference. So you came to bullshit a bit here so that you could say that you were working on the elections in Chicago when you got back, huh?"

"How dare you say that?" the young man got up and started walking towards Hamza, threateningly.

"Hold it!" Hamza raised his voice a bit. "I'm going to be here for a while, drink my coffee, and go home. Now, you can go back to your table and everything can stay cool, or you can come here. In that case, they are going to carry you out of here. It's your choice."

The young man looked around, looking for support from the others, then reluctantly returned to his table. Trying to save face, he pointed his finger at Hamza.

"You'd better leave. And never come back."

The young handicapped guy in the corner got up.

"If somebody is leaving, it's going to be you. Get out!"

The waiter came between them.

"Take it easy, guys. We don't want any trouble."

"You get your ass back to the bar. And you, you little fuck, get out! Now!"

In the sudden silence, Hamza finished his coffee. He paid and approached the guy in the corner.

"Where are you from?"

"Krajina."

"Dudakovic's Fifth Corps?"

"The Heaven's Power!"

"I'm glad to meet you. See you again."

"Just stop by. I'm always here. And don't be afraid. If anybody so much as says a word . . ."

"I'll talk to you."

"Can I tell you something? Don't take it out on the old man. He doesn't have it easy either."

"I know he doesn't. Sometimes I just lose it. But, fuck, do we have it easy? Look at you, look at me, look at those guys from the Seventh Muslim Brigade! What are we doing in the U.S.? It was his job to take care of us."

"He can't do it by himself. Look at the guys around him."

"Well, I told you about Haroon Al Rashid, a minute ago."

"See ya."

Hamza came out of the restaurant with a bitter taste in his mouth. "What just happened to me? Well, it happened and it's over now."

After that, however, he rarely frequented places where Bosnians gathered.

*   *   *

Over the next few months, Hamza saw June regularly. Usually at noon on Sundays, he would walk down Michigan Avenue and run into her at the corner of Ohio or Huron. If one of them was busy on one Sunday, they would definitely meet on the following one. They would walk for a while, June would do some shopping, and then they would go to one of Chicago's many restaurants. June was usually the one doing the talking, but after a while, Hamza opened up and started telling her about his experiences in Sarajevo before as well as during the war.

On one of those Sundays, June asked him if he wanted to go out the following Saturday. She was taking him to dinner. They met, as usual, on Michigan Avenue, and they walked about ten blocks south. June picked an exclusive restaurant. With a profusion of explanations and apologies by the restaurant manager, Hamza had to take off his jacket and replace it with a black tuxedo brought for him. That seemed to be a regular procedure, since Hamza saw a few guys with sport shirts underneath their tuxedos. The restaurant

smelled of an old-world atmosphere. That was probably because
the walls were faded dark beige and all the waiters were older men.
There were no part-time girls there. At the end of the hall, the pianist
was quietly playing "Strangers in the Night," singing a few lines
every now and again.

They ordered dinner. Hamza decided to have a classic cowboy
meal: steak and potatoes.

"If I wrote love novels, I would write that June looks
enchanting," he thought.

"If he wore a shirt and tie and dress shoes, he would look quite
decent," June thought, and then said out loud:

"You look good in a tuxedo. Maybe you could keep it?"

"My jacket is more valuable."

"You mean more expensive?"

"No, I mean more valuable to me. I know I couldn't get much
for it if I wanted to sell it. How was your day?"

"Busy. I have a couple of surgical procedures tomorrow, so I
had to get ready."

"Hard work?"

"No. I love this job, so I don't get tired doing it. What's new
with you?"

"The usual. Go to work, go home, repeat."

"I spoke to my supervisor about you. About Bosnia. You really
know the situation pretty well and are familiar with the current
events. And we are doing some work in psychology. You know, I
think that it might be good if you gave a lecture on Bosnia and the
consequences of the war. You don't mind, do you?"

"A lecture? Me? What would I say?"

"The same things you've told me."

"About Bosnia?"

"Yes, about Bosnia. You were there, you've it seen and lived it.
We, on the other hand, know only that there was a war over there
and that people were killing each other. The reasons for it and most
everything else is not something many people here know."

"I'm sorry. It's not that I wouldn't like to do it. Just the opposite,
actually. I just think that you don't have the guts for it."

"Who doesn't have the guts?"

"You, Americans."

"What do you mean? We're the bravest people in the world."

"You? Of course you are, if Rambo is an American. I mean in real life."

June got up, her eyes gleaming dangerously. "If that's a slur against Americans, I protest. I protest vehemently. I do not let people make jokes about my country."

She sat down, her eyes still shone wildly. Hamza looked at her and nodded.

"Now, that's integrity. That's how one should defend one's country. I apologize. You are right. I didn't mean to make jokes about your country. Anyway, it's always been my country as well, at least for half of me."

They both laughed as the tension dissipated.

"But I still think that you don't have the guts for it."

June raised her finger threateningly.

"Listen, let me explain. You have a strong country. It protects you from everything that can disturb you. It also protects you from the kind of life that is totally different from the one you lead, or any that you've had the chance to experience. Let me give you an example. When I say meat, you think of hamburgers. But that's not what I was thinking of. Or take the steak in front of you. Do you know what I mean? Of course, you do, but you don't think of it the same way I do. It's like this, think about the animal. Somebody had to slaughter it. The blood spews out, the animal screams. They have to hang it upside down so that the blood drains out. Then they skin it using big knives. The meat is steaming hot. They cut the animal open; guts spill out on the floor. They harvest the useful internal organs. Then they slice up the meat and classify it. They grind it and transport it for packaging. And another thing, one hamburger might contain the meat of two or three bulls, since the grinding machines are very big."

June looked at him, smiling and nodding. "And?" She cut a piece of her meat and put it in her mouth.

Hamza was confused. "You can actually eat after what I've just told you?"

"Of course, why not?"

"Then I'll gladly give that lecture."

"Thank you very much. Now, excuse me for a minute." June got up and went to the ladies' room. She ran into the first stall and started vomiting. "We don't have the guts? Bastard!" She came back to the table after five or six minutes, with her eyes a bit red. This time she sat right next to him. Hamza had just lit a cigarette and taken a sip of coffee. Seeing how he enjoyed his cigarette, June said, "Give me one." Hamza lit another cigarette and gave it to her. June took a drag and then slowly exhaled the smoke through her mouth and nose. She laughed with relaxed pleasure.

A violin joined the piano at the far end of the restaurant. They played slow songs from films and foreign countries. June moved her chair closer to Hamza and leaned over so that she rested against Hamza's chest. They were facing the end of the hall and the musicians.

"You know, Hamza, I am happy that you don't have long arms."

"Hold on." Hamza pushed her chair back and got up. He put his arms down against his body and looked curiously at where his fingers reached. He didn't find anything unusual; his arms were neither long nor short. They were just ordinary arms. June started laughing. She forgot that she was smoking and had just inhaled. She began to cough. She coughed terribly, so Hamza took the cigarette out of her hands, slapped her firmly on the back, and gave her a glass of water. The coughing stopped. June laughed again.

"I don't see anything wrong with my arms."

"All right, Hamza, let me ask you something. But, promise that you'll answer right away. Okay?"

"Okay."

"Careful. Remember, I said right away."

"All right, all right."

"Would you like to sleep with me?"

"Yes. No. I mean . . . what did you say?"

June looked at him seriously.

"June, what did you say?"

"Nothing, forget it."

"Okay . . ."

"Hamza, do you know what intelligence is?"

"I think I do. It's something that is not visible, but everybody claims to possess it."

"Seriously."

"Intelligence is the ability . . ."

" . . . of adjusting to new, unknown situations with the help of past experiences. Something like that," June completed the sentence.

"Yes. And . . . ?"

"And nothing. My question was just a little IQ test. Nobody has ever asked you that question before?"

"No. In Bosnia, it is usually the guys who ask the girls that question. So, how did I do on the test?"

"Great."

"Ha-ha," Hamza laughed. "Really?"

"Here are the official scores of the test." June took out her glasses, put them on, and looked at Hamza.

"Seriously, now. Your response was immediate and that is the most important thing. If you had taken any time to think about it, the scores wouldn't be valid. So, your first answer was 'Yes.' That means you like me. A lot. I mean physically, and you would like to have sex with me. No, no, please, Hamza. Don't interrupt. These are serious test results. Your second answer was 'No.' It shows the other side of your feelings—the more subtle and sensitive side. You care about me, and you were scared that you might have insulted me with your first answer, and you don't want to lose me. And finally, your third answer, like 'I didn't catch what you said,' shows your intelligence. Since you found yourself between a rock and a hard place, you decided to buy some time and see how I would react. That was more subconsciously than consciously though. A subconscious attempt to control the situation. The speed of your reaction tells me how intelligent you are. Yes, you can be proud of your intelligence."

"Well, perhaps there's a grain of truth in that."

"But you would never admit it. And which part is true? The one about you wanting to sleep with me or not?"

"Let's change the subject."

"Okay, Hamza. We can change the subject, but we can't change the situation".

"Fine, let's move on."

The violin in the back of the room started playing a Hungarian dance. Hamza closed his eyes and enjoyed the music. June looked at him and thought, "What is with that violin in his head? I think I really confused him with that test, but the scores are correct. Even if they weren't, his behavior afterwards confirmed them even more." The violin ended with the well-known wild rhythm and Hamza opened his eyes and asked, "How did you picture that?"

"What? The sleeping thing?"

"Come on now, we said we were going to move on. That lecture thing, if that's what you want to call it."

"Oh that. We have a lecture hall at our hospital. Do you know what a lecture hall is?"

"Sort of. There are rows of chairs which go sloping downwards and the speaker is at the bottom."

"Great. I'll figure out a time slot. We'll invite the potentially interested people from the hospital and maybe from the Psychiatry department at Northwestern. You'll come, give a lecture, Q-and-A, and that's it."

"What am I going to talk about?"

"Whatever you feel like. Whatever's on your mind."

"Okay. You just mention that stomach part to your boss. I don't want to hold a lecture in front of an empty hall."

"You just make sure that you don't start stuttering. Doctors of Psychology are going to be watching you, and they'll know what you're thinking even before you open your mouth."

"We'll see."

The rest of the night, June talked about Montana, the lakes and rivers at the foot of the Rockies, life on a big farm, hunting, horseback riding, and fishing with her brothers and father. Around midnight, Hamza walked her to her car. June kissed him on the cheek and drove away.

*   *   *

June had finally managed to arrange the time and date for the lecture. The lecture was entitled "Discussion of the Psychological and Sociological Aspects of War." Hamza tried to look a little more suitable for this occasion. His gray turtleneck matched his cords. June's supervisor was a nice old gentleman, very kind and helpful. Underneath that gentle and smooth surface, Hamza could sense the tiger who, using his strength and enormous energy, kept this hospital among the top clinics in the world.

"So, you are Hamza." He shook his hand powerfully. "June told me about you. All good things, of course."

"The devil is not as black as he seems."

"You mean an angel is not as white as it seems?"

"Something along those lines." Hamza smiled and thought, "I don't know how the sheep react to you, but you can't fool this wolf with your Mr.-Nice-Guy routine. There is more energy and strength in you alone than the rest of them combined."

The lecture hall was almost full and Hamza felt a little stage fright. At the same time, he was glad to be able to tell Americans at least a part of the truth about Bosnia. He doubted he'd get any applause afterwards.

"Ladies and gentlemen," June's supervisor addressed the participants. "We don't usually hold this kind of lecture or discussion. However, seeing that we have a very special guest here who happens to come from an area that was recently involved in a war, we've decided to host this lecture today. Our knowledge about that conflict is very limited, which was all the more reason to have this lecture. Seeing the number of participants, I think that the subject is interesting, and we hope that it will clear up some misconceptions we have about the war, as well as help us understand some of the behavior we can see every day in our work."

He motioned Hamza to approach.

Hamza came out onto the stage. He positioned the little microphone on his shirt. He coughed to check that the microphone was on, took a deep breath, and began:

"Honor! Honor is, ladies and gentlemen, a term and something recognized not only among humans. The concept of honor is found among other creatures, especially the more intelligent animals. Thus, we can find honor among elephants, horses, dogs, dolphins, wolves, and others. The concept of honor is not known among animals such as snakes, jackals, coyotes, hyenas, or rats. These species are not familiar with honor. The concept can be contemplated in diverse domains of life. For example, the honor of a family, of a nation, the honor of a profession, religion, the honor of a woman, a sister, and so on. Or, for example, all of you have taken the Hippocratic

Oath upon the completion of your studies, swearing to exercise your profession with honor. Throughout the history of humankind, there have been wars because of honor. People have killed others as well as themselves for honor. The Japanese hara-kiri is only one of the extreme ways of protecting honor that we know about.

I will limit myself to the idea of how honor applies to the family, a wife, and the country. The honor of the wife is one of the oldest forms of honor. The honor of the male when protecting his female exists in the animal kingdom.

Take a stag for example. He'd rather die in battle than flee like a coward. The Trojan War was fought over the honor of a woman, and Odysseus killed everybody who tried to cast aspersions on his family or his wife. A friend of mine was a witness to a double murder once. A betrayed husband killed his wife and her lover. His honor as head of the family, and as a man, was at stake." There was some murmuring in the lecture hall. Hamza looked around the hall.

"Are there any questions?"

"Excuse me," a young doctor said, rising from his seat. "Dr. O'Brian. I thought you were going to talk about Bosnia."

"Patience, please. I am talking about Bosnia and I hope I won't disappoint you. So, if you can follow me. Imagine that one morning you get up to go to work. You are taking your spouse to work and your daughter to school. After a few miles, you come to a barricade and a sign reading 'This is Serbia.'" You rub your eyes, but it doesn't help. The barricades are there, and the signs are there. So are the people with black stockings over their faces and guns in their hands. You think maybe they're shooting a movie and you're going to be late for work. You approach them to ask them to let you through, but they point their guns at you and say, 'Back off!'"

"So now, what do you do? You have to go back. You try to take a different street, but the same thing is going on. 'Serbia,' again. You go back home to call at work, to try to explain why you haven't shown up, but the person you were supposed to call hasn't shown up either. You turn on the radio or the TV. They say that it's a group of irresponsible individuals. The police are going to take care of the incident. You head to work the next day, and there it is, 'Serbia,' again. You go back home. By now, you're sick and tired of it. On TV, they keep on saying that the police are going to take care of it. On the third day, now utterly furious, you put your family in the car and leave. You're close to the barricades. Then suddenly, 'Bam, Bam, Bam!' Sniper fire. Under fire, you manage to turn around and drive back somehow. The car is filled with blood. You turn to find your wife and daughter are dead. You think, 'This is crazy,. That can't be true. It just can't be! Why, for God's sake, why?' But, there's nothing to be done for it, dead is dead. You have to bury them. The cemetery is at the other end of town. You take sleeping bags and put your wife into one and your daughter into another. You'll bury them in the park, but find that the park is already overflowing. Your neighbors, people just like you, are burying their loved ones. You manage to find a bit of free space in the corner. You too dig a grave and bury them. You say a prayer for them, the one you still remember from childhood. You're not the same man anymore! You've had more than enough of it. You're crazy. This is my country! You motherfuckers! This is not 'Serbia.' This is my country! 'Serbia' is somewhere else and if you want Serbia, then go there. This is my country! I don't have anywhere else to go, even if I wanted to!

So, your honor as a husband, a father, and a citizen has been shattered. You were not able to do what every religion in the world says you need to do; you weren't able to protect your wife and child. You were not able to uphold this fundamental principle of all human societies. You were not able to protect your family. What are you? Who are you? Your family had the right to expect you to protect them. Your daughter, your flesh and blood! Okay, fuck it, you failed! But there are other families, there are other children who have to live. You have to at least try to save the country for future generations. You have to fight! Fight! You wander the streets and find others like you: other unfortunate souls. You all want to fight back, but you have nothing to fight back with. Can you charge at tanks and MIGs with rocks? If necessary. You break into a weapons shop. There are a few knives, guns, and some ammunition for hunting rifles. Somebody realizes that the barrels of the rifles are the same as standard plumbing pipes. You find a plumber who knows how to weld and begin making guns out of pipes. Their range is about fifty or sixty yards. Well, at least they shoot. The shelling of the city begins. From ten to fifteen miles away, the city is shelled by weapons

241

of all possible calibers: tanks, artillery pieces, rocket-launchers, airplanes. There's no electricity, water, phone, gas . . .

"The economic system collapses. Money loses all value. There's no gas for the car, no food, nothing. In hidden places, people are digging wells, trying to get to any source of water. The sewer system stops working. Garbage litters the streets. It's the Apocalypse! Why? All because somebody thinks that they can rip out the heart of your country and take it to 'Serbia.' Fires burn night and day. The assholes shoot extra hard at the firefighters trying to put out them out. The gems of your city's architecture are disappearing—religious buildings, nurseries, hospitals, libraries, hotels. Thousands die.

"You fight. With bare hands if necessary, but you fight. A few of you go behind enemy lines to the occupied part and take a few mortar shells, but you have nothing to launch them with. You take some metal pipes, drop the shell into it, and strike it hard with a hammer from the other end. It flies, but it can't be more precise than a quarter-mile radius. It doesn't matter.

"Somehow, you succeed in getting together a delegation that manages to get out of the city. They go to the democratic countries of the world and say, 'Hello. You know so and so? Well, they attacked us. The cities are burning, thousands are dead, we are fighting, but we have nothing to fight with.' The democratic world says, 'We're with you. We lit ten thousand candles for ten thousand of your dead citizens.' You thank them for the candles, but you need weapons. Anything. You can't fight with pipes against tanks. They say, 'We're sorry, but we've decided to impose an arms embargo on the entire region.'

"You don't understand. An arms embargo? The assholes took all the firepower there was—all the weapons that were produced. Now, they're bombing you with shells produced in 1956. This means that they have mortar shells from every year, from 1956 to 1992. That's a lot of mortar shells. That means the embargo is just for you.

"The democratic world says, 'We're sorry, but more weapons equal more bloodshed.' Okay. But that also means that a couple of the killers are going to die as well. Otherwise, the killers can do whatever they want and keep on destroying your country. That's insanity.' But, the democratic world is the democratic world. They made the decision and they respect it. The democratic world is on your side. They are going to give you food. Then, they send you food with an expiration date that passed years ago, baby food that has been sitting in containers for twenty years, lunch packs that were made decades ago, beans that can't be cooked, rice that's rotten.

"The democratic world sends you medicines for venereal diseases or for diseases that no longer exist, expired medicines they would have had to spend millions of dollars to destroy. Yet you watch people dying because of the lack of antibiotics, saline infusions, and so on. You come back with your spirit and morale wiped out. But it is what it is. You have to fight. The assholes have established concentration camps: a new Auschwitz and Dachau. The assholes are grinding your citizens into pet food. They are selling the eyes of your kids on the international black organ market. Hundreds of those asshole soldiers rape your imprisoned women and young girls. But, that's not enough for them. They keep them locked up until they are seven months pregnant and an abortion is all but impossible, and then they exchange them for their captured soldiers. They wipe out entire towns. They are destroy your religious buildings and make parking lots out of them. They are raze your cemeteries with bulldozers.

"You fight, whether you want to or not. You fight with rocks. Rocks! Many die, but you move on. You get weapons. Finally, you somehow have enough to fight back. You've come to the point where you can fire one mortar shell for every ten of theirs. The pacifists of the world organize demonstrations in support for your fight. You feel all warm and fuzzy inside. A little city under a three-year siege. The Bosnians are still managing to survive there. The democratic world orders Bosnians to surrender their arms to the UN units assigned to protect them. You trust them. It will be a 'safe haven' after all. The general of those UN units comes to the town himself. In the name of the democratic world, he promises to protect the citizens. The Bosnian defenders hand over their weapons. Shortly after, the assholes go into the defenseless town and kill ten thousand people. The hunt for the escaped civilians lasts several days, encompassing the mountains and forests around the town. During that time, the UNPROFOR colonel, the one who is supposed to protect the people in the town, is seen drinking with main asshole general. Afterwards, he states that all the people in the town weren't worth the little toe of one of his soldiers. He says: " . . . Their children are dirty and they beg for food."

The main UN general and colonel return to their countries, where they receive praise and acknowledgement for the success of their mission. At night, before going to bed, they tell their grandchildren about the honor of the military profession. When you finally get the weapons and go on the offensive, the democratic world cries out, 'STOP! If you don't stop now, we're going to attack *you*.' And then, the democratic world says you have to live with these assholes. And to them, the democratic world gives forty-nine percent of your country an 'A' for effort. Thus, the assholes who produced and executed the war become part of the government. Two hundred thousand dead, one million two hundred thousand displaced, hundreds of thousands wounded! Why? Because of honor!

The democratic world has lost its honor. The term honor has been redefined. Once upon a time, people fought wars and died for honor. Once upon a time, people walked with their heads held high. Once upon a time, generals committed suicide for honor, and captains went down with their ships.

Once, a long time ago.

Today, spineless politicians become presidents. Spineless officers become generals and receive medals. Spineless countries get spineless presidents. People with a spine get broken, because they stand out. In a mass of crooked people, the straight ones stand out and have to be broken. That is, ladies and gentlemen, the psychological and sociological aspect of war."

Hamza stopped speaking.

The silence echoed through the lecture hall. The participants looked at each other, or stared straight ahead with a shocked expression on their face. After a minute or two, the silence became uncomfortable. It seemed as if nobody had questions, but nobody got up either. One doctor decided to break the silence and discomfort.

"A question. How is it possible that something like that could happen in Europe at the end of the twentieth century?"

"I think . . . well, it's better that . . . Excuse me. Is there a Psychology expert in the room?"

An old, gray-headed doctor, with a short beard got up.

"Dr. Meyer. Doctor of psychology and psychiatry," he said, introducing himself.

"Doctor, psychology is your profession and you have obviously dealt with it for years. How is it possible that something like this can happen in Europe at the end of 20th century?"

The doctor took off his glasses. He took a tissue from his pocket and started wiping them. He thought. He switched the glasses from one hand to another. He put them back on his face, then took them off again. He raised his eyes and looked at Hamza.

"I don't know."

The lecture hall fell silent again.

"I can't remember where, but I read that your officials argued that it wasn't a civil war," asked another participant.

"You see, by definition, a civil war means a conflict between two opposing groups from the same nation. In Bosnia, that was not the case."

"How about religion? It was a conflict of Christians and Muslims, wasn't it?"

"I would say that it was a war waged by the unfaithful. There is no religion that promotes killing. And the way the Muslims were slaughtered in Bosnia points to the absolute lack of any kind of religion on the part of the killers."

"I'm sorry, but I still don't understand."

"Bosnia was a victim of the aggression of two different countries. Their presidents decided to divide it up, and they tried to bring that about through war. The fact is that Bosnian civilians died in Bosnia, and soldiers of the Bosnian army were killed only on Bosnian territory. What were Croatian and Serbian soldiers doing there? What were so many paramilitary units from Serbia doing in Bosnia? These organized groups of killers were sent to Bosnia and promised a good time and loot by their government."

"A question. You're saying that there were two hundred thousand dead in Bosnia. Recently I have heard that the figure was less."

"I've read something about that too. Unfortunately, we'll never know the full extent of the truth. But if you'll allow me, if we found out that the Nazis killed four million eight hundred thousand Jews in World War II rather than the believed six million, would that change our view on Nazism?"

"Question? I've heard that Iran was helping Bosnia. Who was helping Serbia?"

"The Chetniks! Everybody helped them; the whole world. By not helping Bosnia, the world *de facto* participated in genocide. I said genocide. Please remember that. Ge-no-cide. The West exposed its rotten state and immorality by introducing the term 'ethnic cleansing.' Do you know why that term was introduced? It was introduced because the term 'genocide' is automatically associated with the fascism of the Nazis and the suffering of the Jews in World War II. Because, there was a real danger in using the term 'genocide,' which, by the way, precisely and undoubtedly in a single word gives a complete depiction of the suffering of the Muslims in Bosnia and Herzegovina and the horrible crimes committed against them. Because, by using the term 'genocide,' a 'danger' existed that the public opinion in the Western countries might force their governments to react more strongly and take decisive action to stop the war and punish the war criminals. That is why the Western countries invented the term 'ethnic cleansing.' So that while you were hearing about 'ethnic cleansing,' you automatically thought about cleaning, tidying up, a harmless duty we all perform daily. In no way were you thinking about the mass slaughter of civilians. That term cannot be associated with concentration camps."

"Are you including the United States?"

"For one part, yes. Do you know how many resolutions were passed on Bosnia? Only one was respected the whole time. It was the one about the arms embargo. I don't think that America helped the Chetniks. They just failed to do anything to help the Bosnians or stop the war by military force. American ships controlled the Adriatic Sea among others."

"But, they stopped controlling it."

"Yes, Bill Clinton finally made that decision. Although it came too late for the two hundred thousand dead, it was just in time for the survivors. Finally, Bill did not decide that he would give us a chance, but at least that he would not take it away from us either."

"Please, can you be more specific about which UN generals you were referring to?"

"Why not? If they could do what they did, there is no reason for me not to mention their names. I was talking about all the generals sent to Bosnia by the UN. The Canadian general Mackenzie, the Indian general Nambiar, the British general Smith, and so on. This thing about Srebrenica was done by the French generals Morillon and Janvier, as well as the Dutch general Karremans. Morillon was the one who promised to protect the people of Srebrenica if they gave up their weapons, and General Karremans was the one who surrendered Srebrenica to the Chetniks. The next day, July 12, 1995, while the Chetniks were killing thousands in and around Srebrenica, General Karremans was the one having a drink with the biggest of the war criminal, the Chetnik general Mladic. I have the newspaper with me, with that photo that went around the world. Besides that, there are also records of General Morillon's speech in Srebrenica. If you're interested, I can get them for you too."

"Is it possible that the blame lies only on one side?"

"As I've said, our only fault was that we were living on the territory where the assholes decided to build their own state."

"What do you think about your politicians?"

"That's a long story, but, you said it yourself, they are my politicians. Maybe they could have played it better. Still, it's hard to play when you have two hundred thousand people dead and the rest have a knife to their throat."

"Could you have anticipated the behavior of the European powers?"

"Yes, but unfortunately too late. Although in retrospect, there were many little things which indicated the way they were going to behave. For example, when Lord Carrington used the expression 'parties to the war,' we should have known that it was said deliberately and not by any mistake of ignorance. I read that he was appointed an arbitrator in the negotiations between the U.S. and Canada on fishing rights.

"No more questions? I thank you for giving me this opportunity to talk about Bosnia."

After the lecture, a little luncheon in the hall was organized. Hamza came over to June.

"They didn't really strain themselves with applause."

"Applause? Hamza, they're in shock. That was too many facts in too short a time. I don't think they ever participated in this kind of lecture, or will participate ever again."

"Young man, it seems to me that you don't have a sense of politics at all," June's supervisor said with a reproachful glance.

"A sense of politics is for politicians. I am satisfied with the sense of truth," Hamza snapped back.

"Very well, but for statements like that, people go to court in the U.S."

"Yes, in the United States. But, the purpose would be the protection of honor, don't you think? Don't you think that would be a joke? Another thing; did you know that France banned its soldiers from testifying at the War Crimes Tribunal at The Hague? 'Vive la France,' huh? The national honor of France is defended by just one man with a small group of friends. The philosopher and cosmopolitan Bernard Levi."

"Excuse me." An older female doctor came up to him. "That thing about rape, is that really true?"

"Unfortunately yes, madam."

"How many cases were there?"

"Officially, as far as I know, thirty thousand were registered. However, you have to keep in mind that for every registered case, there are at least three unregistered ones. In any case, it is a huge number. There is rape in every war, but in this case, it was premeditated, systematic rape, which was a part of the their war program. That crime was planned well in advance."

"Unbelievable."

"There are records and testimonies. A certain number of those unfortunate women are in the U.S. now. Your media, though, presented censored footage, toned down the news, so you wouldn't get upset."

"I guess they did."

"Maybe it was better that way."

"Perhaps."

*   *   *

The new year began with snow. The temperatures plummeted, especially near the shore. The wind, coming from the north, raised the cold air from the lake and threw it against the city with all its might. The show swirled between the skyscrapers, broke up, and rejoined, making it impossible to tell which direction it came from. The most confusing thing for Hamza were the Americans who acted as though nothing unusual was going on. Women in dresses and guys in suits would come out of their office buildings and head off to lunch, seemingly unaware of the cold. Hamza felt cold just looking at them.

The days went by monotonously. The rare meetings with Ekrem, the colonel, and especially June were like holidays. As much as Hamza felt depressed and lost after seeing Ekrem, he felt good when he was with the colonel, and happy with June. When he visited Ekrem, they would mostly talk about the war and its consequences. The Dayton Peace Accord was the single, most aggravating issue for them. Ekrem would start yelling, swearing, and working himself into a fury. His wife and mother would look at Hamza with disapproval for getting Ekrem into such a state. "Do you know, that Dudakovic needed only a few more days to take over Banja Luka? He needed just a few days for Prijedor. Oh I wish they would start shooting again. Then Ekrem would be off to Bosnia."

"They couldn't, my friend. You know how they pressured them, they had to sign."

"Pressured? What do you mean 'pressured'? Did they put a knife to their throats? Or did they capture their families and threaten to kill all of them if they didn't sign? Huh?"

"You don't understand, that's politics."

"There is no politics, my Hamza. There is only our dear Almighty God. With all the military might the Chetniks had, they should have killed us all within ten days. But Allah didn't let them. And our guys ran to sign the agreement."

"Yes, but if they hadn't signed it, we would have had another three hundred thousand dead."

"So what? So what?! They destroyed my family, my entire family. My son is the only one who'll carry on our name. There were more than thirty of us—uncles, cousins, brothers . . . Another three hundred thousand dead? So what? Those motherfuckers. God willing, there will be war. And Ekrem will be going back to Bosnia."

After a visit, Hamza would try for days to find arguments to present to Ekrem, to help both Ekrem and himself heal pieces of the past.

*   *   *

At the colonel's, the atmosphere would be completely different. Usually, the colonel started talking about some issue from world politics or history, and they discussed it all day long. They talked about the native Americans, the Spanish conquest of South America, Alexander the Great, Genghis Khan, Napoleon, all the way to the Vietnam War. They debated about the world's greatest traveler—Marco Polo or Ibn Batutta. Hamza cooked something in the colonel's big kitchen, or they ordered from one of the better restaurants.

Still, the best times were with June. He felt relaxed and comfortable. They never planned their dates. They met accidentally on her way back from work or going shopping. Hamza's consistent walking route along Michigan Avenue made it possible for June to find him whenever she wanted to. Hamza went shopping with her or they would go to a restaurant or bar in downtown Chicago. They talked about anything and everything.

On one such occasion, June needed to buy a few things, so they went into a store with enormous escalators. Before they got on, June turned to Hamza, "Be careful."

"Oh my God! These stairs are moving!" Hamza pulled her back.

"Yes, this is an escalator."

"Oh, do they have normal stairs in here?"

"What's the matter with you? You're not scared, are you?"

"No, I'm not afraid, but I would like to take normal stairs."

"We're going to the fourth floor. It's a long way. Come on, we'll go together."

"That's okay. Why don't you go up and down once, so I can see?" June stepped on the stairs, went to the first floor, and came back.

"You see, it's not dangerous."

They stepped on the escalator and went up. While she was shopping, Hamza walked around, looking for other things.

"Have you never seen an escalator before?"

"Get out of here. What's wrong with you? We had escalators when you were out hunting buffalo for breakfast."

"Oh, you." She glared at him, then swung her hand and slapped Hamza really hard. Suddenly realizing what she had done, she let out a gasp and put a hand over her mouth.

"I'm sorry. I'm so sorry. I don't know what came over me. I'm really sorry."

Hamza held his cheek. It seemed like he might have a female Musa on his hands, as if one wasn't enough.

"Hey, Musa."

"What did you say?"

"I said, 'hey Musa.'"

"What's Musa?"

"Not a what, but a who."

"Let's go." She took Hamza's hand and they left the store.

While they were sitting at Giordano's, Hamza spoke. "In Sarajevo, just down the street from me, lived a friend of mine. His name was Musa."

"Just a minute. Did he live there or is he still living there? I mean, is he dead?"

"He's alive. At least he was when I left Sarajevo."

"Have you talked to him on the phone? Have you sent a letter?"

"No."

"Why not?"

"I just haven't!" It wasn't worth an explanation. Nobody who hasn't left Sarajevo could understand that. The feeling when homesickness and desire are slowly killing you from inside, but you can't call, and no one can call you. Everybody has to go through that on their own. One day, when they know who they are, what they are, and so on, they will call.

"So, this friend of mine, Musa . . . ," Hamza went on. June kept interrupting with what she thought were reasonable, and Hamza thought they were silly questions. Once again, when they looked at the clock, it was almost midnight. It happened to them regularly. Time simply flew.

*   *   *

It was the thirteenth of January. Hamza pulled his wool cap deep over his face as he came out of a fast-food restaurant. The snow crunched under his feet. He ran to his truck. He paid the parking attendant and drove off. Parking was a luxury in Chicago. "The Chicago police have me trained like a dog." His car had been towed three times, and he had paid about twenty parking tickets before he realized that if area was marked as a 'no parking zone,' there really was no parking allowed, and he could be sure that the police was going to tow the car or at least give him a ticket.

He drove around the city, killing time. It was too early for him to go home. He had to buy a radio for the truck. He just could not figure out a way of doing it without having it stolen the very same night. Maybe a little stereo that would run through the car's lighter outlet would work. While thinking about it, he came to a part of town he had never been to before. He looked around and drove slowly. A bright sign attracted his attention. It hung above a restaurant: *Tasmaydan*. Turkish for "Stone Mine," but also the name of a part of Belgrade.

"It must be either a Turkish or Serbian restaurant."

He found a parking spot and went inside.

It was definitely Serbian. The restaurant was decorated for the New Year's festivities. It was New Year's for the Serbs. That was why this place was so fancied up. They had musicians from Serbia playing Serbian music too. An elegant waiter came to him.

"May I help you?"

"Speak Serbian, my brother, speak Serbian." Hamza patted him on the shoulder like a friend. "I didn't know you had music today."

"You must be new here. Everybody knows that we have music from the old country every New Year's. Would you like a table?"

"I'm more or less new, and no, I'll sit at the bar for a while. Thanks."

Hamza sat at the bar and called the bartender.

"Do you have *Tikves Kavadarci* brandy?"

"Man, where did you pull that one from? We have everything except that."

"All right then, let me have a Manastirka."

"All right, brother. Coming right up . . . glittering like gold."

Hamza drank slowly and looked around the bar. He couldn't recognize a single face. That was good. He didn't know why, but he was suddenly in a good mood. Here he was in Chicago, in a Serbian bar, drinking Serbian brandy. Once the music started, it would even be better.

"Oh, Hamza," he thought, "if your friends could see you now, how would you explain it to them? Hell, let's see happens."

The band was great, but the singer was a catastrophe. She covered her lack of voice and talent with a micromini skirt and low-cut tight shirt. The band played one song, while she sang another, and danced to a third. Despite all of this, she received a huge applause after every song. The most important thing was that she sang songs from the homeland. He could hear a throat clear behind his back. Hamza turned around.

"Your first time here? I'm Risto, the owner of the restaurant."

"Nice to meet you." Hamza avoided introducing himself, since his name would give away his nationality. "Yes, I came here not too long ago. I don't know the area. I'm glad I found you guys."

"Where do you live?"

"With my cousin. He doesn't live too far from here."

"How come he doesn't know anything about us?"

"Maybe he does, poor guy. He married American. She doesn't let him breathe, never mind going out to our restaurants."

"A lot of them like that. They think they are lucky when they marry an American, especially if she has some money. Then the devil comes for his due, and they pay through the nose for every minute. You see, I've been here for thirty years, but when I wanted to get married, I went to Serbia and picked out my wife. Anyway, do you want anything? We have everything—pork to lamb, fresh off the grill."

"I'll have some lamb."

"It's great, just like from back home."

"Get me the ribs and a mixed salad and another drink. And send those guys something to drink too." He motioned towards the waiters.

"Right away, my friend, right away. I hope you come more often."

"Bet on it."

The singer finally finished the song and took a break. People started talking. Everybody spoke at the same time and still somehow understood each other. Midnight approached. With every drink, the idea forming inside Hamza's head took a definite shape, and he decided to go for it. He called Risto over.

"Hey brother, do you mind if I sing a song or two?"

"That would be great for the mood, but I wouldn't want the guests to . . ."

"Just watch and enjoy." Hamza came up to the stage and greeted the musicians.

"Happy New Year, brothers."

"Same to you, brother. Same to you. Would you like to order a song?"

"Yes, but I want to sing it too." Hamza took out a fifty-dollar bill and put it into the singer's shirt.

"Which one do you want?"

"I sing everything."

"Have you had a bit too much to drink?"

"Don't you worry about a thing. They used to tell me that I'm better than Ilic."

"Don't overdo it. Let's go, the man is paying, we're playing."

Hamza whispered something to the accordion player and took the microphone off the stand. Music started and the room grew silent. The guests stopped talking, and they all looked at the young man with the long, ugly scar. There were three married couples sitting at one table. One of the guys nudged his older man next to him, "Hey, Simo, if I had a face like that, I'd stay home. And look at him, he wants to sing."

Hamza stood on the stage with his head bowed. His left arm relaxed next to the body, he held the microphone with his right. When the band finished the intro, he began.

> *"If you just wanted, I would take you to the stars*
> *If you had nothing, I would steal for you*
> *If you wanted the sun, I would burn for you*
> *That is how much, my dear, I've loved you."*

His clear, strong voice filled the room. He saw the approval on the faces of the guests.

> *"Cry tonight, oh, autumn rains,*
> *Life goes on,*
> *My sweetheart loves me no more,*
> *She's forgotten what happiness is."*

Hamza leaned forward closer to the microphone and put his hands together as in a prayer. While the music played the chorus, he kept time with his foot.

> *"When you said leave, I understood,*
> *Because of you, I hated myself*
> *That is how much, my dear, I loved you."*

He raised his arms above his head.
"Everybody!" he shouted in the break between the chorus.

> *"Cry tonight, oh, autumn rains,*
> *Life goes on,*
> *My sweetheart loves me no more,*
> *She's forgotten what happiness is."*

The whole room sang with him.

By the end of the song, Hamza was on his knees with his arms hanging limp and his head bowed.

"Bravo, bravo!"

"Yeah!"

"Good job!"

"Another!"

At the table, Simo had a grimace on his face.

"What's up now, Simo?"

"I don't know. I don't like this."

"Oh, for God's sake, what is it now?"

"Well, it's like he's being sarcastic, like he's fucking with us."

"C'mon."

Hamza sang another song. When he had finished, he noticed two policemen had entered the restaurant and sat at the bar. He thanked the audience and hurried to the bar. One of the policemen asked him, "What did you to make them that happy?"

"Songs from back home. We are all a bit homesick."

Risto rubbed his hands together in satisfaction. The waiters were running across the room with new orders for food and drinks. He was happy about the policemen too. There hadn't been any incidents in his restaurant for a long time, and he liked it when the police came by. Hamza called him over.

"I would like to offer these gentlemen something to drink. Please don't refuse. My father was a policeman his entire life, and I really respect your profession. Certainly here in the U.S. and especially in Chicago."

"All right, just one drink."

"Risto, bring us a bit of lamb too. If you still have any left. My father loved lamb." The policemen took the drink.

"So, what were you singing about?"

"Some love songs. I'm afraid that this crowd is not really the type for anything more serious."

"What, were you looking to sing an opera?"

"Not an opera, but a short recital from a theater piece. I sing well, but theater is in my blood. I would really like to recite something to them, but I'm afraid that they wouldn't understand it."

"What do you care? Give it a shot."

"You don't know our people. If they don't like something, they are ready to fight. Hell, they're ready to kill somebody."

"We're the law here. You just go ahead. We'd like to see that."

"You think that you can protect me if something goes wrong?"

"Absolutely."

"You promise?"

"Promise."

Hamza put his glass down and got up on stage.

"Great guy," Risto said to the policemen.

"Yes, and he respects our profession. His father probably taught him this is a hard way to earn a living," said the other policeman while trying the lamb.

Hamza talked to the accordion player, cleared his throat, and started singing a well-known children's song, with slightly altered lyrics.

> *"But still, it must be known,*
> *We sent our dads to Bosnia . . ."*

"Bravo!"
"Where did he pull that one from?"
"That's right!"
Hamza continued singing:

> *"To slaughter and steal for a while,*
> *And then come back to us,*
> *To set fires and burn the houses for a while*
> *and then come back to us."*

"Fuck! Is this his idea of a joke?"
"What's wrong, Simo? Let him go on for a while."
"Leave him alone, for God's sake. Let's hear some more."
Hamza continued singing:

> *"Say hello to my dad,*
> *Somewhere near Poljine,*
> *Say hello to my dad,*
> *On Hresa and near Borije."*

"Well, fuck it now!"
"What the hell is wrong with you?"
"What's wrong with me? Those are the hills from where we bombed Sarajevo."
"So what? The man is joking a bit."
"Fuck the joke."
Hamza finished and there was a short applause.
"Okay. My first and greatest love is the theater. Tonight, for you only, I'm going to recite a little something from a drama that I personally love very much."
Hamza turned to the orchestra, "Just softly, all right?" He took the microphone, took a deep breath, and started reciting in full voice:

> *"Swear, oh, my people!"*

"This sounds familiar."
"Let it go, Simo, seriously."

> *"Swear, my people,*
> *On the blood of the babies killed in Sarajevo nursery,*
> *By missiles, by shells,*
> *By those Chetnik motherfuckers . . ."*

"What is he talking about?"
"Stop him!"
"Stop, you motherfucker!"
Hamza continued, raising his voice above the din of the room:

> *"Swear, my people,*
> *And don't forgive.*
> *Whoever forgives,*
> *May his children curse him . . ."*

"Stop the motherfucker."

> *"We didn't want this war,*
> *But if they want it, they can have it.*
> *Until the last Chetnik escapes*
> *To their shithole, or Chicago."*

Hamza finished, and deflected a bottle headed for his head. He got hit by a few glasses. He jumped from the stage, ran around a few tables, and made his way behind the policemen. The guests ran toward the bar. The policemen watched the situation escalate, confused. Hamza did tell them that there might be trouble, but they couldn't have imagined that somebody would react this way to a poem.

"Stop! Hold it!" They reached for their guns. With a hand on his gun, one of them stretched out his left palm.

"Chicago Police Department! Stay where you are!"
The other one turned to Risto.

"If you don't stop them, I will personally make sure this place gets shut down."

"Hold it people! Take it easy!" Risto jumped in.

"What do you mean take it easy, Risto? Fuck the both of you!"

"Come on guys . . ."

"Where the hell did you find him, Risto?"

"You can consider this the last time you'll see me here."

With a hand on their weapons, the policemen backed toward the door, with Hamza about half a step behind them. From behind the cover of the two officers, he raised his right hand, and gave the angry guests the finger. The guests started yelling and closing in on them again. One officer looked back at Hamza, but he had already lowered his hand. Finally, they managed to leave the restaurant and run to the police car.

"Should we call for back up?"

"What are you going to tell them? That a guest recited something to them and they went crazy?"

"Okay, we need to keep an eye on this restaurant."

"And you? What did you recite to them?"

"A section from Hamlet."

"Whatever. First they applaud and cheer you like a national hero, and then they almost kill you."

"I told you they didn't have a sense for theater."

"It's one thing not having a sense for something, but it's a different thing when you want to kill somebody for it."

"So, you say your father was a policeman?"

"His whole life."

"Is it as dangerous a job there as it is here?"

"It's dangerous, but not as dangerous as here."

"You see, I told you, Chicago is the most dangerous city in the world," one of the cops said aloud.

"It really is, man. Up until now, people just got killed for drugs, money, love, but now they've started killing for theater. Where's your car?"

Hamza showed them.

"Get in and get lost. And don't come back here for at least a few months."

"Thank you." Hamza got into the car and left. He sang "Autumn Rains."

Back in the restaurant, the guests commented on what had just happened.

"You were right about him, Simo."

"Fuck it now."

"Oh, that son of a bitch . . . he really fucked up our New Year's."

Simo stared at the table with a serious look on his face.

"No, he didn't, brother. We did it ourselves. The New Year's and everything else."

"What do you mean?"

"Well, we ran like idiots to a lunatic who promised us a better life through the blood of others."

"Well, it wasn't exactly like that, Simo."

"Wasn't it? What was it like then? Look at us, we're just a group of pathetic bastards."

"Come on Simo, it's not like that. Is there anything we don't have?"

"Look at us! Look at us!" Simo screamed, turning red in the face. The veins in his neck bulged. "What could we be missing? Why are you even asking that? Nothing! Everything is great! We have everything! Except that when I meet someone, I can't say where I'm from."

"Well, it's not exactly like that."

"No? When Americans ask you where you're from, what do you tell them? Huh? From former Yugoslavia? They have to squeeze it out of you that you are really from Serbia! And right away, you have to add that you've been in the U.S. for a long time, so they don't think that you have anything to do with the war in Bosnia! And that's nothing for you?"

"Now the New Year's is officially fucked."

"Yes, and we've deserved it. It's not only him; everyone's going to shit all over us for the next hundred years—maybe longer. In any case, I won't live long enough to call myself a Serb with my head held high. All right, let's go home. This party is over."

*   *   *

The winter ended abruptly, and spring was suddenly in Chicago. The warmer days and clear, blue skies made Hamza feel relaxed.

The calmer way of life was like an herbal remedy for the soul. His frequent meetings with the colonel and June soothed him even more. Life could be beautiful after all.

It was a sunny April day, and Hamza couldn't decide which way to go when he got out of a restaurant. Maybe it would be best to go back to Michigan Avenue. Maybe he would run into June. He missed talking to her. He walked around slowly, people-watching. He tried to figure out what social class they came from. Even though Americans generally dressed well, he could differentiate between the wealthy businessmen, their secretaries, lower-level employees, and the young, ambitious experts who were climbing the corporate ladder at top speed. He discovered a cause-and-effect relationship between the brand of the suit, tie and shirt, and the cramped facial expressions. Important businessmen, who weren't on the streets all that often, wore expensive suits, shoes that ran upwards of a thousand dollars, and silk ties, but the veneer seemed kind of sterile. They walked along, pretending to look around, but in fact, they never saw anything. They were always in their world of big numbers. Around them, without fail, ran a pack of young, ambitious employees, wearing wide smiles on their frustrated faces.

They seemed to be flashing their fangs, rather than smiling. Lower-level employees usually wore cheap suits in dark colors—black, dark blue or dark gray—and white shirts and ties that usually did not match the suit. It was interesting how just a small number of people knew how to pick a tie. Hamza often thought that those young career-minded people should go to Italy for a short course on dressing properly. Nobody knows how to match colors and combinations like the Italians. Businesswomen were much paler, and tried to cover it up with a lot of makeup. Judging by the way they walked, the happiest people on the streets of Chicago were the young black guys, effortlessly swinging while listening to their walkman.

Hamza sat on a bench to rest a bit. Then he changed his mind. He was going home. He needed to buy some food and milk, so that he wouldn't have to worry about it the next day. He got up off the bench and looked around. He did a double-take. Impossible! He screwed his eyes shut, then opened them again. The image was still there, right in front of him, some twenty yards away. On the corner of Ohio and Michigan, through the crowd, he saw Best Man.

"Impossible. Impossible!" Hamza threw away his cigarette and ran. A girl stepped out in front of him, and he ran into her. The girl swayed and would have fallen if he hadn't caught her. She dropped her bags, spilling their contents on the pavement. "I'm sorry, I'm terribly sorry!" Hamza picked her up, and ran. The girl, frightened, watched him run down to the corner. He looked to the left, the right, up, and down the street, but couldn't see him anywhere, as if he had vanished into thin air. He caught sight of a white car turning the corner. He walked back. The girl was kneeling on the ground and picking up her things. Hamza helped her.

"I'm really sorry. It was my fault. Let me help you."

"Is everything all right here?" an officer stopped had stopped next to the girl.

"Everything is fine, Officer. We just bumped into each other."

The officer looked at Hamza. "Are you sure?"

"I'm sure. As you see, he is helping me."

The officer walked off, and Hamza handed her the things.

"Thanks. The police are always suspicious because of my face."

"It can happen to anybody."

"I'm really sorry. Bye"," Hamza said as he left.

Just then, he noticed he was shaking. It was a warm spring day.

*   *   *

From the moment he caught a glimpse of Best Man, days full of agony and nights full of nightmares began for Hamza. He took out the Tantohidden inside the mattress. Sharpened and oiled, it rested in its case. He worked out like never before. In the morning, at night, he worked out until he bathed in his own sweat. He couldn't remember ever being in such good physical condition. He felt life pumping through his veins. He was ready. Right after work, he would go to Michigan Avenue and walk around until late at night. He would enter exclusive restaurants, go around fast-food joints, walk around cheap stores and exclusive boutiques. Slowly, he expanded his search radius. There wasn't a bar, a restaurant, or store that he hadn't gone into. So intent was he on finding Best Man that he hadn't noticed that summer had come.

On one of those days, tired of walking, Hamza sat down on a bench on Michigan Avenue and watched the people rushing by. He enjoyed the sun and the newspaper, and looking at the interesting collection of busy people. When he had finished reading, he threw the newspaper in a trash can and continued walking. Three black guys were coming his way, talking and laughing loudly. Hamza thought for a moment and then headed straight for the guy in the middle. He bumped into him.

"Hey man, what do you think you're doing?" Strong fists grabbed his chest.

"Hey, neighbor. What's up, man?"

The black guy looked at him for a second, and then burst out laughing. He turned to the other two.

"All right guys, cough up the cash! Ha-ha! Baby, you don't even know how happy I am to see you. You got no clue!"

His friends each counted out some money, and handed it to him.

"Okay, baby, let's go have a drink. It's on me. Ha-ha! I love you, I really do, man. And you two, don't ever bet against me again." He hugged Hamza and led him forward.

"Let's go to Blue Chicago."

"I don't get it! What was the money for?"

"I told them that there was this white guy who had lived in my building and invited me for coffee. They didn't believe me, so we had a bet. Now I bump into you. That is what I call luck, baby!"

They entered the bar and headed for the table in the back. None of them liked having their backs exposed. Hamza ordered a coke, and the rest of them ordered beers.

"Baby, tell them how you invited me for coffee."

"I don't see anything strange in doing that. We were neighbors."

All three of them laughed.

"Baby, that was a good one. And how much money did you have on you in cash?"

"Well, around $20,000."

"What do you think, how long would he have survived if I hadn't sent him away from the hood?"

"Five days."

"I was there for five days."

"Yes, and on the fifth night, I had to persuade some guys that you were a tough guy."

"I do remember hearing some voices coming from the hall that last night."

"Man, if I had known that you had $20,000 on you, I would have capped you the first night," added the other guy.

Hamza smiled. He held the Coke in his left hand, the right one was on the table, holding the cigarette. The black guy on his left was checking his arm out. He raised Hamza's hand with his right palm and looked at it carefully.

"Man, you're so puny. I could snap you like that." He picked up a toothpick and snapped it between his two fingers.

Hamza looked around the bar. The place was mostly empty, and nobody was looking at them. He slowly put the glass on the table, and suddenly the Tanto found itself in his hand, pressed against the black guy's Adam's apple.

"Could be, man. Could be. Or I would cut you into pieces first."

The black guy froze. He didn't breathe. The neighbor and the other guy stared in shock.

"Be cool, baby. Be cool! It was just a joke."

As quickly as it had appeared in his hand, the Tanto disappeared under his collar.

"Of course, it was a joke. That was a joke too." Hamza smiled at him.

"Huh. That was a surprise,." The neighbor sighed.

Hamza patted the frightened guy on the back.

"Come on man, it was a joke."

"Fuck your jokes, man."

"Where did you learn that?"

"In Bosnia."

"You guys had a war over there?"

"Yeah."

"Were you in the war?"

"Yeah."

"I didn't think you were dangerous."

"What, did you think you're dangerous? Gangs? There are no gangs in my country. Look at the three of you. I could wipe you out in fifteen seconds."

"Shit, man."

"Okay, baby." the neighbor tried to change the subject. "Where do you live now?"

Hamza told him.

"Shit, man. You should have stayed in our hood in the south. You would have been better off."

"You convinced me otherwise that night."

The frightened guy came out of shock and ordered another beer. He drank it in one swig.

"You've been lucky so far. You're still alive. Wait a minute man, that's Big Mike's territory." The neighbor looked at Hamza carefully. "Do you know Big Mike?"

"Yeah."

"Have you met him?"

"Yeah."

"Let me guess. They beat you up? Took all your money, and now they take your money regularly? Am I right?"

"Yes." Hamza said with a frown.

"All right baby. It's your life. You can keep getting jacked if you don't want to move. Anyway, we got to go now. Take care."

"You too. Thanks for the drink."

"You earned it."

After he had paid, the neighbor and his friends left. Hamza ordered a coffee and lit another cigarette. A minute later, the neighbor returned.

"I'll give you some free advice, baby. When you decide to take care of Big Mike, don't kill him. No matter what it looks like around here, you do go to jail for murder. Remember that." He turned around and started for the door.

"Hey, what's your real name?"

"I told you already. Whatever you want," he answered without turning around and left the bar.

*   *   *

That hot summer of 1997, Hamza rarely saw June. He was preoccupied with the search for Best Man. June noticed the changes in him, but didn't press him for an explanation. She asked him just once, "Hamza, is there anything I can do for you?" Since she got a negative reply, she didn't broach the subject again. She knew him well enough to know not to insist on anything. Subconsciously, with a woman's intuition, she knew that it wasn't about another girl. It was time. He simply needed time. After that lecture, she could only think of the terrible things that he had been through. With time, everything would be all right. Time heals everything.

She tried to have a conversation about Bosnia. If you repeat terrible stories over and over, they become normal with time. You become numb to them. But Hamza was so unpredictable. She could never know where the conversation would lead. One time, at the end of that summer, while they were sitting in a well air-conditioned restaurant, June started a conversation about a different issue. "Hamza you're a Muslim. So you don't believe in Jesus?"

"That's not true. Nobody—not you or anybody else—believes in and loves Jesus more than I do."

"Hey, wait a minute. Where's that coming from?"

"You know what? The main problem with humanity is ignorance. People are afraid of the unknown. And to know something superficially is worse than ignorance."

"You want to say that it's all about not knowing the facts?"

"Almost. Would you like me to give you a short introduction to the history of humanity?"

"Yeah, I really would like that, though I doubt that you can tell me something I don't already know."

"Why not give it a try? Just the facts, without an intention of convincing each other?"

"All right. You start."

"Let me just warn you. I have been in these discussions since I was a kid."

"Just go ahead."

"Stop me if I say something that you don't agree with. Well, it's like this. God created the universe and the earth. He created the first people out of earth. We call them Adem and Hava. Christians call them Adam and Eve. He gave them a place to live, Paradise. He had already created angels from light. Then he created the Jinns—beings of fire. He ordered them to bow to people. All the angels did, except for one Jinn—Satan or Lucifer—who God allowed to be in their company. So, that was the first sin in the world: disobedience. The devil had refused to bow. He thought he knew better. In Paradise, Adem and Hava ate the forbidden fruit. That's why they were sent down to earth."

"That's almost a completely biblical story."

"There is only one history. It's just that people adjusted it as they saw fit. So, the whole of humanity is derived from Adem and Hava. From time to time, God sent prophets to earth. There were many of them. They all had the same mission: to return people to the true faith and to teach them God's laws. So, history is the same here too. Only the names of the prophets are a bit different. Nuh, the Christians call Noah. Musa is Moses, Ibrahim is Abraham, Isa is Jesus. God's prophets were many. Basically, all the way to Isa—Jesus—the Bible and the Qur'an are fairly identical. The difference is that Christians consider Jesus to be God, and Muslims consider him God's prophet, just as many prophets before and just as Muhammad after him."

"I didn't know that. I thought that Muslims didn't believe in Jesus."

"That's it. We believe and love all God's prophets, including Isa. It's even known where he's going to be buried after he rises again."

"Where?"

"In Medina. Next to prophet Muhammad. There is a space left for him at the entrance."

"Do you think that is the only difference?"

"What seems like a minor difference to you and me is light years away for most people."

"Let's change the subject."

"All right."

Fall came again. Hamza was tired of looking for the best man. He was still wandering around Chicago, but without the zeal that once drove him. His best man had probably been in Chicago by chance and had already left. Hamza caught himself thinking about June instead of the best man. Maybe he should invite her to go away with him for a few days? It would be fun to visit a different state. But what if she says no? Hamza's mind felt trapped in a maze. He'd ask her the next time they meet.

*   *   *

Walking through a store, he noticed some newspapers from Croatia. He went up to the salesman.

"Do you have any newspapers from Bosnia?"

"No, but you can find them at Borders in Oak Park, about five miles west of here. If you want, I'll get you the directions."

The kind salesman talked while drawing the map.

"Take the 290 west, then Harlem north, and then a right on Lake street. It's easy to find. If you hurry, you might even find something tonight."

Hamza hadn't been in the greatest of moods, and the rain only made it worse. He couldn't stand in one place for very long. After work, he would walk through the city with no apparent purpose or direction. He hadn't seen June in a while. She was probably very busy. She hadn't been to Michigan Avenue in a few weeks. He felt uncomfortable calling her at work, and she didn't know his address. He didn't have a phone either.

He decided to head to the bookstore. He hadn't heard anything about Bosnia in a long time and felt depressed. He thought about the American expression *homesick*—one who feels sickness longing for his home. Hamza made his way through the city traffic and got on interstate 290. The car flew. After a few minutes, he caught up to a limousine driving slowly. Agitated, Hamza swerved around it, came back to the left lane, and sped forward. Too late, he noticed that he was stuck in the off-ramp lane. Different from many highway exits, the off-ramps for Harlem and Austin, six or seven miles out of Chicago, were on the left side of the highway. Hamza cursed quietly, knowing he would have to exit, and find another entrance.

As he approached the traffic lights at the exit, he slowed down. Just before the light, a young man stood in the pouring rain with a sign reading "HOMELESS" hanging over his chest. Although the sight was a common one, Hamza always felt uncomfortable. Sarajevo had its fair share of the poor, but this was different. The word homeless was associated with abject poverty and misery. Poor man, Hamza thought to himself. But, that was just another one of the numerous sides of America. The light turned green, and Hamza started driving. Subconsciously, he felt that something was wrong. Something wasn't the way it was supposed to be. But what? Maybe it had something with that poor, homeless man? Homeless, homeless . . . Hamza shook his head, trying to clear it. Was it the arm? The arm! The young man didn't have a left arm. And that face. Now he figured what was wrong. It was the homeless young man, without an arm.

"Dino!"

Hamza screamed and slammed on the brakes. The car screeched to a halt. A line of cars behind him started braking in panic. Hamza jumped out of the car and ran back to the highway exit.

A driver had stopped and handed the homeless man a few dollars. Hamza ran faster.

"Dino, Dino!"

The homeless man turned around. Hamza ran toward him.

Recognizing him, Dino turned around and started running away.

Hamza ran after him.

"Dino, hold it! It's me, Hamza!"

"Help! Help!" Dino was screaming.

A man came out of his car.

"Hey you, leave him alone!"

Running at the man, Hamza pulled out his wallet, flashed it, and yelled, "Police! Move!"

The driver retreated to his car and drove away.

Soon, Hamza caught up with Dino and grabbed him by the shoulders.

"Hold it! It's me, Hamza!"

Dino kept screaming and calling for the police. Hamza grabbed him by the arm and pulled him back toward his car. Behind his truck, a long line of cars had formed. The impatient drivers were honking. Some of them would have gotten out of their cars, but having seen Hamza dragging Dino along, they decided to stay inside. In Chicago, everybody minds their own business anyway. Hamza looked at the cars and shouted, "Sorry, Sorry!"

He opened the passenger door and pushed Dino inside. He dashed around the truck to his seat and started the car. As he circled the car, Dino opened the door and tried to jump out. Hamza grabbed him by the collar.

"Oh no, you don't. I looked after you for three years and now you want to run away from me? No way. What's wrong with you? It's me."

Realizing there was nowhere to go, Dino leaned back in his seat and closed his eyes.

"Dino, it's me."

"I know. I recognized you right away."

"Well, aren't you happy to see me?"

"No."

"What the hell is wrong with you?"

"Nothing. Would you please stop the car so I can get out?" Dino was almost crying.

"Where do you want to go?"

"I'm minding my own business, and you should mind yours."

"You're crazy, acting like you never saw me before. Are you on drugs?"

Hamza meant that as a joke. Dino put his head down. Hamza could feel goose bumps going all over his body.

"Dino, look at me. Look me in the eyes. Look at me, you motherfucker."

Dino turned around and looked at Hamza. At the same moment, he tried to pull the door handle. Hamza slammed on the brakes, Dino slammed forward into the windshield. Hamza pulled him by the collar again, very firmly this time.

Dino lost his balance and fell into the seat. His head ended up in Hamza's lap.

"You want to go, huh? Well, now we're going together!" Hamza slammed the gas pedal down to the floor. The tires squealed and the truck swerved and danced forward on the rain-slicked road. Hamza went faster and faster. He drove across several lanes until he had entered the oncoming traffic lane. The oncoming cars had to avoid him either by braking suddenly or climbing up onto the sidewalk.

"Hamza, slow down, you're going to kill yourself."

"I won't kill myself. *We* are going to kill *our*selves."

"I can't die twice."

Something in his voice made Hamza slow down. He turned into a side street and came to Oak Park again. He parked the car and helped Dino out. He flagged down a cab, pushed Dino into the backseat, and jumped in next to him.

"Just drive"

They drove off. For a while there was silence. Then Hamza began talking.

"Out of everything you could do in the whole world, you chose drugs."

"What do you care?"

"What the fuck do you mean? I took care of you for three years. And now, 'what do I care?' So, you're really not glad to see me at all?"

"I'm glad to see that you're alive."

"Well, at least that's something. Do you know how many times I came looking for you? You were never home."

"I know how many times you came looking for me, and I was home every time."

"But your old man said . . ."

"I know what my old man said. But all of you hid too. Like a bunch of . . . But, why do I need to tell you any of this? Dado was the only one who cared."

"Why Dado?"

"Well, when he came to my house the second time and my old man again told him I wasn't there, he pushed him aside and came in."

"Yeah, so what, I should have pushed your father around too?"

"You don't know anything, Hamza. Do you know what it is to cry for a year and pray to God that somebody comes and finds you? Anyone, just to help you. Do you know what I have been through? You don't. Do you want me to tell you about the desperation I felt within those four walls? Fuck you. Just don't give me that 'I couldn't find you' routine."

*   *   *

They were passing just north of Cicero. Hamza saw a bar. The sign above the entrance said "Saigon." Another minute in the car, and he thought he might suffocate. "Pull over!" The cab stopped, and Hamza and Dino got out. Hamza leaned in through the window and paid the driver. He held Dino firmly by the shoulders, afraid that he might try to run away again. He opened the door of the bar and practically threw Dino inside. He followed. Without thinking, he sat Dino at a table in the middle of the bar and then took a seat himself. He turned his head to the bartender.

"Two whiskies, doubles!" He turned to Dino again. "Here's something much better than heroin." He turned back to the bartender. The bartender sat on the other side of the bar with no apparent intention of serving them. Hamza went up to the bar and quietly took two glasses, grabbed a bottle of whisky, and poured. He grabbed a few ice cubes with his fingers and dropped them into the glasses. He nodded to the bartender and came back to the table.

"Hold this, good. Cheers. Where do you live?"

"In Oak Park."

"Or near Oak Park." Hamza knew that Oak Park was a pretty expensive neighborhood.

"A bit to the east."

"That's not a nice neighborhood. Do you live alone?"

"With Rosita."

"Rosita?"

"That's what I call her. She's Mexican. We live together."

"Wow! Do you love her?"

"I don't. She doesn't love me either. But she takes good care of me."

Hamza was about to comment on her care, given that he was out begging on the highway, but stopped himself in time.

"It's better than nothing. So, what do you do?"

Hamza put a glass in his hand. They both drank at the same time. They then both coughed at the same time.

"When did you get to Chicago?"

"Five months ago."

"So, what's happening over there?"

"I don't know now."

"Oh, come the fuck on. Just tell me. Don't make me drag every word out of you. What was going on when you left?"

"Nothing special."

"What about our guys?"

"Depends on who you're talking about."

"Dino! Buddy! Look at me."

"All right! Right after you left, the war stopped."

"Damn! If I had known that, I would have left earlier."

"It's like this. Sakib got married to a carpenter's daughter. Her old man bought them an apartment and furnished it. Then he bought them a car. Sakib works with him now."

"Sakib? Yeah, he was always a bit on the dull side, but he was reliable. You could be sure to find him where you had left him."

"Mustafa is in politics now."

"The forester? Ah Mustafa, he'll be fine over there. Bosnia is a forest full of wild creatures."

"Everybody thinks that he's a good guy. He's honest."

"Honest, and smarter than ninety percent of the others."

"Musa went to Canada."

"Musa? To Canada?"

"Yeah. Something's strange with that story. I saw him before he left. He said he was going to see your best man. He'd heard he had left for Canada. He said your best man owed him something big, so he had to go get it back."

"Musa?"

"Yeah. I don't understand that. Everybody knows Musa never had money. How come your best man can owe him something so big that it's worth the trip to Canada?"

Hamza combed his fingers through his hair, considering. "Oh, my best man, you poor bastard. Now you're really fucked. Even if I get tired and stop looking for you, even if I could give up, Musa will always be on your back."

"What about Dado?"

"Dead."

"Dead? Dado? How?"

"He was murdered."

"You mean he got shot."

"No. He got murdered in his apartment in Dobrinja."

"How?"

"Nobody knows. You know how cautious he was. He had three locks on his door and a gun in his hand at all times. I thought about that for a long time. I figure that he was killed by a friend."

"What do you mean?"

"Dado must have personally opened the door for the killer. He ended up getting three bullets to the back of the head."

"What about money? He must have had a million."

"No money."

"Dado, Dado. He snuck through mine fields, caught Chetniks like rabbits, and got shot like a punk. What about Kemo?"

"He opened a bar."

"You're kidding me? Where did he get the money?"

"No one knows."

"When did he open the bar?"

"Shortly after Dado was murdered."

"Wait a minute, don't tell me you're thinking . . ."

"I'm not thinking anything. I'm just telling you the facts. Anything is possible, Hamza. It was war."

"Dino, the war can't be an excuse for all the fucked up things in the world."

"As you can see, yes it can."

"Wait a minute. Hey! Two doubles."

The big bartender didn't move this time either. Hamza got up and went to the bar. He reached for the bottle. The bartender grabbed his hand and held it.

"The money."

"You know, where we come from, only hoes are paid up front, but if you insist . . ." Hamza reached into his pocket and took out a big wad of cash. He gave the man a hundred-dollar bill. The bartender released his grip. Hamza poured the drinks and came back to the table.

"Well, now we're fucked, proper."

"Why are we fucked, Dino? What's the matter?"

"Do you see where we are, man? Look around. Just slowly though."

For the first time since they had entered the bar, Hamza looked around. Was it a bar or a nightclub? The space itself couldn't have been more than sixty by ninety feet. Along the wall, there was a stainless steel bar with some barstools. The tables were randomly scattered around the room. In the corner was a guitar, saxophone, and a drum set. The walls held photographs of the Vietnam War. Behind the bar was a military jacket with a hole near where the heart should be. Next to it, a poster of the movie "Deer Hunter." There were roughly twenty people in the bar. Two old guys sat at the table nearest to them. In the far corner were four young bucks with a menacing air about them. They were talking quietly, looking at their direction. The same type of people sat at other tables as well. Two hookers sat at the bar. It was probably lunch break.

"Hamza, Rosita, the one I told you about, works the streets. She's not afraid of anything or anybody, and she warned me not to come to this neighborhood. Now we walked right into the middle of it."

"Fuck it, we'll think of something."

"If only you hadn't pulled out that wad of cash. There is no way we're getting out of here alive now. Even if we do, we'll be dead within ten yards."

As if he had understood what they were talking about, the big bartender moved like a mountain of muscle and came to their table.

"Hey, you sons of bitches! I don't know what you're doing or why you're here. But, as long as you are here, you're going to speak English. Leave Russian for when you go back to your fucking country."

"It's not Russian. It's Bosnian."

"Bosnian? Well, then leave Bosnian for later or get out of here."

"Fine, English."

When the bartender left, Hamza turned to Dino, "You said we were screwed?" He spoke more quietly and in English. "If, after all we've gone through, we get killed here, then we really don't deserve any better. Do you know what we are to them? The Mafia. They're nothing but kids compared to us, Dino. Now, listen to me carefully and do exactly what I say, okay? Get up slowly and start emptying your pockets. Take out everything and turn your pockets inside out, so they can see that you don't have anything else on you."

Dino finished his drink and got up. He started emptying his pockets. About ten dollars, a letter, a syringe, some change . . .

Hamza took the syringe and snapped it on the table.

"You won't need this anymore."

Dino sat down. Hamza got up and started emptying his pockets: a big wad of cash, a pocketknife, and his documents. He took the watch from his hand and put it on the table. On the other side of the bar, the bartender looked at them silently. The other guests turned to them and watched in amazement. Hamza motioned to the bartender. He came this time.

"How much for a cab to Kedzie?"

"I don't know."

"Guess."

"No idea."

"Maybe fifty?"

"Maybe."

"Okay. Here is fifty for the cab and here is the address on Kedzie for the cab driver. The rest is for drinks, for everybody."

"There's a lot of money here."

"Yes. And if you have something to eat, like cheese, or . . ."

"I'll find something." The bartender grinned. He had figured out Hamza's plan, and he liked it. "Drinks for everybody! Come on people. You don't think that I'll bring them over, do you?"

The group in the corner looked at Hamza furiously. The bartender brought them two bottles of whisky and some ice. The guests took their drinks from the bar and returned to their tables.

"So you were saying, Dado came and saw you. Shit, he never told anybody about it."

"My dear Dado. He was the only one who never lied to me."

"What do you mean by that?"

"When he saw me for the first time, he said, 'Kid, you're screwed'. You know Hamza, all the others kept telling me it was nothing, that it was more important that I was still alive and shit like that."

"That's Dado for you. He hits the nail right on the head."

"He said, 'Kid, there is nothing here for you. The ones who are still healthy don't have food to eat, so what do you expect?' He said that we should go to America until things settled down a bit, and then we'd go back to Europe. Then he said, 'We're going to hunt Chetniks. No matter how many we eliminate, it'll be worth it.'"

"What happened to that Chetnik?"

"Which one, the one whom I didn't let them shoot?"

"Yeah."

"Nothing."

"Did he kill him or not?"

"No, he didn't."

"He told you that?"

"Yeah."

"And you believed him."

"Of course, I did. He's never lied to me."

"So, how did your parents let you go to America? What did your old man say?"

"You didn't hear about it? Of course you didn't, you left in fall of '95. Did you know that I got an apartment? Yep, I got an apartment in Hrasno—a two-bedroom—from some Chetnik."

"Great."

"Yeah, I thought so too. We settled in a bit. My old man stopped drinking. He made furniture for the whole place, shelves too. He painted the apartment. It looked really good."

"So what went wrong?"

"One day, the Chetnik came back. He said he had the right to the apartment as long as he wasn't accused of war crimes. And the fact that they had killed and burned for four years that didn't matter at all. Shortly after, we received an eviction notice."

Hamza saw darkness and despair.

"That's impossible."

"So, the Chetnik came with the police. In this condition, I couldn't be of any help. Dado was on a trip, so I called the captain from my neighbor's phone. He came over right away. He started a fight with the cops. They clubbed him with nightsticks and took away his gun. They threw him out by force. Chaos, yelling, screaming. My dad got a bottle of brandy from somewhere and started drinking. All of a sudden, we heard my mother scream. We ran into her room. She wasn't there. The window was open. I looked outside. She was lying facedown on the concrete. She jumped out of the window."

Hamza stared at the floor with a frozen expression on his face.

"So, that's peace in Bosnia."

He took the bottle and drained it, then threw it into the corner of the room. The bottle shattered. He felt his brain absorb the alcohol. Big beads of sweat rolled down his forehead. Dino drank more slowly.

"Hamza, how many people have you killed?"

"None."

"Don't fuck around with me."

"You mean how many Chetniks have I killed?"

"Yeah."

"I don't know."

"Approximately."

"I don't even know approximately."

"Did you kill ten of them?"

"Dino, come on."

"All right, did you kill ten?"

"More."

"Twenty?"

"More, Dino. Many, many more."

The bar became deadly silent. The guests had turned around and were listening with curiosity to their conversation. Hamza's and Dino's inhibitions were long gone. They talked loudly, draining the glasses of whiskey.

The bartender brought them two new bottles of whisky and remained nearby.

"In the last mission, there were about fifteen of them in that dugout."

"Do you remember when you killed the first person?"

"Chetnik, Dino. Chetnik. Not a person."

"All right, fuck it, a Chetnik. Do you remember?"

The world around Hamza disappeared. He no longer noticed anybody else in the bar. The guests, who had inched their tables closer to theirs, disappeared. Even the four rough-looking guys had brought their drinks to the bar and listened to the story carefully. Hamza got up. He staggered to the switch and turned off the main light in the room. He came back to the table, downed another glass, and then smashed it against the wall.

"It was night. April 1992. I crossed the hills above the tunnel at Bembasa."

Hamza had completely transferred himself to that rainy night. The guests listened to the strange story.

"Rain, mud, slippery."

Hamza stalked around the bar, mimicking his movements through the dense bush. He was obviously reliving the event: He grabs a branch to keep from sliding backwards. Suddenly, the wind brings the smell of a cigarette to him. Hamza stands with his head raised high, sniffing the air like a bloodhound. He tries to figure out the direction the smell is coming from. He drops down to the floor of the bar and continues to crawl. He gets up and sits one of the guests behind the support pillar in the middle of the bar. The guard. He's smoking while leaning against a tree. Hamza crawls to get closer to him. When he's close enough, he takes a stone and throws it in the other direction. The guard turns around. Hamza springs forward. He grabs him by the jaw. With his left hand, he searches him. He finds the knife and stabs it through the guard's temple. The black guy held by Hamza struggles. He can't breathe. Hamza stands up. He holds the knife up high. He screams loudly and licks off the blood and pieces of brain.

Hamza came back to the table. He drank another glass and smashed it against the wall. He raised his hands high and began singing. Dino translated the words of the song for the guests:

> *"Sing me only that song, Koshtana.*
> *Take off your vest, raise your hands above your head"*
> *"If only you knew, girl*
> *How sorry I am*
> *That my youth is gone."*

Hamza's voice, normally clear and resonant, was hoarse from the alcohol, giving the song a special, somewhat rougher tone. His voice trembled and rose above the tables and guests, disappearing into the heavy cloud of smoke that clung to the ceiling. Hamza felt his eyes brimming with tears. Something warm and salty poured down his cheeks. He sang at the top of his lungs, while images of his lost loved ones flashed before his eyes.

"You would, my beloved . . ."

With his arms raised high, Hamza walked around the bar. He took short breaks in the middle of the song to drink more whiskey and smash the empty glasses against the wall.

"Hamza, when did you kill the last person?"

"Chetnik Dino, Chet-nik. I remember. In the last mission. We thought that we had finished when Dado brought in that colonel, captain, whatever the fuck he was. Do you remember when I cut his head off? You cried. I went outside. I was shaking. I stood near the dugout to calm down. All of a sudden, I heard somebody crying from the next ditch. I crawled forward, slowly. I saw the shadow of a man. I threw myself at him. With my right hand, I grabbed his machine gun and pulled him by the hair. I pulled his head back to expose his neck. The knife was in my left hand, raised high above me. But, it wasn't a real Chetnik. This was a kid, more a child than a man. I hesitated. What now? How am I going to kill a kid? He went for his gun. BANG!" Hamza pulled his sweater up, revealing a long scar along his chest. He indicated the path of the bullet with his finger.

"Along the chest, to the jaw, across the eye, and along the forehead. I swung down and my knife drove into that kid's head. I jumped up and turned around. There was no one left."

Hamza shook his head. He had returned to the real world. He drank another glass of whiskey.

"Hamza, sing something for us. Something from home. One of our songs."

Hamza raised his arms.

> *"Moj Dilbere, kud se setes?*
> *"Aj, sto I mene ne povedes?"*

Dino translated.

> *"My dear, where have you gone?*
> *Why didn't you take me with you"*

Two old men had inched so close that they almost sat at the same table with Hamza and Dino. One of them took out his harmonica and tried to pick up the melody. The other one drummed the beat with his hands. The music turned into the blues.

"Ah, sto te volim,

Ah, sto te ljubim

Aman Boze moj"

"Oh, how I love you

Oh, how I kiss you

My God."

"Povedi me u carsiju,

Aj, pa me prodaj pazardjiji

"Take me to town,

Oh, and leave me in a pawnshop."

"Oh, how I love you,

Oh, much I kiss you,

My God."

"Uzmi za me oku zlata

Pa pozlati dvoru vrata."

"Take for me a bag of gold

Oh, and cover your house doors in gold."

"Oh, how I love you,

Oh, how I kiss you,

My God."

"Ko god ide neka pita

Haj, cija li su ono vrata

To su vrata moga zlata."

"Whoever walks down the street let them ask,

Oh, whose doors are these?

Those are the doors of my darling."

"Sing the one 'The Young Man Plays the Tamburitza'"

"Okay, my dear friend."

Tamburalo momce uz tamburu

Tambura mu od suhoga zlata

Tanke zice kose djevojacke a terzija pero sokolovo

The young man played the tambourine
The tamburine of pure gold
The thin strings, the hair of a girl
The pick, a feather of a hawk.

Gledala ga Ajka sa cardaka
Vidi majko lijepa junaka
Da mi ga je u dvoru gledati
Na njegovim grudma sevdisati

Ajka looked at him from the castle
Look, mother, what a handsome hero
I wish I could watch him in my castle
I wish I could rest upon his chest

Karanfil bih pod njega sterala
A pod glavu rumenu ruzicu
Nek mirise nek se cesto budi
Ceto budi i cesto me ljubi

I would scatter carnations beneath his body,
And place a red rose 'neath his head
So he could smell it, and wake often
Wake and love me often.

Dino translated the song to the guests quietly.
Hamza finished yet another bottle and smashed it.
"Dino, do you trust me?"
"I trusted you when our lives were at stake."
"The important thing is that I've found you. Everything is going to be all right. You'll see. I have a good job. I work for the union. You won't believe how much I earn—$25 per hour. We can have everything. We'll find an apartment in a good neighborhood. We'll settle down. We'll go fishing on the lake. I've been meaning to get some fishing equipment for a long time now. We'll hang out in bars every once in a while. We'll find some girls. We'll put you through school. There's a thousand jobs you can do. Check you out—homeless? Bah!"

"Forget about that now, Hamza. Sing to us."

"I will, Dino, I will. Which one do you want me to sing?" Hamza wanted to grab the bottle and then realized there wasn't one on the table. "Hey boss, are there any drinks left? Is there any whiskey for the former warriors? For the former kings? Dino! We were kings, weren't we?"

The bartender snapped out of his daze. While listening to those weird stories and songs, he had completely forgotten about the bar and the guests. He pulled out a few new bottles and poured drinks all around. Dino was already hammered. Hamza's question seemed to wake him up. Suddenly, his face changed. He became a different person. His eyes cleared and he looked tough. He drained his glass and smashed it.

"Yes Hamza, *we were kings.*" He got up, hugged Hamza, and started singing. Hamza joined in.

> *Da je meni leci umrijeti*
> *Lane moje leci umrijeti,*
>
> *"I wish I could lie down and die,*
> *Oh, my sweetheart, just lie down and die.*
>
> *Umrijeti smrti ne vidjeti*
> *Lane moje smrti ne vidjeti*
>
> *To die, and not see death*
> *Oh, my sweetheart, not see death*
>
> *Da ja vidim ko ce me zaliti*
> *Lane moje ko ce me zaliti*
>
> *To see who will cry for me*
> *Oh, my sweetheart, see who will cry for me."*

At the midpoint of the song, they stopped, grabbed their bottles, and started drinking. The whiskey filled their throats, overflowed, and started spilling out—running down their cheeks, clothes, and finally, the floor. Before they reached the bottom, they lost their balance and started falling. Two rough guys caught them just before they hit the floor. The bartender motioned to lay them on the floor.

"George, you got your car here?"

The rough guy nodded.

"Put them in the car and take them to this address." He looked at the paper. "I'll be damned, I'll be damned. Ha-ha-ha. George, take them. Watch out, I don't want anything to happen to them."

"Hey, Chris, what's the matter with you? I know how to judge . . ."

"I hope you do. And you can call me Funny Chris from now on."

"You won't get mad? You're hard to deal with, you know."

"No problem. Look here. I'll put their money back in their pockets. They won't miss a thing. Tonight was on me."

"Did they remind you of Saigon?"

Funny Chris nodded silently.

"Yeah, George, they did. They certainly did."

*   *   *

While the car sped along, Dino opened his eyes.

"Hey, driver, where are we?"

"I'm taking you to a place on Kedzie."

"Please, could you drop me off first? 5400 West Addison."

"Nice neighborhood. Okay, brother, I'll get you there."

Dino got out of the cab, never waking Hamza.

*   *   *

Hamza opened his eyes when the car stopped in front of his house.

"Where is Dino?"

"I left him at 5400 West Addison."

"5400 West Addison." Hamza repeated. "Okay, I'll find him tomorrow. Thanks man."

"Take care, brother!" responded the driver as he drove off.

Hamza looked for his keys for a long time in front of his house. He mumbled a song under his breath. Finally, he unlocked the door and went up the stairs to the apartment. He fell asleep next to the couch, Dino forgotten for the moment. In the room on the first floor, Don't Worry Andy looked at Mary.

"This is his first time. I hope he doesn't keep it up. I already feel so sorry for that guy."

*   *   *

Ocean waves crashed in Hamza's head when he woke. The slightest move of his head brought new ones. Trying to move his head as little as possible, he put the coffee on and got into the shower.

"Let it hurt. It doesn't matter. The important thing is that I've found him. It's a miracle. Out of eight million people, I ran into him."

The shower had made him feel better, and he sat by the window. The strong coffee felt good. A cigarette did too. "A man has to be like coffee, strong and warm," he thought, recalling what Avdaga had once told him. "What's he doing now? Probably having coffee with Azra." While he drank coffee, smoking his cigarette, he thought about the conversation he'd had with Dino. "What did he say about his mother? Dear God, why do the good ones always have to die? Well, what's done is done. And Musa? He loved Amra and the Little One so much I often wondered whether he should have married her. It's a small world, Best Man! We'll find you. Whether Musa or I get there first doesn't matter; the same fate awaits you. Dado and Kemo? Is it possible? I don't believe it. Still, everything seems to fit. And Mustafa? In politics? I'm really happy for him. Our forester will know how to deal with politicians. Just like in the forest, he'll sneak up, and wham! He catches a war profiteer! As the old saying goes, 'There are very few people who maintain their integrity when tempted by gold coins and beautiful behinds.' Sakib? Got married. Funny guy. It's a good thing that at least one of us managed to lead a normal life. And I'm sitting here, wasting time when I should be picking up Dino."

Hamza got dressed quickly. He put his knife into the mattress. "I don't think I'll need you tonight. Maybe, God willing, never again. Dino and I can start over."

He stopped on the stairs. He wanted to tell Andy that Dino would stay with him for a while. No, there would be time enough for that when they got back. He might have more trouble with Big Mike. He'd have to take care of him eventually. There was no way one of his cronies could even look at Dino the wrong way, let alone hit him. Mike'll be really surprised when I smack him around a bit. Hamza imagined Big Mike's face as he flew to the ground. But, he'd have to be fast. There were too many of them. He'd have to be so quick and convincing in getting Mike down that the others wouldn't even dare try anything. If he could just tape it somehow and send it to Musa. Hamza laughed. Hamza sang old songs as he drove his truck toward Addison. He found his documents, money, and the watch in his pocket. What did that mean? He tried to come up with an explanation, but couldn't think of anything reasonable. He gave up. He'd have to go back to that bar. He'd find it again somehow.

After a short drive, he found 5400 West Addison, but it was a store. Maybe it's across the street. The cabbie is usually given some better-known reference point. Hamza parked and knocked at the door of the house across the street. Nobody answered. He went to the next house. After knocking for a while, he heard someone walk up to the door.

"Who is it?"

"Excuse me. I'm looking for a young man. His name is Dino."

"There is nobody by that name here," answered a rude voice from the other side of the door. Hamza turned around and crossed the street. He went into the store. It was a small grocery store. Large iron bars protected the windows. A big Mexican lady sat at the cash register. She looked at Hamza suspiciously.

"Excuse me. I'm looking for a young man. His name is Dino. He's missing his left arm."

"I'm sorry. I don't know anybody like that."

"Please, try to remember. He's really . . ."

"You were told that there was nobody like that here," bellowed a rough voice from the back of the room. Hamza couldn't see who had spoken.

"All right, I'm leaving. Have a nice day." He left the store. It wasn't their fault. It was simply that type of neighborhood. The important thing was for him to avoid trouble today. He looked around the street. On the corner, there was a group of black guys and a couple of Mexican girls. Hamza approached them.

"Hey, man, you got a couple of dollars for these guys?" asked a young black guy with a nasty expression on his face. He came up to Hamza.

"Of course," Hamza said, pulling out a ten-dollar bill. "I'm looking for a friend. His name is Dino. He's missing an arm."

"White?"

"White."

"Man, this is a black neighborhood. There are no whites here."

"He lives with a Mexican girl, Rosita."

"Man, every Mexican girl around here is called Rosita. Try somewhere else."

Hamza felt himself starting to sweat. He spent the whole afternoon looking for Dino. First he went around the block, then the next block. He went around the whole neighborhood. He checked all the bars and restaurants. He talked with drug dealers and prostitutes. He knocked on countless doors. Some of them didn't open. At others, people tried to remember. Some would just shake their heads. Some just slammed the door in his face.

He was stopped by police in the evening. Somebody had called saying that a suspicious white man had been walking around the neighborhood all day. The policemen were kind but strict. They searched him from head to toe. They searched his vehicle too. They brought him down to the station for interrogation and verification. After almost an hour, the policeman gave him a friendly piece of advice—get lost.

"Your story might be okay, but we can't guarantee your safety. It's a miracle that nothing happened to you so far. Now, get lost and look for your friend somewhere else."

On the verge of panic, Hamza went back. He was close to the house when he realized that Dino might be on the highway again. He turned on Western Street and got on interstate 290, westbound. He exited at Austin. Dino wasn't there. He came back to the highway and exited at Harlem. He wasn't there either. He thought that Dino might be near the opposite exit. So, he parked the car and went back to the intersection on foot. He questioned people at nearby gas stations, bars, and restaurants. It was almost midnight when he finally got back home.

"I'll find you, God willing, and you won't get away again. Chicago is big, but I'll find you."

While making plans on how and where they were going to live and what they were going to do, Hamza fell into a sleep filled with a bizarre mixture of hope and nightmares. The next day he had to go to work. He could hardly wait for his shift to end. Somebody had to know about Dino and where he lived. Maybe in the Bosnian restaurants or the bar "Jaran." He didn't feel like going, but he had to. Dark faces greeted him at "Jaran." Hamza calmly went through to the bar. In a loud voice, he asked the waiter about Dino, hoping that everybody in the bar could hear him. The waiter silently shook his head. Since the so-called incident from the previous spring, they didn't like him very much. He turned and looked around the room. None of the guests showed any signs of recognizing the name. Hamza left. He didn't have any luck at the place called "Ljiljan"—so named after the Lily on the Bosnian coat of arms—or at any of the other Bosnian restaurants either. Not knowing where to go next, he decided to head back to Highway 290. Nothing again. He called it a day and went back home to sleep.

A whole week passed in the fruitless search. After that, he started wandering west of Chicago— Berwyn, Cicero, Oak Park . . . He would ask around and search. He didn't work on Saturday and so he made plans to go to a Bosnian mosque in Northbrook, and then from there he'd go around to different churches from Chicago to Oak Park.

Maybe there was a welcome group that knew of him. Those welcome groups were a good thing. A few volunteer families would get together and help Bosnians for a few months until they settled in. They usually gave them used furniture, dishes, clothes, food, and sometimes they would help them with finances too. Hamza was going crazy thinking about Dino, probably sitting hungry in some cold, bare apartment, or standing near a different highway off-ramp, begging again. If he didn't find him by Saturday, he would go to the police. They had to have him on file somewhere. Yes. That was what he was going to do. He felt a bit better after coming up with a plan.

*   *   *

He woke up early. It was cloudy outside; the morning promised rain. He drank a few cups of coffee and smoked almost half a pack of cigarettes, and then it was time to continue the search. He was already out of the house when Andy called to him.

"Good morning. Do you a minute?"

"Morning. Not really. I'm in a real hurry."

"Please, just five minutes."

"All right." Hamza thought that he might have forgotten to pay the rent. But there were still five or six days until the first of the month. He came into the kitchen. Andy drank coffee. He poured another cup and handed it to Hamza.

"No, thanks, I'm in a hurry. Maybe some other time."

There was a huge pile of photos in front of Andy. He took one and gave it to Hamza.

"That's me in Vietnam. That was our commander. He died a few days after this photo was taken."

Hamza looked at the photo and gave it back to Andy.

"You can smoke if you want to. Mary is not in the house. She's gone grocery shopping, and then she's visiting some friends after that. I could use a cigarette too." Mary didn't allow him to smoke, so he would ask Hamza for a cigarette every once in a while when Mary wasn't at home.

Hamza pulled out a pack and gave it to him.

"Here you go. I'm on my way to buy a pack anyway. I have to go."

"You can stay ten minutes. Every girl will wait that long."

"No, it's not a girl, Andy. But, all right, if you insist. Ten minutes."

Hamza lit a cigarette and poured himself a cup of coffee. He took a sip.

"This is me in Saigon." Andy handed him a second photo. He looked young, strong, in the company of an Asian girl, grinning.

"Do you know how I got the nickname 'Don't Worry Andy'?"

"I have no clue."

"Out of my whole division, four-fifths of us didn't make it back from Vietnam. They stayed in the jungle forever. While some units didn't even see a jungle in Vietnam, or the Vietnamese for that matter, we were sent out there mission after mission."

"That's what usually happens in life."

"Yes. We went from mission to mission until we were completely worn-out. I was constantly terrified. I was scared worse than anyone else, but I still had to go. Before every mission, I used to tell myself, '"Don't worry Andy, don't worry Andy."' And so, slowly they started calling me 'Don't Worry Andy'. You know, I believe in God, and I was sure that God would not let Andy stay in the jungle. That's why I kept repeating 'Don't worry.' God will worry for you. Your duty is to do the best you can. Don't worry, don't worry."

"Okay Andy, that was Vietnam, but how did you get that name in Chicago?"

"Great, I see you're following along. You see, there was a guy from Chicago who was in my unit. Chris. We used to call him Funny Chris. The funniest thing is that he wasn't funny at all. Just the opposite. The people from the headquarters were afraid of him, so were we, and so were the Vietnamese. He was a head taller than me, and weighed at least twice as much."

Hamza quickly did the math, about one hundred fifty kilograms. That was definitely not a funny guy.

"He used to shave his head and grow a long mustache. Drugs, prostitution, murder, blackmail, and everything else you could think of was linked to him."

"Wait a minute. So, how did he get the nickname 'Funny'?"

"Good question. You know, when it gets really bad, so bad that you can actually feel how bad it is with every inch of your body, Chris would get a laugh attack. And the interesting thing was that he never laughed unless it was really bad. And those attacks were terrible. First, his shoulders would start shaking. Then he would burst out laughing. Not a pretty sight at all. He would laugh like a lunatic, jump out of the ditch, and start shooting. After getting off a few shots, he would charge. So, we had to follow him, whether we wanted to or not. Poor Vietnamese. They probably thought that the devil himself led the attack."

"I have never heard of something like that."

"And you know what's especially bizarre? Bullets didn't like him. He went through the whole hell of Vietnam without so much as a scratch."

"And?"

"And nothing. I came back from Vietnam wounded in both legs. A few months had passed and the wounds were still healing. One night, somebody knocked on the door. He was laughing. And, just so you know, once you hear Funny Chris laugh, you never forget it. Mary opened the door. It really was Chris. He asked where 'Don't Worry Andy' was, and so he ended up telling Mary all about how I got the nickname. Mary told her friends and relatives. So, by the time I was healthy enough to leave the house, everybody called me 'Don't Worry Andy.'"

"An interesting story."

"I still see him from time to time. He still has the nickname 'Funny,' although nobody is allowed to call him that. He owns a bar now, officially. Unofficially, he holds a few suburbs. Drugs, prostitution, gambling, and so on. They accused him of some murders too. Nothing could stick though. The police stay away from him. I don't know. People tend to exaggerate sometimes."

"That's true. People do exaggerate sometimes. But, I really have to get going now."

"Wait a minute. On Thursday, Funny Chris called me up. He just told me to come right away. And you know how it is. When he calls you, you need to go right away. And, I figured, we're old friends now, and I don't do the kind of things that could get me into trouble with him. So, I got dressed and went to the bar. He saw me at the door, came over and hugged me. I wasn't really comfortable, like being hugged by a bear. He could feel it and said 'Don't Worry Andy. We went to the bar. He poured us a couple of shots. He downed his right away and poured another one. And listen to this. He said, "So, that's how you are. You have a lion and you don't tell me anything."

"I was silent, just looking at him. I didn't understand what he was talking about, but I never dare counter what he says anyway."

"You have a golden lion, and you don't say anything to your old friend," he said as he slapped me on the shoulder. My whole back hurt.

"What lion, Funny?" the nickname slipped out of my mouth. I didn't say it on purpose. He burst out laughing, just like he used to in Vietnam.

"It doesn't matter, Andy. Your lion was here a couple of nights ago. He's great. The way he played all the thugs in here. They were starting to measure him up, you know, see how much they could take him for, when he emptied his pockets and gave everything to me. He said he wanted to drink and that he was paying for everyone. Then he and his friend started talking about the war. Singing. His friend translated for us. It was the best night of my life since getting back from Saigon."

Hamza looked at him silently. Impossible. It seemed as though Chicago was a big neighborhood and not a big city. Just like Sarajevo. People knew everything. Out of about half a million bars, restaurants, and pubs, he came upon Saigon. And the bartender did look just like Andy had described. That was it! He had written Andy's address on the piece of paper. That was why he had decided to give him the money back.

"So, I got drunk that night, Hamza. I couldn't say no to him even though I knew what's waiting for me at home. Now, tell me. I've been thinking about what he said for two days now, and you know what conclusion I've come to? Don't get mad but it seems that you are that golden lion. You have golden blonde hair. You look and walk like you're going hunting. You know those stairs of mine that go to the second floor? The only time they don't creak is when you and my cat go upstairs. So, it has to be that you're the golden lion."

"I'm sorry, Andy, I don't know what you're talking about. Thanks for the coffee. I have to go."

Hamza got up and went to the door.

"I didn't think so either. Never mind, I'll have to ask Funny Chris what he meant by that. By the way, have you been watching TV?"

"No, why?" Hamza had already opened the door that lead from the kitchen to the hallway.

"It was on Channel 5 last night. They found the body of a young man in the lake. Twenty-five, twenty-six years old. In a military jacket. With one arm."

Hamza stopped; his heart, blood, brain, and body all came to a screeching halt. With one hand on the door knob, he turned to Andy. He staggered back and hit the wall. His legs went numb and he slid down the wall. His lower jaw started trembling uncontrollably. With his left hand, he pressed against his jaw to stop his teeth from chattering. He stared straight ahead, in shock, without seeing anything. Andy moved quickly.

"Hamza, Hamza!"

Hamza sat, motionless. He held his jaw and stared with a distant look in his eyes. Andy tried to lift him up. Hamza motioned with his hand for Andy not to touch him. Andy started walking up and down the room.

"Oh, shit! Oh, God!"

Hamza and massaged his temples. He was losing his grasp on reality. The explosions in his head grew into a deafening roar. His eyes turned glassy. The room spun before his eyes, fading to black. Suddenly, a huge hurricane appeared, and the whole room and everything in it started spinning. Faster and faster. He felt as if he would be sucked into a giant, black hole. His brain was getting torn apart. The amount of negative information had overflowed his brain. And just like when he was wounded, his brain began to look for a way out. Salvation: insanity. The way out was through insanity. Just delete everything. Destroy all memory centers. Reject the memories. Keep the survival centers at all costs. Life. Life was the only important thing. Reject all senses, they are not necessary. Sight, hearing, smell, all that was ultimately unnecessary. Just hold on to the fine thread of life.

Hamza felt himself sliding into a bottomless pit. He felt himself on the edge, the mysterious and unexplored roads of the subconscious, balanced on the fine line separating this mind from eternal insanity. In front of his frozen eyes, the colors of the hurricane were changing. For a moment, it was white, then green, purple, pink, black, and back to white. His eyes wide, he stared ahead in shock. The hurricane was still sucking him in. Just a bit more. Just a little longer and the brain would make its irreversible final decision. Still in shock, yet somehow aware of what it meant, Hamza stared at the hurricane, awaiting the outcome.

Splash!

Andy had finally come to his senses. He found the whiskey that Mary had been hiding from him. He filled two big glasses. He splashed the first into Hamza's face. The second one he pressed against Hamza's lips. Since he couldn't manage to open Hamza's mouth, he poured the whiskey against it, hoping that at least a few drops would go through his clenched teeth. Hamza was still staring ahead blankly. Andy pinched his nose. Hamza instinctively opened his mouth and Andy poured the whiskey down his throat. Most of the whiskey went down and Hamza coughed. All the colors and the hurricane vanished. Suddenly he could see Andy's terrified face six inches in front of his own.

"I always wondered what a black guy looks like when he 'turns white. Come on," Andy said as he picked him up and carried him to the chair.

"Drink!" There was no more whiskey left and Andy gave him a cup of hot coffee. Hamza obeyed him mechanically. The hot coffee burned his tongue, and he started to breathe loudly in order to cool off his mouth.

"That's it, just stay with me."

Andy lit a cigarette and put it in his mouth. He lit one for himself. They smoked in silence for a few minutes.

"Man, oh, man! You were almost gone. You were a breath away from the other side. Man, I've seen it in Vietnam. Death is a reward in comparison to that."

After a few minutes, Andy started talking again.

"Why didn't you tell me? If you had told me, we could have done something for you. Funny Chris would have found him in half an hour. Wherever he hid, Funny Chris would have found him. But you didn't say anything. Now you're not saying anything either. How long have you been here? A long time, huh? Good morning, good evening! Nothing else. You know what? I've been thinking about that for a long time. Silence is a global problem of warriors.

"Cowards talk, warriors are silent. They are silent when it hurts, silent when it doesn't. You have to speak, you have to hear your own voice."

Andy's words seemed like an unintelligible murmur to Hamza. Andy talked and talked. Hamza's head fought against all thought. You will survive. Don't think. Change your train of thought. Go back to your childhood. Go back! That's it. Think about the neighbor's pear tree that you broke. That's it, that's good. The big, old tree in the fall. Big, juicy pears. No, don't go that way. Trees, fruits, cherries. Three kids who were picking cherries on Kobilja Glava, a couple of miles north of downtown Sarajevo, were killed by the Chetnik killing machines. Think about something else. There, Hamza is skiing, the snow, in the sun. Clear blue skies. From somewhere, other memories of snow are emerging.

The first snow in Sarajevo in the winter of 1993. A part of Sarajevo called Alipasino Polje. Kids are out sledding. A direct hit from a heavy missile. Seven little ones die. A father carries his little son, five or six years old. A shell fragment has completely ripped off his skull. The skin off the face is hanging down to the neck, like a rubber mask, while the father, white as a ghost, turns around helplessly. A few yards away, in the snow, lies a child's brain, red and white, like a lost hat. No, not the snow, not the pears or the cherries!

Think about the water, the fields. Thank God. The image is there. Green fields of a warm summer long passed. The whole family is picnicking next to the river. The field is big. At the end of the field, there is a river flowing slowly. You can see fish swimming about lazily. Everything is in slow motion. Keep that image.

" . . . And do you know what cured me? My Mary did. She made me talk. Thousands of questions. Why? Where? Who? What? How? Thousands. I thought I was going to kill her. She was worse than the Vietnamese. She kept asking until I finally broke down. As a matter of fact, I didn't break down. I came back. Then I cried, for days. Are you listening to me?"

"Yeah. Where do they take the bodies of people who have committed suicide?"

295

"I don't know. But, we can find out. Hang on a second," Andy said as he took the phone book. After making about ten phone calls, he came back.

"I've found it."

"Do you have the address? I have to go there."

"No way. I'm going to drive you. Let me just write a note for Mary. She'd worry without it."

The streets were packed with cars. On the busier streets, pedestrians milled about. In the park, there were parents with children and a few young couples in love. The sky was a navy blue. Suddenly, Hamza could smell the sweet, all-too-familiar smell of death. His dreams of escaping the horror with Dino were tasted like ashes in his mouth.

*   *   *

They arrived at the city morgue.

After briefly explaining the situation, they went to the mortuary.

The attendant pulled out a long iron drawer with Dino in it. His beautiful face was now blue. His hair was glued to his forehead. His eyes were closed. It seemed as if he was asleep. Hamza looked at him for a long time. Then he combed Dino's hair with his fingers.

"Sleep, kiddo, sleep."

Whether it was real or just imagined, there was a look of peace and relief on Dino's face.

"You've reached the end of the road. I'm sorry, kiddo."

"You know him?" asked the worker, pulling his sleeve.

"Yeah."

"Could you give us some information about him?"

"Of course."

They entered the office. Hamza answered the questions quietly. First name, last name, date and place of birth, address, occupation.

The worker offered him a cigarette. Hamza accepted gratefully. He really needed one.

"Who performs Muslim funerals in Chicago?"

"I'm not sure. Check the Islamic Foundation. I'll give you the address."

"Could I bury him? I mean . . ."

"Of course. As soon as we're done with the formalities, you can have him."

After the hospital, Andy took him to Villa Park. The Islamic Foundation was actually an elementary school with a small mosque. New construction was expanding the mosque further. The biggest mosque in North America. From the reception desk, they were sent to the director of the center.

"*Assalamu alaikum.* Brother Hamid?"

"*Alaikumu salam*, brother."

"My name is Hamza," he said to introduce himself and shook hands with the lively old man. He had a long beard, darker skin. A Pakistani. The old man radiated with true peace. He reminded Hamza of Sarajevo. Only deeply aware, religious people could glow with that kind of peace.

"How can I help you, brother?"

"I would like you to do the funeral for my friend."

"He died?"

"Yes, he died."

"Where is his body now?"

"In the hospital."

"Was he killed?"

"No, he wasn't. He killed himself."

The old man looked at him for a long time, silently.

"You know, son, suicide is . . ."

"I would leave that for God to judge. It's not up to us," Hamza nervously interrupted him.

"Yes. Allah is merciful." Both of them stood silently. "Were you close to him?"

Hamza nodded.

"All right. We'll take care of it. Give me the information so we can go and pick up the body. I'll see if we can get a place in the cemetery in Skokie. That's where Bosnians are buried. Was he Bosnian?"

"Yes, he was. Can I pay right now?"

"No. We'll finance it. We have funds for such funerals."

"But I want to pay."

"Son, what he needs right now, you can't buy. There's a mosque at the other end of the building. Go there and pray for him, if you know how to."

"I do."

"And if you have any extra money, there are donation boxes outside, for the school, for Bosnia, for the mosque. You can donate something if you like. You can take the ablution of 'wudhu' in the hall on the left."

"Thank you, brother. *Assalamu alaikum.*"

They shook hands and Hamza left. He took "wudhu" and went into the mosque.

He knelt down and started praying, quietly.

"Bissmillahi rrahmani rrahim . . ."

He whispered the well-known words from the Qur'an. He hadn't prayed for a long time. It's interesting the way he never forgot prayers from the Qur'an once he'd learned them. Just like riding a bike. It was one of the miracles of the Qur'an.

Hamza was focused while praying. Before every prayer, known to him as a *surah*, he would start, "In the name of Allah, the most magnificent and beneficent, the most merciful."

He didn't know how long he had been in the mosque. Suddenly, somebody coughed behind him. He turned around. Andy stood behind him. Hamza said the final words, *"Sadek allahulazeem,"* meaning, "The truth was spoken by Glorious Allah." He ran his palms down his face and joined Andy. They left the mosque together.

"I'm sorry, Hamza, but it's dark outside. And you know, Mary is going to get worried . . ."

Hamza nodded.

Andy was silent on the drive back. He spoke when they reached the house. "Interesting place. I didn't know that there was a place like that in Chicago."

"Neither did I."

"Now we're going to eat dinner at my place. Mary is going to fix us something. She's a good woman. She talks a lot, but she's all heart. And don't tell me that you can't eat. From now on, for the next few days, I'm your mother and father. By the way, are your parents alive?"

"Yes."

"And they live in Bosnia?"

"Yeah."

They entered the house. Mary appeared at the kitchen door. She turned on him with a menacing look, when Andy discretely put his finger over his lips. "Mary, dear. Here are two hungry, old men. Come on sweetheart, please feed the tired warriors."

Judging by his voice and Hamza's lost look, Mary figured that something bad had happened. Hamza was only a tenant to her, perhaps a bit more pleasant than the others, but still just a tenant. However, a small, expensive painting which he had given them the Christmas before had secured him a special place in her heart. Not because of the price but because of the fact that he had thought that they deserved to have a painting like that in their house. A bit surprised, she turned around and went into the kitchen. She was happily talking about harmless things, while sneaking peeks at Hamza. No matter what had happened, Andy would have to have a good explanation for that empty bottle of whiskey and the stench of alcohol everywhere.

"I'm going to prepare dinner now. Hamza, you're going to forget everything you have ever eaten in your life."

"I'm sorry, I don't eat pork."

Andy and Mary laughed.

"We don't either. Cholesterol. The doctor told us to stop eating it a few years ago."

Soon, there was fried chicken, potatoes, salad. Mary brought a bottle of wine to the table.

"No thanks, I don't drink."

Mary glanced at the empty bottle of whisky on the shelf, then at Andy. Andy just shrugged his shoulders.

After dinner, Andy brought Hamza two pills. Hamza shook his head.

"Listen, Hamza. I don't know how your father raised you. But I know I've told you that I am your mother and father now. Now, you're going to take these pills and go to sleep. I'll shove them down your throat if I have to."

Hamza obeyed. He took the pills and then they both lit a cigarette.

Surprisingly, Mary didn't say a word.

When Hamza had gone to bed, Andy poured some wine for Mary and himself and then they went to sit next to the fireplace.

"You know why I got drunk on Thursday, my dear Mary? The phone rang. I answered it. It was Funny Chris. He told me to come right away. What could I do? I went. I went to 'Saigon,' and Funny Chris said, 'You, Don't Worry Andy, have a golden lion and you didn't say anything.'" I couldn't think which lion he was talking about . . ."

Midnight passed and Andy was still telling Mary the strange story about their Hamza and the young man without an arm.

It rained the next morning. Andy didn't feel well, so Hamza went to the funeral alone.

                    *   *   *

The cemetery in Skokie, a North Chicago suburb, wasn't particularly big or old. It had a part where Muslims were buried according to their custom. The funerals were almost like those in Bosnia. The only difference was that the people were buried in coffins.

Aside from an employee of the cemetery, there were just a few people at the funeral: an imam—a Muslim priest from Northbrook—with a friend, brother Hamid with two people, and Hamza. The coffin was suspended right above the grave. The little engines turned on and the coffin was lowered with the help of leather belts. A concrete plate covered the coffin. The cemetery employees left. Hamza, together with the others, took a shovel and began piling the earth on the grave. The earth was muddy and stuck to the shovel. After they had finished, they wiped the mud off their shoes on the grass. They squatted and started praying silently. The well-known prayers reminded Hamza of many funerals in Sarajevo. When the imam had finished praying, he told Hamza to say something too.

Hamza turned his palms to the sky and started reciting prayer "Ihlas"—the final prayer in the Qur'an: "In the name of almighty Allah, the most magnificent, beneficent, the most merciful. Say, Allah is one . . ."

It was still raining. His clothes were soaked. With his head bowed, Hamza prayed for his friend's soul. When they had finished, Hamza introduced himself to the imam and his friend. The imam asked him to come to the mosque in Northbrook to talk a bit.

He then went to greet brother Hamid.

*   *   *

He drove back slowly. He ate at a restaurant on the way and bought some things at a corner store. It finally stopped raining. It grew dark by the time he arrived. The parking spots in front of the house were taken, and so Hamza drove around the block and came back to the street again. This time he had better luck and found a parking slot about a hundred yards away from the house. As usual, he just slammed the car door. It wasn't worth locking. If somebody wanted to get in, they would smash the window anyway. This way was better. He didn't look around. With his head down, he walked toward the house.

"Hey, Black Soul, come here!"

Hamza turned around. Big Mike sat on the stairs, surrounded by his buddies. With the wave of a finger, Mike beckoned him to come over.

"Not tonight," answered Hamza silently as he continued walking.

He heard footsteps behind him. Then Mike's furious voice: "Don't you walk away from me!" He put his big right hand on Hamza's shoulder and pulled him back.

"Arrrrhhhhhhh!" Hamza screamed horribly. All the negative energy built up inside him exploded. He grabbed Mike's fist. He turned quickly, holding Mike's hand firmly drove his right shoulder through Big Mike's elbow. There was a dull echo from the sound of the elbow popping out. It was muffled by Mike's scream. While Mike's body was still moving, Hamza grabbed Mike's massive bicep with his left, pulling him along. At the same time, he drove the palm of his right hand up into Mike's right armpit. Mike's body stopped for a split second.

His shoulder, between the force of his own momentum and Hamza's hand, tore apart with a sickening pop.

Big Mike's head hit the street before his feet did.

"Aaargh!" Mike screamed and writhed in pain on the ground. Mike's friend, who had held Hamza down while they had beaten him, charged Hamza. Hamza waited until the guy threw the punch.

With a small step, he dodged the punch, grabbed the fist, and twisted it viciously. He drove the forearm of his free hand through the extended elbow. It popped. As the body fell forward, Hamza kicked him in the face.

"Anyone else?" Hamza dared the others.

"You're dead, motherfucker! You're dead! There is no place you can hide! I'll fucking kill you!" Big Mike screamed and tried to get his legs under him. Hamza approached him. He drove his heel into Mike's chest, slamming him to the ground. He leaned over Mike.

"Next time, big guy! Next time, I'll rip your heart out and eat it! Like this!" Hamza put his hands together with the palms turned outward. He stabbed his fingers beneath the rib cage, pushed deeper, and pulled up. The rib cage strained between Mike's weight and Hamza's hands. Big Mike started screaming in panic.

"Like this! Next time. You know where to find me." Hamza got up.

He remembered that he had forgotten his bag in the car, so he went back. While he passed the group on the stairs, he said, "Take them to a hospital."

Andy waited for him in the hallway.

"I knew it. I knew it as soon as I saw you, especially after they had beaten you up the last time. Oh, man . . ."

"Okay Andy."

"Where are you going? It's dinner time."

"I'm really not hungry."

"Then the pills."

"I don't think I need them."

"I don't think you need them, either."

*   *   *

Andy couldn't resist.

"Hello, Funny Chris?"

"Hey, Don't Worry Andy! You still alive?"

"Hey, Funny Chris, do you know Big Mike?"

"Everybody knows Big Mike."

"Well, listen carefully . . ." Andy began telling him the story, slowly. After the first few words, Funny Chris interrupted, "Wait,

wait, wait. You can't do it by phone. That story needs to be told the right way. Get ready and get over here."

"No way, man. Mary would kill me."

"Bring her with you."

"Are you kidding?"

"Okay. I know that 'Saigon' is no place for ladies. But if I kick some guests out and clean up the place, it's going to look decent. All right? I'm sending a guy to pick you up."

Mary talked on and on. She mentioned all the possible vices and crimes that were tied to Chris. In fact, the truth was that she had wanted to see that hole for a long time now. Saigon? When one of Chris's thugs rang the bell, she was ready. The neatness of the thug, coupled with his attempt to be nice and polite, clashed so much with his appearance that Mary burst out laughing. The tense atmosphere was broken, and they headed to "Saigon" in a good mood.

Funny Chris was a surprise himself. Snow-white shirt and red bow tie with white polka dots. A big bouquet of flowers for Mary. She felt like a queen. When he had announced the arrival of his guests, he banned the patrons from using any foul language, or else. Nobody wanted trouble with Funny Chris.

When Chris asked if they wanted drinks, Mary nodded to Andy. Whisky for Andy, wine for Mary. The drinks came and they sat comfortably. Andy lit a cigarette, and started,

"So, I'm standing next to my window tonight. I see Hamza driving down the street. He is looking for a parking spot. His truck really stands out. I see him park down the street. In front of the building, on the stairs, is Big Mike with his guys. I ask God to spare him tonight. You know that they beat him up once? You do? All right. And that he's been giving them money regularly? He never says anything. So, I don't hear what they say to him. I see him ignore them. Then, Big Mike runs after him . . ."

Andy talked. Funny Chris leaned against the table, listening to every word Andy said. When he was done, Funny Chris jumped in, "Wait, I didn't understand the end part. How did he do it?"

"Fine. He put his hands together. Say you were Big Mike. Just like this and he jammed his fingers under his ribs and pushed up."

"I'll be damned. I'll be damned. I judged him well. Even if I have never seen that move. Poor Big Mike. My lion wasn't scared here, either. He just wanted to avoid trouble. Huh, the Golden Lion? Did I give him a good name or what?"

Two old men were sitting at the table in the corner. The same two who had accompanied Hamza on the harmonica and drums when he had sang. They were whispering.

"Hey, Funny Chris, could these two old guys get a beer?"

Funny Chris looked at them, "There are no IOUs in this bar. Not for anybody."

The old men looked at each other, smiling, and winked, "Now, it's coming."

"Like I said, for nobody. N-o-b-o-d-y. Except . . . except for my old friends."

He took two bottles of beer and brought them to their table.

"Do the gentlemen need glasses?"

"Sure."

"Two glasses on the way." Funny Chris brought glasses.

"You know, Funny Chris, I'm an old man. I've seen a lot in my life. Lately they've been saying that Madonna and Prince sing some sexy songs. But believe me, I have never heard a sexier song as the one that white man sang the other night. How did the lyrics go? I would put lilies on his bed and roses under his head. So he could wake up often and kiss me often."

"To me, that other song was even stranger . . . then sell me to a pawnshop . . . What do you think, did she love him or was she a hooker?"

"I think that she was a hooker," the first old man responded. Chris listened to them silently.

"I think so too," the other one said. "I told my old lady about that. She never heard anything like that before either. Can you imagine that? He should pawn her for gold and then make his doors gold. Or something like that. Yeah, I think that she was a hooker too. But, he sang about her so tenderly. She must have loved him anyway."

They finally quieted down. Their thoughts flew off to that mysterious, faraway country full of strange and beautiful love.

"I think we'll never be able to understand those people from those foreign countries and their customs."

Funny Chris nodded and went back to the table where Andy and Mary were waiting for him.

Andy and Mary got home at dawn.

It was an unforgettable night for Mary.

*   *   *

When he entered the house, Hamza took the bottle of whiskey from the bag he brought with him. He opened the bottle and took a swig. He undressed and went to the bathroom. He stood under the warm shower and looked at his body as if seeing it for the first time. He touched the scars on his chest, back, and face. He looked at his fists.

"I thought I would make architectural plans and build things. That, as an old man, I would walk around Sarajevo and show my grandchildren what I had built. And now? What now? Is it possible that these hands are only capable of destruction? Breaking, tearing down? Poor Big Mike. Poor idiot. Hamza! What do you think, Hamza? How much longer? Is there an end to this? You knew that it was just a matter of time before you kicked Big Mike's ass! You knew it and you were secretly hoping it would happen. You were looking forward to it. That's why you were working out so hard."

"No, I would be working out anyway. Even without Big Mike. Maybe . . ."

"Dino lost his arm trying to save your life. And, what have you done? You've lost him. He's gone, and it's your fault."

"No! I just wanted to . . ."

"You just wanted to? What?"

"Actions speak louder than words. You wanted to?"

"You wanted to film the house for your cousin. You didn't believe Amra when she kept telling you that she was scared. And you lost both her and the little one.

"You wanted to save Dino? You wanted to save him?"

Hamza left the bathroom. He sat next to the window and started drinking. "And now what? How many people did you kill? Wasn't there enough blood? Did you know that your license to kill has expired? They say there is peace in Bosnia. What peace?

The murderers are walking around the city they destroyed and the citizens they killed. What's happening to me? What's happening to my hands?"

Questions without answers piled up. He emptied the bottle and opened another.

When he woke in the morning, his eyes were bloodshot with dark circles beneath them.

He didn't enjoy work as much as he used to. He would work quickly, thinking about the very next thing he would do. At the end of the workday, he would go straight home. He would read something while drinking whiskey. Soon, he had to drink more than one bottle to fall asleep.

It was Thursday when his boss came to him.

"Do you have some time?"

"I'm busy," Hamza answered, not interrupting his work.

"It doesn't matter. The work can wait. Put your tools down. I'm taking you to lunch."

Hamza rarely spoke with his supervisors. He tried to do his part of the job and let them do theirs. He silently put away his tools, wiped off his hands, and followed the boss. There was a well-known restaurant very close to the construction site. The restaurant staff had already gotten used to the occasional worker coming in for lunch.

"Smoking or non-smoking?"

"Non-smoking."

"Smoking," said Hamza, interrupting the conversation between his boss and the waiter.

"Of course," the boss turned to Hamza. "I'm sorry," the boss conceded and then let him go first. They waited in silence for the food after they ordered. Only after they had started eating did his boss begin the conversation.

"How long have you been working for us?"

"Seven or eight months."

"Is that so? It's a pretty long time. You're good and we're lucky to have you."

"Thank you."

"The only thing is that the guys say that you're kind of withdrawn."

"I don't know. They're probably right."

"I've been watching you work. Especially this week."

"Is something wrong?"

"No, everything is fine. I can see that you are having problems though. But if you don't want to talk about it, that's fine. Can I do anything to help? Anything? Money or anything like that?"

"No, thank you."

"All right. I was born here. My ancestors came from Ireland. A long time ago. I think I know America. I think I know another thing . . . that you're in some serious trouble."

"It just seems like that to you."

"Look, I can show you at least ten easier ways to kill yourself than the one chose."

"Huh?"

"You are killing yourself with work. It doesn't work that way. It's not that simple. It's suicide."

"I think that's my own private business."

"I don't think so. You're good. I would like to work with you long-term. If you continue like this, you'll wear out in a few months."

"And?"

"And another thing. We're in the union. Now we have a problem because you're breaking the 'rules.' People are killing themselves working to catch up with you. I haven't said anything to the big boss because if I had, you would have been in trouble long ago. The workers say you're weird."

"So, what can I do about it?"

"Well, you can do something. Take a vacation. You are entitled to a week of paid vacation. Considering how much you've worked in the past few days, I can give you another week and write it off as if you worked."

"If I have to."

"You don't have to do anything in this country, except die and pay taxes. I would like to see you back to normal. Go somewhere, man. Tour the States. Go to Florida, Disney World. Relax."

"Okay, starting Monday."

"No. Starting right now. Put your tools away and get lost. I'll see you in a couple of weeks. And, I'm telling you as a friend, take it easy on the alcohol."

"Is it that obvious?"
"I'll say."

*　　*　　*

Hamza took care of his tools at work, got changed, and headed to his truck. "Now what? Go see June? No sense in doing that. There is no sense in doing that anytime, particularly now. Go see the colonel? No. And Ekrem left for Bosnia long ago. With normal people around me, I'd feel out of place." He got into his truck and starting driving around the streets of Chicago aimlessly.

Without really paying attention to where he was going, he headed east and found himself on Highway 294. He drove until late at night. He passed through the monotonous regions of the America. In fact, it often seemed as if he wasn't moving at all.

He stopped briefly for gas and continued driving. Sometime after midnight, he began to feel his eyes getting heavy and pulled into a parking lot. He spotted a small motel next to the parking lot and decided to check in for the night. In a nearby corner store, he bought two bottles of whiskey and cigarettes.

The room was small yet clean. It smelled of transience—transient people, transient love. How many true and how many false loves had this bed witnessed?

Hamza took a shower, holding the bottle of whiskey in his hand. He turned on the TV. While flipping through the channels, he drank an entire bottle and fell asleep soon after. It was a dreamless sleep. A black nothingness.

He woke up in the afternoon. The room had the pleasant sense of twilight. Hamza went to the window and pulled the shades up. He was blinded by the bright light of the day so he pulled the shades down and went back to bed. He lit a cigarette, opened the other bottle of whiskey, and took a drink. He drank quickly. His thoughts were empty. From time to time, his thoughts would reach something relevant, but he would cut them off fast. He was on vacation, and you are not supposed to *do* anything on vacation.

After he had emptied the bottle, he fell asleep again. He woke a little before dawn. The person at the front desk told him that he was in Pennsylvania, close to Lake Erie. What the hell was he doing here? He remembered that somebody had once told him that Wisconsin was a great place for a vacation. All right. He'd go to Wisconsin then. He drove the whole day again. His head cleared up slowly. At dusk, he drove through Chicago again. He got off the highway and, in an auto-parts store, had the mechanic install a stereo CD player. He picked up a few CDs and got back on the road. Around midnight, he stopped at a motel again, this one in Wisconsin. And just like the night before, he bought more liquid amnesia.

He stayed in the motel for three days. He would only leave the room to buy food and alcohol. Each time he would come back, the room would be freshly cleaned as if they were waiting for him to leave just so they could clean it.

After the third night, he checked out, bought a map, and went to a restaurant. After eating, he opened the map and slowly ran his finger across the different states.

Colorado or Montana? Montana. June had spoken so highly of Montana. It must be beautiful. June? What was she doing? Hamza bought some food for the trip and left.

Music was definitely a good thing.

*   *   *

June was distracted at work. Nothing worked out the way it was supposed to. She made mistakes on the computer, dialed wrong numbers, and addressed her patients by the wrong name. Around noon, JK came to see her.

"June, you wanna grab some lunch?"

"I don't know. Nothing is going right today."

"Nothing's been going right for you for the last month or two. Let's go, we'll talk in the restaurant."

They walked to a nearby restaurant. While they were waiting for the food to come, JK started, "June, it's not working out this way. You have to do something. I've been watching you for the last two months. You're not the same anymore."

"I realize that I'm pretty jittery."

"It's not only the jitteriness. You're distracted, you can't concentrate. You are absentminded almost all the time."

"Okay! I can notice that much myself."

"Hey, take it easy. I'm not trying to lecture you."

"I know, I'm sorry."

"Are you in trouble?"

"Not really. Everything is the same as usual."

"I don't think so. I think that you don't want to admit it to yourself."

"What don't I want to admit to myself?"

"Hamza."

"What about Hamza? What does he have to do with anything? I haven't seen him in two months anyway."

"Bingo."

"What are you talking about, 'Bingo'?"

"You've been different for the last two months."

"Nonsense."

"Hey, hey! I know something about psychology too. I just can't understand how you could have fallen in love with him."

"With whom, Hamza? You're crazy."

JK looked at her sadly. "So that's it, huh? I have known you for such a long time. I've always thought that you needed time to realize that I care about you."

"JK, are you serious?"

"Serious? I couldn't be any more serious."

"I never thought of you that way. You're a very good friend to me."

"I see. That's unfortunate. Maybe I should have been more direct."

"JK. You are a sweetheart."

"Yeah. The only thing is . . . you love Hamza."

"Where did you get that from? I never mentioned anything like that. We've never even touched each other."

"That's my point. I could hug you. I could kiss you. And nothing would happen. But, if he touched you . . . You both deliberately avoid touching each other. You know, after his lecture on Bosnia, I read up on it and the Balkans. It's a cursed region. Nothing good can come out of there. As for Hamza, he might be good, I don't know. But they all carry the curse with them, a curse of history and blood."

"I don't want to hear about it."

"See? I have to tell you, whether you like it or not. He's trouble. Did you see his eyes during the lecture?"

June remembered and felt a chill pass over her.

"He's trouble. And everything around him is trouble. I hope to God he's gone and never comes back."

"Hey!"

"And if he does . . ." JK paused, "There is an air of death about him, hanging over him. You can feel it. I'm just afraid he'll take you with him."

"You're wrong. He's great, kind, and gentle."

"Fine, let's change the subject."

June thought about his words for days. "He's trouble . . . If he ever comes back . . ."

"To hell with him! I just wish Hamza would call."

Time passed and Hamza still hadn't appeared.

*   *   *

Hamza returned to work in an even worse state. He worked without his usual energy, just enough to meet the basic requirements. November was rainy and cold. His mood went from bad to worse. At the end of every day, Hamza asked himself what to do next. Where to go? On one of those rainy nights, Hamza left a bar and walked back to his truck. He walked slowly despite the downpour. On the corner, a dark figure came up and offered him heroin and cocaine. Head hanging low, Hamza waved him off. He drove home, distracted by the event. He had finally hit rock bottom. He looked so bad that a drug dealer couldn't tell him from an addict. It was an offer to a desperate-looking guy, the final step down the stairway to hell. Hamza got home, got undressed, and went to the bathroom. He stood in front of the mirror.

He was sickened by what he saw. A thin, drawn face with heavy bags under the eyes. Long, matted hair and a three-week-old beard. He looked at the stranger in the mirror. Deep wrinkles were visible around the eyes. From the bridge of his nose, there was a deep cavernous wrinkle that went vertically up his forehead until it disappeared into his matted hair. Still, nothing could compare to the way his eyes looked.

"Hamza, this is not you. This is not you! This is a stranger who somehow stole your body. Thank God June hasn't seen you for a few months. Hey, Hamza!" he slapped himself in the face a few times. "This is not the way! This can't be the way!" He looked around for something to cover the mirror with, found a towel, and threw it over the miserable impostor. "There you go. A person looks the way they think they look.

"My, my. You're bullshitting *again*, Hamza."

He smacked himself on the head and entered the shower. The hot water felt good.

"This is great. It's relaxing. It feels good." He suddenly came to his senses. "It feels so good you almost destroyed yourself? No more relaxing things, Hamza. No more"." He turned off the hot water. The icy cold water hit him hard and left him gasping for air. He took a few deep breaths to steady himself.

"Are you feeling good now, Hamza? This ought to do you good. Fuck you and your whiskey."

He stood in the cold shower until he shook from the cold. He dried himself off with a towel and went to the kitchen. The fridge was empty. Tomato juice and a stale bag of chips were all he found in the cabinets. That and many empty and half-empty bottles of Jack Daniels, of course. "Goodbye, Jack." Hamza picked them up and threw them out. He came back to the apartment, poured the juice into a pot, added water and every spice he could find. After a few minutes, he had the soup ready, or at least something that resembled soup.

"Let's see you work out, Hamza." He dropped to the floor and started doing push-ups. After twenty, his arms were shaking. After the next thirty, his whole body shook. He broke into a cold sweat.

"Workouts instead of whiskey. Let's see how you're going to sleep now."

He came back to the bathroom and noticed he didn't have a razor. He took out the package from under the mattress. The sharp side of the Tanto shone dangerously. He soaped up his beard. Once, on Igman, he made a bet that he could shave using the Tanto. This time he was luckier. He only nicked himself twice. After shaving, he carefully cut the ends of his hair. It almost looked professional. His hair still fell to his shoulders, but it didn't look as bad. He laid down on the mattress and fell asleep immediately.

He woke early the next morning, turned on the coffeemaker, and started exercising. He worked out until he shook and dripped with sweat. After a cold shower, he poured himself a cup and lit a cigarette. At work, he actually greeted the other workers. Most of them looked at him with surprise, as he hadn't acknowledged anybody in the past few months. "Americans are good, you just have to give them a chance," he thought. He wolfed down three burgers for lunch.

The shock of being approached by the drug dealer had brought him back to his senses. He still didn't have the answers to the many questions troubling him, but at least now he knew what he didn't want. The hell of loneliness and alcohol was behind him. Never again. He was certain he had won.

Everything that had happened was a part of him. It was in every pore of his being. Forgetting wasn't the way out. He didn't want to forget anything, not Amra or the Little One, not Dino. He would gladly have laid down his life for any of them. On the other hand, even if he had wanted to, he wouldn't have been able to forget anything. His face alone was a daily reminder. He would have to find the inner peace and strength to deal with everything that happened. And it was "haram," or forbidden, to think about what could have been.

"Haram?"

How long had it been since he had thought about that simple word that prohibited everything that wasn't righteous. Avdaga, Azra? How were they, and what were they doing? What did Avdaga say when he gave him the Qur'an? "You'll find all your answers here"."

After work, Hamza stocked up on food and got a few magazines. When he got home, he made dinner, prayed, and then read the Qur'an. Between two of the pages, he found a little envelope. He opened it. It was a little gold coin minted in 1478. There was a little note with the coin; "If you ever need money, exchange this with a numismatist."

"Oh, Avdaga. This is definitely one of the coins the French generals were looking for during the war. If they were willing to pay five thousand Deutsche marks for one back then, it would fetch well over twenty thousand U.S. dollars now."

On the inside cover of the Qur'an, in Avdaga's meticulous handwriting: "To my Hamza, who I love especially—October, 1995."

Hamza opened the Qur'an and started praying. On the right side of the book, the text was written in Arabic and on the left side stood the Bosnian translation. Hamza first read the translation and then started praying in Arabic. He recited many parts from memory. After twenty pages, he said, "The truth was spoken by the Almighty." He closed the Qur'an and pressed it gently against his lips. He made coffee and sat by the window. He suddenly realized, much to his satisfaction, that the cigarette and coffee once again tasted good. Before going to bed, he worked out, showered, and read the Qur'an again. He prayed quietly and listened to his own voice as if to music. The murmur of familiar prayers calmed him.

For the first time in a long while, he had a restful sleep. Hamza would go straight home after work. He would spend all his time reading the Qur'an, cooking, reading magazines, and working out. The recitation of the prayers, together with the reading of their translation, was slowly bringing him back to the road of optimism. The nightmare in his head was slowly going away, and things were getting back to normal. Still, he wasn't able to find his way out of the situation he was in.

Sometimes he thought the solution was to go back to Bosnia. He would be able to think through things more clearly there. He dismissed such thoughts right away, and returned to the ascetic routine. The end of December was fast approaching.

One day at work, Avdaga's words in the Qur'an came to his mind: "To my Hamza, whom I love especially." There was something about that sentence. Hamza thought that it might be a hidden message instead of a dedication. Perhaps that was what Avdaga had intended when he said that the answers to all his questions would be found in the Qur'an.

"Hamza, you want to get a drink?" asked three co-workers standing in front of him.

"I'm sorry, guys . . ." Hamza started to say no, but then he remembered that it was the first time they had invited him. "As I said, I'm sorry guys, but only if it's on me."

"In that case, we'll go with you every day."

The dedication could wait. They went to a nearby restaurant. Hamza had a Coke while the rest of them ordered either whiskey or beer.

Hamza was haunted for the next few days by the idea of a message in the dedication. "To my Hamza . . ." Avdaga always called him "my Hamza." That was fine. The answer must be in the second part. " . . . whom I love especially." Avdaga always loved him. " . . . love especially." What did he mean by that? Maybe nothing. Avdaga always loved him, regardless of whether he made trouble or not. Oh, Avdaga! Why couldn't you have written what you were thinking?

*   *   *

December twenty-third. Hamza worked as usual, despite the fact that the Western world prepared for Christmas and little work was getting done. Around noon, he started thinking about the dedication " . . . whom I love especially"." Wait a minute. Let me try again. Avdaga loves me. Avdaga has always loved me. He doesn't have ten kids, so why would he put that he loves me especially. And he can't compare me with Azra. No, that's not it. Maybe it's "To my Hamza, whom I love especially—sometimes?" In certain situations? Maybe Avdaga wanted me to be the way I was, when he loved me especially? And when did he especially love me? He had always loved me the same. Wait a minute, Hamza, maybe you're close. When did he especially love me? When I graduated from high school, college? He was a bit happier, but that can't be it. No, definitely not. When then? When I fell in love with Amra, when I got married? Of course, that's it! When I was with Amra. When I loved! Love? That's my Avdaga."

Hamza stopped working. He sat down and lit a cigarette.

"How's it going, Hamza?"

"Fine, just doing a bit of thinking."

"What a coincidence. I was just thinking, how come you take five breaks while the others only take three?"

"Yeah, I got it." Hamza got up.

"Sit down. Sit down and relax for once. Be a bit more American. Besides, the union recognizes the need for holiday frivolity too.

Give me a chance to yell at you. If everybody worked like you do, I'd get fired. And you know I got a wife and kids. You don't want me to get fired, do you?

"God forbid!"

"Okay then. Relax for a while. Just say, 'Sorry boss, I got it.' And when I leave, you sit down again. That's how it's done."

"Okay, boss. Do you mind if I leave early today? I have a very important meeting. I'll stay longer some other time."

"Hey Hamza, you learn fast. All right, but only if you promise not to make it up. Be a bit more American, man."

"Okay, boss."

Hamza considered as he drove. So that was Avdaga's message: love. The answer to all questions. Dervo said something like that too. But, I do love. I love Avdaga and Azra, I love Sarajevo, Bosnia, people. What then? You have love? Easy does it. All these years, what is it that drives you, that pushes you forward? Love?

No, Hamza. Hatred. Hatred drives you. Since that day, there has been no love inside you, just hatred and revenge. Look at yourself in the mirror. Look at those wrinkles around your eyes. As soon as you think about your best man, your eyes start gleaming. Out of love? No Hamza, out of hate. But I have to find him! Okay. He did kill your Amra and the little one. And now he's killing you. He's been doing it all these years. Love, Hamza. Love. But is love possible after Amra, after the little one? Is love possible after Sarajevo, Igman, Manjaca, or Srebrenica? Or is the only way out to spend your life, as Dado used to say, hunting? Blood for blood. More blood and even more blood.

"Hey!" Hamza smacked himself in the head and stepped on the brakes.

The lane behind him came to a screeching halt as well.

"Hamza, love is in front of you! All that time spent searching, when the answer was right in front of you! "Would you like to sleep with me?"

"What seems to be the problem, sir?" asked an officer as he knocked on the window.

"Love, officer. Love."

"Love . . . ?! Move that hunk of junk if it can move."

"Right away officer, right away." Hamza stepped on the gas and was on his way. He drove a bit over the speed limit, taking the main streets to the hospital where June worked.

*   *   *

No one recognized him at the reception desk. A girl from a different shift was on duty.

"I'm sorry, Dr. Thomas is not in today."

"Could I get her number?"

"I'm sorry, but I can't do that. It's against hospital policy."

"Her pager number?"

"I don't have her pager number. I'm sorry."

"Just a minute. There has got to be a way for me to contact her. Here, I'll turn around and you call her."

"I don't know . . ."

"Don't worry. Dr. Thomas won't get mad."

"All right, I hope I won't regret this later."

"I assure you, you will not be sorry."

"Hello, Dr. Thomas? I apologize for disturbing you at home. Yes, this is the hospital. I have somebody here, he says it's very important. What? Yes, I think he's a patient. I don't know. Um, he has a long scar on his face. Yes. Here you go." The girl passed Hamza the phone.

"Hello, June? Yes, I'm fine, thank you. Yourself? I'm good. What do you think about dinner tomorrow? I would like to see you. All right, I'll hold."

Hamza covered the receiver with the palm of his hand, "I told you she wouldn't get mad."

The twinkle in Hamza's eyes told her that he would not be getting mad about anything too soon either.

*   *   *

June paced around the room, her thoughts a whirlwind. She hadn't seen Hamza since the beginning of October. That was almost three months ago. She had walked around their usual places almost every day. She thought he had left Chicago, or even the U.S. She asked herself where she had gone wrong. Maybe she had pushed him too hard.

Their relationship was unique. He had made no attempts to get her into bed. They'd known each other for two years. He had never kissed her. Holding hands was the most that went on between them. She loved him with a subtle kind of love that gave him the opportunity to see what, if anything, he felt for her. She knew that he carried hell in his heart and that it would take a long time to overcome it. He needed to free himself. She felt that he was strong and kind. She had seen him a few times when he was relaxed. His true nature, buried deep beneath the evil and sorrow he had been living with for years, would come out. It would come out with his spirit, smile, and joy of life.

Maybe her friends were a little too hard on him. No, that couldn't be the reason. She had spent three months searching for him in vain. Perhaps she was lucky that it wasn't three years. And now a phone call? From the hospital, of all places. Well of course! He didn't have her phone number. She didn't have his either, though he probably didn't have a phone. But he knew where the hospital was. What should she say to him?

In the middle of the room stood a pair of suitcases, all packed and ready to go. She was supposed to leave in three hours. Off to Montana, going to the "gas station." They were waiting for her; everything had been arranged. And now his voice sounded as if it had been three hours, not three months, since they last spoke.

No. She was going to Montana. Hamza could wait . . . unless he disappeared again. She returned to the phone energetically.

"Hello?"

"I'm here."

"When do we meet?"

"At eight. On the corner of Ohio and Michigan."

"All right."

She hung up. Eight o'clock on the corner of Ohio and Michigan . . . just like in the movies.

"I'm here," he said. As if he hadn't disappeared. He's here after three months. She kicked the nearest suitcase. "Maybe a shower will calm me down."

She sang under the shower.

*   *   *

To his boss's pleasure, Hamza asked to leave work early again the next day. He drove to the mall and went shopping. He went to a few exclusive boutiques until he finally found a store with European clothing. A lifetime ago, he loved suits. After a short search, he settled on a dark gray suit with a very subtle spotted pattern. He picked out a silky, olive green shirt and a dark red tie with patches of light green scattered throughout.

"Very eclectic combination," the attractive saleswoman noticed.

"You don't like it?"

"I'd like you to try it on."

"Just a moment, let me find matching shoes."

In this world there are two types of shoes, Italian and everything else. Hamza knew this well.

Hamza immediately chose a pair of black Italian heeled boots. Not that he wanted to look taller, but the heels made him walk straight. When he came out of the fitting room, the saleswoman complimented him on the extremely successful combination. Hamza also picked out an elegant black raincoat with removable natural fur lining. When he topped it off with a black hat, the saleswoman applauded.

"Wonderful! You're not from around here, are you?"

"Nope. Europe."

He thought about using Dervo's credit card. No. He'd leave it for another occasion. If there would ever be another occasion to use it. Hamza drove home and entered the house, but didn't go upstairs. He opened the door to Andy's kitchen.

"Hey, Aunt Mary! What's for dinner?"

Mary turned around and, at the sight of him, nearly dropped the plates she held. She looked at Hamza, amazed.

"Nothing yet. But I'll fix something soon. Come on in."

"Hey, 'Don't Worry Andy'! How's it going?"

"Hey, Hamza! Man, I haven't seen you in a while. I thought that you had moved out."

"Hey! You can't get rid of Hamza that easily."

"Would you like something to drink?"

"I can't drink on an empty stomach."

"Mary, make lunch, will you?"

"I'm kidding. Coffee's fine."

"Coming up. I've never seen you in such a good mood."

"It's love, Andy, love!"

"Seriously?"

"Seriously. By the way, could I use your phone?"

"Of course, you don't need to ask."

"I'd like to call Bosnia."

"Call the moon if you want. I'm really glad to see you like this. Take the phone over by the fireplace so you don't bother Mary, else we'll never see that lunch."

Hamza sat next to the phone and dialed. The other end of the line was silent. Hamza decided to call directory information in Sarajevo.

"Yes, yes, the number has been changed. New lines. Yes. Do you have a pen?"

"Andy, give me a pen, please. Yes, go ahead. Thank you."

Hamza dialed the number again. It was late in Sarajevo. The time difference was seven hours. Finally he heard a voice on the other end of the line.

"Hello?"

"Dad?"

"Hamza!"

"How are you? How is Azra?"

"Great! How are you?"

"Great."

"I knew it."

"What did you know?"

"That you were going to call."

"You always know everything."

"You're my son. My Hamza."

"I most certainly am."

"How has it been?"

"Hard."

"Have you been alone?"

"Yes."

"Loneliness is hard."

"Very hard."

"You survived."

"I survived."

"Who's the lady?"

"What lady?"

"Your lady. Tell me her name, who is she, what is she?"

"June. How did you know?"

"Because you wouldn't have survived if it wasn't for her."

"That thing in the Qur'an . . ."

"You figured it out?"

"Yes, but it was hard. You could have written it a little more simply."

"It was better this way. Now you know how a man feels when he has reached the summit of a mountain."

"I think I do. What's new in Sarajevo? Do you hear from Musa? How's the captain?"

"Hey, take it easy. Sarajevo is the same as it was when you left it. People think that all kinds of things happen after they leave. Everything is exactly the same. We're just a bit older. Musa is in Canada. He doesn't call. He needs time too. The captain has moved in with us. He retired. He helps me with the store. We go to the Tekija. Tell me about that girl. Is she nice?"

"Yes."

"Is she like Amra?"

"I knew you'd ask that. You hit the nail right on the head. She doesn't resemble her physically, but, she's nice. She has a bit of Amra in her. She slapped me recently."

"That's good. That's love. I talked about that with the captain recently. You never got into a fight with your best man. But with Musa . . ."

"Hold on, Avdaga. Let's not talk about that."

"What are you doing now?"

"I work for the union. Maybe I'll come next spring."

"Bring the lady with you so we can see her. How do you look, physically?"

"I'm fine. Never been better."

"Thank God. Did you exchange the coin?"

"No, I didn't need to."

"Feel free to do it. Avdaga has a lot of them. I just don't want to exchange them now because of you. I don't want to lower their market value yet. By the end, that general who paid five thousand for it is gonna cry."

"Avdaga, my Avdaga."

"Do you drink?"

"Not anymore."

"That's good. What about the girl, does she know you love her?"

"I think so."

"You haven't told her?"

"I will, tonight."

"Oh, my Hamza. Hold on, here's Azra. Make sure you call from now on. The most important thing is that you have gotten over the loneliness. Now it doesn't matter where you are. You can even come back to Bosnia. Here's Azra."

"Hamza?"

"Mom!"

"Son! How are you?"

"I'm fine, mom, I'm fine."

"You've never called me mom before, you know that?"

"When I was little and I used to call you by your first names, you all used to laugh. Afterwards I was too embarrassed to call you mom or dad."

"My son, how are you doing?"

"Where are you from, mom? I mean, where are you really from?" Hamza switched to English.

"It's a long story."

"I know the story is long. You can give me the details when I come there, or you come here, God willing. Just tell me where you're from."

"Montana."

"Okay. That's all for now. I love you all. Say hi to the captain and everybody else."

"We love you too, our Hamza."

Hamza hung up. He rubbed his sweaty palms.

"Feels like I got a mountain off my back."

"That was the first time you called since you got here?" Andy confronted him.

"You wouldn't understand it, Andy. I could spend years explaining it to you, and you still wouldn't get it. We're from Sarajevo, we're simply different."

"If I had known, I would have kicked your ass. Then you'd really be different, black and blue at least. If I'd known, I would have called them myself. Your poor parents."

"Believe me, I did the right thing. Anyway, they didn't expect me to call until I had dealt with some things on my own. You and Mary helped a lot."

"Hamza, get up, please. Let me have a look at you. You look so sharp!"

Mary couldn't wait. Hamza got up and walked around the room, strutting like a model. He took off the coat, unbuttoned the blazer, and showed them the brand of the suit.

"Hugo Boss!" Andy laughed.

"You look great!"

"Thank you, thank you." Hamza bowed theatrically. "And now I must excuse myself. There's a young lady waiting for me, and I don't want to be late."

"Go on, get lost. And, if she's not afraid of the neighborhood, bring her with one of these days so we can meet her."

"I think you'll like her. Bye!"

Hamza left the house with a spring in his step. He got into his car.

*   *   *

"Drive slow, I'm in a hurry." Musa used to say to the cab drivers when he was running late. That's the way Hamza drove that night. He found a parking spot close to Michigan Avenue. A cold north wind awaited him as he got out of the truck. He pulled up his collar, pulled his hat down over his head, and headed north. There was a Tiffany & Co. store a few blocks away from Ohio Street. Hamza entered. Tonight was no ordinary night. He decided to buy something for June. He was quite convinced, although not absolutely certain, that she cared about him. At least a little bit. He scanned the showcases. A platinum ring with a soft green stone caught his eye. A little ring, a small soft green stone, and very many green dollars. Hamza paid and put the box into his pocket. Walking to the rendezvous point, he stopped at a florist and bought a single, beautiful long-stemmed red rose. He carefully put it underneath his blazer. Now he was ready.

On the corner of Ohio, he waited a few minutes before June arrived. She stood a few yards from him, scanning the crowd. She couldn't recognize him. Hamza came up to her and cleared his throat. June turned around surprised.

"Whoa! There you are. Hold on, let me get a look at you. Very good! Turn around. That's great. A totally different Hamza."

Hamza leaned in and kissed her on the cheek. June acted as if it was a perfectly normal thing for him to do. Still, Hamza noticed her shiver slightly.

"Would you do something for me?" June asked.

"Anything."

June dipped her hands under his collar, and golden hair spilled out over the coat.

"That's better."

"You look beautiful," Hamza said, just to say something.

"Oh no, you look beautiful. I look the same as usual."

"Still, there is something unusual."

"You're imagining things."

"If you say so." Hamza pulled the rose out of his blazer and handed it to her with a flourish.

"This is from Avdaga."

"Av-da-ha?"

"Av-da-ga. My father, Avdaga."

"Your father? You talked to him?"

"Yes, just a while ago."

"And?"

"They're doing fine. He and Azra."

"Who is Azra?"

"That's my mother. She's from Montana."

"You're lying!"

"I don't lie. Ever."

"I wasn't serious. Where from, in Montana?"

"I didn't ask her. I have to ask her things bit by bit."

"You'll tell me about it when we sit down. Where are we going anyway?"

"Navy Pier."

"Great. We've never been there together. I love Navy Pier. That place has the feel of an adventure, probably because of the lake. Which restaurant?"

"We'll see. Whichever one we like. This way, we're taking my truck tonight."

"The $500 one?"

"Actually, $520. Now you'll see what it looks like. It's much better on the inside than the outside. Just like its owner."

"What's the matter with your outside?"

"Let's say . . . nothing."

"Of course."

They walked slowly, holding hands.

"Well, here it is! My truck."

"Wow! Are you sure this thing runs?"

"You'll see."

"Hey, these blankets look great and warm."

"Just like the owner."

"The owner is warmer, at least as far as I can tell."

They drove along Michigan Avenue. They headed north to Navy Pier. In between traffic lights, Hamza really stepped on the gas and the truck flew.

"Hey, this thing can really move! Wow!"

"Not bad for $520!"

"Can you find me something like this?"

"They don't make junk like this anymore. Here we are." They left the truck and walked along Navy Pier. A cool wind blew in from the north. June squeezed in closer to Hamza. He hugged her, shielding her from the wind.

"Shall we try this place?" He almost had to scream so that she could hear him over the wind.

"This is the restaurant here where Clinton ate when he came to Chicago on an unexpected visit."

"It must be good."

They hurried inside.

*   *   *

They had entered a different world. The elegant glass door completely protected the inside of the restaurant from the terrible whistling of the wind.

"Ugh! I don't like the snow in this city."

"The snow is good. I don't know why, but I always looked forward to the snow for Christmas."

"Today is Christmas?"

"Didn't you know?"

"I forgot. I wasn't thinking about it at all. Oh, maybe you wanted to spend it with your family?"

June was about to tell him about the plane tickets, but stopped herself in time.

"I will, don't worry."

Hamza looked at her.

The night, snow, and the Chicago cold contrasted softly with the warm, pleasant restaurant. He picked up an old familiar fragrance, one that he hadn't smelled for a long time. One he thought he would never smell again. The fragrance of love.

The maître d' approached them.

"Good evening and merry Christmas!"

"Merry Christmas!"

"Do you have reservations?"

"I'm afraid not. I hope you can find us a table for two?"

The maître d' had plenty of experience with guests. With a glance, he could tell whether he had a quarrelsome married couple in front of him, lovers, or just people in love. These two were in love. Terribly in love. And he loved people in love.

"I'll have a look. I think something can be found. If not, I'll personally see to it that a table is brought in. Don't worry. You can check your coats."

"Thank you. That is very kind of you."

Hamza helped June with her coat and then took off his own. He handed their coats to the attendant.

"Excuse me. I"ve found a table in the corner, close to the music. Don't worry, the music is soft, it won't bother you."

June took Hamza's hand and they followed the maître d'. When they entered the dining area of the restaurant, Hamza looked around. Music came from the back, close to a large, well-lit, Christmas tree. The restaurant was filled with decorations, a festive atmosphere for the holidays. A few hundred people were seated throughout. Hamza looked about, taking in the hall. Suddenly, he stopped, and did a double take. At the far end of the room at a table next to the window, along with a small group, was his best man!

*   *   *

His best man!

Hamza stopped mid-stride. He lowered his head so that his face couldn't be seen, hugged June, and turned and walked toward the exit.

"Hey, what's wrong?"

"Nothing! Let's just get out of here!" Hamza pulled her toward the exit.

June followed along, confused.

"What's wrong?"

"I'll tell you outside. Please, hurry." They went back through the reception area. The maître d' went after them.

"Is something wrong?"

"No, no. Everything's fine. We've just forgotten something. We'll be right back."

They got their coats and left. Heavy snowflakes, chased by the howling wind, greeted them outside.

"Hamza, what happened? What's the matter?" June yelled, trying to speak over the wind.

Hamza put his hands on her shoulders. He tried to look her in the eyes.

"June, June, I . . ."

"Hamza, what's the matter? You're shivering."

"Listen, June. Please. Don't ask me anything. Just listen. Please."

"Okay, I'm listening. I'm listening."

"This is very important. Please. It's a very serious matter. Try to remember what I'm telling you. Do you know where I live? You don't? I'll write it down for you. Do you have a pen? Thanks. Here's the address. Be careful, it's not the best neighborhood."

"Hamza?"

"Please, just listen, okay? Take a cab. Here's some cash. Have him take you right to the door. *To the door*. And make him wait for you with the engine running. Here are the keys. This one is for the outside door and this one is for the upstairs door. If Andy sees you—he's my landlord—don't be afraid. If he sees you, tell him that you're my girlfriend."

"Finally."

"Please, listen to me. On the bed in the room, actually on the mattress, there is a label. Do you know what I'm talking about?" June nodded." Tear it off. Underneath it, there is an opening, and there is a package wrapped in black cloth. Bring it to me. I'll be here."

"Hamza, what's this about?"

"I can't tell you right now. You'll have to trust me. This is very important."

"I thought that I, that we were important."

"You are. We are."

"So, what is it then?"

"This is something bigger than you and me."

"Hamza, should we go to a different restaurant?"

"Honest to God, I'd love to. But I can't."

"Hamza, I have a feeling like something terrible is about to happen. You're being too mysterious. I don't like that look on your face. You had that same look the day of the lecture. I don't like the way you're shivering. I'm scared."

"Everything's going to be all right."

"Hamza, you've never shivered before."

"June, please. Do it for me."

"But . . . all right! I'll do it, although . . ."

"Just do it. I'll be here."

June turned around and left. Hamza went past the nearby souvenir shop and stood in a dark corner. He crossed his arms and waited.

*   *   *

"I thought that it was over. That it was behind me. But it's not over. Five years later I feel the same fire in my veins. I'm shivering again. June was right. Something terrible is about to happen. Terrible? For whom? Is there anything terrible that hasn't happened to me already? No, no. Everything terrible has already happened—been seen, been done. What's left is simply the payback. For Amra, for the little one, for Dino, for Senad, for Nihad, for Caki, for . . . The list is too long. The best man is not the first one. He won't be the last one either. Maybe for me, but, there are many Hamza's out there. We're scattered all over the world.

That's enough Hamza! Think about something else. Let your mind rest."

And he actually did. He stood still, watching the entrance to the restaurant. The snow fell hard. The wind carried and swirled it around. The sky was almost black. From time to time it, would be lit by the lights of a plane that had just taken off from O'Hare, trying to break through the clouds and reach the altitude needed for its flight to Europe.

*   *   *

June found a cab. It was nice and warm. The cab driver, an Arabic guy, probably from Syria or Morocco, talked about nothing in particular. June listened to him without paying attention to what he was actually saying. She was preoccupied with her worries for Hamza. What had happened? He probably saw somebody. Yeah, he definitely saw somebody. An old friend? You don't run away from friends. Not like that anyway. He had lowered his head and turned fast, probably to keep from being seen. Was it an enemy? Well, we could have left. What a shame. It was such a beautiful night. A promising night. He probably would have told her . . . What would he have told her? Maybe he wouldn't have spoken of love. And the rose? From his father. He is, as Hamza said, a "beh"? No, maybe it was a "bey." Yes, a "bey." He must be an old, gray gentleman. And his mom is from Montana? Great, maybe we'll end up being long-lost cousins . . ."

"I think we're here, lady."

"Hmm. It looks like it. Would you please get all the way up to the house, on the sidewalk?"

"But, lady . . ."

"Don't worry. I'm paying for it. And keep the engine running. I'll be right back."

"Okay, lady, it's your money."

June left the car and climbed the stairs. She had just taken out the key when the door opened.

"Are you looking for somebody?"

June jumped back in surprise.

"Good evening." Good thing Hamza had warned her.

"I'm Hamza's girlfriend, June."

"Oh, you are? Come on in. Hamza just left. He said he had a date with you."

"Yes, we were together. You must be Andy?"

"Yes."

"Hamza told me a lot about you."

"A lot less than he's told us about you. Definitely."

"Huh?"

"Never mind. He's a good guy. Thank you for bringing him back."

"What do you mean bringing him back?"

"He was on his way to the bottom of rock bottom, I'm telling you. He's a good guy. And today, he was a different person. He said it was love."

"Are you sure that was what he said? *Love*?"

"Yes, and now I can see why."

"Thank you. I'm sorry, but Hamza sent me to take something out of his apartment. May I?"

"Sure. Oh, merry Christmas."

"Merry Christmas to you too."

June ran up the stairs. She went into the apartment and turned on the lights. She looked around. Spartan! A mattress lay near the window, next to it there were magazines and books, all in order, and an empty ashtray. June looked in the kitchen. Everything was clean and empty, as if no one had lived there. She looked in the closet. Hamza's jacket, a couple of shirts, a few sweaters, and some T-shirts hung on hangers. Nothing else. June looked around in disbelief. Next to the window was a small reading stand. A book lay open on it. She leaned over to look at it. One side was written in Arabic, the other in a language that June couldn't understand. Probably Bosnian, she thought. She came to the mattress and lifted the blanket. She smelled it. It smelled like Hamza. She pressed it against her cheek for a moment. There was a factory label on the mattress. June grabbed it by an end and pulled. The stitching gave, and she tore it off. Inside the mattress, she saw a wrapped black package. It was long and heavy. She started to unwrap it, but stopped. She really did not want to know what was in the package.

"It wouldn't be fair," she placated her curiosity. She took it and left the apartment. She ran into the cab and they sped back.

"What is in here? I can feel it at least." She carefully touched the unknown object with her fingers. A small box. At one end there was something like a handle. A knife? But at the other end there was something softer than the blade of a knife. Like leather. Maybe it was a case? A knife in a case?

"A knife? Hamza, Hamza!"

"Yes, lady?"

"Nothing, I was talking to myself."

"Here we are, lady."

June took out the money and paid the cabby. "Thank you. And have a merry Christmas."

"Merry Christmas to you too, lady, and have a great night."

*   *   *

"A great night, right," June thought as she walked down the Navy Pier. When she got close to the restaurant, Hamza stepped out of the shadows.

"There you are. But now I wish I hadn't gone."

"Thank you."

June hugged him. He wasn't shivering anymore, which scared her even more than the earlier trembling had. His facial expression also scared her. He was there, in front of her, yet somehow far away.

"Hamza! Hey, Hamza, are you there?"

"What? Oh yeah, definitely. June, please listen. I'm going inside and you're going home. Okay?"

"What do you mean okay? It's not okay. It's just not! Something terrible is about to happen. I can feel it. I know."

"We can't change that."

"Hamza, I love you. Listen to me, I love you. Let's just get out of here."

"It's too late. I have to go. One more thing, if we don't see each other again . . . here, take this little box. Inside is the explanation for everything. And here's another little box too. This is how it should have been." Hamza put the two boxes into her hands. He removed his wallet from his pocket and gave it to her.

"Hamza, please . . ."

Hamza wasn't there anymore. He had turned around and disappeared into the darkness. He quickly took off his coat and blazer. From inside the black wrapping, he removed the Tanto with the case and belts. He put it on his back and connected the belts to his pants. He stretched from side to side, left and right, to check how it sat on his back. Satisfied, he nodded to himself. He put his blazer and coat on again, paying no attention to the snow. He walked out of the darkness and toward the restaurant. June stood frozen in the snow and watched him go.

In the reception area, Hamza took his coat off again and handed it to the person in the cloakroom, along with a tip. The kind maître d' came up to him.

"I kept the table for you."

"Thank you, but I won't be needing it. I have company inside."

*   *   *

Hamza passed the maître d' and made a beeline to his best man's table. He knew them all. The same crew as on that fateful

April day in 1992. His best man, the big bald guy, two guys who looked like professional boxers, and Neno. Neno, whose life and freedom he had bought for two hundred fifty marks. Neno, who had been throwing up after they killed Amra and the little one. Hamza approached them and stopped about a yard away from the table.

"How are you, my best man?"

"What? Hamza!" His best man jumped out of the chair. The others, except for Neno, got up too. His best man stared at him, eyes wide with shock. Suddenly, he remembered that he was in the U.S., in a restaurant full of people, that he was safe. "Oh, Hamza! I'm good, Hamza! How are you?" The best man sat down. The others did the same.

"I'm fine, just fine. Are you celebrating Christmas?"

"Us? Christmas? No, we're just drinking." The guys at the table glanced back and forth between Hamza and his best man, looking for any indication of trouble. Hamza seemed like a lot of things, but not dangerous. He looked at his best man calmly.

"So, how was it, my best man?"

"Tight. You kicked our ass in the end."

"You kicked ours too."

"Thanks for Neno."

"Don't mention it." Hamza kept looking at him. His mind considered millions of possibilities in a moment.

So, this was it. Finally, what he had wanted, what he had worked for through the entire nightmare: to have his best man in front of him. He looked at him carefully, as if seeing him for the first time. Good facial symmetry, high forehead, hair, beard, and mustache. Sloppy, as usual. Intelligent eyes, slightly eaten away by alcohol. He had probably drank a lot in the past few years. Or did he just have trouble sleeping?

His best man. The man that destroyed his life, once. Now it seemed that he would do it a second time, and it wasn't worth it. This guy who called himself a man was not worth Amra's little toe. Not a hair from the little one's head. Not one worried glance from June. That face. He had been fond of it once. Why? What happened in that head of yours that made you decide to do something like that? Kill, all right! But why a woman, why a child? You're living in the past, my brother. You're still at the Battle of Kosovo, in the centuries buried in hatred and lies about the imaginary Kingdom of Dusan. You will never discover love. Even when you get married, when you sleep with your wife, you'll do it out of hatred, not love. You're going to have children. You're going to raise them with the same monstrous values you were raised with by your father—a Chetnik. And his father, and his father's father . . .

You'll raise children to live in the same world of darkness and lies. Lies ruled your grandparents. They will rule your grandchildren too. It will go on and on until the day one of you finally says, "Enough! Hold it! Those are all lies! We have to start over again!" And just like Willy Brandt, you too will kneel in front of the shadows of the innocent and ask for forgiveness. What happens now? Should I kill you? Or should I let you live on until you kill yourself with hatred? I can't bring back the dead. And you? You're already dead. You just don't know it yet. You've probably never been alive. You never felt the beauty, never seen the golden-blue dawns above the city that you destroyed so savagely. You are dead.

June? Where is June? Probably outside waiting for me. Amra, my little one, you do understand, don't you? Dino, Senad, Dado . . . ? I know Dado, I can hear you. Tanto! Tanto! You have him in front of you! Do it! Dado, I'm sorry. I have the choice. I can choose. We were never given a choice, until now. They didn't even leave us the option to surrender when we were being slaughtered. This is my choice now."

"What's up, Hamza?"

"Nothing, my best man. I just wanted to thank you."

"For what?"

"For Amra and the little one. Neno was just a part of the debt."

"Yes, Neno told me."

"Well, I'll be going now. I have a meeting. It was nice seeing you."

Hamza simply waved, turned around, and started toward the exit. The band played a slow Latin tune. The waiters walked around the hall quietly. There was a soft clinking of glasses in the background. The guests were toasting to a merry Christmas. June moved away from the door so that Hamza wouldn't see her. "Thank God nothing happened. Everything is going to be fine."

*   *   *

"Hold on! STOP!"

His best man's voice drowned out all the other sounds in the restaurant. Hamza stopped. The guests at the nearby tables stopped talking. The music continued. Hamza's lips parted to revealed two rows of clenched white teeth. He grinned like a wolf.

The people at the table next to him would later swear they had heard him growl.

"This way is for the better" He thought, "At least I tried. For June. But I know that I would have cursed myself for the rest of my life. Let's end it. Everything has to end. Old debts must be repaid. I'm sorry, June."

Hamza felt the adrenaline rushing through his body. Out of his pocket, he took out a black silk headband. On the front, a message in Arabic was embroidered in white silk: *La Ilahe Illallah Muhammedu Resulullah*," meaning "There is no God but Allah, and Mohammed is his Messenger." It was a band that Muslim warriors wore into battle. He wound it around his left wrist. The moment he turned toward his best man, he was ready. For a second he thought he'd seen June at the entrance. The next moment, he forgot all about her. He forgot about everything around him. With his left hand, he threw his hair back over his shoulder. He walked a few steps back until he stood next to the table.

"What's up, my best man?"

"Enough of this shit. Let's end it."

"End what?"

"You don't owe me anything. Nothing. Do you understand me? Nothing!" His best man screamed. He had obviously lost control.

"What do you mean, my best man?"

"There is no debt! There is no Amra! There is no little one! I killed them! I did it!

"I know. I buried them the same night."

"Impossible!"

"Possible. In the rose garden, behind the house. So you see, there is a debt." Hamza raised his left shoulder a bit and stretched out his right hand toward his best man. "I just don't know why you had to do it. We could have fought as men on the opposite sides of the war and maintained a small bit of respect for one another. Until I killed you, that is."

"Shoot! Shoot, you motherfuckers!" screamed the best man.

His companions reached for the guns hidden beneath their coats.

*   *   *

Afterwards, the restaurant guests gave varying statements to the police. Some stated that everything happened in less than five seconds. Others were convinced that, from the moment the guy with a beard said something and the one with golden hair came to the table, five to seven, maybe even eight seconds had passed.

*   *   *

Neno threw himself backwards. He fell together with his chair, and remained on the floor with his legs over the chair and his arms in the air. As Hamza moved, the guy to his left, the one closest to him, had already drawn a gun. With his left hand, Hamza felt for the Tanto handle over his right shoulder, and bringing the blade across in a wide arc. The blade tore through the flesh and bone with ease, dropping both hand and gun to the floor. The man toppled over.

"Aaargh!" The scream filled the hall. The music stopped. The guests leapt out of their chairs. Hamza tossed the knife, catching it with his right hand in midair and, completing the circular motion, sliced open the throat of the guy on his right. The blood gushed out in a fountain of crimson. Ignoring the dead man, Hamza jumped over the chair and found himself in front of the bald mountain of a man. He had drawn his gun. Hamza threw himself at the man, hugging him closely with his left hand and driving the gun to the side. With an upward stroke, his right hand plunged the Tanto through the heart. He twisted the blade and pulled it out. He pushed the body away. With his left, Hamza grabbed the edge of the table and threw it aside. He stood in front of his best man.

His best man just stood there, eyes wide open, pale as a ghost.

"If you have to kill, make it quick and clean" was Avdaga's advice at the beginning of the war.

Hamza thrust the blade just beneath the navel and pulled up. He felt little resistance as the knife reached the breastbone. He pulled the knife out, and with a short swing of the forearm, slit the best man's throat. He took the knife with both hands, raised it as high, and swung down with all his might, forcing it right through the skull. He grabbed and held his best man up with his left arm, and carefully watched as the last ounce of life disappeared from his eyes.

"BOOM, BOOM, BOOM!" Three shots. The guy who had lost his hand came to his senses and squeezed off the shots with his remaining hand. The bullets struck Hamza in the back. A nearby guest kicked the gun out of the guy's hand.

Hamza smiled.

"It's for the best."

*   *   *

June had already been on her way out to wait for Hamza when she heard his best man's voice. She turned back and looked across the restaurant. The best man's friends had drawn their guns. When Hamza sprang towards them, she covered her face with her hands. After the shots rang out, she moved her hands away, only to see Hamza's body recoiling from the force of the bullets.

"Hamza! No!"

June ran across the hall.

Hamza staggered. He managed to pull the Tanto out, and pushed his best man away. He stood for a moment and then fell to his knees. His head hung forward helplessly. When June screamed, he tried to turn around but he couldn't find the strength and fell forward.

June tripped in her heels, somehow took them off, and ran to Hamza. She turned him on his back and raised his head. Hamza's eyes were glazing over. For a moment she thought that he'd recognized her, that he wanted to tell her something.

"Hamza! Hamza!" She shook him.

But it was useless. Hamza was far away.

"Hamza! Hamza!" She raised her head. "Call an ambulance! Call the hospital! For God's sake, call somebody!"

With nerveless fingers, the manager tried to dial 911.

CPSIA information can be obtained at www.ICGtesting.com
Printed in the USA
LVOW062108110213

319617LV00001B/177/P